D0259779

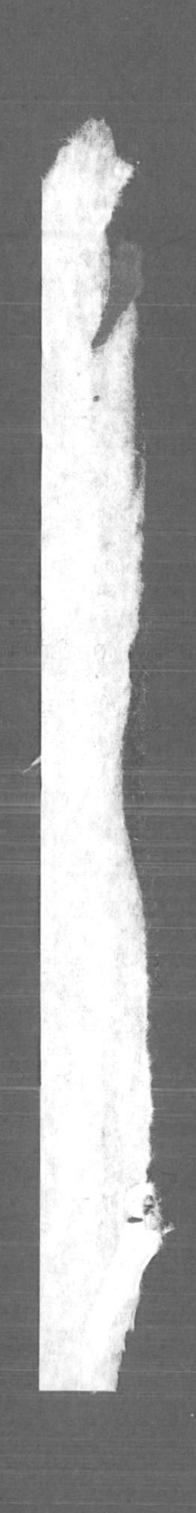

THE KEEPER

Also By Luke Delaney

Cold Killing

THE KEEPER

LUKE DELANEY

HarperCollins*Publishers*

HarperCollins*Publishers*
77–85 Fulham Palace Road,
Hammersmith, London W6 8JB

www.harpercollins.co.uk

Published by HarperCollins*Publishers* 2013
1

A catalogue record for this book
is available from the British Library

ISBN: 978-0-00-748609-0

Set in Meridien by Palimpsest Book Production Limited,
Falkirk, Stirlingshire

Printed and bound in Great Britain by
Clays Ltd, St Ives plc

Dedication

I don't believe we're all lucky enough to find our true soul mates in this life, but I have. I would love nothing more than to write her name in lights high above the world for everyone to see, but unfortunately because of my past life I cannot. So instead of a galactic firework display in her honour, I dedicate this book, *The Keeper*, to my incredible wife – LJ, whose love has done much to shape the man I am today.

At our wedding my Dad gave a little speech and described LJ and I as being a powerful force. It took me a few years to fully realize what he meant, but now the meaning of his words is crystal clear, as anyone who's ever seen us together would understand. We drive each other, push each other forward, challenge each other when it's needed, criticize each other when it's warranted, but above all else we love and support each other. We can do all these things because we belong to each other – are safe and secure with each other – respect and adore each other.

So here's to LJ – loving and dedicated mother, a fearless captain of her industry and inspirational leader both at work and at home – a young girl from a nowhere town who overcame all the significant disadvantages and hurdles life put in her way to reach the very top. And most importantly of all, and as a lesson to everyone, she achieved all this without ever telling a lie, without ever being deceitful, while always being kind and loyal, and with an unshakeable morality.

Without LJ, I could easily have lost my way – at the very least settled for less than I could have been. So for all she has given me I thank her and love her.

For LJ
Love,
LD x

1

Thomas Keller walked along the quiet suburban street in Anerley, south-east London, an area that provided affordable housing to those attracted to the capital who discovered that they could only afford to live on its edges, financially excluded from the very things they had come to London for in the first place. He knew Oakfield Road well, having walked its length several times over the previous few weeks and he knew in which house Louise Russell lived.

Keller was cautious. Although confident he would draw little attention in his Post Office uniform, this was not his normal route. Someone might realize he shouldn't be there and that the mail had already been delivered earlier that morning, but he couldn't wait any longer – he needed Louise Russell *today*.

As he approached number 22 he made sure to drop post through the letter boxes of neighbouring houses, just in case some bored resident had nothing to do other than spy on the street where nothing happened anyway. As he posted junk mail his eyes flicked at the windows and doors of the street's ugly new brick houses, built for practicality with no thought of individuality or warmth. Their design provided excellent privacy, however, and that had made Louise Russell even more attractive to him.

His excitement and fear were rising to levels he could barely control, the blood pumping through his arteries and veins so fast it hurt his head and blurred his vision. He quickly checked inside his postal delivery sack, shuffling the contents around, moving the junk mail aside, touching the items he had brought with him for reassurance – the electric stun-gun he'd bought on one of his rare holidays outside of Britain, the washing-up liquid bottle that contained chloroform, a clean flannel, a roll of heavy-duty tape and a thin blanket. He would need them all soon, very soon.

Only a few steps to the front door now and he could sense the woman inside, could taste and smell her. The architecture of the soulless house meant that once he had reached the front door he could not be seen from the street and nor could Louise Russell's red Ford Fiesta. He held his hand up to ring the door-bell, but paused to steady himself before pressing the button attached to the door frame, in case he needed to persuade her to open the door to him. After what felt like hours he finally pressed it and waited, until a jerky shadow moved from the bowels of the house towards the front door. He stared at the opaque glass window in the door as the shadow took on colour and the door began to open without hesitation or caution. He hadn't had to speak after all. Now at last she was standing in front of him with nothing between the two of them, nothing that could keep them apart any longer.

He stood silently, in awe of her. It felt as if her clear, shining green eyes were pulling him forward, towards her glowing skin, her pretty feminine face. She was only a little smaller than he, about five foot six and slim, with straight brown hair cut into what was nearly a bob. She was about the same age as he was, twenty-eight years old. He began to tremble, but not with fear any more, with joy. She smiled and spoke to him. 'Hi. Do you have something for me?'

'I've come to take you home, Sam,' he told her. 'Just like I promised I would.'

Louise Russell smiled through her confusion. 'I'm sorry,' she said, 'I don't think I understand.'

She saw his arm moving quickly towards her and tried to step back, away from the threatening-looking black box he held in his hand, but he'd anticipated she would and he stepped forward to match her stride. When the box touched her chest it felt as if she'd been hit by a wrecking ball. Her feet left the ground as she catapulted backwards and landed hard on the hallway floor. For a few blissful moments she remembered nothing as her world turned to black, but unconsciousness spared her from reality all too briefly. When her eyes opened again she somehow knew she hadn't been out for long and that she was still unable to command her own movements as her body remained in spasm, her teeth clenched together, preventing her from screaming or begging.

But her eyes were her own and they could see everything as the man dressed like a postman busied himself around her prone body. His stained, buckled teeth repulsed her, as did the odour of his unwashed body. As his head passed close to her face she could see and smell his short, unkempt brown hair, strands of which had stuck to his forehead with sweat. His skin was pale and unhealthy and appeared quite grey, marked with acne and chicken-pox scars. His hands were bony and ugly, too long and thin, the skin almost transparent like an old person's. Long dirty fingernails fidgeted at things he was taking from his post-bag.

Everything about him made her want to turn from him, to push him away, but she was trapped in the unrelenting grip of whatever he'd touched her with, unable to do anything but watch the nightmare she was at the centre of. And all the time he spoke to her using the name of another as the pictures adorning the walls she knew so well stared down at her – happy photographs of her with her husband, her family, her friends. How many times had she passed the pictures and not taken time to look? Now, paralysed on the floor of her own home, her sanctuary, the same pictures mocked her from above. This couldn't be happening, not here – not in her home.

'It'll be all right, Sam,' he promised. 'We'll get you home as soon as we can, OK. I'll get you in the car and then it's only a short trip. Please don't be scared. There's no need to be scared. I'm here to look after you now.'

He was touching her, his damp hands stroking her hair, her face and all the time he smiled at her, his heavy breaths invading her senses and turning her stomach. She watched through wild eyes as he took hold of her arms and crossed them at the wrists over her chest, his fingers lingering on her breasts. She watched as he began to unroll a length of wide, black tape from a thick roll he'd brought with him. She prayed silently inside her frozen body, prayed that her husband would appear in the doorway and beat this animal away from her. She prayed to be free from this hell and the hell that was about to happen because now she knew, she understood clearly, he was going to take her with him. Her pain and terror weren't going to be over quickly, in a place she had no fear of. No, he was going to take her away from here, to a place she could only imagine the horror of. A place she might never leave, alive or dead.

Through her physical and mental agony she suddenly began to feel her body's control returning to her, the muscles relaxing, her jaw and hands beginning to unclench, her spine beginning to loosen and straighten, the unbearable cramp in her buttocks finally receding, but she was betrayed by her own recovery as her lungs allowed a long breath to escape. He heard her.

'No, no. Not yet, Sam,' he told her. 'Soon, but for the moment you need to relax and let me take care of everything. I swear to you everything will be just the way we wanted it to be. You believe that, don't you, Sam?'

His voice was a menacing mix of apparent genuine concern,

even compassion and a threatening tone that matched the deep hate in his eyes. If she could have answered him she would have agreed with anything he said, so long as he would let her live. She felt rape was a certainty now, her mind instinctively preparing her for that, but her very life, her existence, she would do everything she could to preserve that: she would do anything he asked.

Carefully placing the tape on the floor next to her, he took a washing-up liquid bottle from his bag and a rag. He squirted a clear liquid on the rag. 'Don't fight this, Sam. Just breathe normally, it's better that way.' Even before the rag covered her mouth and nose she could smell its pungent hospital aroma. She tried to hold her breath but could only manage a few seconds, then the chloroform fumes were sweeping into her lungs and invading her bloodstream. She sensed unconsciousness and welcomed it, but before the sanctity of sleep could descend he pulled it away. 'Not too much,' he said. 'You can have some more when you're in the car, OK?'

Louise tried to look at him, to focus on his movements, but his image was distorted and his voice warped. She blinked to clear her sight as the first effects of the chloroform began to lessen. She recovered in time to see him binding her wrists together with the tape, the pain of the adhesive being pressed into her skin cutting through even the chloroform. Then his hands moved towards her face, holding something between them. She tried to turn away, but it was useless as she felt the tape being plastered across her mouth, the panic of impending suffocation pressing down on her empty lungs like a ton weight, the effects of the chloroform preventing her thinking rationally or calming herself so she could breathe.

'Relax,' he assured her. 'Relax and breathe through your nose, Sam.' She tried, but panic and fear still refused to allow any normal sense of self-preservation to ignite.

Suddenly he moved away from her, rifling through her handbag and then the set of drawers next to the front door.

Moments later he returned, having found what he was looking for – her car keys.

'We need to go now, Sam,' he told her. 'Before they try and stop us again. Before they try and keep us apart. We need to hide from them, together.'

He struggled to get her to her feet, pulling her torso off the ground by gripping and tugging at her top, her near dead weight almost too much for his slight physique to bear. Finally he managed to wrap her right arm around his neck and began to haul her from the ground.

'You have to help me, Sam. Help me get you up.'

Through her confusion and fear she could hear the growing anger in his voice and something told her she had to get up if she was to survive the next few moments of this hell. She struggled to make her legs work, the tape around her wrists preventing her from using her arms for balance or leverage, her unsteady feet slipping on the wooden floor.

'That's good, Sam,' the madman encouraged her. 'Almost there, just a little bit more.'

She sensed she was on her feet now, but the world was spinning wildly, making her unsure of anything as she began to walk, moving forward into the bright light beyond the home that should have been her refuge. The light and air helped clear her mind further and she could see she was standing at the rear of her own car while this man fumbled with her keys. She heard the alarm being deactivated and the hatchback door popping open. 'You'll be safe in here, Sam. Don't worry, we haven't got far to go.'

She realized his intentions but only managed to mumble 'No,' behind her taped mouth before he grasped her shoulders and steered her towards the opening, making her lose her balance and fall into the back of the car. She lay there, her eyes pleading with the man not to take her from her home. It was the last thing she remembered before the chloroform-soaked rag once more pressed into her face, only this time he held it there until unconsciousness rescued her from perdition.

He looked at her for as long as he dared, all the while smiling, almost laughing with happiness. He had her back now, now and for ever. Pulling the thin blanket from his sack, he carefully spread it over her prostrate body before closing the hatch door. He jumped into the driver's seat and struggled to put the key in the ignition, excitement making his hands shake almost uncontrollably. At last he managed to start the car and drive away calmly, slowly so as not to draw attention. Within minutes he would swap Louise Russell's car for his own and then, soon after that, he would be at home with Sam. At home with Sam for the rest of her life.

Detective Inspector Sean Corrigan sat inside court three at the Central Criminal Court, otherwise known as the Old Bailey, named after the City of London street it dominated. Despite all the romance and mystique of the famous old court, Sean disliked it, as did most seasoned detectives. It was difficult to get to and there was absolutely no parking within miles. Getting several large bags of exhibits to and from the Bailey was a logistical nightmare no cop looked forward to. Other courts across London might be more difficult to get a conviction at, but at least they provided some damn parking.

It was Wednesday afternoon and he'd been hanging around the court doing little more than nothing since Monday morning. Sean scanned the courtroom, oblivious to its fine architecture. It was the people inside the room he was interested in.

Finally the judge put the Probation Service report to one side and looked over the court before speaking. 'I have considered all submissions in this matter, and have given particular weight to the psychological reports in relation to Mr Gibran's mental state now and at the time these crimes – these serious and terrible crimes – were committed. In the case of this defendant, on the basis of the opinions of the expert witnesses for the defence, namely those of the psychologists who examined Mr Gibran, it is my conclusion that Mr Gibran is not fit to stand trial at this time and should be treated for what are apparently serious psychological conditions. Does anybody have any further submissions before we conclude this matter?'

Sean felt his excitement turn to heavy disappointment, his stomach knotted and empty. His attention was immediately pulled back to proceedings as the prosecution barrister leapt to his feet.

'My Lord,' he pleaded. 'If I could draw your attention to page twelve of the probation report, it may assist the court.'

The court fell silent again except for more shuffling of papers as the judge found page twelve and read. After a few minutes he spoke to the prosecuting barrister. 'Yes, thank you Mr Parnell, that does indeed assist the court.'

The judge looked to the back of the court where Gibran sat motionless and calm. 'Mr Gibran,' the judge addressed him, speaking as softly as distance would allow, already treating him like a psychiatric patient instead of a calculating murderer. 'It is the decision of the court that in this case you will not be standing trial for the crimes you have been charged with. There exist serious doubts as to your ability to comprehend what would be happening to you, and as a result you would not be in a position to defend yourself adequately from those charges. I have therefore decided that you should receive further psychiatric treatment. However, in view of serious concerns expressed by the Probation Service that you pose both a danger to yourself and the public . . .'

Sean's emptiness left him as quickly as it had come, squeezed out by the excitement again spreading through his core. He didn't care who the turnkeys were, prison officers or nurses, so long as Gibran was locked away behind bars, for ever.

The judge continued: '. . . I cannot ignore the risk you represent and must balance that with your need to receive treatment. As a result I am ordering you to be detained under the Mental Health Act in a secure psychiatric unit for an indefinite period. Should you in the future be deemed to have made sufficient progress towards recovery then it will be considered again as to whether you should stand trial or indeed be released back into the community. Very good.'

With that the judge stood to signify an end to proceedings. Everyone in the court rose simultaneously to show their respect. Sean was the last to his feet, a suppressed smile thinning his lips as he looked to the dock and whispered under his breath, 'Have fun in Broadmoor, you fuck.' His eyes remained locked on Gibran's as the guards led the defendant from the dock towards the holding cells beneath the old court. Sean knew it would almost certainly be the last time he ever saw Sebastian Gibran.

The events of the past few months raced through Sean's mind as he gathered his files, stuffing them into his old, worn-out briefcase that looked more like a child's oversized satchel. He headed for the exit keen to avoid the handful of journalists who had been allowed into the court, stopping en route to shake the prosecuting counsel's hand and to thank him for his efforts, as unimpressive as they were. He walked from the courtroom at a decent pace, scanning the second-floor hallway for journalists or family members of Gibran's victims, neither of whom he wanted to speak to now, at least not until he'd spoken to one of his own. He walked briskly through the main part of the court open to the public and into the bowels of the Bailey, a labyrinth of short airless, lightless corridors that eventually led him to a Victorian staircase that he climbed until he reached an inconsequential-looking door. Sean pushed the door open and entered without hesitation, immediately hit by the noise of the chitter-chatter that could barely be heard from the other side of the door.

The little 'police only' canteen was enshrined in the force's myth and legend, as well as serving the best carvery meat in London. It didn't take long for Sean to find Detective Sergeant Sally Jones sitting alone in the tiny warm room, nursing a coffee. She sensed Sean enter and looked straight at him. He knew she would be reading his face, seeking answers to her questions before she asked them. Sean wound and weaved his way through the tightly packed tables and chairs, apologizing when necessary for disturbing the rushed meals of busy detectives. He reached Sally and sat heavily opposite her.

'Well?' Sally asked impatiently.

'Not fit to stand trial.'

'For fuck's sake!' Sally's response was loud enough to make the other detectives in the canteen look up, albeit briefly. Sean looked around the room, a visual warning to everyone not to interfere. 'Jesus Christ,' Sally continued. 'What's the fucking point?'

Sean noticed Sally unconsciously rubbing the right side of her chest, as if she could feel Gibran hammering the knife into her all over again. 'Come on, Sally,' he encouraged. 'We always knew this was a possibility. Once we'd seen the psychiatric reports it was practically a certainty.'

'I know,' Sally agreed with a sigh, still rubbing her chest. 'I was fooling myself that common sense might break out in the judicial system. I should have known better.'

'It's entirely possible he is actually mad.'

'He is completely fucking mad,' Sally agreed again. 'But he's also absolutely capable of standing trial. He knew what he was doing when he did what he did. There were no voices in his head. He's as clever as he is dangerous, he's faked his psych results, made a joke out of their so-called tests. He should stand trial for what he did to . . .' Her voice tailed off as she looked down at the cold coffee on the table in front of her.

'He's not getting away with it,' Sean assured her. 'While we're sitting here he's already on his merry way to the secure wing at Broadmoor. Once you go in there you never come out.' Some of England's most notorious murderers and criminals were locked up in Broadmoor; their faces flashed through Sean's mind: Peter Sutcliffe aka the Yorkshire Ripper, Michael Peterson aka Charles Bronson, Kenneth Erskine aka the Stockwell Strangler, Robert Napper the killer of Rachel Nickell. Sally's voice brought him back.

'Gibran killed a police officer and damn nearly killed me. He'll be a bloody god in there.'

'Don't be so sure.' Sean's phone began to vibrate in his jacket pocket. The number said 'Withheld' meaning it was probably someone calling from their Murder Investigation Team incident room back at Peckham police station. Sean answered without ceremony and recognized the strange mixture of Glaswegian and Cockney at the other end immediately. DS Dave Donnelly wouldn't have called unless there was good reason.

'Guv'nor, Superintendent Featherstone wants to see you back here ASAP. Apparently something's come up that requires our "specialized skill set".'

'Meaning we're the only soldiers left in the box,' Sean answered.

'So cynical for one so young.'

'We'll be about an hour, travelling time from the Bailey,' Sean informed him. 'We're all finished here anyway.'

'Finished already?' said Donnelly. 'That doesn't sound good.'

'I'll explain when I see you.' Sean hung up.

'Problem?' Sally asked.

'When is it ever anything else?'

Louise Russell's eyes began to flicker open, her mind desperately trying to drag her from the chloroform-induced sleep that held nothing but nightmares of smothering, darkness, a monster in her own home. She tried to see into the gloom of her surroundings, the blinking of her eyes beginning to slow until finally they remained frozen wide open with terror. My God, he had taken her, taken her away from her home, her husband, her life. The fear fired through her like electricity, making her want to jump up and run or fight, but the effects of the chloroform weighed her down. She managed to push herself on to her hands and knees before slumping on to her side, using her forearm as a makeshift pillow. Her breathing was too rapid and irregular, her heartbeat the same. She tried to concentrate on conquering her fear, to slow the rise and fall of her chest. After a few minutes of lying still and calm her breathing became more relaxed and her eyes better able to focus on her new surroundings.

There were no windows in the room and she couldn't see a door, only the foot of a flight of stairs she imagined would lead to a door and a way out. One low-voltage bulb hung from the high ceiling, smeared with dirt, its light just enough for her to see as her eyes began to adjust. As far as she could tell the room was little more than thirty feet wide and long, with cold unpainted walls that looked as if they'd been white-washed years ago, but now the red and greys of old brick were showing through. The floor appeared to be solid concrete and she could feel the cold emanating from it. The only noise in the room was water running down a wall and dripping on to the floor. She felt as if she must be underground, in a cellar or the old wartime bunker of a large house. The room smelled of urine, human excrement and unwashed bodies and, more than anything else, absolute fear.

Louise pulled the duvet that covered her up to her neck against the coldness of her discoveries only to add to her chill. She looked under the duvet and realized all her clothes had been taken and the duvet left in their place. The duvet smelled clean and comforting against the cold stench of the room, but who would do this, take her from her home, take her clothes, but care enough to leave her a clean duvet to cover herself and keep out the cold? Who and why? She closed her eyes and prayed he hadn't touched her. Her hand slowly moved down her body and between her legs. Fighting the repulsion she touched herself gently. She felt no pain, no soreness, and she was dry. She was sure he hadn't raped her. So why was she here?

As her eyes adjusted further to the gloom she discovered she was lying on a thin single mattress, old and stained. He had left a plastic beaker of what looked and smelled like fresh water, but the thing she noticed most, the one thing that brought tears stinging from her eyes, was when she realized she wasn't just in this terrible room, she was locked in a cage inside the room. All around her was thick wire mesh interwoven through its solid metal frame, no more than six feet long and four feet wide. She was locked inside some sort of animal cage, which meant there were only two possibilities: he'd left her there to die, or he would be coming back, coming back to see the animal he'd caught and caged, coming back to feed his prize, coming back to do whatever he wanted to her.

She wiped her tears on the duvet and once again tried to take in all of her surroundings, looking for any sign of hope. One end of her cage was clearly the way out as it was blocked with a padlocked door. She also noticed what appeared to be a hatch in the side, presumably for the safe passage of food between her and her keeper. Fear swept up from the depths of her despair and overwhelmed her. She virtually leapt at the door, pushing her fingers through the wire mesh and closing her fists around it, shaking the cage wildly, tears pouring down her cheeks as she filled her lungs ready to scream for help. She froze. She'd heard something, something moving. She wasn't alone.

She looked deep into the room, her eyes almost compl[e]tely

adjusted to the low light levels now, listening for more sounds, praying they wouldn't come, but they did, something moving. Her eyes focused on where the sounds had come from and she could see it, on the opposite side of the room, another cage, as far as she could tell identical to the one she was locked inside. My God was it an animal in there? Was she being kept with a wild animal? Was that why he'd taken her, to give her to this animal? Driven by panic she started shaking her cage door again, although she knew it was futile. The sound of a voice made her stop. A quiet, weak voice. The voice of another woman.

'You shouldn't do that,' the voice whispered. 'He might hear you. You never know when he's listening. If he hears you doing that he'll punish you. He'll punish us both.'

Louise froze, the terrible realization she was not the first he'd taken paralysing her mind and body. She lay absolutely still, listening, disbelieving, waiting for the voice to speak again, beginning to think she had imagined it. She could wait no longer. 'Hello,' she called into the gloom. 'Who are you? How did you get here?' She waited for an answer. 'My name's Louise Russell. Can you tell me your name?'

A short, sharp 'Sssssh,' was the only reply. Louise waited in silence for an eternity.

'We need to help each other,' Louise told the voice.

'I said be quiet,' the voice answered, sounding afraid rather than angry. 'Please, he might be listening.'

'I don't care,' Louise insisted. 'Please, please. I need to know your name.' Frustration brought more tears into her eyes. She waited, staring at the coiled shape lying on the floor in the other cage, until eventually the shape began to unfold and take on a human form.

Louise looked at the young woman now sitting, legs folded under herself in the cage opposite. She looked around and confirmed to herself there were no more cages in the room, her eyes soon returning to the other woman. Louise could see that she was still pretty, despite her unkempt appearance – her short brown hair tangled and her face pale and dirty, any signs of make-up long since washed away by tears and sweat. She had bruises on her body and face, as well as a badly split lip. She looked to be in her late twenties, slim and as far as Louise could tell from a sitting position, about the same height as she was. In fact almost everything about her was similar to Louise. She couldn't help but notice the other woman had no mattress or duvet, no covers or bedding of any kind, and all she had to wear were her filthy-looking knickers and bra. She looked cold, despite the fact the room was reasonably warm, although Louise couldn't see an obvious source of heating. She guessed the room might be next to a boiler room or maybe the fact they were underground, as she suspected, kept it warmer than outside. But why was this other woman apparently being treated so much worse than she was? Was she being punished? Was that why she wouldn't speak, for fear of further punishment? What would he do to her next – remove her underwear, the final humiliation?

'My name's Karen Green.'

The sound of the voice froze Louise. It took her a few seconds to find her own voice.

'I'm Louise. Louise Russell,' she answered. 'How long have you been here for?'

'I don't know. He's got my watch.'

'Can you remember what day it was when he took you?'

'Thursday morning,' Karen told her. 'What day is it now?'

'I don't know. I can't be sure. I remember it was Tuesday morning when he . . .' Louise struggled to find the word. 'When he attacked me. Do you know how long I've been here for?'

'Quite a while. Maybe even a day. You've been out the whole time.'

Louise slumped against the wire mesh of her cage, trying

to comprehend the fact she could have been missing for a day and still not been found. And then a more chilling thought swept over her; Karen had been missing for almost a week and yet here she was, rotting in a mesh cage and, up until now, alone – except for him.

'Do you know what he wants?' she asked Karen in a sudden panic. 'Why are we here?'

'No. I don't know what he wants, but he always calls me Sam.'

Louise remembered he had called her Sam too. *I've come to take you home, Sam. Just like I promised I would.* She felt the sickness rising in her stomach, the foul, bitter bile pushing up through her throat and into her mouth. They were replacements for someone else – replacements for whoever the hell Sam was.

Another wave of exhausting fear washed over her, a tangible, physical pain. They were being held by someone who was insane, someone impossible to reason or rationalize with. Hope drained from her.

Louise looked across at Karen and was reminded of her lack of clothing and the only thing she feared almost as much as death itself. 'Has he touched you?' she asked. There was a long silence and she watched Karen shrinking and coiling into the foetal position, hugging herself silently.

'Not at first,' Karen answered in little more than a tearful whisper. 'When I woke up he'd taken my clothes, but I don't think he'd touched me. He left me a mattress and duvet, like he has for you, but later he took them away and he . . . he started to hurt me. At first he was almost gentle. He injected me with something that stopped me struggling and then he did it. But now he's always angry with me. He does it to punish me, but I haven't done anything wrong. I haven't done anything to make him angry.'

Louise listened as if she was listening to her own future being described, her body stiff with panic, her muscles cramping with tension. 'What happened to your clothes?' she asked. 'You said he took them when he brought you here, but he gave you back your underwear. Why didn't he give you the rest back?'

'These aren't mine,' Karen explained. 'My first few days here he let me wash, then he gave me some clothes and made me wear them. But last night – I think it was night, he came and took them off me, except for what I'm wearing. I didn't know why he took them until he brought you here.'

Louise too realized why he had taken the clothes and knew that soon she would be wearing them. She retched bile, capillaries in her eyes rupturing, leaving them pink and glassy. The silence was suddenly shattered by the metallic clank of something small and heavy hitting against what sounded like sheet metal. A padlock being opened, Louise guessed, and for a second dared to believe it could be their rescuers. The fear and dread she heard in Karen's voice soon chased her hopes away as she instinctively backed into the furthest corner of her cage.

'He's coming,' Karen told her. 'Don't speak to me now. He's coming.'

Sean and Sally entered their murder inquiry incident room at Peckham police station shortly before four on Wednesday afternoon. The office was both unusually busy and quiet, the detectives from Sean's team taking advantage of the lull between new investigations to catch up on severely overdue paperwork. They hadn't picked up a murder case in weeks, despite there being no shortage to go around. The other Murder teams working South London were getting more than a little annoyed that the regular flow of violent death seemed to be passing Sean's team by. Though glad of the respite, Sean increasingly had the feeling he was being saved for something he knew he wasn't going to like.

As they crossed the room he saw Detective Superintendent

Featherstone through the Perspex of his partitioned office. He caught DS Donnelly's eye as he walked and with a barely noticeable twitch of his head indicated for Donnelly to follow them. As Sean approached Featherstone, he began to get the feeling this was the day he'd been dreading. They entered the office and Featherstone stood to greet them. 'A little bird tells me it didn't go so good at court today,' was Featherstone's hello.

'Depends on your point of view,' Sean answered.

'And what's yours?' Featherstone asked.

'Well, he'll probably spend the rest of his life banged up with the worst of the worst in Broadmoor. That sounds like a result to me.'

'And who would disagree with that point of view?' Featherstone enquired. Sean said nothing, but his eyes flicked towards Sally. 'Nobody gets out of Broadmoor, Sally. That bastard will rot in there. Think of it this way: he's got a life sentence and we didn't even have to go to trial. All it takes is a couple of dimwits on the jury who like the look of him and he walks free. Trust me, Sally, this is an outstanding result.'

Sally was unmoved. 'He should have stood trial,' was all she said.

Sean decided it was time to move the conversation on. Cops never dwelt on old cases long. It didn't matter whether they'd had a good result or a disastrous one; within a few hours of the court's decision the case, though not forgotten, was put aside, rarely to be mentioned again. However, the investigation surrounding Gibran had been significantly different from anything any of them had dealt with. And bad as it had been for the rest of them, it had been much, much worse for Sally – she had almost died, almost been killed in her own home. Physically she had survived, just, but Sean felt that something had died inside her. She'd spent two months in intensive care and then another three with the hospital general population. A month later she'd gone back to work, but it was too soon and she couldn't cope physically or mentally. A few weeks later she'd returned again and he couldn't persuade her to take more time off, no matter how hard he tried. That was two months ago; nine months after she was attacked. She couldn't hope to have truly recovered in that time.

'There's no point dwelling on what did or didn't happen any longer than we have to. What's done is done. We can't appeal a decision made at committal so we all need to move on.' Sean glanced at Sally, who was silently staring at the floor, then turned to Featherstone. 'I assume you've gathered us together for a reason, boss.'

'Indeed. I've got a missing person for you to find.'

Featherstone's words were greeted with disbelieving silence.

'A what?' Sean queried.

'A missing person,' Featherstone repeated.

'Must be someone very important to have an MIT assigned to their case,' Donnelly surmised.

'Important, no,' Featherstone told them. 'Or at least, not to the general public. No doubt she's important to her family and friends, and certainly to her husband who reported her missing.'

'Are we talking foul play?' Sean asked. 'Is the husband a suspect?'

'Yes to the foul play, no to the husband. He's not a suspect.'

'How long's she been missing for?' Sean continued.

'Best guess is yesterday morning. The husband, John Russell, left her at about eight thirty to go to work and hasn't seen her since,' Featherstone explained. 'He got home at about six that evening and both his wife and her car were missing. Her handbag was there, her mobile phone etc, but Louise wasn't. Clearly something's happened to her and clearly she could be at risk.'

Sean didn't like what he was hearing. Women who ran

off with secret lovers didn't leave their handbags and phones behind. 'How far have we got?' he asked.

'About as far as I've just described,' Featherstone told them. 'The local uniform inspector who picked up the missing persons report didn't like the look of it so he passed it up to their CID office who in turn thought it might be something we'd be interested in.'

'And when or if they find her body, we will be interested,' Donnelly chipped in.

'The idea is we find her before it comes to that,' Featherstone snapped back.

'That's not our brief,' Donnelly continued to argue. 'We deal with murders, nothing else. Why don't they give it to the Serious Crime Group or even leave it with the local CID?'

'Because,' Featherstone explained, 'the powers that be, sitting in their ivory towers in Scotland Yard, have decided to trial a new policy with vulnerable MISPERs who at first sight appear to have come to harm. It's an extension of the murder suppression and prevention programme.'

'Then why not give it to the Murder Suppression Unit?' Donnelly refused to back down. 'Seems tailor-made for them.'

'Not quite their remit,' Featherstone continued. 'They need a suspect to concentrate on before they'll take a job.'

'And we need a body,' Donnelly insisted.

Sean broke the argument up with a question. 'How old is she?'

'Sorry?' Featherstone's mind was still tussling with Donnelly.

'How old is the missing woman?'

Featherstone flicked through the file he'd been holding throughout the meeting. 'Thirty.'

'Prime running-away-with-another-man age,' Donnelly sniffed.

'She hasn't run away,' Sally joined in. 'A woman wouldn't leave so many personal belongings behind unless something had happened.'

'Like what?' Donnelly asked.

'Like she was taken,' Sally answered.

Sean sensed another argument was about to flare. 'We'll look into it,' he announced.

'What?' Donnelly turned to him, indignant.

'Look at it this way,' Sean told Donnelly. 'If we can find her before something happens to her, we'll save ourselves a lot of work.'

'Good,' Featherstone said. 'I want to be regularly updated on this one, Sean. The powers that be are keen for a positive result to keep the media off their backs.' He handed the missing persons report to Sean who passed it on to Sally. 'There are a few photographs of her in the file. The only distinguishing mark is a scar from when she had her appendix removed when she was a teenager.'

'Get some copies of this run up please, Sally, and spread them around the team,' Sean told her. 'Dave can give you a hand.'

Donnelly looked as displeased as he felt. 'Waste of our time,' he insisted. 'She'll be home in a couple of days smelling of aftershave and demanding a divorce.'

Sean gave him a hard look. 'I don't think so,' was all he said. Donnelly knew when to stop pushing and left the office in Sally's wake.

Featherstone waited until they were well out of earshot before speaking again. 'How's Sally?' he asked.

Sean sucked a breath in through his teeth. 'She's getting there,' he answered.

'Bollocks,' snapped Featherstone. 'Any fool can see she's struggling, unsurprisingly.'

'She'll be OK,' Sean assured him, a little disappointed in Featherstone's lack of faith in Sally's ability to recover. 'She needs some time and a decent investigation to take her mind off what happened, that's all.'

'Is that why you so readily agreed to take on a missing persons inquiry?' Featherstone asked. 'To help Sally.'

Sean avoided the question. 'I didn't realize I had a choice.'

'For what it's worth,' Featherstone told him, 'you did have a choice.' Sean said nothing as Featherstone headed out of his office. 'Make sure you keep me posted and if there's anything I can do, give me a call. I know you're allergic to the media, so if you need me to deal with them, no problem.'

Featherstone was halfway out the door when Sean stopped him with a question. 'Do you think she's already dead? Is that why you want me to take this on?'

'I was hoping you would tell me that, Sean,' Featherstone answered. 'And her name's Louise Russell and she's someone's wife, someone's daughter – and if we do our jobs properly, one day she might be someone's mother. I think we all need to remember that, don't you?'

Sean said nothing as he watched Featherstone close the door behind him.

He suddenly felt very alone, sitting in his small warm office, surrounded by cheap furniture and out-dated computers with monitors that belonged in a museum. Even the view out of his window offered nothing but the sight of sprawling Peckham council estates and the travellers' caravan site on the wasteland next to the police station itself. He started to think about Louise Russell, to imagine what had happened to her and why. Where was she now? Was she still alive and if so why? Had somebody taken her, taken her to do horrific things to her? Should they expect a ransom note? No, he didn't think so. This felt like madness, as if madness had come into Louise Russell's life without any warning or reason.

Sean rubbed his face and tried to chase the questions away. She's a missing person, he told himself. Stop treating her like she's dead. But he knew it was pointless – he'd already begun. He'd already begun to think like him. Like the madman who'd taken her.

2

Natural light flooded down the staircase and into the room, its brightness temporarily blinding Louise Russell as she blinked to adjust to its harshness, before the noise of a door being quickly but carefully closed took the light away. Louise's eyes welcomed back the twilight she had grown accustomed to and looked across the room at Karen Green, who was sinking further into the corner of her cage, her fingers curling through and around the wire mesh as if she was bracing herself, anchoring herself against a tide that was about to sweep her away. Louise could hear her trying to stifle her tears as the footsteps on the stairs grew closer. She listened to those footsteps approaching, but they weren't heavy and dramatic, they were light and made little more than a shuffling, scraping sound that filled her with a fear worse than anything she'd ever experienced.

It was as if her senses were tuned in to the minutest sound, shade, smell, movement in her prison. This was the darkest most desperate place and time of her life, yet she'd never felt so alive. She found herself mimicking her fellow captive as she backed into the furthest corner of her cage, the beat of her own throbbing pulse almost drowning out the gentle footsteps that tentatively crept down towards them.

After what seemed both an agonizingly long time and a desperately short time he appeared at the bottom of the stairs and stepped falteringly into the makeshift dungeon. Louise watched as he paused before slowly moving inside, keeping close to the wall. As far as she could make out he was wearing a dark or grey tracksuit top and bottoms. Still he said nothing as he moved deeper into the room, then suddenly disappeared as if by magic. A second later she heard the springy click of a cord being pulled, followed by the yellow glow of a low-wattage bulb spilling into the subterranean room. The light wasn't strong enough to trouble her eyes or vision, but it made a huge difference to what she could see clearly. She saw that he'd walked behind a fabric screen, the type used on hospital wards to provide some degree of privacy.

It was like watching a silhouette in a puppet show, as he stood on the other side of the screen, his legs still, his arms and hands moving, busying themselves with something that made dull chinking sounds. Louise heard the rasp of a stiff tap being turned and then running water. He was cheerfully humming a tune she didn't recognize, a sound more terrifying than any scream or screech in the night. Her mouth was unbearably dry with fear, her throat glued shut with rising panic, her eyes as wide as a wild animal that knows it's about to be torn to pieces by its tormentors, her fully dilated pupils increasing her night vision at a time when she almost wished she could see nothing, hear nothing and feel nothing.

Louise watched as the silhouette became still, although somehow she knew he had turned to face them. She could hear him breathing deeply, as if he was preparing himself to walk on to a stage and meet his audience. Finally he stepped from behind the screen, this unimpressive man, average height, too slim, with scruffy brown hair and waxy skin. But to her he was vile monster, a hideous beast that threatened her in every way – her dignity, her freedom, her very existence. How could this wretch suddenly have so much power over her?

She could see he was smiling, a non-threatening, friendly smile. She remembered his stained teeth and the stink of his breath from when he took her, the memory pushing vomit-tasting saliva from her stomach into her mouth. Other memories rushed forward now – the smell of his unwashed hair, the stench of his stale sweat infested with stinking microbes, and his hands, his witch's hands, lingering too long on her breasts. Without warning the deluge of noise from her heart and blood fell silent. She realized he was speaking and it was enough to make her stop breathing, for her heart to stand still, just for a second.

'Sam? Are you OK? I brought you something; something to drink and a bite to eat if you can manage it. It's not much, but you'll feel better if you can manage to eat and drink a little.' He began to walk towards her carrying a tray on which he balanced a plastic mug of water and plate with a sandwich that looked like something a child would make. He walked in a crouched position as he circled her cage, peering in through the wire bars, smiling all the time while his eyes, wide and excited, darted over her body, stabbing her with a thousand needle points and making her skin crawl.

'I'll have to put the tray through the hatch,' he told her. 'It's better that way, until you understand more. You know what I mean, don't you, Sam? You always understood what I meant, even when nobody else did. That's why we're supposed to be together.'

He took a small key from his tracksuit pocket and unlocked the padlock securing the bolt to the cage's hatch. Louise watched his every move, wary of his hand suddenly stretching out for her through the hatch, but he merely pushed the tray in and held it, waiting for her to take it. 'Take the tray,' he told her. 'It's all for you. I'll come back for it later, when you've had enough.' Louise shuffled forward slowly, tentatively, her eyes never leaving his as she took the tray, which she immediately placed on the ground before shuffling back into the furthest corner of her prison.

'Try some,' he encouraged. 'Drink first though, the chloroform can leave you a bit dehydrated.'

She picked up the plastic mug and looked at it suspiciously, trying to detect any scent that didn't belong in an innocent drink of water. Finally she sipped it, a sense of relief soon overtaken by the clean, cold taste of fresh water. Suddenly aware how thirsty she was, she gulped it down quickly.

'Good, eh?' he said. 'Don't drink too much too quickly though, it might make you feel sick.'

Louise stopped drinking and began to dab some of the water around her lips and face, pausing as she remembered the woman locked in the other cage. Was she strong enough to speak to him yet? She decided she needed to try, do something to establish a relationship. She'd seen a programme about a kidnapped woman who'd built a bond with her captor that ultimately saved her life when he could no longer bring himself to kill her as he'd planned. 'What about her?' she managed to ask, barely recognizing her own weak, scratchy voice.

'Who?' he asked, his smile twitching now, blinking on and off.

Louise looked towards the other animal cage then back to him. 'Her. Karen. She said her name was Karen.'

He stared coldly into Louise's face, his smile nothing more than a memory now. 'You mustn't talk to her. She's a liar and a whore. She made me think she was you, but she isn't.'

Louise watched his face contorting with hatred, his lips pulled back over his teeth like a hyena laughing, the veins in his neck swollen and blue with anger. Sensing that she had put Karen in real and immediate danger, she hurried to undo her mistake. 'No,' she told him. 'She hasn't said anything, I promise. I made her tell me her name. It wasn't her fault. Please, there's too much water here for me. You can give her the rest of this. Please.'

Her desperate attempts to calm his anger towards the woman cowering and whimpering in her cage on the other side of the room seemed to go unheard. He was stalking across the floor, his eyes fixed on Karen.

'The whore gets nothing!' he shouted, his voice echoing hollowly in the brick tomb. 'The whore gets nothing, except what all whores really want.'

Louise covered her ears with her hands, instinctively curling herself into a tight ball pressed against the wire mesh, watching in horror as he drew closer to the only person in the world who shared her nightmare.

'It wasn't her fault,' she forced herself to call out, somehow certain his anger would not be turned on her. 'Leave her alone, please. She's done nothing wrong.' Tears slid down her cheeks, salty through dehydration. Strands of dry, sticky saliva stretched across her mouth like a spider's web as she silently pleaded with him to stop.

He fumbled in his trouser pocket, trying to remove an object that was bulkier than the keys he had produced earlier. Whatever it was caught on the fabric of his pocket and he tugged violently to free it, his eyes never leaving Karen Green's cage. 'I'll give you what you fucking want, whore.'

Louise tried to close her eyes, tried to look away as Karen desperately pushed herself into the wire at the back of her cage, trying to find a way to escape the approaching madness. She could see what he was holding now. It was the strange box he'd touched her with when she'd first opened the door to him – the thing that had left her paralysed and helpless.

Almost dropping the key in his fury and excitement, he struggled to unlock Karen's cage, his words slurred and incoherent. Finally he opened the hatch and leaned into the cage. Karen's scream pierced through the hands that covered Louise's ears and penetrated into every millimetre of her body.

Karen was pressed hard against the wire, the skin on her

face patterned with the squares of the wire cage, blood running down her chin from the split lip that opened raw and painful as she tried to push her body through the tiny holes, all the time imploring him to stop in her faint, defeated voice. 'Stop. Please stop.' But he didn't. Instead he kept getting closer to her, inch by inch. Moving cautiously, as if she was a wild animal that might turn on him, he stabbed out at her with the stun-gun. He repeated the action several times, missing his target and then backing away, extending her misery and dread, until finally he struck her at the base of her spine.

For a split second Karen's body went rigid and as hard as mahogany, then she collapsed in a jerking, convulsing wreck. Still he maintained his distance, watching her agony with a slight smile spreading across his lips until her convulsions began to subside. Then he moved in, rolling her on to her back and pulling her legs straight. Louise again tried to look away, but couldn't, any more than she could have looked away from a crystal ball showing her own future. She watched as he tugged and wrenched at his tracksuit pants, exposing his white buttocks, then his long fingers reached for Karen, pulling her filthy knickers down to her knees and shuffling forward as he lay on top of her. Louise heard him moan as he entered Karen, his buttocks moving rhythmically, slowly at first then quickly, brutally, guttural animalistic noises filling the room. Karen, who had stopped convulsing, was lying under him motionless, sobbing, her eyes wide and staring at Louise, accusing her.

Less than a minute later, screams of joy and pleasure signified his climax. His cries faded away to silence. No one spoke and no one moved for what felt like hours, then he tugged at his trousers until they covered his buttocks and still swollen genitals. He backed out of the cage without a word, replacing the lock and bolt, coughing to clear his throat before speaking. He was calm now, but appeared embarrassed, his eyes avoiding Louise's.

'I'm sorry,' he told her. 'I'm sorry you had to see that, but that's what she does. She tricks me. She makes me do it. She knows I don't want to. She knows I don't like being with her. She makes me feel dirty. I won't let her trick me again. Not now you're here, Sam. I promise,' he told her. 'I have to leave you for a while. I'll come back later for the tray. Try to eat something.'

He turned off the light and moved to the staircase, head bowed as if ashamed. She listened to the slow, soft footsteps as they climbed the unseen staircase and then the clank of metal as the unseen door was unlocked. Again there was a flood of daylight that stung her already sore, red eyes. Then gloom once more as the door gently closed.

Louise peered through the gloom towards the figure lying motionless on the concrete floor of her cage making no attempt to cover herself with the little clothing she had. She whispered into the darkness: 'Karen. Karen. Are you all right? Please, Karen. I'm sorry. I'm so sorry.'

But there was no reply. Instead Karen curled into a tight ball, hugging herself, and began to sing a barely audible song. Louise struggled to make out the words. When she did, she realized it wasn't a song Karen was singing, it was a nursery rhyme.

Sally and Sean pulled up outside 22 Oakfield Road, the home of Louise and John Russell, early on Wednesday evening. Sally saw an ugly but practical modern townhouse. Sean saw much more – a concealed front door providing privacy from neighbours and passers-by, state-of-the-art double-glazed windows that were virtually impossible to break in through, a street full of near-identical houses inhabited by neighbours who never spoke to one another, a street where only men who lingered too long and youths clad in hooded tracksuits would draw attention.

'Why's this place not been preserved for forensics?' he demanded.

'No one's saying anything happened here,' Sally told him, defending someone else's decision as if it were her own. 'This is just the last place anyone saw her.'

'"Anyone" meaning her husband?'

'Apparently.' Only day one of the investigation and Sally already sounded weary.

They abandoned their car at the side of the road and walked the short distance to the driveway of the house. Sean stopped and looked around, silently surveying every inch of the house and street, looking up as well as at eye level. Only cops looked up as they walked. Many of the surrounding houses had lights on although it wasn't fully dark – people still used to the habits of winter. Sean searched the windows without thinking, his eyes waiting to be attracted to something they hadn't yet seen. Across the street a curtain twitched as his eyes passed – a neighbour who'd been spying on them guiltily trying to disguise their curiosity. Good, Sean thought, nosy neighbours were often the best witnesses. Sometimes they were the only witnesses. He made a mental note to shake up the neighbour's world as soon as he'd finished with Russell.

He turned towards the house and saw Sally was already waiting for him at the front door. Impatience was not a trait he'd associated with Sally until Gibran almost ripped the life from her. He reasoned that, like most people who'd sailed too close to death, she could no longer bear to waste a second of life. He strode to the front door faster than he wanted to and reached for the bell before hesitating and using his fist to pound on the door instead.

'That doorbell must have been pressed a hundred times since she was taken,' Sally told him. 'If indeed she was taken. Any forensic use it might have had is long gone.'

'Good practice is good practice,' was all he said.

A silhouette inside the house moved quickly to the door and opened it without caution. A tall slim white man in his early thirties stood in front of them. He looked tired and despondent. Everything about him reeked of desperation, not least the way he rushed to the door. He looked disappointed to see them. Sean knew he'd been hoping it was his wife, coming home to beg forgiveness for her infidelity, forgiveness he was all too willing to offer. 'Yes?' he said, his voice no less strained than his body and face.

'John Russell?' Sally asked.

'Yes,' he confirmed.

'Police,' Sally informed him bluntly. 'We're here about your wife.'

Sean saw the blood drain from Russell's face and knew what he was thinking. 'It's all right,' he tried to explain. 'She's still missing.' He watched Russell start to breathe again and held his warrant card at eye level so that even through his panic Russell could see it clearly. 'Detective Inspector Corrigan and this is Detective Sergeant Jones.' Sally's face remained blank. 'May we come in?'

Locked in his moment of private torment, Russell took a few seconds to react and step aside. 'Sorry. Of course. Please, please come in.' He closed the door behind them and led the way to a comfortable kitchen-diner.

Sean glanced at the bric-a-brac of the couple's lives: photographs of holidays together, more elaborately framed photographs of their wedding taking the prime spots on side tables and hallway walls. They looked happy living their un-extraordinary lives, content with their lot, blissfully ignorant of the things he saw every day. He guessed they were planning to have children soon.

'Would either of you like a drink?' Russell offered.

'No thanks. We're fine.' Sean spoke for both of them. 'We just wanted to ask you a few questions about your wife, Louise.'

'OK,' Russell agreed. Sean could tell he was nervous, but not in a way that suggested guilt.

'When did you last see her?' Sean asked.

'Tuesday morning. I left for work at about eight thirty and she was still here, but when I got home she wasn't.'

'And that was unusual?'

'She nearly always got home before me. I work longer hours.'

'Did she say she was going out after work? Maybe you didn't hear her when she told you. Maybe you were distracted. We all live busy lives, Mr Russell,' Sean suggested. 'My wife reckons I only hear about a third of what she actually says.'

'No,' Russell insisted. 'We don't live like that. If she'd been going somewhere or if she was going to be late she would have made sure I knew and I would have remembered. This is all a waste of time anyway. She didn't go out for a night out with her friends and she hasn't run off with another man. If you knew her, you wouldn't think that, you'd be looking for her.'

'We are looking for her,' Sean reassured him. 'That's why we're here and that's why I have to ask some difficult questions.' Russell didn't respond. 'Even the people closest to us sometimes have secrets. If we can find out any secrets Louise had then maybe we can find her.'

'Louise didn't have secrets from me,' Russell insisted.

'What about you from her?' Sally asked clumsily. It was a question that needed to be put, but not now. Not yet.

Sean swallowed his frustration with Sally. 'Maybe something that seemed innocent to you, but that you didn't want her to know, something that might have upset her enough to make her want to be alone for a few days?'

'Such as?' Russell asked.

'Anything,' Sean answered. 'An old girlfriend contacting you or a large bill you've been hiding from her because you didn't want her to worry about it. Maybe she thought it was a breach of trust.'

'No,' Russell slammed the door of possibility shut. 'There are no old girlfriends, no money worries. We're careful.'

Sean took a few seconds to consider before making his final judgement. Russell had nothing to do with his wife's disappearance and couldn't help Sean find her. There would be no secret lover and she wasn't going to return in a couple of days telling anyone who would listen that she'd needed a little time alone. Something terrible had happened to her, something beyond her husband's imagination, beyond almost everyone's imagination. But not Sean's.

Despite the warmth of the central heating Sean felt the hairs on his arms and neck begin to tingle and rise. He found himself looking back towards the front door. He saw the faceless silhouette of a man coming through the door, knocking Louise Russell to the ground, somehow overpowering her and taking her, dragging her from her own home, the place she felt safest.

He didn't know how many seconds he'd been absent for when Sally's voice dragged him back.

'Guv'nor?'

'What?' he replied like a man caught daydreaming.

'Anything else we need to know?'

'Yes . . .' Sean turned to Russell. 'You said her car was missing too?'

'That's right,' Russell answered. 'That was when I realized something was wrong, when I saw her car wasn't on the drive. I just had a bad feeling. Then I came inside and found her handbag and phone, but she wasn't here. I've already given your colleagues a description of her car and registration number.' Sean glanced at Sally, who confirmed with a quick nod of her head. 'Is there anything else you need?' Russell asked tiredly.

'No,' Sean told him. It was obvious the guy had had enough of giving the same answers to the same questions. 'You've been really helpful, thanks.' Russell said nothing. 'If I could just ask you to try and avoid the hallway by the front door as much as possible until I can get our forensics people to have a look at it.' Russell looked at him accusingly. 'I like to be sure,' Sean reassured him. 'Check every possibility.'

'If you think it's necessary,' Russell agreed.

'Thank you,' Sean said. 'And one last thing, before I forget. Who is her best friend? Who would she confide in?'

'Me,' Russell told them. 'She would confide in me.'

Sean and Sally heard the door close softly behind them as they walked down the Russells' driveway without looking back. Sally spoke quietly: 'Well?'

'He's got nothing to do with it and he can't help us find her any more than he already has. We both know she hasn't run away, not without her bag and phone.'

'We're not all addicted to handbags,' Sally reprimanded him, holding out her arms to indicate the absence of a bag.

'Phone?' Sean asked, indicating the mobile clutched in Sally's guilty hand.

'OK,' Sally conceded. 'So what happened?'

'I don't know yet,' Sean answered. 'He either did her in the hallway by the front door and took her body away in her own car, or he took her alive.'

'He?' Sally challenged. 'You sound like you already know him.' Sean merely shrugged in reply. 'So what next?' she continued.

'I need you to get hold of Roddis. Have him examine the house properly, concentrating on the hallway, front door, etc. The scene, if it is one, has been well and truly trampled, but you never know your luck. And make sure her car details are circulated if they haven't been already, then get them marked for forensic preservation – that won't have been done yet, you can put your mortgage on it.'

'I'll see to it,' Sally assured him while following his eyeline across the street to the house he was staring at. 'Something I should know?'

'A twitching curtain,' Sean told her. 'When we first pulled

up, someone was watching us. The question is, why?' He started walking towards the house, offering no explanation. Sally followed.

Sean used the doorbell this time and waited impatiently – he already knew someone was at home. There was no glass in the front door, just a spyhole. Clearly the occupier preferred security to natural light. Sean noticed the pristine Neighbourhood Watch sticker attached to the inside of the front-room window. He went to press the doorbell again, but delayed when he felt a presence on the other side of the wooden barrier. They listened as at least two good, heavy deadbolts were withdrawn. Not many people used security like that when they were at home and awake.

The door fell back into the warm house revealing an elderly man in his late sixties or early seventies. He was still quite tall, about Sean's height, and he held his back straight military-style, although Sean doubted he'd ever actually been a soldier. He wore smart grey trousers and a brown cardigan over a blue shirt that contrasted with the reddening skin pulled over his bony, angular face. His hair was grey and wavy, but still had traces of the blond that had only recently deserted him. He knew who they were but asked them anyway: 'Who are you and what do you want?'

Sean had already formed a dislike to him. Sally had no opinion; to her he was one more face, one more witness to be spoken to, assessed and categorized before she could escape to the solitude of her own home, away from prying eyes and stupid questions about how she was coping.

Holding up his warrant card for the wannabe soldier, Sean announced: 'DI Corrigan and this is my colleague DS Jones. We're making some local inquiries about a missing person. Mind if we ask you a couple of questions?'

'Do I know this missing person?'

'I don't know,' Sean answered. 'Do you? Louise Russell, she lives across the road, number twenty-two?' Sean didn't let him answer. 'Do you mind if we come inside? This inquiry's at a sensitive stage, you understand.'

The man stepped aside reluctantly. 'Fine, but this won't take too long, will it?'

'No.' Sean passed by him into the neat and orderly house, immediately looking around, his eyes studying every detail. 'Sorry, I didn't catch your name,' Sean prompted as Sally entered the hallway, making a little too much of checking her watch.

'Levy,' the man answered. 'Douglas Levy.' Sean's eyes turned from scanning the house to surveying the occupier, dissecting him layer by layer. Was this the man responsible for Louise Russell's disappearance? Had he watched her every day from behind his twitching curtain, fantasized about her, about having her, taking her, doing things to her that no woman would ever let him do to them? Had he masturbated while thinking about her, did he take himself in hand while he watched her from the window, ejaculating embarrassingly into his own hand, too overcome by his excitement to fetch tissues from the bathroom before he started? And then, after months, maybe even years, had he decided he needed more? Maybe just to touch her once, maybe a kiss, an innocent kiss on the cheek, something to add spice to his fantasies and masturbating. Had he gone too far, touched her in the wrong place, tried to kiss her too hard until she started to scream and fight, and he panicked, hit her, hit her hard and all the time the excitement rising in his groin, the material of his underpants tightening uncomfortably around his swelling penis and then she was unconscious and he was inside her, grunting and rutting like a pig until all too quickly it was over and then he had to kill her, he didn't want to, but he had to, to stop her telling everyone what he had done, his hands closing around her throat, her eyes bulging, the whites turning red as a thousand unseen capillaries ruptured. Sean found himself studying Levy's hands for scratch marks. There were none, but Sean knew he was at least partly right about him.

'Do you live alone, Mr Levy?' Sean asked.

'I don't see what that's got to do with anything,' Levy responded, indignant.

'No,' Sean agreed, his question unwittingly answered. 'I see you're a member of the local Neighbourhood Watch.'

'Actually, Inspector, I'm the coordinator of the Neighbourhood Watch. You can check with the local police if you don't believe me.'

'Why wouldn't I believe you?' said Sean, enjoying the discomfort creeping over Levy's features.

Sally looked on, disinterested and excluded, already convinced Levy was a waste of time as a witness or a suspect.

'As coordinator of the Neighbourhood Watch, you no doubt keep an eye on things, look out for strangers in the street, keep a watch on your neighbours' houses when they're at work and you're at home alone . . . I'm sorry,' Sean finished with an insincere smile, 'I've made an assumption you're retired.'

'I am,' Levy told him, straightening his back as if he was proud of his retired status, although Sean could tell it was killing him, knowing that he'd passed his usefulness sell-by-date.

'And did you?' Sean asked.

'Did I what?' Levy was struggling to keep up with the conversation, his pink face growing redder with anger and frustration.

'See anything or anyone in the street the last few days that made you suspicious?'

'I don't spend all my time looking out of the window,' Levy protested.

'But when you hear something, like a car coming or going, you do,' Sean suggested.

Levy grew more flustered. 'Sometimes . . . maybe . . . I don't know, not really.'

'But you heard us arrive earlier and you watched us

through the window. So you like to keep an eye on the comings and goings of the street, yes?'

'What's the point of all of this?' Levy snapped. 'I know nothing about the woman across the street's disappearance. I didn't hear anything and I didn't see anything.'

Sean studied him in silence for as long as he felt Levy could stand. 'OK,' he said finally. 'Just one more thing. Did anyone ever arrive at the Russells' house after Mr Russell had left for work but before Mrs Russell set off?'

'Not that I noticed.' Levy answered with his eyes closed as if he could somehow block Sean out of his consciousness.

'Did they ever argue or fight that you know of?' Sean continued.

'No,' Levy insisted. 'They're a decent, quiet couple who keep themselves to themselves. Now please, I'm very busy and I think I've helped you as much as I can so—'

'Of course,' Sean agreed. Levy opened the door a little too quickly and moved aside, waiting for them to leave. 'Thanks for your time.'

They walked past him and into the growing darkness. The street was quiet with the onset of night and their words would travel too far if they spoke outside, so they waited until they were back in the car. Sally spoke first.

'Do you mind telling me what that was all about?' she asked. 'Given that I doubt even you are seriously considering Levy as a suspect.'

'Why not? Lives alone, bored out of his skull, nothing to do, nothing to look forward to. The devil finds work for idle hands. He watches her, fantasizes about her until finally he can't resist it any more so he waits for the husband to go to work and decides to pay Mrs Russell a little visit. But he goes too far and before he knows it he's a killer. It's nothing we haven't seen.'

'Christ!' Sally exclaimed. 'Even if he did fantasize about her – which I doubt – he would never have the balls to try and do something about it. If there's one thing that terrifies the likes of Levy it's change. He would never risk upsetting his pointless life.'

Sean could see that Sally had had enough. 'Fair point. I guess I just didn't like him. I guess I just don't like any of them.'

'Any of who?' Sally asked.

'The stuffed shirt Neighbourhood Watch brigade. We might as well get rid of the lot of them for all the good they do. Stickers in windows and monthly meetings, for fuck's sake – who are they kidding? Some madman came to this street and killed or kidnapped a woman right under their pious noses and nobody saw a damn thing. Neighbourhood Watch? Bunch of sanctimonious wankers.' Tiredness suddenly swept over him, reminding him to check his watch. It was gone eight. By the time they got back to Peckham and tidied up the first day of inquiries and prepared for the next it would be close to eleven. He had a chance of making it home before midnight.

'So you're sure then?' Sally asked. 'She's either already dead or someone's taken her and she probably soon will be.'

'I'm not sure of anything,' Sean lied. 'Let's head back to the office. It's getting late, there's nothing else we can do tonight. In the morning you go see her parents and I'll have a word with her workmates, just in case we're missing something.'

'Fine,' was all Sally replied.

Sean forced himself to ask her the obvious question, fearful she might answer truthfully, making him listen to her fears and pain, but Sally wasn't about to share herself with anyone yet. 'Sore and tired,' she told him. 'I need tramadol and sleep.'

'Sort out forensics for the house and check her car details have been circulated and then get yourself home,' he instructed her. 'Don't stick around for anything else.' He watched as

Sally again subconsciously rubbed her chest where the knife had entered. He could imagine the scars beneath her jacket and blouse, still red, raised and ugly; one above her right breast and one below. It would be years before they faded, but they would always be clearly visible.

'I will,' Sally promised. 'And thanks.'

'Don't thank me,' Sean insisted. 'Just look after yourself.'

Louise Russell sat in the gloom of her cage, knees pulled up to her chin, arms wrapped around her lower legs, hugging the thin duvet close and rocking subconsciously as she tried to judge the time. She guessed it must be the early hours of the morning, whereas in fact it was earlier, not quite ten at night. She'd tried to get her fellow captive to talk, but Karen Green just lay motionless on the floor of her wire prison. Louise already suspected that if either of them were ever to see the sun again they would have to work together. Somehow she needed to break through to Karen and persuade her to talk.

The sudden noise of metal striking metal fired her alert, her eyes open impossibly wide, like a frightened deer, her heart beating like a cornered rat's. She heard Karen shuffling around in her cage, scratching at the floor looking for somewhere she would never find to hide. The noise and movement fleetingly reminded Louise of the pet mouse she was allowed to keep as a child, always searching in vain for a way to escape its wire world.

Gripped by fear, Louise waited for more sounds. She heard the heavy metal door swinging open and waited for the flood of light to sting her eyes, but it never came and she remembered it was night. A thin beam threw a circle of light on to the floor at the bottom of the staircase. As the soft footsteps made their way down towards them the ray of light bounced around. He stepped into the room and swung the torch slowly and deliberately from one side to the other, ensuring everything was as it should be, exactly as he'd left it. Temporarily blinded, Louise could no longer see his silhouette, only the harsh glare of the torchlight touching her skin, making her shudder as surely as the touch of his hands. She couldn't see his face, but she was sure he was smiling.

A minute or two later the light behind the screen clicked on, the string cord swinging after he released it. Louise squeezed her eyes shut for a few seconds while she prayed this was all a nightmare, an unusually long and realistic nightmare, but one that must end soon. If she could only chase the sleep away and wake herself then this would be over. It would leave her shaken for the rest of the morning, but by lunchtime it would have faded like a watercolour left in the rain. But when she dared open her eyes again he was standing there, peering into her very being, a torch in one hand and a tray in the other with a happy smile on his face.

He carefully placed the things he was carrying on what she assumed was some kind of table behind the screen and began to nervously approach her, one or two small steps at a time, his right hand outstretched in front of him palm up, as if he was approaching a stranger's dog. 'It's OK, Sam,' he tried to reassure her. 'It's me. I didn't wake you, did I? I didn't mean to disturb you. I only wanted to make sure you were all right.' He fell silent as if expecting her to answer. She didn't. 'You should be feeling a lot better by now, the effects of the chloroform should pretty much have gone.' Still she didn't answer him, but she watched him, watched his every tiny move. He gestured to the tray hidden behind the screen. 'I've brought you more food and something to drink, a Diet Coke – I remembered it's your favourite.'

Some deep survival instinct told her she had to answer him or soon she would become to him what Karen Green already was. Had that been Karen's failure, her damnation, that she hadn't been able to answer him? 'Thank you.' She forced the words out, her voice sounding weak and broken.

A wide, relieved smile spread across his face. With his new-found confidence he moved too quickly towards her cage, startling her. He froze for a second, aware his impatience had frightened her.

'Don't be afraid, Sam,' he almost begged her. 'I would never hurt you, you know that. That's why I brought you here, so I could look after you, protect you from all those liars, all those liars who told you all those things about me to keep you away from me. I always knew you didn't believe them, Sam. And now they can't hurt us any more. We can be together now.' More silence as he waited for her to answer.

'I need the toilet,' she told him, the thought and words coming from nowhere.

He stared at her for a while, his mouth still holding a thin smile, but his eyes darted around in confusion and fear. 'Of course,' he eventually answered. 'I thought you probably would.' It wasn't how she'd expected him to answer. 'I'll have to let you out,' he continued. 'Where you won't be as safe from them, Sam. They're still in your mind, you see. All the things they did to you, they're still in your mind. They might try and trick you, get you to do something you don't want to do. They might try and make you hurt me.'

'I won't,' she forced herself to say. 'I promise.'

He pushed his hand into his loose tracksuit bottoms and fished around awkwardly for something, before finally tugging the black box free and showing it to her. She recognized it immediately, the stun-gun he'd used to take her. The thing he'd used to defile Karen Green. 'Don't worry,' he assured her. 'If they try and make you do something you shouldn't, I'll use this.' He looked puzzled by her expression of fear. 'It won't hurt you,' he promised. 'It'll just stop them making you do things. It keeps them away.'

'I need to clean up, that's all,' she told him.

He considered her for a long time before speaking. 'OK,' he said, and moved towards her cage slowly and carefully, his eyes never leaving hers. Within a few short steps he was at her cage, almost as close to her as he'd been when he took her, his pallid skin and stained crooked teeth clearly visible, his arms thin, but sinewy and strong, the arteries and veins blue and swollen. He took a key carefully from his other tracksuit pocket and tentatively held it close to the lock. He considered her again, then gave a broad smile, pushed the key into the lock and turned it. A slight moment of hesitation and then he swung the door open, the hinges squealing and the wire of the cage reverberating. He stepped back, the stun-gun in his hand at his side. 'Please,' he said, 'this way,' and pointed towards the old hospital screen.

Louise walked in a hunched, squatted gait towards the opening, the pain of her muscles cramping matched only by the fear that made her heart send shock waves through her chest. She paused for a moment at the entrance and waited for him to take a few more steps back, at last pushing herself through into the room, stretching her sore, stiff body, straightening for the first time in a day and a half, but all the time careful not to let the duvet slip from her shoulders and show him her nakedness. 'Behind the screen,' he instructed her. 'You can get cleaned up there and there's a toilet you can use. It's only a chemical one, but it works well enough.'

'Thank you,' she forced herself to tell him, when all she really wanted to do was spit in his face. As she rounded the screen she saw her facilities – an old, stained sink barely attached to the cellar wall; rusty, limescale-crusted metal taps and a new-looking chemical toilet set low on the floor. She guessed he had recently installed the toilet, but clearly he had been planning for this for some time. Her eyes searched around for anything she could fashion into a weapon. There was nothing. She swallowed her disappointment and her rising tears.

She could feel him on the other side of the screen, watching her through the thin fabric, waiting for her to drop the duvet, his imagination removing the barrier, his eyes flicking across her skin. 'Are you all right in there?' he asked, as if she was in a separate room.

'Yes,' she stuttered in reply. 'Just getting things ready.'

'The hot water tap's the one on the left,' he warned her.

She let the water run hot before putting the chained plug in the sink and allowing it to fill, looking over her shoulder at his silhouette behind her, allowing the duvet to slip to the floor, leaving her standing naked and vulnerable in a way she'd never felt until now. Quickly she began to wash, using the sliver of soap he'd left on the sink to try and cleanse her skin of as much of him as she could. All the time she knew he was watching her, watching her hands moving over her own damp, shiny body. She rinsed herself clean of the soap and looked around for a towel, a sense of panic rising as she realized there wasn't one next to the sink, the panic easing when she saw it on the table by the tray of food he'd brought. Hurriedly she patted herself dry, the stale smell of the scratchy towel making her want to retch. She could hear him, breathing heavily as he watched her. Pulling the duvet over herself, she stepped out from behind the screen.

'Take the tray,' he said. 'It's all for you.'

She studied the tray and the items on it suspiciously. A white-bread sandwich, some crisps emptied into a plastic bowl, a few biscuits and a can of Coke. The emptiness in her stomach and the rasping dryness of her throat told her to take it. 'You'll have to eat it in your room,' he instructed, his eyes pointing to her cage. 'I'll get the tray later.'

She did as he wanted and walked as quickly as she could back to her prison, almost relieved to be behind the wire again, a barrier between her and him, even if she knew it was a barrier he controlled. 'I'll bring you clean clothes in the morning,' he said as he closed her cage door and replaced the lock. 'You need to get some sleep, Sam. We have so many plans to make. I have to go now.'

He was moving towards the light cord when a weak voice stopped him.

Karen's head raised slightly from the floor. 'Please,' she asked desperately. 'I need a drink and I'm very hungry. Can I have something, please? I promise I'll be good.' The room waited silently for a reaction, Louise looking from Karen to him and back, praying he wouldn't hurt her cellmate, praying she wouldn't have to watch again.

'What?' he demanded, the friendliness in his voice replaced with a quiet menace. 'You want what, whore?'

'Please,' Karen pleaded, her voice trembling, her throat almost shut with dryness and terror. 'I'm so thirsty. I don't feel very well. I need some food. Please. Anything.'

'Lying whores get nothing!' he shouted.

'No, no,' Karen sobbed. 'Please, I don't understand what you mean. I don't know why I'm here. Just let me go, please. I swear I won't tell anyone what you've done.'

'Shut up,' he screamed, agitated, behaving as if he was the one who was trapped, as if he was the one in danger. 'You're trying to trick me. You're trying to fuck with my head again.' He was pointing at Karen, accusing her, close to tears himself now. He turned to Louise. 'See what they do, Sam? See what they're trying to do to us?'

'Just let me go,' Karen was almost shouting. 'Please, let me go.'

'Shut up. Shut up. Shut up. Shut up. Make her stop, Sam!'

Louise covered her ears with the palms of her hands, pressing so hard that her inner ears began to hurt under the pressure. She couldn't stand to listen to this a moment longer.

'You're a whore, a lying whore! She tried to pretend she was you, Sam. She tricked me. She made me bring her here, but I found out she's a liar. She's one of them, trying to ruin everything for me.'

'That's not true,' Karen pleaded with him through the

strings of saliva that webbed across her contorted mouth. 'I'll do anything you want me to, I swear.'

'Shut up, lying whore,' he shouted in her face through the wire, holding his stun-gun in front of her so she could see clearly. 'I know what you're trying to make me do, it's what all you whores want me to do to them, but you won't make me.' He looked back at Louise, a smile mixing with his fear, his face shining with the sweat of anxiety. 'Sam's with me now. You can't stop us.' He began to walk backwards, silently, his eyes never leaving Karen's, wagging his finger at her as if warning her against doing whatever it was he imagined she was about to do. He pulled the light-switch cord, sinking the room back to its deathly gloom as he stepped behind the wall of the staircase and out of sight. They could hear him breathing, deep and panicked, but calming once he couldn't be seen, then they could hear him no more. They waited a few minutes until the torchlight returned with a click, followed by his familiar soft footsteps climbing the stairs. A metal door being pulled open and then swung carefully shut; the locked padlock clanging against the sheet metal. Then nothing – silence and darkness. Nothing.

Shortly after ten on Wednesday night Sally squeezed her hatchback into virtually the last parking space in the street. Even the necessity to display your residents-only parking permit couldn't keep the road clear of vehicles abandoned for the night. Her neighbours had been home for hours, most already thinking about sleep before the dawning of another day exactly like the one they'd just lived. Sally almost envied them. She waited in her locked car, lights on and engine running, until she saw some other sign of life in the street. A young couple appeared in her wing mirror, walking arm in arm along the pavement, the man muttering and the woman giggling. At this time of night it would have to do. Sally quickly turned off the lights and engine and jumped from her car, locking it without looking as she walked towards the smart three-storey Victorian terrace her new flat was in: a two-bedroom place on the top floor. By the time she reached the front door she already had her house keys ready and she entered the house quickly and quietly, the way she'd practised hundreds of times. No one could have followed her inside.

She heard the young couple walk past outside, reminding her of one of the many reasons she'd chosen this flat, in this house, on this street: because it was often quite busy, even at night – Putney High Street was just at the end of the road. Sebastian Gibran may not have taken her life, but he'd killed so many things that had been important to her, that she'd loved. She'd not been back to her old flat since he attacked her there. It held nothing for her but nightmarish memories of horror and pain. The selling estate agent had been very helpful and had visited the flat whenever necessary so Sally hadn't had to.

As quickly and efficiently as she'd entered the house, she climbed the stairs and entered her flat. Only when she was inside did she breathe out the tension she'd been carrying for the last few hours. Standing with her back to the front door, she surveyed the interior, the lights she'd deliberately left on all day – another new habit, to avoid those panicked moments in the dark, fumbling for the light switch. Everything seemed fine as she scanned the sparse furniture and removal company boxes spread around the floor, still waiting to be unpacked. If this latest case went the way she was sure Sean thought it would, the boxes would have to wait a few more days or even weeks.

Sally stepped into the room that served as both her entrance and lounge and searched for the television remote. She found it on the coffee table, hiding under an unread newspaper, and clicked the TV on for background noise. She kept moving deeper into the flat, along the corridor and into the gleaming new kitchen equipped with everything a keen cook would need, things that she would hardly ever use. Stabbing pains in her chest strong enough to make her wince reminded her of her mission. From an overhead cupboard she pulled a pack of tramadol prescription painkillers free, grabbed a glass from the neighbouring cupboard and headed for the fridge. She yanked the door open and checked the barren contents, discovering half a bottle of white wine, still drinkable. Trying unsuccessfully to steady her hand, she poured a full glass, spilling a few drops that ran down the outside of the glass and dripped annoyingly on to the kitchen table. She pushed three tramadol from their foil surrounds, one more than she'd been prescribed to take, and swallowed them in one go with a good swig of the wine.

Closing her eyes, she waited for some relief, some elemental change in her mind and body, but the effects were too slow. She grabbed another glass from the draining board and headed for the freezer, hesitating for a second before surrendering to the idea and opening the door. Her old friend seemed to look at her, that bottle of vodka that had been ever-present in her freezer since her early days in the CID, wedged between a packet of unopened frozen vegetables and a once-raided bag of French fries. The vodka had become more necessary of late, an everyday requirement rather than a treat after a particularly tough day. By five o'clock her mind would already be drifting to the thought of that first taste, first hit, mixing with the tramadol and ibuprofen, a legal narcotics cocktail that rushed straight to her brain and took the world away just as sure as any junky's fix could. She poured two fingers' worth into the short, fat tumbler and drank half in one gulp, the freezing liquid numbing her throat and empty stomach, warning her brain of the delights it could soon expect.

She waited for the chemicals to ease her pain and anxiety, but as the storms calmed the quieter ghosts began to sweep forward. The tears seemed to start in her throat, but no matter how hard she tried to swallow them back down they found their way to her eyes and escaped in heavy drops that ran down her face, each finding a new route, dropping on to her hands and into her drink. Once the tears were flowing she knew there was no point fighting them, better to let them come until she would be too exhausted to cry any more; then she would sit quietly, motionless, her mind still and blank, her heart fluttering in the silence until finally sleep would take her. In the morning she would feel a little better, hung-over, but a little better, just about able to face the world.

Since she went back to work she'd been holding it together OK during office hours, getting the job done, not asking for any special treatment, but there were frequent moments of burning anxiety, when she'd been scared to speak for fear of her voice shaking, scared to hold a pen in case someone noticed her hand trembling. And every morning before leaving for work she stood frozen by her front door, physically unable to reach out and open it, hyperventilating with fear of the world beyond. Two weeks ago she'd suffered one of her worst attacks, remaining slumped against her door for more than an hour while she desperately tried to gather up the courage to leave her sanctuary. Even on the days when she overcame the fear and made it to her car, she would drive through the streets pretending nothing was wrong, sit at her desk pretending that she didn't have to endure this daily ritual of personal torment.

Sally drained the glass and reached for her old friend in the freezer to pour a refill.

It was midnight by the time Sean arrived home, a modest semi-detached Edwardian house in the better part of Dulwich that he shared with his wife Kate and their two young daughters, Mandy and Louise. He knew Kate had been working the late shift as the attending physician in the Accident and Emergency Department of Guy's Hospital and would therefore not long have got home herself. Probably he'd find her awake, eager to talk about her day and the children. On a normal day at a normal time he'd have looked forward to sitting with Kate and chatting about the unimportant and important alike, but this had been no normal day. His mind was swimming with images and ideas he wouldn't share with her – images and ideas that would make it difficult to concentrate on anything she said. He reminded himself that women needed to talk, that somehow he would have to focus on his wife's conversation. All the same he was hoping she'd be asleep so he could grab a drink and watch the TV in the kitchen and pretend to himself he wasn't thinking about Louise Russell.

He turned the key and quietly pushed the door open. The lights were on in the kitchen. Dropping his keys as noisily as he dared on the hallway table, hoping Kate would hear the noise and know he was home before he accidentally startled her, he took a breath and walked to the kitchen.

Kate looked up from her laptop. 'You're late,' she said matter-of-factly. 'I'm the one who's supposed to be on lates this week, remember?'

'Sorry,' Sean told her. 'We picked up a new case.'

'So you won't be around much the next few days?'

'Sorry,' he said again. 'You know what it's like when a new one comes in.'

'Yes, Sean,' she answered. 'We all know what it's like when you get a new one. Shame,' she continued, 'I was hoping to save some money on childcare this week.'

'Kirsty's all right looking after the kids, isn't she?' he asked. 'She probably needs the cash.'

'So do we,' Kate reminded him. 'At least if you were still a sergeant, you'd get paid overtime. The hours you work, we'd be rich.'

'I doubt it,' Sean scoffed.

'So what's the new case?' Kate asked. 'What tale of horror do you have to untangle this time? I assume it's another murder?'

'Even if it was a murder, you know I wouldn't tell you about it. Work stays at work.'

'Even if it was a murder,' Kate pointed out. 'Meaning it's not a murder this time. So why is a Murder Investigation Team investigating something other than a murder?'

'As it happens, it's a missing person,' Sean told her.

'Oh,' Kate said, interested and concerned. 'A missing person who you think is dead. Get you on the job early, ready for when the body turns up. That's not like the Met, planning ahead.'

'I don't,' Sean said.

'Don't what?'

'Think she's dead. I think someone's taken her.'

'A kidnap case?' Kate asked.

'I'm not expecting a ransom note.'

'Then what?'

'Like I said, no details.' Sean changed the subject: 'How are the girls?'

Kate paused before answering, unsure as to whether she should try and prise more details from him. She decided she'd be wasting her time. 'Last time I saw them awake they were fine, but they miss their dad.'

'I suppose that's good.'

'I think I know what you mean,' Kate smiled. 'Next time you're home they'll mob you – you have been warned.'

'I look forward to it.' Sean headed for the fridge, searching around inside for a beer. Kate waved her empty wine glass in the air. 'While you're in there, a top-up please.' He grabbed the bottle of wine and poured as little as he thought he could get away with into her glass, not wishing to delay her going to bed any longer than was absolutely necessary, before putting it back in the fridge and grabbing a beer. He took his favourite glass from the cupboard and sat at the table with Kate, using the remote to click the TV on.

'I take it that's the end of conversation for the night,' Kate accused.

'Sorry.' Sean turned to her with a mischievous grin. 'I thought you were playing on your computer.'

'Ha, ha,' Kate replied. 'Working, Sean. Working. All we ever do is work. Work and pay bills. That's it.'

'It's not that bad,' Sean argued, now glad she'd waited up, pleased to have the distraction of conversation.

'We should think about New Zealand again. Remember, after what happened to Sally, you said we ought to get the hell out of here, start a new life, one where we actually see each other. Where we see the kids.'

'I don't know,' Sean answered. 'It just feels like running away.'

'Nothing wrong with running away if it's running away to a better life.'

'There's no guarantee of a better life,' Sean argued. 'I did my research. New Zealand's not all green fields and blue skies. They've got plenty of problems too. You don't really think they'd stick me in a plush office somewhere overlooking the Pacific with nothing to do but twiddle my thumbs and admire the view all day, do you? They'd find some shithole to stick me in and we'd be back where we started, only stuck on the other side of the world.'

'It can't be as bad as it is here,' Kate insisted. 'I've lived with you too long not to know your job and how it works. If you were to so much as hint that you want to go home and see your family once in a while, they'd all look at you like you've gone mad, like you're somehow letting the team down. Only losers want to actually go home now and then, right?' Sean shifted uncomfortably in his chair. 'And as we both know, there's no way you could ever, ever walk out on a job and let somebody else deal with it. You're way too conscientious for that. True?'

'I can't walk out in the middle of a job. There's no one

else to pass it on to. A case comes in, it lands on my desk and that's it. It's mine until it's finished. If I don't get to come home for a week then I don't get to come home for a week. That's the way it is. It goes with the territory. It's the job. It's what I do. I can't run off to New Zealand. I can't run off anywhere. I am what I am. I do what I do. You don't want to see me sitting in an office in the City pushing paper around, living for my bonus, another clone – that would kill me. I wouldn't be me any more. I'd bore you to death.'

Kate thought for a long while before answering. 'You're right,' she told him. 'I know you have to be a cop. You thrive on it. It makes you proud – and so it should. But the kids are getting older. At least one of us needs to be here more for them.'

'Meaning?'

'I'm just saying,' Kate went on. 'The fact is I earn almost twice what you do and I don't have to nearly kill myself to do it.'

'What are you suggesting?' Sean asked, his voice thick with suspicion.

'I don't really know,' Kate admitted. 'I think we need more of a plan, that's all. I have no idea where we're going.'

'Who ever knows that?' Sean questioned. 'All anyone can do is live in the day, try and get something out of every day. All these books and gurus spouting plans for a better life – it's a load of crap. You have to just try and live your life the best you can.'

Kate studied him a while. 'I am happy,' she told him, 'but surely there's more for us somewhere. Something better.'

Sean searched her brown eyes for signs of happiness. He saw no signs of unhappiness and decided that was good enough, for now.

'I do love you,' she continued, 'which is why I worry about you, which is why I don't want to share you with the bad people, the psychos, the drug dealers, the angry madmen. I want you all for myself and the kids.'

Her words made him smile. 'I know,' he said. 'But I want you and the kids to be proud of me. I want them to know what I do.'

'Christ,' Kate replied. 'You'll scare the bloody hell out of them.'

'I'll spare them the details, but you get what I mean.'

'So,' Kate surrendered, 'we carry on as we are, ships that pass in the night, absent parents?'

'I'm not ready to walk away yet,' Sean told her. 'Let's give it a couple more years, then we'll see.'

'I wouldn't ask you to walk away if you don't want to,' she assured him.

'A couple more years,' Sean almost promised. 'Then we'll see.'

'I'll remember this conversation, you know,' she warned him.

'Of course you will,' Sean conceded. 'You're a woman.'

3

Thursday morning shortly before nine o'clock and Sally was knocking on the door of a nondescript house in Teddington on the outskirts of West London, steeling herself to ask the occupants a set of questions that even their closest friends wouldn't dare to broach. Though she'd never met these people, experience told her they would see her as their potential saviour. This morning she felt more like an intruder come to wreak havoc. So long as she got the answers to her questions – answers that could progress or kill off this new case – she didn't really care what impact her visit might have on their lives.

While she waited for an answer, she took a couple of steps back from the door, surveying the large ugly house that would have been the pride of the street when newly built in the seventies, but now looked tired and out of place amongst the older, more gracious houses.

She heard the approach of muffled footsteps, comfortable slippers or soft indoor shoes, moving rapidly, but shuffling, the effort of lifting feet too much for ageing, tired muscles. There was a hurried fumbling of the latch then the door opened to reveal a grey-haired couple who resembled each other: both small and slightly dumpy, curly hair long since abandoned to nature, tanned skin from too many cruise-ship holidays, cardigans and elasticated trousers, thin-framed spectacles magnifying bright, hopeful, blue eyes. They answered the door together, something that only happened in times of joyful or fearful expectation. Sally thought they looked like children sneaking into a room in the middle of the night where their parents had lied to them that Father Christmas would have left their presents, excited by the promise of toys, afraid of being caught.

'Yes?' the old man asked, his wife peering over his shoulder. Sally flipped open her warrant card and faked a smile.

'DS Jones, Metropolitan Police . . .' She managed to stop herself adding *Murder Investigation Team*. The last thing she needed was two old people passing out on her, or worse. 'I'm looking into the disappearance of your daughter, Louise Russell. You are . . .' Sally quickly checked her notebook, silently cursing herself for not having done so before knocking, '. . . Mr and Mrs Graham – Louise's parents?' They were too desperate to notice her hesitation.

'Yes,' the old man confirmed. 'Frank and Rose Graham. Louise is our daughter.'

Frank and Rose, Sally thought. Old names. Strong names. 'Can I come in?' she asked, already moving towards the door.

'Please,' said Mr Graham, stepping aside to allow her to enter the hallway.

Sally felt the carpet under her feet, worn and thin, too colourful for today's tastes, like the floral wallpaper and framed prints of famous paintings, Constable mingling with Van Gogh.

'Have you heard anything?' he asked, his patience failing him. 'Do you know where she is?'

'Frank,' Mrs Graham reprimanded him. 'Maybe Sergeant Jones would like a cup of tea first?'

'Of course. Sorry,' Mr Graham apologized. 'Perhaps you'd like to come through to the lounge. We can have tea in there – or coffee, if you'd prefer.'

'Tea will be fine,' said Sally.

'I'll put the kettle on,' Mrs Graham announced and scuttled away to where Sally assumed the out-dated kitchen would be. 'I'll be back in a couple of minutes,' she called back over her shoulder.

'This way,' said Mr Graham, indicating the nearest door as if he was showing her to a seat in the theatre.

Sally entered the room, taking everything in: more cheap-looking prints of paintings, moderately expensive bric-a-brac, china figurines of women in Victorian dresses holding parasols, a mustard-coloured carpet so thick it was bouncy, and as the centre piece an old oversized television newly adapted to receive a digital signal. Sally doubted they even knew why they needed the strange box that now sat on top of their former pride and joy.

'Please,' Graham invited her. 'Take a seat.'

Sally looked around for a seat no one would be able to share with her and decided on the fake leather armchair, the type she'd seen in old people's rest homes.

'Thanks,' she said, perching herself on the edge of the chair, dropping the computer case that she used as a briefcase on the floor by her feet. Graham sat in what she assumed was his usual chair, prime of place for TV viewing.

'This has all been very difficult for my wife,' he began.

'I'm sure it has,' Sally empathized. 'And for you too.'

'I've been OK,' he lied. 'Bearing up. Someone has to, you know.'

'Of course,' Sally pretended to agree.

'Ten years in the army teaches you a thing or two about coping with, with difficult situations.'

'You were in the army?' Sally asked, warming him up for the hard questions still to come.

'I was.' His voice and posture suddenly became more soldierly. 'I did my National Service and, unlike most of my mates, I loved it. So I signed up for regular army when my year was up. The Green Jackets. But it's a young man's game, the army. After ten years I moved to civvie street.'

'What did you do there?' Sally asked, already knowing she wouldn't be interested in the answer.

'Sales,' he answered curtly, as bored by his life as Sally would have been. An uncomfortable silence hung in the air until Sally thought of something to say.

'Was . . .' she began clumsily. 'Sorry, is Louise your only child?'

'Yes. How did you know?'

'I didn't,' Sally lied. She'd recognized the desperation of single-child parents the moment they'd opened the door. Once Louise was gone they'd have nothing. 'Not for sure.'

'Oh,' was all he replied, then more silence. 'If you'll excuse me, I'll just go and check on that tea. Rose has been a little distracted the last couple of days. Won't be a minute.'

'Of course,' said Sally. As soon as he was gone she stood and began to move slowly and silently, scrutinizing the room's contents, careful not to touch anything. She homed in on the framed photographs on the mantelpiece above the old fake-flame electric fire. One or two showed Frank and Rose Graham in exotic locations, but most were of Louise, a collage of her life from young girl to womanhood. Sally liked the photographs. They were very different to the one and only photograph of Louise she'd seen up to now, the lifeless passport photo her husband had given them. These pictures were full of energy and joy, hope and expectations: a child beaming for the school photographer, a teenager posing with friends on a trip to the London Eye, a young woman receiving her graduation diploma outside some university. 'Where the hell are you, Louise?' Sally found herself saying. 'What's happened to you?' Her peace was snatched away as the Grahams clattered back into the room, Mr Graham carrying the tray of tea and accompaniments as his wife opened the door and made sure his path was clear.

'Here we are,' Mrs Graham said almost cheerfully. 'Pop it on the table, Frank, and I'll sort it out from there.' He did as he was told and retreated to his comfortable old chair as Sally returned to hers. 'How do you take it, Sergeant?'

'Milk and one,' Sally told her. 'And please, just call me Sally.'

'All right, Sally,' Mr Graham replied. 'How can we help you find our daughter?'

'Well,' Sally began to answer before pausing to accept the cup and saucer Mrs Graham held out to her. 'Thank you. Well, there may be questions that you're best able to answer, about Louise – things that only a parent would know.'

'She's a good daughter,' Mrs Graham insisted. 'She always has been, but I shouldn't think there's anything we could tell you that John hasn't already.'

'Her husband?' Sally sought to clarify.

'He may be her husband,' Mr Graham sniffed, 'but he doesn't know her like we do.' So, Sally thought, Louise is a daddy's girl and Daddy sounds a bit jealous.

'You have a problem with him?' Sally asked.

'Yes, he does,' Mrs Graham answered for him. 'He's had a problem with all her boyfriends. None of them were ever good enough for his Louise, including John.'

'She could have done better,' Mr Graham said coldly.

'He's a good husband and a good man,' Mrs Graham scolded. 'She did well to keep hold of him, if you ask me.'

Mr Graham rolled his eyes in disapproval.

'Is she happy?' Sally asked. 'In the marriage?'

'Very,' Mrs Graham replied. Mr Graham chewed his bottom lip.

'Any problems that you know about?' Sally continued to probe.

'None,' Mrs Graham answered bluntly. 'They're hoping to start a family together. Louise is so excited, she always wanted children, you see.'

'A waste of her education if you ask me,' Mr Graham reminded them he was there.

'A higher diploma in graphic design,' Mrs Graham scoffed. 'She was never going to light up the world with that, was she? She only went to college because he made her.' She jutted her chin towards her husband. Another roll of his eyes.

'Was that where she met John?' Sally asked.

'No,' Mrs Graham shook her head. 'She met him through mutual friends a few years ago.'

'I'm sorry to ask this,' Sally apologized in advance, 'but was there anybody else?'

The Grahams were confused by her question. 'Sorry?' Mrs Graham frowned. 'Anybody else? I don't understand.'

Sally sucked in a deep breath. 'Is there any possibility that Louise could have been seeing another man?' She watched their blank faces and waited for the reaction.

'Another man?' Mrs Graham asked.

'It does happen,' Sally told them. 'It wouldn't make her a bad person. It's just something that can happen.'

'Not to Louise,' Mr Graham answered, more stern now; offended.

'Are you sure?' Sally persisted. 'I need you to be absolutely sure.'

'We're sure,' Mr Graham spoke for them both.

Sally waited a while before continuing, studying Mrs Graham, looking for a contradiction in her face, a hint of shame or lying eyes avoiding hers, searching for a place to hide. She saw nothing.

'What about John?' Sally asked. 'Did Louise ever have suspicions about him? Could he have been seeing anyone?'

'If he is, Louise never mentioned it to us,' Mr Graham assured her. 'But we would hardly know, it's not like we live in each other's pockets. I mean, we see them regularly enough, but they live on the other side of London. Their business is their business.'

'I understand,' said Sally. 'And I'm sorry I had to ask, but when a young woman goes missing we need to cover every possibility, no matter how unlikely.'

'Of course,' Mrs Graham said, ever understanding. 'Anything to help try and find her.'

Sally could see the pain and loss swelling in Mrs Graham's chest and throat. She felt a sudden sense of panic, something screaming at her without warning to run from the house, to get away from these people before they began to transfer their nightmares on to her, before she would be expected to comfort Mrs Graham, to tell her everything would be fine. Sally stretched out of her chair and placed her untouched tea on the table.

'You've been very helpful, but I've taken up enough of your time.' Sally found herself almost backing out of the room before Mrs Graham stopped her.

'You don't think anything bad has happened to her, do you?' she asked. 'Nothing really bad's happened to her, has it?'

'I'm sure she'll be fine,' Sally reassured them, desperate to escape the house and the Grahams.

'If anything's happened to her, I don't know what we'd do,' Mrs Graham tortured her. 'She's our only child. She's always been such a wonderful daughter. She's a good person. No one would want to hurt Louise, would they? She's not the sort of person anyone would want to hurt. I mean, these terrible men you hear about, they go after prostitutes and young girls whose families don't care about them, let them wander the streets at all hours, don't they?'

Sally almost grabbed at the pain that suddenly throbbed in her chest, Sebastian Gibran's face looming in her mind, straight white teeth and red eyes. Nausea gripped her body, the blood rushing from her face, her lips turning blue-white as she tried to swallow the bile seeping into her mouth. She wanted Mrs Graham to stop, but she wouldn't.

'Louise just isn't the sort of person these people go after.

She goes to work and then goes home. I've seen programmes on the telly, they always say murderers select their victims, don't they, that somehow the victims attract these terrible men, they do something that draws these lunatics to them, as if there's something wrong with them.'

Sally knew she was close to vomiting, even if her empty stomach forced out nothing more than saliva and bile. She managed to speak.

'Could I please use your toilet?' she asked, clamping her lips closed the moment the words were out.

Mrs Graham spoke through rising tears. 'Of course. It's off the hallway, second on the left.'

Sally staggered from the lounge into the hallway, trying to remember Mrs Graham's directions, pushing every door she came to until she found the toilet and fell inside, somehow managing to close the door before pulling her hair back with one hand and thrusting her face deep into the bowl. Instantly her stomach compressed and her eyes rolled back into her skull as she violently retched, time after time, the agonizing pain in her belly yielding nothing but a trickle of bile, thick, green and yellow, as bitter as hate. Finally the retching ceased. Sally blinked and tried to focus through watering eyes, standing and checking herself in the mirror. Her eyes were red – she'd ruptured tiny capillaries – but some colour was returning to her face and lips. She rinsed her mouth and dabbed a little of the cool liquid on to her eyes, carefully drying them with a towel without rubbing too hard. After a few minutes she decided she looked passable and headed back to the Grahams, a rapid escape uppermost in her mind.

As she re-entered the lounge, the still-seated Grahams looked up at her like two Labradors waiting for their master's command. 'Are you all right?' Mrs Graham asked.

'I'm fine, thank you,' Sally pretended.

'You don't look very well, dear,' Mrs Graham pursued. 'Are you sure you're OK?'

'Just a virus,' Sally invented. 'Anyway, thanks for your time, and if there's anything you think of, please let me know.' She recovered her computer case, pulled a business card from the side pocket and handed it to Mrs Graham. 'In the meantime, if we have any news we'll let you know straight away.'

'Thank you so much.'

Mrs Graham's gratitude only added to Sally's rising guilt. 'No problem,' she called over her shoulder, heading for the front door, both the Grahams in pursuit. Rather than wait for them to open the door for her, she fumbled at the locks and handles herself, tugging the door open and stumbling into the driveway, pulling in chestfuls of fresh air through her nose. 'We'll be in touch,' she promised.

'Please find her,' pleaded Mr Graham, his eyes glassy. 'We don't care what she's done, tell her. We just want to know she's safe.'

'Of course,' Sally answered as she stretched the distance between them and her, only stopping when Mr Graham said something she didn't understand.

'We have some money,' he called to her.

'Excuse me?' Sally floundered. Was he trying to bribe her to find his daughter?

'If someone asks for money to let her go, we have money Not much, but it might be enough,' he explained.

'No,' Sally told him. 'This isn't about money. We're not expecting a ransom demand.'

'Then what is it about?' Mr Graham demanded.

'We don't know yet,' Sally answered truthfully, the need to escape now overwhelming. 'Let's just hope she comes home safe and well soon.'

'And if she doesn't?' Mr Graham asked. 'What then?'

Sally searched frantically for an answer, trying to think what the old Sally would have said to him, but nothing came.

'I don't know,' she replied. 'I'm sorry, but I don't know.'

* * *

Sean sat at his desk feeling hungry, tired and thirsty. He'd kept promising himself he'd stop for a quick breakfast, but another intelligence report, another door-to-door inquiry questionnaire, another possible sighting of Louise Russell would catch his eye and delay rest, food and water for a few more minutes. It would be the same once the time for breakfast became time for lunch. A rapid-fire knocking on the door frame of his office made him look up from an intelligence report about a night-time prowler seen in the vicinity of the Russells' house some weeks before Louise's disappearance. DS Dave Donnelly's considerable bulk filled the entrance.

'Morning, guv'nor,' he began. 'How's everything in the garden today? Bright and rosy, I assume.'

'It'll be a lot brighter when you get the door-to-door organized properly,' Sean reprimanded him.

'I'm only trying to save resources,' retorted Donnelly. 'I don't want to waste any more time and people on this than necessary. String it out for a couple of days and then she'll be home and we can get on with what we're supposed to be doing.'

Sean needed Donnelly on side, he couldn't allow him to keep believing the case was a waste of their time. Donnelly was the mirror image of Sean – he dealt only with what was in front of him. He processed evidence, pressed witnesses hard, interviewed suspects skilfully, but he did it all on the basis of tangible evidence, not theories and hypothetical conclusions. And he got results doing things his way. Sean, on the other hand, was instinctive, imaginative, using the evidence as a guide not a rigid map, unnerving suspects in interview by telling them what they had been thinking as they were committing their crimes rather than relying on things he could prove. They complemented each other – and if the team was to be effective, they needed each other; a fact Sean grasped better than Donnelly.

'Listen to me.' Sean looked him in the eye, his voice full of conviction. 'You're wrong about this one. Something bad's happened to Louise Russell. Is she still alive? I don't know, but I think so, which means there's a chance we could find her before she turns up floating in a river somewhere. I need you with me on this, Dave.' He sat back in his chair, ran a hand through his hair. 'God knows Sally isn't exactly her old self. I can't afford to lose both my DSs.'

Donnelly stood silently for a moment, weighing up his response. 'Are you sure?' he asked. 'Sure she's not just run off with a rush-hour-Romeo? One last time around the block before settling down to a life of kids and coffee mornings?'

'I'm sure,' Sean told him. 'Unfortunately.'

'Fine,' Donnelly agreed reluctantly. 'So what do you want me to do?'

'See to it that door-to-door's finished for a start,' Sean answered, 'and keep everyone on their toes. I want this handled as if we already had a body. No taking it easy because it's only a MISPER.'

'Your wish is my command,' Donnelly assured him.

'Really?' Sean questioned before lowering his voice. 'And keep an eye on Sally. She's a bit up and down, know what I mean?'

'No problem,' said Donnelly.

They were interrupted by Sean's phone ringing. He held a hand up to prompt silence and ask Donnelly to stay while he took the call.

It was DS Roddis from the dedicated Murder Investigation Forensic Team. He greeted Sean in his usual manner, avoiding any reference to rank.

'Mr Corrigan, good morning.'

'Sergeant Roddis. You have something for me?'

'I'm at the Russell home now,' he said. 'We're concentrating our examination on the hallway and front door, as you requested.'

'Good,' Sean answered. 'Anything?'

'It would appear so . . .' Sean's heart rate began to

accelerate with anticipation. 'Unfortunately, the scene hasn't been preserved as I would have liked, but at least whoever took her didn't make any attempt to clean up after him. There's no indication that he wiped any surfaces, nothing's been polished or scrubbed. And when we got down low to the wooden floor we found a full palm print with fingers attached. We've compared it to John Russell's. It's not his and it's too big to be Mrs Russell's.'

'Can you lift it off the floor without damaging it?' Sean asked, a picture forming in his mind of the man who took Louise Russell kneeling next to her prostrate body, his hand on the floor to balance himself, fingers spread to take his weight . . . while he did what to her?

'We've already lifted it,' Roddis said gleefully.

'Is it good enough to get a match from?'

'If he's in the system, we'll be able to get a match. I'm having it sent straight to Fingerprints.'

Sean was certain whoever took Louise Russell was a previous offender. It wouldn't be anything as big as this, but there'd be something in his past. The question was, had he been convicted? If not, his prints wouldn't be on file.

'There's another thing,' Roddis continued. 'The traces are very faint, but on the floor, close to where we found the print, there seems to be evidence of a non-typical chemical. We've swabbed it for the lab, but my first guess would be chloroform.'

Another piece of the film playing in Sean's head became clearer: the man kneeling next to her, pouring chloroform on to material, placing it over her mouth. Sean saw bindings too, being wrapped around her hands, but not her feet – he would have needed her to walk. He blinked the images away and spoke into the receiver. 'OK, thanks. Let me know as soon as you have more.'

Beckoning for Donnelly to follow him, he got up and went through into the main incident room where his team of detectives were busying themselves at their desks.

'Listen up, everyone,' Sean shouted across the room. 'Forensics have just confirmed there are indications that Louise Russell was abducted from her home by an unknown male. If this isn't already a murder case it soon will be unless we can find her. I know this is different from our usual, but we are now her only hope, so I want you to give it everything. Chase down every lead, every piece of information and intelligence we have, no matter how irrelevant it looks. Let's find her before it's too late.' Sean looked around the room at the faces of his team. The message seemed to have got through.

'Just for once,' Donnelly said, 'I hope you're wrong.'

'I'm not,' Sean told him. 'But what I can't be sure of is how long we've got. How long before he tires of his new plaything? And after he throws her out with the rubbish, what then for our man? Somebody else? Will he take another?'

'You tell me,' Donnelly answered.

'I don't know,' Sean replied. 'Not yet anyway.'

Mid-morning Thursday and Thomas Keller should have been at work, but his supervisor had agreed to let him have a few hours off so long as he made the time up in the afternoon. As he walked across the cluttered courtyard from his cottage towards the metal door that led to the cellar his excitement and nervousness grew in equal measure. He picked his way through the old tyres and oil drums that littered his land, land that was dotted with old, disused outhouses and corrugated-iron barns that once housed battery chickens and God knows what else. Even the cottage he lived in was hideous, made of large grey breezeblocks sometime in the sixties and never painted.

He wore his usual loose-fitting tracksuit, the stun-gun pushed into one pocket bouncing awkwardly off his hip as he walked, the keys in his other pocket prone to becoming entangled in stray threads from the fraying seams. This morning he also carried a breakfast tray and a holdall thrown over his shoulder.

On reaching the heavy metal-clad door that led to the cellar below he carefully placed the tray on the floor. Cursing himself for not having moved one of the old oil drums to the door so he could use it as a temporary table, he resolved to do it later, after he'd taken Sam her breakfast.

As he unlocked the oversized padlock that held the door secure he felt his heart begin to race with anticipation and anxiety. He'd barely been able to contain himself during the night, barely been able to keep himself from sneaking in to see her, even if it was just to watch her sleep, to curl up on the other side of the wire next to her and listen to her breathing. But he knew he should leave her alone and let her rest. Now that he was only seconds away from seeing her, the longing to be with her, be with her the way he knew she wanted him to be, was almost overwhelming. He practised his breathing like the doctors had shown him – breathing was the key to being able to control his actions, his temper, his desires.

He pulled the big door back slowly, allowing the light to flood into the cellar, and stood at the entrance, head cocked to one side, listening for any noises that might drift up from the darkness below. After a few minutes, having heard nothing, he picked up the tray and began to move stealthily down the stone stairs, still listening. If he heard anything that alarmed him he would drop the tray and run back to the light, slam the door shut and lock it for ever, never returning to the cellar no matter what.

At the bottom of the stairs he craned his head around the corner of the wall that hid the staircase from the rest of the room and peered into the gloom, allowing his vision time to adjust to the poor light, searching for any sign of change, anything that should make him run. After a few seconds he could clearly make out the two figures cowering in their cages, both sitting with their knees pulled up to their chins, arms wrapped around their legs, Karen in her filthy underwear, Louise naked but covered by the duvet he'd given her.

Finally he stepped into the cellar, their dungeon, all his concentration on Louise, as if Karen wasn't there any more. 'Did you sleep OK, Sam? I've brought you some breakfast.' He lifted the tray a little so she could see. 'You'll probably want to get cleaned up first though, eh?'

Placing the tray on the makeshift table behind the old hospital screen, he tugged the cord, the bright bulb flooding the cellar with harsh white light. Louise squeezed her eyes tightly shut against the onslaught, tears seeping out from her eyelids as he pulled the stun-gun and key from his trousers and moved slowly towards her cage, careful not to alarm her by moving too fast like before. He unlocked the cage and allowed the door to swing open, his head ducking inside. Seeing her eyes focused on the stun-gun in his hand, his own eyes were drawn to it.

'I do trust you, Sam, you need to know that, but they could still try to keep us apart. If they do, I'll need this to protect you. You do understand?'

She nodded a frightened yes, her eyes wide with fear. He thought she looked like a kitten waiting to be plucked from its mother's side, and it made him feel good, made him feel strong, wanted, needed and in control. He backed away from the entrance to allow her to emerge and watched as she shuffled forward, bent double, clinging to the duvet that hid her nakedness. He knew what she was hiding, remembering the first day he'd brought her here, when he'd taken her clothes, the clothes they'd made her wear. Excitement coursed through him, his penis swelling as the blood rushed into it, making it uncomfortable and obvious under his tracksuit. The memory of seeing, of touching her soft, warm, slightly olive skin was almost too much for him to bear. He closed his eyes and tried to keep control, but the image of her round breasts, dark circles at their centre, and the soft pubic hair almost entirely covering her womanhood, burnt itself into his mind. The need to be with her here and now was so strong it was threatening to overtake him. He knew she wanted him too, wanted him as her lover, but first he needed to show her that he respected her. When they were finally together it would be so much better because they had waited.

She disappeared behind the screen, becoming a shapeless shadow with a silhouette of a human head. 'There should be plenty of hot water,' he managed to say through his pain, the need to release growing ever stronger, 'and the towel should still be there.' He heard the sound of running water and waited, knowing what was coming, until at last the duvet slipped from her shoulders to the floor, the perfection of her silhouette standing so clearly in front of him now, the shape of her back, the curves of her hips and buttocks, her beautiful breasts, the points of her nipples, her hands running over her body, touching it as he so desperately wanted to, her shadow a template on to which he projected the memory of her nakedness. He realized his mouth was hanging open and emitting an ugly guttural moaning he hoped she hadn't heard above the running water. The sound of water ceased as he watched her hurriedly dry herself and pull the duvet tightly around her body. 'Don't forget the tray,' he rasped through his dry mouth. 'You must eat. You'll need your strength.'

She appeared from behind the screen, looking from the floor to him and back again, heading for her cage, speeding up as she passed him, glancing at the stun-gun in his hand, ducking obediently back inside the safe place he'd made for her. He waited until she'd settled, watching her examining the items on the tray: cereal, milk, some fruit. Yes, he thought to himself – she was becoming as he wanted her to be, as he needed her to be. He eased the cage door shut and replaced the lock, all the time watching her in wide-eyed excitement and anticipation of the moment when he would be with her, as it had always been meant to be.

Needing release, to untie the knot in his guts, to stop the throbbing in his head, the pain in his groin, he looked across at Karen Green. He was disgusted by her, yet drawn to her, drawn to the odour leaking from her cage. Slowly he moved towards her, his face ugly and threatening, his uneven stained teeth bared. Sensing danger, she tried to escape his approach, but all directions led to cold wire.

'You disgusting whore,' he accused her, his voice quiet, but full of hateful intent. 'You've pissed yourself. Do you want me to punish you? Do you?' shouting now.

'No, please,' she begged him. 'I couldn't help it. Please, I tried not to. I knew it would make you angry, please.'

His teeth clenched together in rage, the words squeezing through them, each one shouted with a pause between to emphasize his fury as he edged closer to his desperately needed release. 'If . . . you . . . knew . . . it . . . would . . . make . . . me . . . angry . . . then . . . why . . . the . . . fuck . . . did . . . you . . . do . . . it?'

'I tried so hard not to,' Karen pleaded, bright tears making clean stains down her increasingly filthy face, her mouth round as if trapped in a scream, her eyes wild with panic as he approached.

He opened a hatch in the side of the cage that was just big enough for a human arm to fit. 'Put your arm through the hole,' he demanded.

'No,' she sobbed.

'Put your arm through the fucking hole or you know what'll happen.'

'I can't,' Karen gasped between terrible childlike sobs. 'I can't.'

'Put your arm through the fucking hole!' His scream intensified, making both women jump in fright.

Slowly Karen inched her way across the cage and slid her

arm through the gate, looking away, knowing pain would soon come. He leapt forward and stabbed the stun-gun into her exposed flesh, sending her flying through the air to the rear of the cage where she crashed into the wire and fell on to her side.

Then he waited. Waited until the convulsions became little more than twitches. Finally he darted to the cage door, dropping the key in his rush to unlock it, fumbling on the floor in a panic to locate it, giggling when he did. The lock undone, he jerked the door open in a desperate rush to reach her before she fully recovered.

The desire was overtaking him, everything beginning to feel dreamlike, as if he had left his body and was watching someone else in the cage with her, someone else rolling her on to her stomach, tearing at her flimsy underwear, pulling himself free and searching for her, thrusting and missing, thrusting again, searching for a warm opening to push himself into her, until finally, when he was so close to releasing the demons that pounded inside of him, he felt himself enter her, the feeling of being inside her making his eyes roll back with excruciating pleasure like he'd never been able to feel before – before he started taking them. In the midst of his ecstasy he wondered if the others would be as good as this, his first.

He rutted like a wild animal, almost unaware of the human being lying underneath him, crying in pain, humiliated and desolate, while he forced himself on her, grunting with absolute pleasure, the warm flesh around his sex driving him to push harder and deeper until the release rushed free from his body and into her. He pushed himself as deeply as he could inside her as the release began to fade, at last allowing his body to relax, bringing him back to the world and the realization of what he had done, shame attempting to wash him clean of his terrible sin.

Keller looked down at the sobbing creature pinned

underneath him, his erection fading fast. He pulled himself out of her and tugged his trousers up, already backing out of the cage, unable to look at her. His eyes were immediately drawn to Louise, looking on in horror.

Pointing at the figure discarded on the floor of the other cage, he protested, 'She made me do it, Sam. She always makes me do it. She knows how to trick me. She's one of them. That's how I knew she wasn't really you, because of the things she makes me do to her. You would never make me do those things.'

Slamming the door to Karen's cage shut, he snapped the lock back into place then stood clinging to the wire mesh, fighting back the tears that tried to escape from his red eyes, self-loathing and hatred tearing away the ecstasy he'd felt only moments earlier. He scrunched his eyes tightly together, shame giving way to an anger that without warning swept through his being like a raging fire ripping through a bone-dry forest. He straightened, his body frozen with tension as he released his fury, screaming 'I hate you!' into the room.

Then he turned and ran sobbing from the cellar, up the stairs and into the daylight, cursing his lack of control, his weakness, the fact they had seen his weakness. Humiliation kept his legs pumping as he ran across the derelict courtyard, bouncing off oil drums, tripping on old tyres until he reached his dilapidated cottage and fell through the door, clutching his chest, desperate for his burning lungs to fill with air, to slow his heart and stop the throbbing pain in his head.

Collapsed on the floor of his neglected kitchen, he waited, staring at the ceiling, as images from his childhood taunted him, joined by other, more recent images of torment. But he didn't try to push them away. Instead he embraced them like a welcome dream, and gradually the ugly images calmed him, slowed the torrents of his mind and body until finally he was in control again.

Realizing he was lying on the kitchen floor, he sprang to

his feet, confused and distrustful of how he came to be there. The memories of what had happened in the cellar came seeping back, and with them his anger, but it was controllable now. He could turn this weakness into his strength, but in order to do that she needed to be taught a lesson. He would have to show the whore he knew what she was.

Keller made his way to the shed attached to the side of the cottage and pulled the unlocked door open. Undaunted by the disorganized chaos that confronted him, he began to scoop armfuls of items from their shelves, kicking the things that landed on the floor out of his way until he found what he was looking for: a bag of litter and a tray he'd bought months ago when he was trying to domesticate one of the feral cats that patrolled his land. He paused for a second, the memory of the ungrateful cat pricking his thoughts. It had got what it deserved, but at least he'd given it a proper burial, in one of the few green and picturesque spots on his land, under the sole willow tree that shaded the back of his cottage. He shook the memory away and examined the items he held.

Satisfied that this would teach the whore who was in control, he set about filling the litter tray, then made his way back to the stairs that led to the cellar, taking care to avoid the obstacles that littered the way. Once inside, he raced down the stairs, abandoning caution now, revelling in his power when he saw them cowering in the corners of their cages. He saw the holdall he'd dropped on the floor earlier and the clothes inside. No matter. First he'd deal with the whore.

He unlocked the padlock to Karen Green's cage and pulled the door open. This time there was no need to brandish the stun-gun; she wouldn't dare cross him now. The terror in her eyes told him she knew it was no use trying to escape. He threw the tray of cat litter on to the floor of her cage. 'When you need to piss, whore,' he shouted, 'you piss in there. You piss in there and you shit in there.' He watched as she hugged herself, rocking rhythmically back and forth. Again he pointed at the tray. 'In there – understand, whore?'

Neither waiting for an answer nor expecting one, he slammed her door closed and carefully replaced the padlock. Then he crossed the cellar to retrieve the holdall, a smile changing the shape of his face as he pulled the clean and pressed clothes from within: a sky-blue blouse, grey knee-length pencil skirt, a cream V-neck sweater and white underwear. Next he removed two bottles: Elemis body lotion and Tom Ford Black Orchid Eau de Parfum.

'This is for you, Sam,' he told Louise. 'Your own clothes, not the ones they made you wear. These are your own. And look – your favourite perfume and lotion. Use the lotion before you dress. Understand?' Louise nodded that she did. 'Put the perfume on after,' he added. 'Understand?' She nodded again. He moved to the side of her cage and opened the hatch just wide enough to fit the items through once he'd rolled them into a single package. 'Take them,' he demanded, making her stretch out and snatch the package away, falling back into the corner of her cage.

'I have to go to work now,' he said. 'But I promise I'll come and see you when I get home. And don't worry about her.' He flicked his head towards the other cage. 'She can't hurt us any more. Nobody can. Nobody can keep us apart, Sam. They'll never find us here. They'll never take you away from me again. I swear it on my life, Sam, I'll never let that happen.'

Mid-morning Thursday and Sean waited in the comfortable office of Harry Montieth, owner-manager of Graphic Solutions, the small business in Dartmouth Road, Forest Hill, where Louise Russell should have been at work. He heard Montieth knock on his own door before ushering in two women in their late twenties. They both looked scared and anxious; the darkening around their eyes a clear indication that neither had slept well since learning of their colleague's disappearance.

He liked them already because of their concern, their self-inflicted sharing of her pain.

'This is Tina,' said Montieth, fumbling for the best way to introduce them to a cop. 'Tina Nuffield. And this is Gabby – Gabby Scott.'

'Thank you,' Sean acknowledged, examining his face for any signs of guilt or shame, searching the women's faces for telltale indications of disgust. Having concluded there was nothing untoward going on between Montieth and his female employees, he set about questioning them. 'Mr Montieth has told me that you are Louise's closest friends.'

'We're good friends,' said Gabby, brushing her short blonde hair behind her ear. Tina remained silent, chewing on her bottom lip, in danger of opening the partly healed cut she'd already made.

'How good?' Sean probed.

'I've known her since she started here, must be nearly five years ago.'

'And what about you, Tina?' Sean wanted to drag her into the conversation.

'About three years,' she answered quietly. 'That's when I started here. Louise really looked after me, and Gabby too,' she added, so as not to upset her friend.

Sean had already decided there was nothing here for him. He continued the standard questions, barely listening to the replies.

'Things sometimes happen at work that stay at work,' he suggested. 'Things that never find their way home. You know what I mean?' Everyone in the office did.

'Not Louise,' Gabby said firmly. 'If anything like that had happened, we'd know about it for sure and I'd tell you now if it was. I wouldn't risk lying to you.'

'You're her best friends, so I guess you would know,' Sean encouraged.

'We would,' Gabby reaffirmed. 'And there wasn't. If Louise

went out without John she would be out with us. We would've known. She loves John. All she ever talked about was John and how they were going to start a family soon.'

'What about an unwanted admirer?' Sean asked as a last procedural question. 'Someone hanging around outside the office waiting for her? Someone other than the husband sending flowers, cards?'

The three colleagues looked blankly at each other before Gabby answered for them all.

'No. Not that I ever saw and not that she ever mentioned.'

'What about at home? Anyone making a nuisance of themselves?'

'Same,' said Gabby. 'Nothing. If there had been, she would have reported it to the police.'

They were interrupted by Sean's phone ringing on the borrowed desk. He glanced at the caller ID. It was Donnelly.

'Excuse me,' he said, snatching the phone up, turning his back on them for false privacy. 'What's happening?'

'We've found the car,' Donnelly told him.

'Where?'

'A place called Scrogginhall Wood, in Norman Park, Bromley.'

'Bromley!' Sean exclaimed. 'That's only a few miles from her home.'

'You were expecting something different?' Donnelly queried.

Sean realized he'd been thinking out loud. 'No,' he muttered. 'Not necessarily.' He already had a strong feeling that whoever had taken Louise Russell was local. She hadn't been snatched by some long-distance lorry driver or salesman on a trip down South. No, this one was from somewhere within the borders of this forgotten part of London. 'What state's the car in?'

'Locked and secure, apparently. No signs of damage or a struggle. A routine uniform patrol found it in the car park while they were looking for local toe-rags who screw the cars there with annoying regularity.'

'Are you already with the car?' Sean asked.

'No,' said Donnelly. 'I'm on my way. ETA about fifteen minutes.'

'Fine. I'll meet you there as soon as I can. Travelling time from Forest Hill,' Sean explained. 'Make sure uniform preserve it and the car park for Forensics. And have the AA meet us there to get the thing open. I don't want any over-keen constables smashing the windows in.'

'It'll be done,' Donnelly assured him.

Sean hung up and turned to his waiting audience.

'Have you found something?' Montieth asked, his lips pale with dread.

'We've found her car,' Sean told them, seeing no point in keeping it a secret. Montieth's eyes widened, while Gabby started to cry and Tina covered her mouth with both hands, as if pushing the scream of anxiety back inside her. 'It's just her car,' Sean tried to reassure them. 'There's no sign of a struggle, nothing to suggest anything untoward has happened to her.' Gathering up his belongings, he told them, 'I need to get to where the car was found as quickly as I can, so I'm afraid I'll have to cut our meeting short. Thanks for all your help. I promise I'll be in touch if we find anything.' During the long months without Sally at his side, covering for his abruptness, he'd had to learn to be a lot more subtle and polite with the public.

'Of course,' Montieth agreed. 'Please, you do what you have to do.'

Sean headed for the door, only to be stopped by Gabby grabbing his arm and locking eyes with him.

'If someone's hurt her,' she told him, 'and you find them, you do the right thing by Louise. You understand?'

'I understand,' he assured her, resisting the temptation to rattle off a spiel about justice, courts and trials, knowing it wasn't what she wanted to hear. She continued to hold his arm and eyes. 'I understand,' he repeated, his gaze dropping to the fingers coiled around his forearm. She slowly released her grip. 'I'll be in touch,' he promised.

The moment the office door closed behind him he broke into a run, virtually jumping down the stairs, desperate to get to the car before any more evidence could fade. Before the last lingering traces of the man he hunted drifted away in the next spring breeze.

4

Thomas Keller arrived for the afternoon shift feeling content and calm, almost happy. He walked through the gates of the Holmesdale Road Royal Mail sorting office in South Norwood and headed towards the large grey building he'd worked in as a postman for the last eleven years. It had changed little inside and out since he'd started there not long after leaving school at seventeen. To begin with he'd been restricted to menial jobs, working his way up to helping with the sorting. It took several years before he was finally given his own round. He'd never sought to go further in the Royal Mail and knew he never would. He entered the main building and clocked on, the same time-card-punching machine noting his arrival now just as it had done eleven years ago.

Without acknowledging his colleagues he walked to his station in front of the seven-foot tall wooden shelving system and began to prepare the mail for his round, placing the letters and parcels into pigeonholes according to postcode. He found the work easy and relaxing; its repetitiveness allowed his mind to wander to more pleasant thoughts and recent memories.

He was unaware that he was smiling until a voice too close behind him broke his reverie.

''Allo,' the scratchy voice accused, thick with a south-east London accent. 'Someone looks happy.'

Thomas Keller knew who the voice belonged to. Jimmy Locke was one of his regular tormentors.

'D'you get your end away or something, Tommy?' Locke bellowed, the smile broad on his face as he looked around at the other men working their stations for approval. Their laughter indicated that he had found an appreciative audience.

Keller looked sheepishly over his shoulder and smiled briefly before returning to his task, doing his best to ignore them.

'Oi!' Jimmy demanded, his face suddenly more serious, the Crystal Palace Football Club tattoos on his biceps stretching as he flexed the sizeable muscles that helped offset his growing beer-gut, his cropped hair making his head look small. 'I asked you a question, Tommy.'

The room fell quiet as the men waited for an answer.

'My name's not Tommy,' Keller responded weakly. 'It's Thomas.'

'Is it now?' Jimmy mocked him. 'So tell me, Thomas – is that Thom-arse or Tom ass?'

More laughter, the other men enjoying Keller's impending humiliation. Keller continued to try and ignore them.

'So what are you, son, an arse or an ass?' Locke turned to face his audience, pleased with his wit, his daily ritual of destroying Thomas Keller bit-by-bit almost complete. 'I'm waiting for an answer, Thom-arse, and I don't like being kept waiting, especially not by little cunts like you.'

Keller felt the shame crawling up his back, hatred and fear swelling in his belly in equal measures. He felt his skin tingling, growing hot and sweaty, his face and the back of his neck glowing red, super-heated by his crushing embarrassment and feelings of uselessness. He heard Locke moving closer to him, readying himself to spit more venomous words into his ear, but still he couldn't find the strength to turn and face his torturer. He cursed the power for deserting him, the power he felt when he was with them, alone in his cellar with them. If he had that power now he would tear Locke apart. He would tear them all apart. One day, he promised himself. One day he would turn and face them, and then they would all be sorry.

Locke's mouth moved in close to the side of his face, the smell of stale beer and tobacco unmistakeable. Keller tried to lift his arms to pigeonhole the letters, but they refused to rise.

'Are you a queer, Thom-arse?' Locke demanded. 'Me and the boys reckon you're a fucking queer. Is that right? Because we don't like working in the same place as a fucking queer. Some of the boys are worried you might give them AIDS. They reckon you dirty faggots are all disease-ridden. Is that right, Thom-arse? Are you infected?' Locke's face, twisted with bigotry, was inches from his.

'I'm not a homosexual,' Keller managed to stutter, barely a whisper.

'What?' Locke almost shouted into his ear, flecks of spittle pricking the side of Keller's face.

'I'm not a homosexual,' Keller repeated a little louder, wishing he had a knife in his hand, imagining how he would spin on his heels, keeping the knife low and tight to his own body, flashing it across Locke's abdomen, stepping back to watch the red streak spread across the fat bastard's belly as his intestines slowly tumbled out like eels from a fishing net, with Locke struggling to push them back into the cavity of his gut, a look of horror replacing the smug expression on his face.

'What did you say, queer?' Locke snapped, making him jump as he yelled into his ear. 'Can't you faggots speak properly?'

Without warning, Keller turned on his tormentor, the

imagined knife in his hand slashing at the soft flesh of Locke's over-sized belly just as he'd planned. The movement was enough to make Locke jump back, fear flashing across his features for a split second. Keller had never dared turn to face him before. He would make sure the little faggot never did again. His fingers curled into a well-practised fist, miniscule scars bearing witness to the teeth he had punched in the past.

Keller waited for the blow he knew would come. Instead he heard a voice demanding, 'What's going on here, men?'

The strong calm voice that carried a trace of Jamaican belonged to the shift supervisor, Leonard Trewsbury. He peered at Locke over the top of his bifocals, refusing to be intimidated by the younger, bigger man. The man who he knew detested being supervised by a black man.

'Nothing for you to worry about, Leonard,' Locke pushed.

'I'll be the judge of that,' the supervisor warned him, knowing Locke would back down. 'And you can call me Mr Trewsbury.' He maintained eye contact with Locke, daring him to give him an excuse to put him on report or, better still, dismiss him altogether. 'OK, everybody, let's get back to work,' he ordered.

Eyes glaring and vengeful, Locke slunk back to his workstation.

Trewsbury pulled Thomas Keller to one side. He liked the boy. Keller kept himself to himself and worked hard. He came to work on time and was always looking for and willing to do overtime. What he did with his money was a mystery. Trewsbury never asked and Keller never told.

'You shouldn't let them push you around,' Trewsbury told him.

'It's all right,' Keller lied. 'It doesn't bother me. They're just joking.'

'That's not what it looked like. Next time Locke or any of his cronies bothers you, you let me know, OK?'

'OK,' Keller agreed, the pounding in his heart mercifully receding, the throbbing pain of self-loathing and rage easing in his temples.

'Good man,' said Trewsbury. 'Now let's get back to work before we fall too far behind to catch up.'

'Sure,' Keller replied, trying to sound cool and in control. But inside his soul, where nobody could see, the images of his revenge were playing out cold and cruel, bloody and excruciating. When he was with Sam, when they were finally together as they were meant to be, as he knew she wanted them to be, she would give him the strength to be the person he knew he really was. And then he would make Locke and the others regret their tormenting. He would make them all regret everything they had ever done to him.

Sean turned on to the access road in Norman Park, Bromley, heading towards Scrogginhall Wood. Only in a city would such an insignificant patch of forest be given the title 'Wood'. His car bumped along the uneven track, bouncing him around inside and causing him to swear out loud. As he passed between the wooden posts that marked the entrance to the car park, he saw there were a number of cars parked there in addition to the police vehicles he'd expected to see. Presumably their owners hadn't returned from walking dogs or liaising with their extra-marital lovers. He hadn't decided yet whether he was going to let any vehicles be taken away. One could belong to the man he hunted. He could be lingering in the trees, watching the police, laughing at them. Laughing at him.

He spotted Donnelly sitting on the boot of his unmarked Vauxhall, which was parked next to the uniform patrol who'd found Louise's red Ford Fiesta. An AA man was standing by in his van, waiting to be given the order to use his box of tricks to open the abandoned car.

Sean pulled up at a forty-five-degree angle to the car

that was now a crime scene, blocking any other vehicles from driving too close to potentially precious tyre tracks or footprints. He swung his feet from the carpet of his car to the surface of the car park, disappointed to feel a rough mixture of compressed dirt and solid stone connecting with the soles of his shoes; not a promising surface for recovering useable prints or tracks.

Catching sight of him, Donnelly flicked his cigarette as far as he could away from the found car, aware of his own DNA soaked into the butt, not wanting to end up the subject of ridicule at the next office lunch for having contaminated the crime scene.

Sean made a beeline for the car, calling out to Donnelly while scanning the ground. 'Let's start tightening things up a bit, shall we?'

'Meaning?'

'Meaning securing the entire area as a crime scene, not just the car itself. And not dropping fag butts close to the centre of it.'

Donnelly looked in the direction of his discarded cigarette, disappointed by Sean's lack of appreciation for the distance he'd managed to flick it.

Sean tugged the rubber gloves he'd produced from his pocket over his hands, all the while surveying the ground around Louise Russell's abandoned car, a mute mechanical witness to her fate. He could see nothing obvious so moved closer to the car, slowly circling anti-clockwise, his eyes passing over every last millimetre of the ground. Donnelly watched silently, knowing when best to leave Sean to himself – to his own methods.

After a few minutes Sean was back at the spot he'd started from. Again he began to circumnavigate the car, clockwise this time, his eyes concentrating on the vehicle itself, searching for anything, anything at all. A trace of the suspect's blood drawn from his body by a fighting, scratching victim. A scrape from another vehicle that might have left a paint trace or imprinted a memory in the mind of whichever motorist had been struck by a red Fiesta that failed to stop after the accident. Louise had kept the car spotlessly clean – any visible evidence would have been relatively obvious, but he could see none.

If there were clues to be found on the exterior of the car they must be invisible to the naked eye. Perhaps they might yet be retrieved with the use of powders and chemicals, ultraviolet lights and magnification. In the meantime Sean needed to see inside the car, to feel its stillness before Roddis and the forensic boys turned it into a science circus.

'Let's get it open,' he said.

Donnelly strode across to the waiting AA van and tapped on the window. The driver dropped his copy of the *Sun* and eagerly jumped out, grabbing a bag of unusual tools from the back.

'Will you be able to get it open?' Donnelly asked, more out of the need for something to say than because of any doubts.

'It's a Ford,' the AA man answered, heading for the car. 'It'll only take a few seconds. Which door do you want opening?'

'The passenger door,' Sean told him. 'I'd appreciate it if you could touch as little as possible.'

'I'll do my best,' he answered, already tugging what looked like an over-sized metal ruler with a hook at one end from his bag. Sean recognized it, known to AA men and car thieves alike as a slim-jim. The AA man peeled back the rubber window seal and slid the metal deep down into the door panel. His face twisted in concentration as he manoeuvred the slim-jim blindly around the mechanics of the door, before suddenly jerking it upwards, an audible click letting all present know the door was now unlocked. The AA man immediately reached for the door handle, but Sean's hand wrapped around his wrist and stopped him.

'Hasn't been checked for prints yet,' Sean told him.

Once the AA man had been moved away, Sean's gloved hand stretched carefully towards the handle, one finger hooking under it in the place the suspect was least likely to have touched. He pulled his finger up and waited for the door to pop open a fraction, his other hand poised to stop a sudden breeze swinging it fully open before he was ready. He checked around the now broken seal that separated the door from the main body of the chassis, keeping an eye out for any evidence the wind might threaten to take away – a hair pulled from the suspect's head as he closed the door too quickly, a piece of material torn from his clothes as he fled from the abandoned car. He saw nothing and allowed the door to open by a few inches, the smell of the interior flooding out and catching him unaware, making him recoil at first. He steadied himself then breathed all the scents in eagerly: cloth, vinyl, rubber and above all else, her perfume, floral and subtle. But there was something underlying the other smells, something trying to disguise itself, trying to stay hidden in the cacophony – the faint trace of something surgical, clinical.

Chloroform, Sean decided. It was not something he'd ever smelt before, but he knew it had to be. Donnelly broke his concentration.

'Anything?' he called out.

'Chloroform, I think,' Sean answered. 'Get hold of Roddis and have him take a look at the car in situ before towing it away to the lab.'

'Will do.' Donnelly immediately started punching keys on his phone.

Sean opened the door more fully now, all the while searching for anything that might be evidence, touching nothing, seeing all as he crouched next to the opening, bothered by something he couldn't think of, something missing. Without warning the answer jumped into his head. It was too quiet. He stood upright and spoke to no one in particular: 'There's no alarm.'

Donnelly looked up from his phone. 'Excuse me?'

'Why's there no alarm?' Sean asked. 'He locked the car, but there's no alarm.' His heart was beginning to pound a little with the conviction he'd found something relevant, but his hope was cut short by the watching AA man.

'It's a Ford,' he said.

'So?'

'You lock it with the remote key. One press to lock it and another to arm the alarm.'

Did that mean anything? Sean asked himself. Had the man he hunted been in so much of a panic that he'd fled the scene without making sure the alarm was on? Or had he not wanted the beep of the alarm setting to attract attention to him? Why lock it at all? He'd already left his palm and fingerprints at the Russells' house.

Sean had to remind himself not to get too tied up in the knots of possibilities. All the same, he couldn't stop this man from invading his mind. As the case went on he would gradually start thinking like his quarry, until the thoughts of the man he hunted would become his own thoughts. A cold, uncomfortable feeling washed over him. The days ahead would be joyless and stressful, his only hope of relief would be finding Louise Russell and the man who took her. The man who had her now.

He desperately wanted to enter the car, to sit in the driver's seat as her abductor had done. To check the position of the seat, the mirrors, the steering wheel. Louise's limp body flashed through his mind, bound and gagged, lying behind the back seat in the boot of the hatchback. He saw a faceless shadow driving the car through London traffic with his prisoner, his prize, in the back, moaning muffled pleas for him to let her go from behind the material wrapped around her mouth. He saw the faceless shadow looking over his shoulder, talking to her as he drove, reassuring her everything would be all right, that he wouldn't harm her, wouldn't touch her. But Sean wasn't about to enter the car and risk damaging or destroying any invisible evidence waiting to be found within.

Donnelly came up behind him and made him jump. 'Roddis is on his way,' he announced.

'Good. Thanks,' Sean replied, hesitating before continuing: 'I need to have a look in the back.'

'Are you sure that's wise, guv'nor? Roddis will not be pleased.'

'I won't touch anything,' Sean promised. 'I just need a quick look.' He moved to the back of the car and searched with one finger under the lip of the hatchback door for the handle, the handle he absolutely knew the suspect would have touched. He pulled the handle and watched the hatch door rise open with a pneumatic hiss. He bent inside as much he could without over-balancing and falling forward, noticing immediately how clean the boot was, like everything else in the car. Everything was perfect, everything except for the slight scuffing on the carpeted surface of the boot and the smallest of scratch marks on the interior panelling close by. Sean knew what it meant.

He pulled away and stood. 'This is where he had her,' he told the listening Donnelly. 'He tied her, probably gagged her and put her in the boot. You can see where her shoes have disturbed the carpet and marked the plastic panel. He's a bold one, our boy. He snatches her from her own home in broad daylight and casually drives her through mid-morning traffic to this spot. And this is where his own car was waiting,' he continued, indicating with a sweep of his hand that the suspect's car would have been on the driver's side of Russell's. 'He pulls up here and waits a few seconds, just long enough to be sure no one's around. Then he gets out, moving fast, but smoothly. He knows exactly what he's doing, no panic. He unlocks his own car or van, pulls Russell from the boot of the Fiesta and forces her into the boot of his. If he used chloroform in the house then he's unsure whether he can control her without it, so he probably gives her another dose before trying to move her – but not too much, he doesn't want to knock her out and end up with a dead weight. He's not strong enough – if he was, he wouldn't be so reliant on weapons and drugs – he'd physically overpower her instead. Once he transfers her to his own car, he locks hers and takes the keys with him. He doesn't stop to wipe any prints or check for anything else he might have left behind because he doesn't care whether we find it or not. He has what he wants, the one thing that he cares about. He has her. He closes the hatch door and carefully drives away. Have you checked for CCTV?'

'There is none,' Donnelly told him.

'Then he knew there wasn't,' Sean insisted. 'He's a planner. None of this happened by accident. Have the access road checked for cameras. You won't find any, but check anyway.'

'It'll be done,' Donnelly promised.

Sean closed the hatch door carefully. He looked into the woods, just as the suspect would have done when he was checking the car cark before moving her. He still couldn't see the man's face, but already he felt as if he would recognize him in a second if he saw him. Something he didn't yet fully understand would enable him to pick this one out in a crowd if only he could get close enough. That's what he had to do now: let the evidence, let the facts get him close enough to allow the dark thing inside of him to take him the rest of the way to finding this madman.

In the early spring the trees still looked wintery and foreboding. Sean felt himself shiver, as if he was being watched. As if he was being watched from the inside by some spectre he knew he would eventually find himself face to face with.

'I've got a really bad feeling about this one,' he confessed to Donnelly. 'I don't think it's going to end well.' He pinched his temples between the middle finger and thumb of one hand and tried to squeeze the growing pressure in his head away before it exploded into a full migraine. 'You wait here with the motor,' he said. 'I need to get back to the office and start trying to piece all this together. People are going to be sticking their noses into our business, so we might as well be ready with a few answers. When Roddis gets here, leave him with the car and head back to Peckham for a scrum-down.'

'I'll be there as soon as I can.'

Sean didn't hear Donnelly's reply; he was already climbing into his car looking for Superintendent Featherstone's mobile number with one hand while starting the ignition, releasing the hand brake and fastening his seat belt with the other. He still hadn't got around to setting his phone up to be hands-free. Again he cursed the uneven road as he bounced along, driving too fast and making it even worse. He had to wait longer than he'd wanted to before Featherstone answered.

'Boss, it's Sean.'

'Problem?' Featherstone asked bluntly.

'Your missing person case,' said Sean. 'I'm afraid it's an abduction case now.'

'Any idea who took her?'

'Whoever it was, I don't think she knew them.'

'A stranger attack,' Featherstone said. 'That does not bode well.'

'No, sir,' Sean agreed. 'It does not.'

'What do you need from me?'

'Have you got anyone in the media who owes you a favour?'

'Maybe,' Featherstone answered cagily.

'I need to get an appeal out tonight,' Sean explained. 'Ask for public assistance. He took her in broad daylight and transferred her from one vehicle to another in a public place. It's possible someone saw something.'

'If someone has taken her, won't an appeal spook him?' said Featherstone. 'We don't want to force his hand. I don't want to push him into—'

'I understand,' Sean agreed, eager to cut to the chase, 'but I have no choice. Her family have already worked out what's happened, and now we've found her car dumped close to a wood in Bromley. If we don't pull out all the stops to find her, we're leaving ourselves wide open. It's a shitty call to have to make, but we have no choice.'

'All right,' Featherstone reluctantly agreed. 'I'll call in a few favours, see if I can get my face on the telly tonight – but no promises. I'll catch up with you later.' He hung up before Sean could reply.

He tossed his phone into the centre console, finally controlling the car with two hands, relieved to be back on a smooth road, suddenly remembering he needed to call Sally, again cursing himself for not having set up his hands-free system. He found Sally in his contacts and called her number while pushing his car through the increasingly dense traffic, all the while wishing he had more time – more time to simply sit and think, to try to become the thing he had to stop. The sooner he did, the sooner they would catch the man who dumped Louise Russell's car near the wood. The man who Sean knew would soon dump her body as casually as he'd abandoned her car, unless he could find him first. Find him and stop him, any way he knew how.

Sally paced up and down the street outside the Russells' home under the pretence of checking on the door-to-door team's progress, but in truth she just needed to get out of the office and get some fresh air, to be away from sympathetic and suspicious eyes alike. She knew Sean was trying to prevent her becoming involved in the main body of the investigation, his way of protecting her, but it wasn't making her feel any better.

She spotted DC Paulo Zukov walking along the street towards her. 'All right there, Sarge?' Zukov asked in his usual chirpy, mischievous manner.

'You're not in uniform any more,' Sally reminded him. 'You call me Sally now. Remember?'

'Just being respectful,' Zukov teased. 'But seriously, how are you?'

'Don't try and sound genuine and caring,' Sally chided him unfairly. 'It doesn't suit you.'

It was water off a duck's back for Zukov. He'd only been in the police six years, but it had been more than enough to harden his shell. 'Harsh, but fair,' he replied with a grin, pleased she perceived him as some cynical old detective, despite his young years and short length of service.

'Have you finished the door-to-door yet?' Sally asked.

'Not quite, but we ain't getting anything interesting anyway and I don't suppose we will. Door-to-door, waste of bloody time if you ask me.'

'No one did,' Sally reprimanded him, her phone vibrating in her hand distracting her from their tête-à-tête. Caller ID told her who it was. 'Yes, guv'nor.'

'We found Russell's car.'

'Any sign of Louise?' Sally knew he'd have said so right out if there had been, but she asked anyway.

'No,' Sean replied. 'The official line is that she's been taken. That's what I believe.'

'What's our next move?'

'As much media coverage as we can get, roadblocks, start canvassing a wider area and wait for forensics to give us something. Where are you?'

'Checking on the door-to-door.'

'They don't need you there. Get back to Peckham as soon as and I'll see you then.'

'OK,' Sally managed to get in before he hung up, leaving her alone with Zukov.

'Problem?' he asked.

'I'll tell you later,' she muttered, a feeling of dread crawling over her skin. A suffocating anxiety was spreading through her body like an unstoppable rising tide turning dry sand wet and heavy. 'I've got to head back to the office.'

The few steps to the car felt like miles and the car door seemed heavy as a drawbridge as she pulled it open, falling into her seat, feeling for the thick scars under her blouse, her breath coming in short sporadic bursts. She grasped the computer case she used as a holdall and frantically searched inside until she found the two small cardboard packets she needed. She popped two tramadol from one and six hundred milligrams of ibuprofen from the other into the palm of her hand and threw them down her throat, swallowing drily. She was glad now she hadn't concealed a bottle of vodka in the bag as she'd considered doing.

Leaning back with her head on the headrest she closed her eyes, waiting for the drugs to give her some relief, both physical and psychological. To expel the memories of Sebastian Gibran breathing into her face as he waited, expected her to die – of Sebastian Gibran sitting opposite her in an exclusive London restaurant, smiling and flirting and her liking it. The memories forced her eyes open. She found herself gazing up the branches of a nearby tree, dead-looking limbs beginning to burst into life, the little green buds forcing their way through the hard bark. She thought of Louise Russell's parents, so normal and unsuspecting, dragged from their comfortable life of cruise-liner holidays and early evening soap operas into a world they'd only ever seen fleetingly on the news. She hoped Sean wasn't planning on putting them in front of the cameras – a tearful appeal from loving parents wanting their precious child returned to them unharmed. She had a horrible feeling he was, but as she shook the thought away more unwelcome images rushed her consciousness. Where was Louise now, right now? Was she looking into the eyes of the man who'd taken her, the man who meant her harm, the way Sally had looked into Gibran's eyes? Was she feeling sick with fear the way Sally had? Did she feel suddenly weak and vulnerable, as impotent as Sally had – like a victim?

A victim. Sally had never realized how much she feared becoming a victim until it happened. All the power and prestige she'd built up as a detective, a cop, stripped away by a man whose madness ran so deep even Sean had struggled to grasp his motivation. She felt the tears beginning to force their way to her eyes, the pressure of holding them back numbing her brain and dulling her senses, and all the while the questions banging inside her head – could she face another killer now each case was all so much more personal to her than ever before? Could she sit across an interview room from them and resist the instinct to flee or worse? Would she be able to chase a suspect into a dark alley in the middle of the night, alone? 'You bastard,' she whispered to the car. 'I hope you rot in hell.'

A loud rap on the window put her heart into her mouth. It was Zukov. She wound the window down.

'You OK?' he asked, registering the glassiness in her eyes.

'I'm fine,' she told him. 'Just knackered, that's all.'

Zukov offered his packet of cigarettes to her. 'Smoke?'

'No,' she said bluntly. 'I quit. Remember?' It wasn't true entirely. The fact was she'd been unable to smoke after the attack, lying for weeks in a medically induced coma, then weeks more of drifting between this world and another few would ever see. By the time she could make her own way from her bed to the hospital garden she'd broken the physical habit, but the psychological addiction still burned strongly, only the pain in her chest stopping her from reaching for a packet. 'I need to get back to the office,' she told him, winding up the window and starting the engine. 'I'll see you later.'

She drove away leaving Zukov standing alone, cigarette in mouth.

'Nice speaking to you too,' Zukov called after her, knowing she couldn't hear him. He reminded himself to speak with Donnelly about Sally. No one wanted someone who was going to lose it on the team. The poison of their inability to cope would affect them all. He was young, but old school. He liked everyone around him to be solid and predictable, to pretend everything was fine even if it wasn't. All troubles, be they domestic, health, financial or other, should be left at home, not brought to work. The job took precedence over everything. If Sally couldn't handle it any more, then maybe it was time she was moved on. He dragged on his cigarette and wondered whether they would make him acting sergeant if Sally went. He saw no reason why not.

Louise Russell sat in the gloom of her cage dressed in the clean clothes he'd brought her, but despite their pristine condition they made her skin crawl with revulsion. These weren't her clothes and no matter how much she tried to quieten her mind, it kept asking her the same question. Whose clothes are they? Whose clothes were they? She looked across at the shape she knew was Karen Green and remembered what she had told her: the first few days he'd let Karen wash and then he'd given her some clean clothes to wear, but the night before he'd taken Louise, he'd made Karen remove the clothes, his false affection towards her replaced by violence and lust, an outlet for his sick frustrations. Was she about to become what Karen was already? And if so, what was he going to do to Karen?

Desperation to survive forced her into action. 'Karen,' she whispered, just loud enough to be heard, a barely audible echo reverberating around the hard walls of their prison. No answer. 'Karen,' she said a little louder. 'We have to help each other. We can't just wait for someone to find us.' Still no movement. 'I think he leaves the door open,' she explained. 'When he comes down here, I think he leaves the door open. The door to this cellar or wherever we are.' Karen moved a little on the floor of her cage. 'Please, I'm not your enemy,' Louise promised. 'I know it probably feels that way, but that's what he wants. He does it on purpose, to stop us helping each other.'

'How do you know?' Karen broke her silence with a quiet, defeated voice.

'How do I know what?'

'How do you know he leaves the door open?'

'Because the last time he came here there was daylight. I heard him opening the door and then there was daylight and the light stayed, even once he was down here, the light stayed. Next time one of us is out of these cages we have to try and free whoever isn't. Together I think we can overpower him.'

'How would you get the key to open the cage?' Karen asked, already doubtful and afraid of the consequences of any attempt to rescue themselves.

'Take him by surprise,' Louise explained. 'Throw the tray in his face and kick him where it hurts. Just keep hitting him until he's the one cowering on this stinking floor. Take the keys off him while he's still confused. Then open the cage and free whichever one of us is locked in. Then we can both kick the bastard to death.'

'It won't work,' Karen argued. 'And if we try, it'll only make things worse. He'll be so angry, it'll just make things worse.'

'How could things be worse?' Louise asked, exasperated.

'We could be dead.'

Karen's response silenced Louise for a moment while she tried to come up with another way to reach her. 'Are you hungry?' she asked. 'Sorry. Stupid question. You must be. I have some food left, maybe I could get it over to you.'

'No,' Karen snapped. 'If he sees you've tried he'll blame me and then you know what he'll do. You've seen it.'

They both sat in silence for a long while before Karen spoke again. 'I was supposed to be going to Australia. The day he took me. I had everything packed, everything arranged. Six months of travelling, maybe longer. I might even have stayed there. But he took me and brought me here. Jesus Christ, why is this happening to me?'

Louise waited for the crying to stop, then asked, 'Is there anyone special in your life?'

'No,' came the answer, followed by more silence.

'I'm married. My husband's name is John. We were going to start a family. My God, John. He must be beside himself. Blaming himself. I miss him so much. Please, God, let me see him again.' She felt sorrow and loss threatening to engulf her. It wasn't what she needed now and she pushed all thoughts of home and lovers away. 'Karen, I need to ask you something . . .'

'What?'

'These clothes I'm wearing – are they the same clothes he made you wear? Are these the clothes he took from you before I got here?' There was no answer. 'Please,' she tried. 'I need to know.' She waited, dreading the answer.

'I can't be sure,' Karen lied. 'They look the same, but I can't be sure.'

'They are, aren't they?' Louise pressed. 'Aren't they?'

'Yes,' Karen almost shouted before returning to a whisper. 'Now you know. Now you know what's going to happen to you.'

Trying to comprehend the enormity of what she was being told, Louise looked across the cellar at the wretched creature in the opposite cage, filthy and bruised, covered in his foul scent, with his diseased seed forced inside her. She wouldn't let it happen to her. She couldn't let it happen to her.

She tried to imagine Karen away from this hell, in

Australia somewhere, on a beach, happy and tanned, her attractive young body drawing attention from the men showing off on the beach. No cares, no worries, young and alive, enjoying the adventure of a lifetime. The image almost made her happy, but then it made her sad, replaced by thoughts of herself at home, cooking something in the kitchen while John tried to help but only succeeded in getting in the way. Herself happy and looking forward to having a bump in her belly and shopping for tiny clothes. Feeling safe. Above all else, she feels safe.

What wouldn't she give to feel safe again? Louise closed her eyes, promising herself that she would never undervalue that feeling ever again, just so long as she could live through this.

Karen's voice broke the silence. 'When he takes away your clothes, when he comes to you the way he comes to me, if he offers you drugs, take them. It makes it easier. You'll feel less.' Then she rolled over so her back faced Louise, leaving her alone in the silent darkness, happy thoughts of her home and husband chased away by the gathering demons of things yet to come.

Sean paced the floor of his office, listening to Donnelly updating him on the progress of the forensic examination of Louise Russell's car. Roddis's team had searched the area around the vehicle, but found nothing. The car had then been loaded on to a flat-back lorry, covered in a plastic tarpaulin and carried off to the forensic car-pound at Charlton, where it would be minutely examined inside and out. By the time they had finished it would be little more than a shell, but any evidence would have been carefully and meticulously bagged and tagged before being sent off to the various private forensic laboratories that had taken over from the once fabled do-all government-funded lab at Lambeth. Another stroke of genius from the powers that be, granting access to highly sensitive material to commercial enterprises all for the sake of saving a few pounds.

His eye was drawn to movement in the main office: Sally had come in and was making her way to her desk. He summoned her with a jut of his chin. She dropped her computer case on her chair and headed straight for them, eyes down and shoulders slumped. Watching her, Sean was again reminded how much he missed the person she used to be. She walked into his office and sat without being asked. 'What's happening?' she demanded.

'Not enough,' Sean replied.

'Whatever that means,' she said, oblivious to her own mood. Sean let it slide.

'We've been on this for twenty-four hours. He snatched her in broad daylight in her own car. He's a planner and he's organized. He would have checked her house before he took her, made sure he couldn't be seen.'

'So he's been there before,' Donnelly surmised.

'Yes, but when?' Sean asked. 'Sally, have the door-to-door team ask neighbours to think back at least a couple of weeks for sightings of strangers hanging around.' She scribbled something in her notebook. Sean took it as a sign she understood.

'What else?' said Donnelly. 'Any insights?' Sean knew the question was directed solely at him.

'No,' he answered, not entirely truthfully. 'Other than I believe he's local and probably lives alone in a decent-sized house or maybe somewhere reasonably isolated. He needs space and privacy.'

'For what?' Sally joined in.

'I don't know yet,' Sean answered, 'but I know it's bad. Sorry.' Sally looked at the floor again. Sean wanted to bring her back. 'But you're right. We need to work out why he takes them. When we understand that, we'll be that much closer to catching him.'

'Them?' Sally stopped him. 'You said *them.*'

'I meant her,' he lied again.

'No you didn't,' Sally insisted. Sean didn't reply.

'Oh, bloody marvellous,' Donnelly exclaimed. 'You mean there's going to be more?'

'Only if we don't stop him in time,' Sean pointed out.

'But surely we have to consider the possibility this is a one-off, that for whatever reason Louise Russell was special to him?' Donnelly insisted. 'Special enough to make him want to take her.'

'She was special to him,' Sean agreed, 'but not because of any relationship between them. She was a stranger to him and he to her. He chose her quite deliberately, maybe because of the way she looked or maybe just because of the type of house she lived in – I don't know yet. But whatever he saw in her, he'll see in others. That much I'm sure of. If we don't find him, there will be others.'

Sally came back to them. 'There was no forced entry,' she pointed out. 'So maybe she knew whoever took her.'

'She was young and strong and in her own home. She had no reason to be fearful of a knock at the door. Do you only open the door to people you know?' Sean regretted his question as soon as it was out of his mouth. Sally unflinchingly held his gaze, her misting eyes accusing him. His desk phone saved him from making it worse by ringing before he had a chance to say sorry, the last thing Sally wanted to hear. He snatched it like a drowning man reaching for a life-jacket. 'DI Corrigan.'

'Andy Roddis here,' announced the forensic team leader. 'Bad news, I'm afraid. No match on file for the prints we lifted from the Russell home. Sorry.'

'Damn it,' Sean said calmly, despite the twisting in his guts. 'I wasn't expecting that.'

'Nor me,' Roddis confided.

'What about the car? Anything yet?'

'Too soon to tell, but I expect to at least find his prints. They won't help us identify him prior to his arrest, but once we have him they'll certainly help get a conviction.'

'OK. Thanks, Andy. Keep me posted.' He hung up and turned to the others. 'His prints aren't on file.' They knew what it meant – the man they were looking for had no convictions.

'I was bloody sure this one would have previous, even if it was just a bit of flashing on Bromley Common,' Donnelly said.

'It's unfortunate,' Sean agreed. 'But there must be something in his past. He may not have been convicted, but you can bet he'll have been arrested and charged somewhere down the line. This guy is in our records, we just need to dig around till we find him: run checks on local sexual offenders who've come to our notice but have never been convicted of anything. And let's check on any local stalkers – top-end only though, not ones who've gone after celebrities and footballers. Concentrate on the care-in-the-community types. Our boy hasn't just jumped in at this level, he's been building up to this for years, convictions or no convictions. Anything else?'

'Sounds straightforward enough,' Donnelly said. 'All we need now is about another hundred detectives and we'll have him nicked by lunchtime tomorrow.'

'Well, that ain't going to happen,' Sean confirmed what he already knew. 'So let's do the best we can with what we've—'

A ripple of disturbance from the main office caused him to break off and look through the Perspex that separated him from his team. Featherstone was making his way across the main office, stopping periodically, handing out pep talks to one and all en route.

'Heads up, people,' Sean warned Sally and Donnelly. A few seconds later Featherstone was knocking on his office door frame and entering without being invited.

'Afternoon, boss,' Sean said. 'Only a step backwards since we last spoke, I'm afraid.'

'How so?'

'It appears whoever we're looking for has no previous. Prints found at the Russells' house came back "no match".'

'That sounds unlikely.' Featherstone raised an eyebrow.

'Unlikely or not, it's a fact. And any DNA we find will go the same way.'

'So,' Featherstone continued, 'we'll have to find him by old-fashioned means – shoe leather and hard work, folks.'

'With respect, sir,' said Sally, 'we're going to need more than that if we want to catch him quickly.'

'Agreed,' Featherstone contradicted himself. 'Which is why I've sorted out a media blitz. ITV and BBC will put out an appeal for information on their local channels tonight, with a special appearance by yours truly. I'm still working on Sky, but they're holding out for more details than we want to give them at this time.'

'What about the papers?' Sean asked.

'The papers will follow the TV channels' lead.' He made a show of looking at his watch. 'Right, I need to be at the Yard by six to meet the TV people, so I'm off. Keep me posted.' Dismissing them with a nod, he strode out of the office.

'God save us from senior officers,' Donnelly said when Featherstone was well away.

'He's not so bad,' Sean reminded him. 'We could do a lot worse.'

'If you say so.' Sean let it slide. 'Me, I'm off to chase my daily quota of useless leads.' Meaning he was heading to the pub, Sean thought. 'Care to give me a hand, Sally?'

'Not just now,' she answered. 'I need to tidy a few things up, make a few phone calls.'

'Suit yourself,' sniffed Donnelly. 'Then I shall bid you farewell. If I don't see you later, I'll see you tomorrow.' With that he headed for the main office in search of recruits to buy him a drink.

'He's got the right idea,' Sean told Sally.

'How so?' she asked.

'Get some rest and recreation now, while you still can. I get the definite feeling this will be the last chance for some time. Once that media appeal goes out, the spotlight will fall on us.'

'Just go home and forget about Louise Russell until tomorrow?'

'That's not what I meant,' said Sean. 'It's just things are going to start happening tomorrow, I can feel it. And they're not going to stop until this case is finished, one way or another.'

'You think she's already dead, don't you?'

Sean sat heavily in his chair, caught off balance by her question.

'Maybe not . . . It depends on his cycle.'

'What cycle?'

'Just an idea,' Sean explained. 'A theory.'

'What theory?' she demanded, losing patience with his secrecy.

'He's taking a lot of risks. Calculated risks, but risks all the same. He doesn't just do to them whatever it is he wants to do in their homes, because he needs more time with them. And if he needs time with them then the chances are there is a timescale. I think he fantasized about her for a while before taking her and transporting her into his living fantasy – a fantasy that will have a beginning, middle and end. All of which suggests a timescale. It might be a week, a month – I don't know yet.'

'Or it might be a lot less?' Sally questioned.

'Might be,' Sean admitted. 'There's no way of telling until he releases her or we find her.'

'Find her body, you mean.'

'We have to be prepared for that possibility.'

'Possibility or probability?' Sally asked.

'You know how this works.' Sean shrugged. 'Look, if it's too much too soon, I'd understand. If you want to keep this one at arm's length it's not a problem. I can make that happen.'

'Don't make allowances for me.'

'You've got nothing to prove,' he told her and meant it. She didn't reply. 'Go home, Sally. Get some rest. I'll call you if anything happens.'

She slowly rose and headed for the door, turning when she got there. 'One thing . . .'

'Go on,' said Sean.

'I want to be in on the interviews. When we catch him, I want to sit in on the interviews.'

'OK.' Sean granted the request, knowing why she needed to sit in. She nodded once and left him alone.

Sean scanned the office for anyone heading his way. When he was happy no one would require his immediate attention, he lifted the phone on his desk and punched in a sequence of numbers. It was answered on the fifth ring.

'Hello.'

'Dr Canning, it's Sean Corrigan.'

'And what can I do for you, Inspector?'

'Nothing yet,' said Sean. 'This is more of a heads-up to expect something in the next few days. Something a little more unusual than the norm.'

'Ah,' Canning replied. 'Your speciality seems to be things that are a little more unusual than the norm.'

'What can I say? Somebody somewhere must like me.'

'So what should I be expecting?' Canning sounded intrigued. 'What does that crystal ball of yours tell you, Inspector?'

He nodded as if Canning could see him. 'When it happens it'll be an outside body drop, in a wooded area, possibly in water. The victim will be a white woman in her late twenties. Cause of death will be suffocation or strangulation with evidence of drugs having been administered to her. That's all I'm prepared to speculate for the time being,' Sean explained. 'But I'll need you to examine the body in situ.'

'That's quite a lot of information you have there, considering this person is still alive,' said Canning. 'I am correct in assuming they are still alive?'

'You are,' Sean admitted, but he'd say no more.

'Very well,' Canning agreed. 'I shall await your call – and thanks for the warning. I don't usually get advance notice of such things in my business.'

'No,' Sean answered. 'I don't suppose you do.'

'Until the unhappy event then,' Canning said.

'Indeed,' Sean agreed and hung up, already regretting making the call. He knew forensically it made good sense – forewarning Canning meant he could prepare himself and his pathology equipment for an outside scene examination, possibly saving as much as a few vital hours. Outside scenes could deteriorate incredibly quickly, especially if whoever took her went to the trouble of dumping her body in flowing water, although Sean doubted he would; he'd made no effort to destroy evidence at the other scenes so why would he when it came time to rid himself of her body? Mother Nature was no respecter of the dead or of those trying to gather the evidence to give them justice. But nonetheless he wished he hadn't made the call. He felt soiled, complicit, as if he'd somehow sealed Louise Russell's fate.

Shaking his regrets away, he buried his head in the evergrowing pile of reports spreading across his desk.

Thomas Keller arrived home still upset and agitated by the confrontation he'd had at work. His ageing Ford slid to a stop on the dust road outside his ugly cottage just as the spring day was turning into a cold, cloudless night. His mind was racing so much he almost forgot to turn the lights off and lock the door. He fumbled for his house keys, desperate to release the pressure he felt hammering in his head and tightening in his groin. Once inside, he tore through the cluttered cottage, not stopping to turn on any lights, tripping over unpacked boxes and piles of old magazines in the rush to get to his bedroom. The frantic pace came to a halt only when his hand was within reach of his special drawer, where he kept his special things. He froze, heart drumming on the walls of his chest, listening to the silence, feeling the air around him until he was certain he was alone. With a sudden burst he pulled the drawer open, pushing aside the mish-mash of clothes until he found the bundle of letters bound together with an elastic band. He would have liked to linger, to unwrap the magical package the way he planned to undress Sam when they were finally together, but his excitement was overpowering, forcing him to rush. He yanked the elastic band away and let the letters spill on to his unmade bed, grabbing at the nearest one, running his fingers across the name on the front of the envelope as if he was reading Braille. He looked down at the other envelopes, his eyes leaping from one to the next, all bearing the same name – *Louise Russell.*

Most of the letters were the usual bills and credit card statements, although some were personal, but they were all precious to him, they all brought her closer to him, entwined his life with hers. These letters had been the beginning of their relationship. It had taken him months to collect them, as he couldn't risk arousing her suspicions that her mail was being stolen. Somehow he'd been disciplined enough to limit himself to a few items each month, mostly things she would never miss, resisting the almost unbearable temptation to take everything that looked personal. Every time he needed to be with her, he turned to the letters.

He knew the letter he held in his hand was from an old friend of hers who now lived on the other side of the world, in a place where he suspected mail regularly went missing. He slipped the letter from its envelope and began to read the hellos and how are yous, the apologies for not writing sooner, the references to a past life they'd shared as young girls. The more he read the more agitated he felt, the more his uncontrollable desire engulfed him. He dropped to his knees by his bedside as if he was about to pray, but his hands did not come together. Holding the letter in one hand, he slid the other hand slowly under his waistband, moving tentatively towards his swelling sex. As he touched himself a moan escaped his mouth in anticipation of the pleasure and release he would soon feel washing through his body. He gripped himself tightly and began to move his hand back and forth, gently at first, but then quickly, desperately, as he failed to reach a full erection, the frustration overtaking any thoughts of ecstasy, causing his penis to grow ever more flaccid in his palm.

Cursing and issuing silent threats in his mind, he leapt to his feet and snatched another bundle of letters from the drawer, held together by an elastic band just as the others had been. His eyes fleetingly rested on a third bundle of letters and a fourth and a fifth, before returning to the one in his hand. He checked the name on the top envelope – *Karen Green*. Yes, he told himself, this was all her fault. She was ruining everything with her jealous lies, deliberately coming between him and Sam. But he knew how to deal with her. He knew what he had to do. Throwing her letters on the floor, he tore off his postman's uniform and began rifling through a pile of dirty clothes on the floor until he found his tracksuit. He tugged it on and stomped to the kitchen.

The narrow cupboard by the back door held a number of illicit items. After a moment's thought he selected the electric cattle prod he'd found and repaired when he first bought the buildings and land from the local council for a bargain price, other potential buyers having been put off by its history of animal cruelty and slaughter. The land was everything he'd been waiting and praying for – everything he'd been saving for, putting aside most of his earnings for years until finally he'd amassed enough to buy it, the land and buildings that meant he could begin to prepare for a life with Sam. Once he'd bought the land he'd immediately started his search for her, but it had been difficult to tell who Sam was now – so many years had passed and her mind had been so poisoned, any one of them could be her. He had no choice but to work his way through them until he found the real one. No matter how many of them tried to make him look a fool. He knew what to do with people who tried to make him look a fool.

With a final glance at the double-barrelled shotgun that held pride of place, he grabbed the keys to the cellar from their hook and closed the door. Then he stumbled to the bathroom, pulling the cabinet open and taking out a first-aid box. He opened it and removed one of the syringes and a large phial of alfentanil. Taking the safety cap from the syringe, he expertly eased it into the phial, drawing out fifty millilitres of the anaesthetic before replacing the cap.

Now that he had everything he needed, he made his way outside, striding across the yard, the syringe in his trouser pocket, the cattle prod gripped in his hand. But when he reached the metal door he froze, the absolute clarity of what he had to do suddenly deserting him, the enormity of it almost too much comprehend.

You have no choice, he told himself. *She will destroy everything. She's too dangerous to ignore.* He knew he was right, and with that belief his strength and purpose returned. He unlocked the padlock and pulled the cellar door aside, jumping down the stairs two at a time into the darkness below, his usual caution and fear swept away by the need to rid himself of her.

Both women felt the change in his bold approach. For a

brief moment Louise allowed herself to believe it was their rescuers pounding down the stairs. But as the overhead bulb flooded the cellar with light she saw her hope was a false one and tried to push herself deep into the corner of her wire cell. Like a snake charmer watching for the cobra's strike, her eyes never left him as he crossed the room, his right hand gripping a strange-looking rod. She soon realized he wasn't remotely interested in her. It was as if she didn't exist. He had come for Karen.

His eyes appeared quite red as they reflected the light from overhead, his face expressionless as he moved towards her, intent on some sick purpose. Karen cowered in what was now the safest place in the room for her to be. He pointed the cattle prod at her. 'It's time for you to leave,' he told her.

Karen knew what he meant, knew he wasn't going to simply release her so she could tell the world what he had done. There would be no happy reunion with her friends and family. 'No,' she begged him, 'please let me stay. I'll be good. I'll be very good. I'll do all the things you want me to. I'll make you happy, just like when you first brought me here, remember?'

'Don't talk to me.' His voice was steady and cold, without feeling. She was nothing to him now, merely a problem he needed to deal with.

'Don't do this, please, I'm begging you,' Karen almost shouted, her tears slurring her words, horror and disbelief etched into her contorted face.

He opened the hatch in the side of her cage. 'Put your arm through,' he ordered. 'Put your arm through and I won't hurt you. Do as you're told.'

'I can't,' Karen wailed, 'please God, I can't.'

'Do it or you'll make me very angry,' he growled, lips narrowing as the feelings of anger and disgust towards her began to crawl back into his soul. 'If you make me angry I'll have to use this until you do as I tell you.' He held the cattle prod close to the wire so she could see it, although he doubted she would know what it was.

'I don't want to make you angry,' Karen pleaded, 'but don't make me give you my arm.'

'Damn you,' he suddenly yelled, making both women flinch with fear. 'Damn you to hell – do as you're told.' Without warning he thrust the cattle prod through the wire and into Karen's ribcage. Her scream was deafening in the confined space, the pain it described lingering in the room as she fell on her side, back exposed as she tried to protect her burning ribs.

His eyes grew wider as a smile fattened his lips. He thrust the prod towards her again, his smile turning to a snarl as he pushed it hard into her back. Her second scream wasn't as deafening as the first, the pain in her spine causing her to arch unnaturally backwards, squeezing her already empty lungs.

Louise watched the torture from her own cage with both fear and rage. 'Leave her alone,' she shouted. 'You fucking coward, leave her alone.' But her demands were ignored, as if she wasn't even there.

'Put your arm through the hatch,' he told Karen, sounding calmer now as the room fell silent. After a few seconds she began to stir, struggling to her hands and knees and crawling the three feet to the other side of the cage, her fingers curling around the wire as she slowly dragged herself to the height of the hatch and slid her arm through, quietly crying in surrender. 'Good,' he said, pulling the syringe from his pocket and discarding the cattle prod. He tugged the cap from the needle and took hold of her arm. 'Keep still,' he warned her and began to search for a vein.

It was proving harder than he thought. He regretted not having brought something to use as a tourniquet to swell the blood vessels in the crook of her arm. Tutting in exasperation he plunged the needle in, but was sure he hadn't found a vein. He pulled it out without care and pushed it deep into the crook of her arm a second time, the pain making her struggle. 'Be still,' he hissed into her face, but again he'd missed his mark. Sweat was dripping from him as his frustration mounted. He wrenched the needle free and immediately shoved it back in, a satisfied noise leaking from his mouth as he saw the needle had found its mark. Too quickly he pushed the alfentanil from the syringe and into her vein, the surging drug agonizingly painful as it made the blood inside her body feel as if it was turning to ice, rushing around her body, slowing her breathing and relaxing her muscles, her mind spinning as if she was seriously drunk. He pulled the needle free and released her arm, watching her as she slid to the floor, conscious but defenceless.

Like a predator wary of its wounded prey, he deactivated the cattle prod and used it as a stick to poke his victim, stabbing it hard into her back and ribcage. Karen groaned each time he jabbed her, limply trying to ward away the stick. Satisfied, he smiled a sickly grin and moved to the main door of her cage, unlocked it and entered.

For a few moment he stood over her, still cautious, still using the prod to ensure she was no threat to him. Then he suddenly snapped into action, discarding the cattle prod and rushing at her, just as he'd practised, grabbing a fistful of the hair on top of her head, slipping his other hand under her jaw, dragging her across the floor of her cage and into the main body of the cellar.

Louise shrank into a ball, pressing her eyes shut and covering her ears against the screams.

'Get up,' he told Karen, quietly at first, then louder. 'Get up.' He knew he wouldn't be able to pull her up the stairs; the effort of dragging her from the cage had drained most of his strength. 'Get up!' he screamed.

Karen tried to speak but could only mumble, the alfentanil numbing her mind and tongue. The adrenalin of anger breathed some new strength into him as he crouched next to her and draped her arm around his shoulders, lifting her weight with his burning legs, the veins in his neck swelling blue under the strain. Once he began to walk he found she could take most of her own weight as she moved one leg in front of the other, heading in whatever direction he led her, struggling to recall where she was and why she was there.

'Am I going home now?' she managed to whisper, her eyes trying to focus on the stranger who was going to take her from this place.

'Yes,' he lied, 'just keep walking. I'm going to take you home now.'

Louise had opened her eyes to the unfolding scene and her ears to his lies. 'Leave her alone,' she begged. 'Please don't hurt her. She won't be able to tell the police anything. She doesn't even know where we are.'

'No,' he shouted back. 'I can't do that. She's too dangerous. She could ruin everything for us. I can't let that happen.'

He headed for the stairs, Karen obediently holding on to him. It took him several minutes to reach the top, the task of removing a drugged woman from the cellar far more difficult than he'd thought it would be. Once outside, he propped her against the wall while he slammed the heavy door shut and clasped the lock back into place, Louise's screams from below virtually inaudible now.

'Where are you taking me?' Karen asked, slurring the words.

'I told you,' he replied in a mock-friendly voice, 'I'm taking you home.'

Gripping her around the bicep, he marched her across the yard, stopping several times as she fell, tripping on the clutter she couldn't see in the dark or through the clouds of the anaesthetic. After the short, perilous journey they reached his Ford. He popped open the boot and sat her on the edge, gently pushing her chest so she fell back, lifting her legs and folding them neatly into the tight space. The fingers of her right hand curled around the rim of the boot as she sensed danger.

'What's happening?' she asked, confused, desperately trying to make sense of her situation.

'Shut up and be quiet,' he hissed, lifting his foot and stamping down on her fingers, slamming the boot the second she recoiled in pain.

His heart was pumping so fast as he jumped into the driver's seat he feared he wouldn't be able to keep control long enough to do what he knew he must do. He paused for a moment, breathing deeply and slowly, calming his mind and body, thinking about the task ahead, the route he would take to the place he'd already chosen – the way he'd take her from the car, the way he'd walk her into the woods and finally, the way he'd rid himself of his mistake.

John Russell sat alone in the kitchen of what he and Louise had dreamed would one day be their family home. He sipped his whisky and water, feeling ever more guilty as he remembered the relief when the police had told him they were sure Louise hadn't simply run off with another man.

Detective Constable Fiona Cahill entered the room, disturbing his solitude and grief. 'Are you all right?' she asked gently.

Russell looked up from his drink at the tall, handsome woman in her mid-thirties standing in his kitchen, her short hazel hair cut for style and function, her intelligent green eyes examining him. 'Why are you here?' he answered her question with one of his own.

'I'm the Family Liaison Officer, remember. That kind of makes me your minder until everything gets sorted out.' He didn't respond. 'I'm here to help you with anything you need, to answer any questions you may have about what we're doing and what we intend to do. This can all be a bit confusing if you're not used to it – scary even.' She noticed a slight contraction of his pupils that betrayed his fears. 'It's my job to try and make it that much more bearable – as far as I can, anyway.'

'Why do I need a Family Liaison Officer?' he asked without feeling. 'Aren't they usually assigned to the families of murder victims?'

DC Cahill managed not to look away. 'Not always,' she reassured him, 'there's no fixed rule, really. We often assign Family Liaison Officers in kidnaps, vulnerable people, that sort of thing.'

'But you're not expecting a ransom demand, are you?' he asked, his eyes growing ever more dull and lifeless, reminding her of a stabbing victim she'd held until he was dead, back in her days as a rookie in uniform. She shook the memory away.

'No,' she answered truthfully. 'We're not expecting a ransom demand. If it was going to happen, it would have by now.'

'What then?' Russell snapped at her. 'None of this makes sense. Who would take her? Why would anyone do that?'

'I'm afraid a lot of the people we deal with make no sense, but you mustn't give up hope.' DC Cahill struggled to find words of encouragement. 'If anyone can find her, it's DI Corrigan. Trust me, this case couldn't be in better hands. We all just need to stay positive.'

'But that won't make any difference, will it? It doesn't matter whether I stay positive or whether I think the worst. It won't make any difference. It's like having cancer: some people swear they're going to beat it and then six months later they're dead, while others almost give in to the disease as soon as they're diagnosed, but live until they're ninety. It doesn't matter what we think – it's already been decided.'

DC Cahill knew he spoke the truth, but her training and experience wouldn't let her agree with him. 'You probably need to eat something,' she said.

'No thanks, I'm not hungry.' DC Cahill saw the tears welling in his eyes, eventually growing too heavy and running down his cheeks like tiny spring streams. 'I just want her back, you know. That's all I want. I just want her back. I don't care what's happened to her, I don't even care what happens to the bastard that took her – I just want her back.'

Thomas Keller drove along the single-track road that led to Three Halfpenny Wood, in Spring Park, Addington, a few miles south of London. He drove with the lights off, searching for the spot he'd found several weeks previously, but it had been daytime then and now in the dark and rain, with no street-lighting, it was proving more difficult than he'd expected to find it again. He slowed to a crawl, trying to locate the giant oak tree that marked the place where he would stop. Then he saw it, black branches moving in the wind, making the cold air around it sing. Relief washed over him as he put the car into neutral and let it coast to a stop without touching his brakes. He turned the engine off and stepped into the freezing drizzle that blew into his face making him feel even more alive and awake.

Keller stood by the side of his car, as alert as the nocturnal creatures that hid in the wood watching him, every sense burning with concentration as he listened and watched for movement, tasting the air for the presence of others. Only after several minutes, once he was totally sure he was alone, did he move to the back of the car, filling his lungs with the night air and tugging the hood of his tracksuit top over his head to protect him from the rain before opening the boot and staring down on the terrified woman curled into a tight ball inside.

He reached in and gripped her wrist, pulling her hard, trying to drag her from the boot, but he wasn't strong enough to lift the dead weight she had become. 'Get out,' he ordered her in a loud, flat voice. 'It's time for you to go.'

'No,' Karen pleaded. 'I don't want to.'

'I'm letting you go,' he lied, 'but you need to get out of the car.'

'I don't believe you. I don't believe you.'

Keller felt panic rising in his chest, the fear that someone might discover him here in the woods in the dead of night with a near-naked woman in the boot of his car. He had to do something. Leaning into the boot, he grabbed the small, stunted baseball bat he kept there and waved it in front of Karen's face. 'Get out or I swear I'll hurt you.'

'Leave me alone,' she begged him. 'Please don't hurt me.'

'Get out of the car and I won't.' He spat the words into her face, panic threatening to take away what little control he had left, but still she wouldn't do as he commanded. 'Get out of the fucking car,' he screamed as loudly as he dared, the wind and rain swallowing his words before they could travel more than a few feet, but she continued to cower in the boot.

He raised the bat above shoulder height and brought it smashing down on to her knee, the pain slicing through the alfentanil and making her scream. Again he raised the bat, this time smashing it down on to her elbow, her next scream merging with her first. Wrapping a hank of hair around his fist, he pulled as hard as he could, partially dragging her as she scrambled from the boot and fell to her knees on the wet gravel road. He slammed the boot shut and pushed the bat into the waistband of his loose tracksuit bottoms, his eyes never leaving the cold, wet, shivering creature kneeling before him, the drizzle sticking to her body, making her olive skin look like the sea at night. He slid his hands under her armpits and pulled her to her feet, immediately pushing her towards the forest that waited at the side of the road.

She stumbled across the grass verge and into the dark, foreboding trees, the shadow and musky smell of him close behind her, shoving her forward and then helping her to her feet whenever she fell, marching her deeper into the forest. Soon her feet were covered in cuts from the brambles that snaked across the ground. She tried to turn to face him, wanting him to see her face as she pleaded not to die in this godforsaken place, but each time she turned he shoved her in the back, sometimes knocking her to the ground as she tripped on unseen snares. 'Please,' she implored the trees in front of her, 'just let me go and I swear I won't tell anyone. Please, Jesus, I swear to God I won't tell anyone.'

'You have no god,' he sneered, gripping her hair and twisting it tight. 'You betrayed me, Sam. You let them keep us apart. Your parents, the teachers, they all lied and you believed them. You turned your back on me. You abandoned me and left me alone, Sam, you left me all alone.'

'I'm sorry,' she told him, playing his game, sensing one last chance to save herself. 'I won't ever leave you again, I promise, I swear to God.' The anaesthetic was wearing off, but still she felt so weak and confused, it was difficult to keep up with what he was saying, difficult to pick her way through the labyrinth of his distorted mind.

'Do you know what happened to me after you left me?' he asked. 'Do you know what they did to me in school, in the care home? The things they made me do?'

'I'm sorry,' she tried to touch his conscience. 'It wasn't my fault. I wanted to stay with you, but they took you away. I couldn't find you,' she rambled, hoping something she said would ring true with whatever he was talking about, would make him pause and think before he did to her what she was increasingly sure he would.

'I'm sorry,' he said, his voice devoid of emotion, 'but you betrayed me then and you'd betray me again.' He stopped walking, his hand resting on her shoulders, pulling her to a halt.

'What's happening?' she asked through choking sobs, trying to turn to face him.

'Don't turn around,' he warned her, 'don't look at me. Now, take your clothes off.'

She hugged herself against the drizzle that had turned to icy rain, the wind driving it hard into her face, washing away the dirt and blood from her ordeal in the cellar. She looked up at the tree branches swaying high above her head, clouds sweeping fast across the dark blue night sky, and she knew she was deep in the forest, where no one would see her plight or hear her screams for mercy.

'Take off your clothes,' he repeated.

Karen shivered in the cold, her semi-naked body turning pale with the loss of temperature, her lips sky blue. 'I don't have clothes,' she told him, her voice pathetic with surrender.

'What you have,' he insisted, 'take them off.' Her hands went to the filthy underwear she wore as she realized what he wanted her to do, her legs nearly buckling under the weight of his cursed command. 'Do it,' he hissed, his voice impatient. 'Do it quickly. I'm not going to touch you.'

Karen slowly reached her arms behind her back, the bruises from the previous week reminding her of what she'd already suffered at his hands, the pains in her arms and shoulders making it almost impossible to reach the fastening on the strap of the bra. Eventually her straining, stretching fingers found and released it. She managed to catch the bra as it fell, pressing it hard against her breasts, refusing to let it fall away and leave her exposed. She felt a sharp jab in her spine that stole her breath.

'Let it fall to the ground,' he demanded. 'I need it.'

Once more she tried to face him, to connect with him somehow, but his anger made her quickly turn away.

'Don't look at me!' he snapped. 'I told you not to look at me. Do as you're told and let it fall.'

She felt another jab in the spine, her sobbing ignored. Slowly she released her hold of the bra she'd once hated but now clung to as if it was her life itself. It fell to the ground, almost floating to the brown leaves and dirt on the forest floor. 'The rest,' he said. 'And the rest.' There wasn't the slightest trace of compassion in his voice.

'No, please,' she appealed to him, to any human decency he may have left. 'I'm begging you, please just let me go. I swear, I swear I won't tell anybody.'

'Take the rest off,' he ignored her pleas. 'Do it quickly.'

She felt something solid connect with the side of her head, hard enough to split her ear and dull her world, but not violent enough to knock her down. She clasped both hands to her bleeding ear, her mouth contorted with pain.

'Take the rest off,' he insisted, 'or you'll get more of the same. You'll get everything you deserve for what you did to me, Judas.'

She slipped her thumbs under the sides of her soiled knickers and pulled them down over her hips, letting them slide to her ankles as her arms once more crossed her breasts. She stood in the silence of the night, its purity only spoilt by the sound of him breathing behind her, fast and deep, as if he was close to an asthmatic attack.

Thomas Keller raised the bat above his head and closed his eyes as he brought it down across the back of her head, the skin breaking, a fine jet of blood spraying across his face, hissing as it painted a line across the fallen foliage on the ground. She fell forwards on to her knees, clutching the back of her head, conscious, but seriously dazed, giving in to the fog of pain that overtook her and falling prostrate to the forest floor.

Keller moved towards her still living body, looking down on her as she writhed. He knew he needed to show her mercy now, despite her treachery; he needed to show her mercy and end her suffering. He kneeled and rolled her over just enough so she could see him. His arms felt like lead weights hanging at his side, almost impossible to lift, but somehow he forced them to rise, his hands closing around her throat, his fingers clamping around her jugular as his thumbs, side by side, pressed deep into her trachea.

Her eyes bulged as the pressure inside her head grew, turning red as the blood vessels began to rupture, a hideous cracking sound leaking from her lips as she tried to draw a breath. Her hands wrapped around his wrists and pulled weakly as she tried to save herself, her naked, bleeding feet sliding hopelessly on the wet soil and dead leaves, digging sad little trenches as her heels slid back and forth, slowing as the life eased from her as quietly as a child drowning, unseen by anyone who could save her, who could pull her back to the surface.

His hands remained clamped around her neck for a long time after she'd stopped moving and her hands had fallen away from his wrists. He was frozen with the fascination of how dead she already looked. He hadn't expected such a rapid transition from life to death – it was the first dead body he'd ever seen.

Eventually the cold night rain drifting into his face brought him back to this world. He hurriedly released his grip from her throat as if he'd had an electric shock, as if he had no idea how his hands came to be there in the first place. He shuffled away from the twisted body, aware that he was breathing heavily and that the salt he could taste on his lips was his sweat as it mixed with the rain that ran down his face. A calmness he'd never before experienced began to wash over him. A sense of control surged through him, clearing his mind, giving him focus and purpose.

Remembering what he needed to do next, he crawled around the body using only the light from the stars and moon to search for her meagre clothing, his eyes by now well adjusted. Having found the garments he stuffed them into his pocket, then stood and began to walk steadily away from the patch of forest that would forever be haunted by what it had witnessed. As he walked he thought nothing of Karen

Green. She had already faded to a distant memory, something that had happened a long time ago.

His thoughts had shifted to the next woman he would be visiting, the woman he knew was the real Sam.

5

Friday, seven thirty a.m. and Sean found himself driving towards the scene of another tragedy the rest of the world would probably never even notice. The closer he got to the scene, the more Louise Russell's attractive face etched itself into his mind. But what would she look like now? Would she be mutilated with ugly stab wounds or would the visible damage be restricted to a few telltale signs of strangulation around her neck? Perhaps her scalp would be matted in sticky red hair, like burnt jam, her skull caved in. He couldn't be sure how she'd died yet, at least not until he saw her, but somehow he already knew she would be naked and uncovered – that her killer would have made no effort to conceal her body or destroy forensic evidence, other than possibly dumping her in running water.

He rolled his car along the dirt road through Three Halfpenny Wood, looking for the obvious signs of a police presence and soon spotted two uniform patrol cars and Donnelly's unmarked Ford at the side of the road. Blue-and-white tape cordoned off the road ahead and the forest edge close to the parked cars. Ignoring the aches and tiredness that tried to distract him from what he had to do, he sat on his bonnet and awkwardly pulled forensic protective covers over his shoes before striding towards the two uniform officers who guarded the cars and entrance to the scene, his thin mackintosh coat trailing behind him as he approached. He tugged his warrant card free when he was close enough to the men for them to be able to see it clearly. 'DI Corrigan,' he announced himself. 'Where's the body?'

'About fifty feet into the woods, sir,' one of the uniforms replied. 'Just head straight in and you should find your DS easily enough.'

Sean peered into the woods, pausing for a couple of seconds before turning back to the uniform officer. 'Thanks,' he said, and ducked under the tape. He began to walk into the woods, always studying the ground ahead for evidence before moving forward a few steps. It was difficult to work out which route the killer had taken in and out of the wood as so many paths had been made by people and animals trampling through the vegetation, but he was sure the killer would have taken the most direct route in and out – he wasn't trying to cover his tracks. It would probably be easier to track backwards after he'd seen the body. He looked up and through the trees to a clearing where he could see Donnelly casually chatting to two more uniform officers. A twig snapped under Sean's foot and made all three look in his direction as if he was an unwanted intruder.

'Guv'nor,' Donnelly greeted him.

'Is it Louise Russell?' Sean asked bluntly.

'Who else could it be?'

'Have you seen the body?'

'I didn't get that close,' Donnelly told him. 'It was already confirmed that she was dead, no need for me to trample the scene. But I was close enough to see it's a young white woman with short brown hair, so unless you know different, I'd say it's her.'

'If that's the description, then it's her.' Sean felt his spirits sink further, any last hope it could have been a female vagrant dying of exposure or a young suicide victim leaving him. 'Where is the body?'

'The other side of that raised ground, in a clearing. Do you want me to fill you in on what I know so far?'

Sean shook his head. 'No, I'd rather see her myself first.'

'Fine,' Donnelly agreed. He wasn't insulted – he knew how Sean liked to work.

'Who found her?'

'A man taking his dog for an early morning walk. The dog did the finding.'

'Don't they always?'

'Any suspicions about the walker?'

'No. He's just an unlucky witness, but we've got him at the local nick anyway, reluctantly handing over his clothes and giving samples, intimate and non-intimate.'

'Good,' said Sean. 'Make sure we get hairs from the dog too.'

'You what?'

'I want hair samples from the dog,' Sean repeated.

'Why would we want that? If we find any hairs on the body, DNA will tell us whether they're human or canine. If they're canine, we'll know where they came from – the walker's dog.'

'And how do you know her killer doesn't have a dog? How do you know he didn't bring his dog out here with him? How do you know he didn't keep her somewhere where he also kept a dog or dogs?'

Donnelly sighed before answering. 'I don't.'

'Fine, then let's take the samples from the dog and get someone to do a cast of his paws too, for comparison with any found close to the body.'

'If you really think it's necessary.'

'I do – so let's make sure it's done.' There was a pause, then Sean spoke again. 'I need to see the body.'

'Forensics won't like it.'

'They'll survive. Besides, I want Dr Canning to examine the body in situ before Roddis's team crawl all over the scene.

I've already asked him to meet us here. Are forensics on the way?'

'Aye,' said Donnelly, 'they should be here soon enough.'

'Keep them at bay until Dr Canning's been and gone, OK?'

'No problem.'

Sean looked at the moss-covered patch of raised ground formed by the undergrowth spreading over an ancient fallen tree. He knew what lay on the far side and he knew it was time to enter the other world that existed beyond the world that most walked: a world of pain and suffering, of mindless violence and the death of innocence. 'I need a few minutes alone with her,' he told Donnelly, then set off towards the grassy knoll, moving slowly, making a show of searching the ground in front of him, hoping the watching police would assume he was being careful not to tread on any evidence. The truth was he needed time to prepare himself for what he was about to see – for what he was about to feel. He needed time to prepare himself for the person he was about to become.

He reached the raised ground and circled it carefully, walking a wide arc, unsure of what position the body would be in, not knowing whether he would first see her head or her feet.

As he rounded the tiny hill his heart began to pound, not with fear, but with excitement and anticipation at what he would find – at what bit of himself the killer had left behind for him to discover, for him to experience, knowing the more he shared with the man who had been here in the night, the closer he would be to catching him.

When the shattered body came into view Sean looked away, giving his mind vital seconds to prepare itself for what he had to see and what he had to do. He looked up to the blue sky, his vivid imagination turning the daylight to darkness, the sunshine to cold rain. He imagined the forest in the dead of night, the freezing wind and the pale lifeless body lit by the moonlight that bounced off the clouds. When he looked back at the body he saw his instincts had been right – she was naked and uncovered, lying on her back with her arms limp at her sides, her legs somewhat bent at the knees and slightly spread, as if the killer had deliberately posed her in a sexual position. Sean doubted it was caused by anything deliberate or premeditated, although he was sure she would have been violated at some point, probably repeatedly. He pictured clouds looming over the moon, turning the forest pitch-black as the killer kneeled over her, his hands wrapped around her neck as her legs scraped in the mud. Sean went in closer, almost close enough to touch the imaginary dark figure hunched over his victim, faceless and vague. He drew even closer, moving as slowly as a snake before it strikes, reaching out his hand, only inches away from where the killer would have crouched, the woman's body still writhing under him. Sean's fingers uncoiled and stretched towards where the killer's face would have been, imagining himself staring into the killer's eyes, as if by looking into those eyes he would understand why – why the man he hunted had become a monster, why he felt compelled to do the things he'd done, things no one else could understand – except Sean, perhaps? Understand, but not forgive.

A moment later the vision deserted him as quickly as it had arrived – night turned back to day, rain and wind to spring sunshine and morning stillness. Sean was left momentarily confused and disorientated; the extraordinary vividness of the images from the night before had made them feel somehow more real than the stark loneliness and surrealism of standing alone, inches away from the quiet, still, pitiful body of another murder victim killed and dumped without compassion or mercy.

Usually he was able to control his imagination, use it as precisely as a surgeon would wield his scalpel, but today the images in his mind had been almost beyond his control, taking on a life of their own, showing him all too clearly the last moments of Louise Russell. He knew what it meant – that he was already forming a strong connection with the man who had committed this crime.

A distant-sounding voice pulled him further back to here and now.

'You all right over there, guv'nor?' called Donnelly. 'I thought I heard you say something.'

'No,' Sean answered. 'I'm fine.'

Dismissing Donnelly from his thoughts, he stared once more at the frail body lying amongst the dead foliage, questions rushing into his mind, the answers hard on their heels, preventing him from analysing and ordering them logically and systematically as he knew he must. Closing his eyes, he breathed deeply and slowly, deliberately blocking the flow of information to allow his mind to settle. When at last he felt the peace he needed to move forward, he opened his eyes to see the yellow morning sunlight piercing the branches of the trees. It was as if the light was split into hundreds of individual sun rays, the rain of last night turning to mist as it warmed, magnifying the beauty of the rays as steam swirled in the ghostly light beams. Everything around him appeared magical, like a scene from some enchanted fairytale – everything except for the broken body lying inches from where he stood.

The questions and answers were starting to come again, but this time he was ready for them and able to control them. Sean moved as close as he dared to the body, close enough to see all that he needed to see. He knelt and scanned her from head to toe, over and over, the injuries telling their own tale: the split lip that showed signs of healing, well-formed dark-brown bruises that must have been inflicted days ago, in contrast with the fresh wounds to the side of her head and her blood-soaked ear. New bruises to her right knee and right elbow. Her right hand too had recently been injured, the skin of the knuckles scraped away, the fingers swollen, possibly broken; the lack of bruising suggested these too were fresh injuries, like the countless lacerations to her feet. Her entire body was covered in bruises in a variety of shades, as if she'd been repeatedly stabbed with a blunt object over a period of time.

Sean leaned closer, drawn by something unusual in the crook of her arm: bruising and needle track marks. She'd either been forced to inject herself or he had done it to her.

Glancing around to check that he wasn't being watched, Sean snapped on a single rubber glove and carefully brushed the hair from her face. What he saw stopped him dead as he tried to make sense of it. After a few seconds he began searching in his inside jacket pockets, certain he'd remembered to keep a photograph of Louise Russell close to hand. He found it in the last pocket he searched, holding it in front of him so he could compare it with the face of the woman lying on the ground. He strained to recall the Missing Persons Report, searching his mind's image of it for the Marks & Scars section, recalling that Louise Russell had had her appendix removed when she was a teenager, leaving a four-inch scar on her lower right-side abdomen. His hand moved down her body, floating inches above her skin until he reached the place where the scar should have been, but the skin was pure and unblemished. 'Jesus Christ,' he said quietly, struggling to comprehend what he had discovered.

His eyes searched her body for other signs this was not who she was supposed to be, but he could find no more unique marks or scars visible on her front. Carefully he gripped her right wrist and slowly rotated her arm, exposing the underside and the cheap-looking colourful tattoo of a phoenix. Something about it seemed childlike and unreal. There was no mention of Louise Russell having a tattoo. This couldn't be her.

Sean stepped back, never taking his eyes away from the body. 'Louise Russell wasn't your first, was she?' He spoke to the spirit of the killer whose malignant presence had stained the ground he now stood on so indelibly it was as if he was still here. '*This* was your first. You took her and then you took Louise Russell. But why? What are you thinking? What's making you do these things?'

He stopped, stood in silence, letting his mind roam, exploring each avenue of possibility before speaking again. 'They're the same. The two women are the same – late twenties, early thirties, slim, short brown hair, same nose, face shape . . . This was no coincidence, was it?' Once more he paused, thought in silence, letting the answers come to him, not forcing them. 'They reminded you of someone . . . No,' he reprimanded himself, 'more than that. When you saw them, they became someone, someone you loved, someone who rejected you, who betrayed you. They betrayed you, and so you take these women to be with her again, don't you?' He was unaware that his hands were pushing the hair on the sides of his head back continuously as he spoke, the effort of concentration subconsciously manifesting itself. 'But why this?' His hands now both pointing towards the body, palms upturned, standing, waiting for further revelations. 'Did she reject you as well and you couldn't deal with that again, so you punished her?' He stopped himself, paused, shook his head. 'But that doesn't explain this.' He looked down at the body. 'This was an execution. You killed her as quickly and painlessly as you thought you could. There's no rage here, no leaving the body displayed to humiliate her. So tell me, you sick fucker, what made you go from loving her to dumping her here like a dead animal?'

Realizing he was standing with his arms outstretched, he quickly tucked them into his coat pockets to stop any more involuntary gestures. Then he stood motionless, processing the information, dissecting it with diamond-sharp clarity, drawing conclusions he would never be able to explain to the rest of his team, let alone an outsider. There was only one other person who would understand what he was thinking – the man who had tortured and strangled the life out of the pretty young woman now lying amongst the fallen leaves and crawling insects.

Sean suddenly turned on his heels and strode towards Donnelly, speaking as he closed the distance between them. 'It's not her,' he announced.

Stunned, Donnelly opened his mouth to reply, but before he could speak Sean cut in:

'The victim – it's not Louise Russell.'

'It fucking looks like her to me, guv.'

'It's not her,' Sean repeated. 'Similar in every way, but it's not her. Louise Russell had her appendix removed when she was a teenager. This woman has no post-op scarring and she has a tattoo on her arm. Louise Russell does not. This is not her.'

The weight of what Sean was telling him took Donnelly a few seconds to translate. 'Oh fuck,' he finally declared.

'Oh fuck indeed,' Sean agreed.

'So if she's not Louise Russell, then who the hell is she?'

'I have absolutely no idea,' Sean answered, an admission that spurred him to action. 'OK. I want you to get hold of Sally and tell her to check all the recent missing persons reports for south-east London – but only for women of similar description to Louise Russell. She won't find many, but let's hope there's at least one. When the Lab Team get here, have them photograph the tattoo on the underside of her right forearm – there's something off there, something odd about it. Get a copy of the photo and give it to someone you trust to research it – local tattoo shops, Internet, etc. Someone may remember doing it for her.'

'I'll give it to Zukov. He likes a little project,' grinned Donnelly.

'Fine. Meantime, you stay here and liaise with forensics when they arrive. Tell them we need the scene and everything from it processed as a matter of the utmost urgency. They'll moan like drains that the anti-terrorist boys have got them buried under an avalanche of work, but do it anyway. Make sure they know we still have an outstanding missing person who will be turning up in some other wood making them even more work if they don't get this rushed through.'

'No problem,' Donnelly assured him. 'But there's one thing you may have overlooked, boss.'

'Such as?'

'We can't be sure Louise Russell's disappearance and this woman's death are connected.'

Sean bit back the caustic reply, reminded himself others around him needed more time, more tangible evidence to draw the same conclusions he already had. 'No make-up, no painted nails or dyed hair. No track-marks in her arms or legs – no body piercings. This was no prostitute dragged off the street and murdered.'

'Agreed,' Donnelly answered, 'but that doesn't mean she was killed by the guy that took Louise Russell.'

'Same age, same physical build, hair, face. There'll be a MISPER report somewhere that'll tell us who she is and with it the evidence to all but confirm they were taken by the same man.'

'If you say so,' Donnelly sighed.

'I'm off back to the office to put Featherstone in the picture. Oh, and one last thing . . .'

'Aye?'

'For God's sake cover the poor cow up with something, will you – she's suffered enough already. It'll help preserve evidence if it rains too.'

Donnelly nodded in agreement as he watched Sean picking his way through the fallen branches and tree stumps, heading for the road and his car, just as the killer had the night before.

* * *

Thomas Keller slowly descended the stone stairs to the cellar, the low morning light casting a long shadow that moved across the floor like an evil spirit. He listened for sounds of movement from below without losing concentration on balancing the tray of breakfast items, his mood calm, but somewhat melancholy. As he stepped into the room he placed the tray on the same little makeshift table behind the old screen and pulled the light cord, managing a forced half-smile in Louise Russell's direction. 'I have to go to work soon,' he told her, 'but I thought you might like to get cleaned up a bit and have some breakfast.' She didn't respond. He was pleased to see she was wearing the clothes he had given her, his smile broadening as he admired the well-dressed woman locked in her cage.

'You look lovely,' he told her. 'Did you use the moisturizer and perfume I gave you? I can't smell them.' Still she didn't respond. 'Don't feel like talking, eh? Never mind. I understand. You're upset about . . .' he managed to stop himself before saying the name. 'You're upset about the other woman that used to be here. Well, don't be. She's gone now. She can't make any more trouble for us. We won't have to listen to her lies.'

Louise broke her silence. 'What happened to her?'

'I told you, we don't have to worry about her any more,' he answered, agitation creeping into his previously calm persona. 'So please, let's not mention her again . . . OK?'

'What did you do to her?' Louise persisted, contempt and anger overtaking her fear and caution.

'We don't talk about her,' Keller erupted, his face contorted with rage. 'We don't fucking talk about her ever again. Never again. Do you understand?'

Louise rocked back in her cell, her temporary courage deserting her, her hands pushed out in front of her as if to fend him off. 'OK. Sorry. I won't mention her. I promise.'

'Good,' he said, calmer now. He pulled the key and the

stun-gun from separate pockets, looking at them guiltily. 'I'm sorry about this,' he told her, 'but I don't know how much they poisoned you. There may still be some inside of you, making you think things about me that aren't true. We need to be careful.' He unlocked the cage door and pulled it gently, allowing it to swing open under its own weight, stepping back to give her space. She began to crawl towards the door, but he stopped her midway: 'Wait, don't forget the moisturizer and perfume. I want you to use them today. But make sure you take all your clothes off first. I want you to wash properly before you use them.'

Louise crawled back and gathered the items, clutching them to her chest as if they were something she treasured, despite her revulsion.

As she left her cage she registered the daylight from above pouring down the stairs and knew the door was open. There was nothing she could do though, not with him watching her every move, stun-gun at the ready. She walked past him, using her peripheral vision to watch him, waiting for him to lower his guard and give her a chance, but he stayed alert and the opportunity never came.

She moved behind the screen and began to undress, carefully hanging her clothes over the screen, looking at him sheepishly to show him her embarrassment at being watched. 'Please, excuse me.'

Keller took the hint. 'You want some privacy, of course.' He moved deeper into the cellar, resigning himself to watching her through the thin material of the screen as she removed the last of her clothes and began to wash, wiping the cloth across her naked body. But he felt no stirring today, no delicious anticipation of when they would be together. The events of the previous night seemed to have dulled his senses and lessened his feelings towards the woman he watched in silhouette through the fabric. Doubts began to seep into his mind as to whether she was the true one after all, but he managed to chase them away, for now.

She had begun to dry herself, hurriedly rubbing the coarse towel over her skin. 'Don't forget the cream and perfume,' he told her, watching the silhouette freeze for a few seconds before reaching for the moisturizer, her hands almost frantically rubbing it into her shoulders. 'Slow down,' he demanded. 'Take your time. I want you to put it everywhere. It only works if you put it everywhere.' Again she froze for a few seconds, then carried on massaging the cream into her skin. A satisfied sigh escaped his lips. 'That's better,' he said encouragingly. 'Do it just like that.'

He watched for minutes as she performed for him, but still his excitement failed to reach its previous levels, leaving him feeling disappointed and unfulfilled. 'Now the perfume,' he insisted, watching as her shadow pointed the small bottle towards the base of her throat and pressed twice, the tiny cloud of man-made scent casting its own silhouette as it floated through the air behind the screen.

When she'd finished dressing she walked from behind the screen and headed obediently back towards her cage, the scent of the cream and perfume wafting under his nose as she passed him, its combination intoxicating, but still the excitement he expected to feel was not there. He looked away from her.

Seeing him turn his head as if ashamed, Louise saw an opportunity to reach out him, to try to form some kind of bond. She'd vowed to learn from Karen Green's mistakes. Perhaps if Karen had managed to touch him, he wouldn't have treated her like an anonymous pawn in his game of fantasy. If she'd only tried stepping from the shadows of whoever Sam was to him, it might have made it more difficult for him to force himself on her and finally, when he tired of her, to dispose of her like an unwanted pet.

By getting closer to him, Louise hoped she could confuse him, make him doubt himself and what he was doing. If she had to, she would take him inside of her, pretend she wanted him, but all the time she would be looking, waiting for the opportunity to hurt him – to hurt him like she'd never hurt anybody in her life.

'Are you all right?'

The gentle, caring question seemed to catch him off-balance. 'Sorry,' he said, before realizing he had heard her question after all. 'Yes, sorry, yes I'm fine. I'm just a little tired, that's all. I've been working very hard lately . . . er, things have been a little crazy at work, but I'm fine. Thank you.'

'What do you do?' she asked, aware of his awkwardness, determined to keep him talking.

'You know what I do,' he said. 'You've seen me.'

'You mean you're a real postman? That's a good job. You must be very responsible to have a job like that.' She knew her speech was stuttering and unnaturally bright, but she had to search for the chink in his armour of madness.

'It's OK,' he answered suspiciously, his eyes back on her now, moving up and down her body as if the way she moved would betray whatever treacherous ideas she might be hatching. 'People leave me alone,' he lied, 'and I can pretty much do as I like, so long as I get the job done.'

'That's good.' Without meaning to, she found herself talking to him as she would a child. 'It must be nice to be left alone.'

'What do you mean?'

'Nothing. Just it must be nice to be able to do what you want to do, when you want to.'

'Why?' he asked. 'Do you resent being here? Don't you want to be here?'

'No, no,' she hurried to assure him, realizing she was losing whatever ground she'd made. 'I want to be here with you. I want to understand.'

'Maybe you'll never understand.' He was glaring at her, his voice cold. 'Maybe they poisoned your mind too much for you to ever be able to understand.'

Louise felt herself being dragged towards the edge of the cliff. 'No, you can make me understand, you can take the poison away. I know you can. I'm Sam, remember?'

He remained silent, considering her, waiting for his instincts to tell him how to react. He felt nothing.

'You need to go back inside,' he told her. 'It's not safe for you yet. The lies are still in your head.'

'Why can't I come with you?' she almost pleaded, desperate to escape to the daylight above and the unlimited possibilities of salvation she dreamed it held. 'You don't need to leave me down here any longer.'

'I told you,' he insisted, 'it's not safe for you yet. You need to go back inside now.' He raised the stun-gun a few inches to encourage her. Tears began to roll down her cheeks as she stooped back inside the desolate cage, the door closing quickly behind her, the lock snapping shut, condemning her to more hours alone in the gloom without hope.

He got to the foot of the stairs and then turned back, came right up to the side of her cage. 'I almost forgot . . .' He was smiling again. 'I have something for you, something that will bring us even closer together.' He pulled the sleeve of his right arm up over his bare forearm, slowly rolling it back on itself to expose a tattoo on the underside of his arm, its bright colours vivid against his pale, lifeless skin: the reds, blues and greens of a phoenix rising from the gold of the fire. It was clumsy illustration, like something a child would choose at a fairground. 'This is us,' he told her, 'this is our love, rising from the flames. They all tried to stop it from happening, but you can't stop what is meant to be.'

He bared his small ugly teeth as he smiled at her, his eyes shining brightly as he nervously waited for her reaction. She forced herself to smile through her fear and disgust.

'Here,' he said, reaching into the pocket of his tracksuit top, 'I have something for you, something to show everybody that we were meant to be together.' Carefully he pulled out a flimsy, shiny-backed piece of paper. He smiled as he looked at the picture she couldn't yet see, pinched between his thumb and index finger, eventually twisting his wrist to show her the image of the phoenix, exactly the same as his tattoo in every way.

Suddenly his hand shot out and opened the hatch to the cage. 'Put your arm through,' he said, still smiling.

'Why?' she asked, memories of the torture he'd inflicted on Karen Green too fresh in her mind.

'Don't be scared,' he laughed, 'it's not a real tattoo like mine. You can get a real one later, when the poison's gone – this one's just a transfer. Don't you remember? It's the same one we had when we were kids. It was our secret. Only we knew about them. You put mine on my arm and I did yours. It was our secret sign.'

'Yes,' she lied. 'It was a long time ago, but I remember.'

'Good,' he said, his eyes bright with joy. 'Now put your arm through the hatch.'

She resisted the temptation to close her eyes as she eased her arm through the cage opening, his hand closing around her wrist, gently pulling her forearm towards him. He licked the underside of the transfer, but his swollen red tongue lacked saliva and he had to run it over the transfer several times before it was moist enough to apply. It took every ounce of strength Louise had not to recoil from his vileness, her nausea reaching new levels as he pressed the wet transfer into her forearm, his hand clamped over the top of it, his saliva glistening on her skin.

'You have to keep still for a while,' he explained, 'or it won't work properly.' He held her for minutes that felt like hours before peeling away the transfer underside, leaving behind the ugly image of something that should have been beautiful. As he released her arm she couldn't help but pull it back inside her cage too quickly, turning his smile to a frown of concern. 'What's the matter?' he asked. 'Don't you like it?'

'Of course,' she lied, 'it's beautiful.' Her blinking eyelashes flicked tears across her face.

Keller had learned to trust what he saw, not what people said. The smile did not return to his face. He stood to his full height and filled his lungs with air pulled through his nose and began to walk to the staircase, tugging the light cord and returning the gloom. At the foot of the stairs he turned to her once more.

'Everything can be replaced, Sam.' His voice was flat, devoid of emotion. 'They taught me that, in the home they took me to, they taught me that. Everything can be replaced. Even you, Sam. Even you.'

Sean strode across the incident room, speaking to everyone he passed without stopping, asking quick-fire questions, making sure they knew he was aware of the tasks they'd been assigned and that he needed results fast. They weren't used to trying to save a life yet to be lost and Sean was concerned they would struggle to adapt from the pace of a normal murder investigation, where the victim was beyond saving if not beyond redemption.

Through the Perspex windows of his office he could see Sally talking to Detective Superintendent Featherstone. He went in and joined them.

'Sally's been giving me the good news.' Featherstone's voice was heavy with sarcasm. 'Are you one hundred per cent sure about this, Sean?'

'Yes,' Sean answered bluntly. 'The woman I saw this morning is not Louise Russell. Sally, what you got?'

'Karen Green,' Sally began. 'Reported missing yesterday by her brother, Terry Green. This is a photograph of her.' She handed Sean a picture taken with a flash in some bar, Karen's smile beaming at the unseen lens. 'She's twenty-six years old, five foot six approximately, shortish brown hair, slim—'

Sean cut in before she could finish. 'That's her,' he said. 'Karen Green's the woman I saw this morning. OK, what do we know about her?' He looked to Sally for answers.

'Not much. All we have so far is a basic non-vulnerable MISPER report. It's not exactly overflowing with information. We know she lived and worked in Bromley, and that she lived alone but had lots of friends, two sisters and three brothers including Terry who reported her missing.'

'Have they been spoken to yet?' Sean asked.

'No,' Sally told him. 'Like I said, she was only reported missing yesterday.'

'But when did she actually go missing? When was she last seen?'

Sally scanned the report. 'According to Terry, he hasn't heard from her since Wednesday.'

'This report's not going to tell us anything useful. Get this Terry Green to meet us at Karen's place. I need to speak to him myself and I need to have a look around before forensics pile in.'

'I'll get it sorted now.' Sally was already on her way out of the room.

'What about going back to the media?' Featherstone asked. 'They'll make a connection sooner or later.'

Sean nodded. 'They may be a lot of things, but they're not stupid. I suggest we tell them upfront what's going on, but hold back enough details so we can dismiss any nutters phoning in, claiming to be the killer. Christ,' he exclaimed, 'once the media find out we have one dead and another living on borrowed time, they'll go fucking mental. They'll be all over this every second of the day.'

'I can't do anything about that,' sighed Featherstone, 'but I can probably keep them off your back, keep your name in the background as much as possible.'

'It would be appreciated.'

'But are you sure bringing the media in won't panic him?

We don't want to be accused of pushing him into doing what we both know he's going to do anyway.'

'It won't,' Sean assured him. 'He's working to his own timeline and nothing's going to interfere or change that.'

'How can you be so sure?'

'He didn't just snatch Louise Russell off the street and I'm betting he didn't just snatch Karen Green either. That means he has a plan in mind for the women he takes, even if he doesn't consciously know it himself. He won't let a media appeal interfere with that. Keeping them alive as long as he does is too important to him. It's everything. If Karen Green's timeline is anything to go by, and I believe it is, we have about three days to find Louise Russell before she ends up the same way.'

Sally appeared at the door, already pulling her coat on. 'Terry Green will meet us outside Karen's house as soon we can get there.'

Sean stood and began to load his pocket with items snatched from his desk.

'One moment, Sean,' Featherstone stopped him. 'I need a quick word.' He looked at Sally. 'In private.'

'I'll meet you at the car,' Sean told her. She shrugged and left. 'What is it?' he asked.

'Well,' Featherstone began, 'first off, let me just tell you the powers that be are very happy that you're the one heading up this investigation.'

'But . . .?'

'But they want you to work with someone on this one, especially now a body has turned up that's not the woman we were looking for.'

'They already know about that?'

Featherstone didn't answer his question. 'They want you to work with someone from outside the force – a criminal psychologist, to be exact.'

'Please tell me you're joking.'

'I'm afraid not. Her name's Anna Ravenni-Ceron. She's very well qualified.'

'Anna Ravenni-who?' said Sean. 'Look, boss, I really don't have time to babysit some civi-scientist so she can make a name for herself and get her face on the telly.'

'I'm sorry, Sean, but the decision's been made – it's out of my hands. I know it's bullshit, but you'll just have to put up with it.' He lowered his voice conspiratorially: 'Listen, my advice – give her the mushroom treatment: keep her in the dark and feed her shit as much as you can. Just don't get caught doing it, eh?' He winked and then added cheerily, 'I'll send her over in the next day or so.'

'Fine,' Sean reluctantly agreed, knowing he had no choice. 'But if she gets in my way or interferes with this investigation, I'll personally throw her out on her ear.'

'Have you considered that she might actually be able to help you?' Featherstone asked.

'No,' Sean told him bluntly. 'That's not something I have considered and it's probably not something I will consider. All she needs to do is keep out of my way.'

Louise Russell lay on the filthy mattress inside her cage, the dirty light bulb hanging from the ceiling painting everything in the cellar a miserable yellow. She'd felt so alone since he took Karen away; alone and afraid. A terrible anxiety and sense of panic had gripped her, sending her heart racing and making her stomach tighten painfully. She sensed she was on the verge of totally losing control and descending into madness if she didn't find some way of combating the dread that was engulfing her. So she tried to fill her head with thoughts of home, her comfortable house, the things inside it that suddenly meant so much to her – her pictures, her clothes, her own bathroom and real toilet, warmth and safety. Her mind drifted to her husband, strong and quiet, kind and reliable, moral and loyal, the sort of man she'd always planned on settling down with, the sort of man she wanted to have children with – a happy little suburban family.

All too soon other thoughts forced their way into her consciousness. What had he done to Karen? She was sure he hadn't simply released her. He couldn't risk letting her walk away to tell the world what he had done. Maybe he'd just moved her to another place, to keep them apart? She hoped so, but somehow she doubted it.

Dear God, she thought, why had he taken her, why was she the one lying on a filthy mattress in a wire cage? What had drawn this beast to her? She hadn't done anything wrong, she hadn't hurt anyone, she had no enemies, so why her? And why Karen? Images of Karen being abused and violated flashed behind her eyes, his words as he left her ringing inside her head – *Everything can be replaced. Even you, Sam. Even you.* The inevitability of what was to come consumed and terrified her, the rising sense of panic once again overwhelming her, as if the cage had already become her coffin, the worms and maggots writhing over her skin, spiders crawling across her slowly decaying body. She could feel them and knew she had to escape her crypt.

She launched herself at the cage door, bouncing off it to the floor, ignoring the pain in her shoulder and launching herself again with the same result, tears of pain mixing with tears of frustration and abject terror, as if she only now realized the full extent of her predicament. Again she rammed the door with her shoulder, and again, until finally she could stand the pain no more, falling to the floor sobbing, scratching and digging at the unyielding concrete like a trapped dog trying to escape, her fingernails splintering and bleeding, the futility of her actions increasingly obvious until she finally rocked back on her haunches, hands fallen at her side, her head lolled backwards, staring at the heavens she imagined somewhere above the cold cellar's ceiling. 'God,' she pleaded. 'Please help me. Dear Jesus, please help, I'm begging you, please help me.' Her quiet prayers suddenly turned to desperate screams. 'Jesus Christ help me. Please, anybody help me, please, for God's sake somebody please help me. Somebody!'

But her prayers, both whispered and screamed, were met with silence. She crawled to her mattress, curled into a tight ball and waited, waited for the sound of the heavy metal lock being knocked against the steel door and then the footsteps, the soft footsteps as he descended towards her.

Mid-morning Friday and Sean and Sally waited impatiently outside Karen Green's house for her brother Terry to show. Sally sensed Sean's bad mood. 'Are you all right?' she asked. 'Something seems to be bothering you.'

'I'm fine,' he dismissed her concern. 'I could just do without other people sticking their noses into my business.'

Sally intended to pry further, but Sean was saved by Terry Green's car pulling on to the driveway. He climbed out quickly and almost tripped as he staggered towards them, his face riddled with anxiety.

'Sorry I'm late,' he panted breathlessly.

'Don't worry about it,' Sally replied, 'and thanks for coming.'

'When you said it was about Karen I came straight away. Has something happened to her? Have you found her? Is she all right?'

Sean flashed his warrant card. 'DI Corrigan. Are you Terry Green?' His mood and the urgency of the situation made him abrupt.

'Yes.'

'I need to establish when you or anyone else last saw Karen and I need to do it quickly.'

'Why? What's happening?'

Seeing that Green was becoming flustered, Sally pushed her own feelings of anxiety to one side and stepped between him and Sean, protecting him from an onslaught of blunt questions.

'I'm Sally, we spoke on the phone, remember?'

'Of course. You asked me to meet you here. You said it was about Karen.'

'It is,' she told him, 'and if there was any other way of doing this, believe me we would have, but the urgency of the situation meant we had to meet you here and we have to ask you some questions straight away.'

'But what about Karen?' Green asked, concerned.

'I have to be honest with you, Terry. I have to tell you something that's not going to be easy to hear, but it's only fair you hear it now.' She waited for signs that Green had braced himself for the worst. When she was sure his lungs could inhale no more air she rested a hand on his shoulder and continued. 'We found the body of a young woman this morning and she matches the description of your sister.' His lungs deflated instantly and he seemed to sway, his eyes closing for a second before slowly flickering open. She knew his body had dealt with the blow well, but his mind had gone into temporary shock. Resting her other hand on his opposite shoulder, ready to steady him if his swaying threatened to topple him, Sally continued: 'She matches the description of your sister, but we can't be sure it's her until she's formally identified.'

'When will that be?' Green managed to ask.

'A little later,' Sally told him, 'as soon as we can get it organized. But right now we need to know when was the last time anyone saw Karen.'

'I'm not sure,' he admitted. 'It was probably me, what, last Wednesday, in the evening sometime, the night before she was due to fly to Australia. I was picking up a set of keys for her house and taking care of some other stuff I told her I'd do while she was away.'

'Australia?' Sean queried.

'She was going travelling, looking for something she said she couldn't find here.'

'Was she going with anyone?' Sean asked, excited by the prospect of identifying a now missing travel companion, especially if that companion was a new man in her life.

'No,' Green ended the possible line of inquiry. 'She wanted to go alone, which is pretty typical of her. She has a spirit of adventure, you know. She makes friends easily. She had no fear of going by herself.'

Sean had no interest in her personality at this moment. His priority was gathering hard facts he could use to find Louise Russell. 'So as far as you're concerned she's been missing for nine days?'

'I think so, yes.'

'And you didn't report her missing until yesterday because you thought she was travelling around Australia, yes?'

Green nodded, still looking dazed.

'So what happened? You tried to call her and couldn't get an answer? Then you called around her friends and they all told you the same thing – nobody had heard from her.'

'Yes,' Green answered, struggling to gather his thoughts. 'So I phoned the airline she was flying with and they said she never boarded the flight. That was when I knew for certain something was wrong, so I reported her missing.'

Sally could see Green needed a softer approach. 'You did the right thing, Mr Green. Checking with the airline was a smart move,' she reassured him, flashing a look at Sean that warned him to ease off, at least for a while. 'You look as if you could use a cup of tea, so how about I nip across to that café over the road and get us a drink, then we can get started with the questions?'

'Yeah. Sure.'

'Did you bring keys for the house?' Sean asked. 'I need to take a look inside.'

'Of course,' said Green, fishing in his pocket and handing over two keys.

'Thank you.' Sean examined the keys that he could see fitted quality locks – so Karen Green hadn't been flippant about her home security. 'Have you been inside, since you reported her missing?'

'I checked it out this morning – it was as quick as I could get here. As soon as I found her backpack and travel documents I told the same police I'd first reported it to. That was when they said you'd be taking over the investigation. I should have checked the house as soon as I thought something was wrong – shouldn't I?'

'It wouldn't have made any difference,' Sean told him. 'You did everything you could. You wait here. I'm just going to take a look around.'

Turning his back on Green, he walked towards the front door, already struck by the similarities between Louise Russell's house and this one – small, modern townhouses in quiet, anonymous streets, the dog-leg design of the garage and house frontage meaning the front door could not be seen until you were very close. Sean imagined the faceless killer approaching the property, feeling safe and comfortable with it, the type of house he would stick to now, never changing his approach, never changing his method even though it clearly marked his crimes.

Sean moved around the outside of the building, checking the windows at the front, sides and back for signs of forced entry or disturbance without expecting to find anything. He couldn't imagine the killer searching for a weak entry point, it just didn't feel right – too clumsy and random, too likely to give himself away, to be heard or seen by a nosy neighbour. He moved back to the front of the house and stood by the front door with its opaque glass arches in the higher section. The killer would have been able to see Karen Green approaching, would have been able to hear her, sense her.

This was his way into the house, he was sure of it. He walked in straight through the open front door. But had he waited outside for the random opportunity of the door being opened for some reason, or had he caused the door to be opened?

Sean thought about the entrances to this and Louise Russell's house, the privacy they provided, and decided it would have been possible for the killer to hide in the alcove, concealed from both the road and anyone inside casually looking out. But if they were looking hard, searching for the source of an unfamiliar or suspicious noise, he could have been seen. No, Sean told himself. Too risky. It didn't fit the way this one operated. This one hit fast and hard, sticking to a plan, silent and unobserved, his escape and the transfer of his victims from car to car seamless and unseen. No, this one strode up the drive and rang the doorbell almost without hesitation, pausing only for a second to run through the plan in his mind one last time.

But that didn't explain why both women had opened the door to this monster. Were they so secure in their own homes they didn't think to check who was on the other side of the door? Or had he appeared to be something he was not – something they saw every day that they trusted, that they would never consider a threat? Artifice, Sean decided. The bastard used artifice to get the door open. But if he'd gone to the lengths of planning Sean was increasingly sure he had, then he wouldn't simply knock on the door and tell them he was from the gas board, he wouldn't risk that.

Sean thought for a second, not wanting to chase the answer too hard, afraid if he tightened his grip too quickly the truth of what had happened would ooze between his fingers and be lost. This one wore a uniform, a uniform people trusted: a council worker, a meter reader, a postman or maybe even a police uniform. No, Sean told himself, not a police uniform, people remember the presence of a cop. The man he was looking for would have chosen something bland, a profession people took for granted.

He realized he'd been standing only inches from the front door staring into the warped glass arches for an unnatural length of time. The voice of Terry Green from somewhere behind him further dragged him back to the world of the living and sane. 'Is everything all right?' Green asked. 'Are you having trouble with the keys?'

'No,' Sean called over his shoulder without turning to face him, looking down at the unused keys in his hand and lifting them to the first lock. 'I'll be back in a few minutes. Wait here for DS Jones.'

Unlocking the door as swiftly as he could, he stepped inside, braced for an onrush of senses and images of both the victim and violator, but little came. He eased the door shut and took a deep breath, relieved to be alone, away from the confused, concerned gaze of Terry Green. He stood with his back to the door looking around the hallway, waiting for his projected imagination to be kick-started by some sight or smell, but still little happened. The scene was old now, cold and lifeless. No one had been inside the house for the last nine days. How quickly a home becomes a shell, deprived of the ebb and flow of people that keeps it alive. Still he needed to glean from it what he could, find some trace of what had happened, some imprint of the man who came through the front door nine days ago and shattered the life of Karen Green and everyone who cared about her.

He walked deeper into the house, keeping close to the walls, staring hard at the hallway carpet, though he doubted there would be much to see. This one didn't spill blood at the scene. The best they could hope for was that the forensic team would find a shoe imprint in the carpet or more traces of chloroform. He took a moment or two to look around the hallway, simply and tastefully decorated, the walls adorned with framed colourful prints and multiple photographs of the victim with people he assumed were her friends and family, trapped behind the glass of cheap clip-frames. The door leading into the lounge was already open as he stepped across the threshold. It was decorated in the same simplistic way: prints and photographs on walls, although fewer than in the hallway, a comfortable set of modern chairs with a sofa, a decent television with accompanying electronic adornments, thick cotton blinds instead of curtains. So far the house was providing no real sense of its owner. Disappointed, he moved on to the kitchen, the heart of any home, even one belonging to a person who lived alone.

On re-entering the hallway he found the kitchen door ajar. He paused for a second. Where had she been when the killer came calling – in the kitchen? No. The door would have been fully open if she'd come from there. The lounge then? Again no – it was pristine, no signs of recent use, no indentation on the chairs or sofa, no TV or music playing. He thought for a moment. She was due to fly to Australia the morning she was taken, so she would have been too excited to sit and watch TV, there'd have been last-minute packing to do and arrangements to take care of. So she'd have been upstairs when he called, Sean was sure of it. For a brief moment he felt the panic that had gripped the killer when she took longer to answer the door than he'd anticipated, finishing whatever task she was in the middle of before making her way downstairs. But his connection with the madman faded as quickly as it came.

His thoughts and senses returned to the kitchen he found himself standing in, but it looked and felt like a show kitchen, everything scrubbed clean and put away, its sterile surfaces and unused cooker revealing nothing about her. 'I'm wasting my time here,' he told himself, aware he was speaking out loud. 'Time I haven't got.'

He left the kitchen and headed upstairs, unconcerned about stepping on any unseen forensic evidence, utterly convinced that the killer had never been near the stairs. At the top of the stairway he was confronted by three doors, two partially open and one fully so. He went through the fully open door first and found exactly what he had expected – a brand-new, fully loaded backpack lying on the stripped double bed next to the last few items waiting to be packed away. Alongside the backpack was a larger than normal travel wallet that drew him to it. He flicked it open with one finger and studied the contents: a passport, Australian dollars, travellers' cheques and insurance documents. She'd been well prepared and organized, clearly she'd lived an orderly life, as did Louise Russell. Was that important to the man who took them? Did his knowledge of them go beyond where they lived, encompassing how they lived – and if so, how did he come by this information? What was his window into their lives?

Another question hit him. Why hadn't her brother checked inside and found what he had found? He considered Terry Green for a while, trying to remember what he had felt when he'd first seen him, whether he'd missed something. Could it be that Terry had killed his own sister and then taken Louise Russell in some twisted attempt to replace her, to avoid feelings of guilt and remorse, loss and sorrow? The replacement angle felt right, but everything else felt wrong.

He moved slowly around the bedroom, but again could get no sense of her, no trace of her perfume or shampoo, her body or hand cream. Her house was a desert to him. He checked the other bedroom as a matter of course and found she'd been using it mainly as a storage room; it was full of neatly piled cardboard boxes that had once contained the items now spread around the house, although there was an unmade single bed pushed into the corner for the use of overnight guests who didn't share her bed.

Sean slipped from the bedroom and quietly crossed the hallway to the bathroom, beginning to feel more like an intruder than a cop. The bathroom was little different from the rest of the house, sterile and unyielding, everything cleaned and tidied away before she left for her adventure of a lifetime. He opened the large mirrored door to her oversized bathroom cabinet, looking for some hint of her life before the madness came, and was confronted by a multitude of bottles and jars, lotions and potions that only women would ever consider covering themselves in. Most of them had been at least partially used, seals broken and bottles half-emptied of their strange-coloured liquids. He examined them closely, absorbing their pleasant clinical fragrances, moving things around so he could see deeper into the cabinet and her life now past. She clearly cared for herself, but there was nothing exotic here and most of the brands were familiar to him as they would be to almost anybody: Nivea, Clarins, Radox, Chanel and dozens more, all left behind because they'd been used – people liked to take unopened toiletries when they headed off on a long journey and she'd clearly been no different.

Feeling as if he was being suffocated by the soulless house, Sean hurried back downstairs, needing to get out as fast as he could. He was on the verge of flinging open the front door when he remembered that Terry Green and Sally would be waiting on the other side for him, so he paused to compose himself, only emerging when he was sure he appeared calm.

On stepping out, he immediately noticed an absence on the driveway. 'Her car?' he asked as he approached Sally and Terry. 'She had a car, right, so where is it?'

'It's in storage,' Green answered.

'How so?'

'She had no room in the garage for it, and she thought it would be safer in storage than left on the drive.'

'Storage where?' The urgency in his voice was tangible. 'Did she tell you what storage firm she used?'

Green thought for a moment. 'It was over in Beckenham, I know that. Had one of those obvious names, like We-Store-4-U.'

Sally was already typing the details into her iPhone. They all waited in silence for a couple of minutes until Sally spoke.

'Yep, here they are – We-Store-4-U, Beckenham.' She enlarged the telephone number and tapped it, moving the phone to her ear, walking away from Sean and Green while she made her inquiry. Sean's concentration was so firmly fixed on Sally he all but forgot Green was there, watching as she paced the driveway talking into her phone and waiting. Finally he heard her say 'Thank you' before hanging up. She stepped back towards them, shaking her head. 'The car was booked in for storage, but it never turned up. They tried calling her, but got no answer.'

'Of course they didn't. Son-of-a-bitch took her car just like he—' Sean stopped himself from mentioning Louise Russell in Green's presence.

'Just like what?' Green asked.

'Nothing,' Sean lied. 'I need you to tell me about her car – make, model, colour, registration if you know it.'

'A Toyota, I think,' Green answered, thrown into confusion by Sean's questions. 'I don't know the number plate.'

'Don't worry about it,' Sally intervened. 'The storage people gave me the details – a red Nissan Micra, index Yankee-Yankee-fifty-nine-Oscar-Victor-Papa.'

'Good,' Sean said. 'Get it circulated.'

Sally immediately began typing numbers into her phone.

'And when you've done that, take Mr Green's statement – everything he can tell us about Karen's last-known movements and her intended trip to Australia, names of recent boyfriends, etc, etc.'

Sally nodded as she waited for her call to be answered. 'Anything else?' she asked, phone pressed to her ear.

'Plenty,' said Sean grimly, 'but let me worry about that. You take care of the car and statement – I need to get back to the office, set the ball rolling.'

* * *

Sean had no sooner started the engine than his phone rang. He took the call while pulling away from the kerb, well practised at one-handed driving.

'Inspector Corrigan? This is Dr Canning.'

'Doctor. D'you have something for me?' Sean asked.

'I thought I ought to let you know the body from the woods has been moved to the mortuary at Guy's where I plan to carry out the post-mortem later this afternoon, if you'd care to join me.'

'I'll be there,' he confirmed, images of the terrible wounds the pathologist would be inflicting on Karen Green's body invading his mind.

Trying to keep one eye on the road, Sean scrolled through his phone for Donnelly's number, tapping it to call and waiting a few seconds before it was answered.

'Guv'nor. What's happening?'

'According to Karen Green's brother, no one's seen her for nine days. All the indications are she was taken eight days ago, the morning she was due to travel to Australia.' Sean muttered a curse at a bus pulling out in front of him, then resumed: 'Louise Russell's been missing four days, which means we have at best three or four days to find her before she ends up like Green.'

'What's our next move?'

'Get hold of Roddis, have him divert some of his forensic people to Green's home address. Tell Zukov and O'Neil to expand their checks on the local Sex Offenders Register to include anyone with previous for using artifice to gain entry into private dwellings. Our boy's sticking to what he knows will work.'

'I thought our suspect didn't have previous. How could he be on the register?' Donnelly asked.

'He might have an overseas conviction,' Sean pointed out, 'or maybe somebody just fucked up when it came to printing him, I don't know, but let's not assume anything.'

'OK, I'll see to it.'

'There's one more thing I need you to do, but keep it quiet.'

'And what would that be?'

'Tell Featherstone I need his authority to circulate a request to have all MISPERs of a similar description to our victims reported directly to us. But no rubbish, just ones where there are suspicious circumstances surrounding their disappearance – handbags not taken, phone left behind . . .'

'Hang on, guv – we have two victims, one dead and one missing, we *know* their identities, so why are we looking for more MISPERs? If he'd killed someone before Green, we'd already know about it.'

'I'm not thinking about what he did before,' said Sean grimly, 'I'm thinking about what he'll do next.'

'Next he'll probably kill Louise Russell unless we can find her first,' Donnelly argued.

'No,' Sean told him. 'Next he's going to grab someone else. He needs to replace Green. The way I see it, he's on a seven to eight day cycle. Green went missing eight or nine days ago and Russell four. Green turns up dead this morning, which means for at least three days he kept them together. If he follows that pattern, he'll need to grab another within the next day or so.'

'You mean he kept them at the same time, not necessarily together,' Donnelly corrected him.

Sean was silent for a few seconds, giving himself a chance to work out how to explain his conviction in a way that would make Donnelly buy into it.

'I'm pretty sure he kept them together,' Sean finally explained. 'To keep them separate would mean he'd need two secure and secluded places, plus he'd have to divide his time between them. I can't see him doing that. He wants them together, where he can keep an eye on both of them at the same time. Less work for him.'

Sean wasn't ready to go into the real reason he believed the killer would have kept the women together. If his vision of the man they hunted was accurate, he would be living out fantasized relationships with his captives, relationships that disintegrated as the days passed. He needed his new victim to witness the plight of her predecessor, perhaps as some kind of warning – *Please me, or suffer the same*. Whether this psychological torture was deliberate or subconscious Sean didn't yet know, and wouldn't until he got closer to his quarry, close enough to start thinking like him, feeling what he was feeling. Only then would he have the full picture with no need to fill in the gaps with guesswork.

To Sean's relief, Donnelly accepted his explanation. 'Sounds reasonable,' he replied. 'I'll let Featherstone know what you want.'

'Good. I'm heading to Guy's for the post-mortem. Do me a favour and keep everyone on their toes, if they're not already.'

'They are,' Donnelly assured him. 'They understand the situation.'

Sean ended the call and realized he'd been driving like an unthinking automaton. He checked his mirrors to ensure he hadn't picked up a traffic unit and pointed his car towards Guy's Hospital and the empty shell that used to be Karen Green.

Friday lunchtime and Thomas Keller sat alone in the canteen at work repeatedly stirring a mug of tea that had long ago turned cold, his barely touched plate of food pushed to one side. He was both agitated and excited, unable to settle or concentrate on anything other than the woman he would be calling on later that afternoon. Everything had been planned, from her selection to how, where and when he would take her. He realized he'd started rocking in his chair like an inmate of a lunatic asylum and managed to stop himself before anyone noticed. He tried to chase thoughts of the woman away, aware he needed to appear to be his normal self – meek, mild and unassuming. A nobody. But he knew he would never be a nobody to the one person who had truly loved him. And in a couple of hours he would be seeing her again, saving her from the people who had filled her head with lies about him. Because this time he had really found her. They'd tried to trick him, but despite their lies he'd found her, his one true soul-mate who would never betray him like the others had. He licked his swollen pink lips as his wide staring eyes peered into an unseen distance.

His daydreaming was suddenly shattered as two workers from the sorting office noisily pulled out the chairs next to him and sat down, making an intentional din as they dropped their loaded plates of food on to the table. 'All right, Timmy son?' the older, bigger man asked. 'You don't mind if we sit with you, do you, Timmy boy?'

'No,' stammered Keller, trying not to betray his fear of the men and annoyance at having his sweet daydream interrupted.

'Course you don't,' the same man said. 'Only a sad loser would want to eat on his own all the time, eh, Timmy?'

Keller forced a slight smile and swallowed the hatred he felt towards them. 'I don't mind being alone,' he told them weakly. 'And my name's not Timmy, it's Thomas.'

The smaller of the men leaned across the table, his face uncomfortably close to Keller's. 'We know what your name is, cunt, and we know you think you're better than the rest of us – don't you, Thomas?'

'No,' he protested. 'I don't think anything, I just like to be left alone, that's all. I just don't like the things you like.'

'What – like women?' the bigger man roared. 'Are you a fucking queer, faggot?'

The words stoked the raging hatred he felt towards them and their kind in the very core of his being. He could feel the eyes of other would-be-persecutors focusing on him. All around the canteen, ugly grinning faces were turning in his direction, baring row upon row of sniggering stained white teeth. He pushed back from the table and jumped up to his full height, almost knocking his chair over, but his tormentors didn't flinch. They had no fear of him.

'Better be careful, Stevie,' the smaller man feigned terror, cowering away from Keller. 'I reckon he's gonna do you.'

'Take it easy, Tommy boy,' the bigger man laughed. 'I'm shitting myself here.'

Derisive laughter rippled around the room. To Keller it was the cruellest sound of all, a constant malignant companion that had haunted him since his earliest childhood. He imagined locking the doors of the canteen with chains and pumping petrol through the gaps, savouring the screams of panic from within as his tormentors smelled the fumes, then striking the match, letting it fall from his fingers, watching as it slowly drifted to the floor, the flames igniting and spreading like a forest fire through dry bushland, reducing the men inside to charred, twisted statues.

A voice full of hate and bigotry pulled him back to reality. 'Well, Tommy boy – what you going to fucking do about it?'

Keller turned on his heels and walked as quickly as he could towards the exit without actually running, bursting through the swing doors of the canteen, the slight laughter he left behind amplified into a cacophony in his dysfunctional mind.

He raced down three flights of stairs to the basement and burst into the old storeroom that had become his place of refuge whenever the need to be alone overwhelmed him. There was no lock or bolt, so he had to make do with propping a chair under the handle to ensure he couldn't be followed or disturbed. Only then did he allow the tears to flow.

Thomas Keller was no longer of this time. He was a child

again, abandoned by his mother and a father he doubted his mother had even known for more than a night. They'd promised that he'd be safe and loved in the orphanage, but they'd lied – he wasn't loved, he was hated. The faces of the other children danced across his mind, impish and venomous as only children can be, hunting in packs, seeking out the weak and defenceless. But Thomas Keller wasn't defenceless. He had fought back, attacking the ringleader of his teasing swarm, sinking his teeth deep into the child's cheek until he felt them scraping against bone, the taste of blood sweet and bitter on his tongue and lips. He remembered the child's terrified screams, the other children also screaming in panic and fright at the sight of blood running down his chin and dripping on to his shirt as he snarled like a rabid dog and searched for his next victim. Strong arms had clenched around his waist and shoulders, pulling him to the ground while belts secured his ankles and wrists, pulled so tight he could feel neither his fingers nor his toes. And then he'd seen the syringe in the hands of a faceless adult, the needle being pushed through his skin, the liquid flowing into his blood and making it freeze, his body becoming limp while his mind raced and whirled.

He remembered being gripped under the armpits and dragged across the floor, through a door into the darkness and down the stairs to the cellar that lay hidden and forbidden beneath the children's home. The door to the animal cage had been opened and he was thrust inside, his bonds removed by practised hands, the door slamming shut, the metal wire of his prison shuddering as the adult voices moved away. He'd screamed then, screamed for his mother to come and save him, screamed for her forgiveness, although he didn't know what he'd done wrong, what crime he must have committed to have been sent here. So he kept calling for her, fighting against the drugs that invaded his blood, until a face full of hate and retribution pressed against the wire, hissing at him, 'Call her all you want, you fucking freak. No one's coming for you. She hates you – do you understand? She hates you. This is your home now, so start getting used to it, because you're going to be here for a very, very long time.'

6

Sean dumped his car in the ambulance bay at Guy's Hospital and tossed the police logbook on to the dashboard to warn the hospital's private security guards not to clamp it. He then used his usual entrance to the giant building, walking through the Accident and Emergency Department doors clearly marked 'Hospital Staff Only', nodding at the few faces he recognized and ignored by the rest who rightly assumed what he was. He headed for the main body of the hospital and the relatively new shopping-foodhall complex that was open to staff, public and patients alike. He entered the concourse and searched for his wife, who he'd arranged to meet for a rushed late lunch before he went to see Dr Canning for the post-mortem of Karen Green. He passed the ubiquitous chain cafés and found Kate sitting in Starbucks as they had planned, her head buried in clinical data reports. She hadn't waited for him before grabbing a sandwich and coffee. He considered not bothering to get himself anything, but the service queue was mercifully short so he grabbed something that he wouldn't have to wait to be toasted, ordered the simplest coffee he could find on the overhead menu-board and headed for his wife who hadn't yet seen him arrive. 'Excuse me. Is this seat taken?'

'My, my,' she joked, 'who is this handsome stranger standing before me?'

'A stranger, I'm afraid so. Handsome, I'm not so sure about that,' he replied, pulling out a chair and sitting heavily.

'Anyway, what brings you to my neck of the woods, Inspector?'

'That missing woman I told you about.'

'You found her? She's here in Guy's?' Kate asked.

'No,' he said, unwrapping the sandwich he already knew would taste of nothing. 'We were looking for one woman and found another.'

'I don't understand.'

'The woman we were looking for wasn't his first,' he told her in a hushed voice, checking there were no eavesdroppers. 'The woman we found – he'd already taken her.'

'So now she can tell you where the other woman is?'

'I'm afraid she won't be able to do that.'

Kate immediately understood the inference. 'I'm sorry,' she said, and meant it.

'Me too.' They sat in silence for a moment without pretending to be interested in their lunch.

'So I guess I won't be seeing much of you for a while then?'

Sean shrugged his shoulders. 'You know how it is.'

'Yes, Sean,' she sighed, her frustration at having to share him with so much horror and misery making her sad, 'I know how it is.'

'Things just got a lot worse than I expected. What can I do?'

Kate pulled in heavy lungfuls of air and puffed her cheeks. The coming days, probably weeks, would be hell as she tried to juggle her work and children with little or no support from Sean, but she understood the importance of the job he had to do. She thought of her own two girls and what she would expect of the police if either of them were missing:

she would expect them to work without end, without sleep, without food or rest until her child was found. She wouldn't let herself be a hypocrite. 'What can you do?' she replied. 'You can catch the bastard, that's what you can do.'

Sean actually managed a smile. 'Thanks.'

'So where you going after our luxurious meal?' she asked.

'Over to see Dr Canning for the post-mortem.'

Kate slouched in her chair and smiled without joy. 'Well, I suppose I should feel honoured. I mean, how many wives are squeezed in between a murder scene and a post-mortem?'

'I'm doing the best I can.'

'That's what worries me.'

'You never know, I might get this one wrapped up sooner rather than later. Whoever I'm looking for has been leaving a lot of evidence behind – fingerprints, DNA – and he takes them in broad daylight. He'll make a mistake soon enough, then the evidence will hang him.'

'I hope you're right.'

'I hope so too,' he said, glancing at his watch and standing, taking half the sandwich and leaving everything else. 'I've got to go. Dr Canning'll be waiting for me.'

'Well, that was short and sweet,' Kate said. 'Is there any chance I might see you at home later?'

'Maybe, but don't wait up. I'll try and call you.' He leaned across the table and kissed her lightly on the lips, embarrassed even by such a small show of public affection. She watched him walking quickly across the concourse, weaving his way through the other pedestrians, torn between her attraction to his intensity and the fear that one day she might lose him to his job. It left her feeling melancholy.

Sean pushed the last of his sandwich into his mouth and at the same time felt his phone vibrating in his jacket pocket. He forced the dry bread down his throat and checked the caller ID. It was Sally. He tapped the answer key. 'Sally – you got something for me?'

'Karen Green's Micra just turned up in a car park in Mazzard's Wood, Bromley Common, secure and undamaged.' An image of tall trees leaning in the wind jumped into Sean's mind.

'OK,' he said, 'send someone to babysit the car until forensics can get to it, and make sure they give it a good once-over before taking it off to Charlton.' He swerved to avoid bumping into an elderly couple passing him in the corridor. 'I'll be at Guy's for another hour or so. Keep me informed.' He hung up and immediately searched for another number in his phone, tapped 'call' and waited for an answer.

'Hello,' DC Zukov answered.

'Paulo, how are you getting on with the tattoo inquiry? Any luck?'

'Nothing yet. I've checked the Internet for the design and drawn a blank. And I've emailed a picture of the tattoo to most of the tattoo parlours in the area in the hope someone may recognize their own handiwork.'

'Good. Keep at it,' Sean told him.

He hung up and slid the phone back into his pocket as he exited the main entrance. Cutting across the front car park, he turned left and out of the main flow of pedestrians and headed towards the oldest part of the hospital. He passed the department marked clinical waste, with ominous-looking fluorescent wheelie bins waiting outside and walked through the swing doors discreetly signed 'Pathology'. Pushing his way through the thick rubber strips that hung from ceiling to floor, he entered the autopsy suite.

Sean looked around the large room. Two bodies lay covered, awaiting attention while Dr Canning busied himself with the body of Karen Green. She was laid out on the examination table, a cold stainless steel surface with a shallow channel running along its middle that drained into a plughole, enabling the removal of blood and other fluids. He could see that Canning had already cleaned the body up in an effort to distinguish haemorrhaging from dirt.

At the sound of Sean snapping on a set of surgical gloves, Canning looked up. 'Afternoon, Inspector.'

Sean ignored the nicety. 'Any trouble moving the body from the scene?'

'No,' Canning replied. 'I carried out a close examination of the area around the body, but didn't find anything startling. I should think the evidence we're after will be on or in her body.' Sean nodded his agreement. 'Aside from the throat, I haven't opened her up yet, but I don't expect to find any significant internal injuries other than the crushed trachea I've already discovered, which was almost certainly what killed her.'

'What about the head wound?'

'The skin on the back of her head has been split by a blow from a blunt, cylindrical object, but the wound's not nearly significant enough to have contributed to her death.'

'Could it be post-mortem?' Sean asked. 'The killer for some reason trying to draw us away from the real cause of death?'

Canning shook his head. 'No, there was too much bleeding from the wound for it to be post-mortem, although it was inflicted very close to the time of death, which was about twenty-four hours ago. Perhaps your killer wanted to knock her senseless before committing the terrible deed.'

The image of the faceless man standing behind Karen Green in a dark forest raced into Sean's mind, the blunt, heavy object being raised above his shoulder and then brought down hard on the back of her head, pitching her forward to the soft, wet ground. 'Any signs of sexual assault?'

'Numerous,' Canning answered, 'and probably committed over a period of time – a few days at least. She has semen in her vagina, upper and lower, as well as her anus. Both vagina and anus show extensive bruising consistent with non-consensual intercourse and there are signs of some tearing at the entrance to her anus that are consistent with the same. It would appear you are looking for a rather unpleasant individual.'

'That much I already know,' said Sean.

'Just as you knew I would soon have a female body recovered in woodland to examine.' Canning locked eyes with Sean, waiting for him to blink first. 'I reckon it would take a sharper scalpel than mine to dissect that brain of yours.'

'I'm not as insightful as you think,' Sean confessed. 'This isn't the woman I was expecting to find.'

Canning raised an eyebrow. 'Then am I to expect more ladies of the forest?'

'At this stage, all we can do is hope for the best and be prepared for the worst.'

Eager to conclude the autopsy and get back to the office, Sean directed Canning's attention back to the body on the table. 'When I had a cursory look at the scene, I saw a tattoo on the underside of her right forearm – a phoenix, I think.'

'You mean this?' Canning rotated her forearm to expose the garish little picture. 'Not a tattoo, Inspector – a transfer. Common enough, but not usually found on an adult. Did she have any children?'

'No.'

'Perhaps she worked with children, a nursery or infant teacher?'

'No,' Sean repeated. 'Children weren't a part of her life.'

'Then you have another mystery on your hands.'

Sean thought for a moment. 'She was about to go travelling, to Australia and possibly beyond. Maybe she wanted to appear more exotic, but didn't have the courage to get the real thing?'

'That I wouldn't know, Inspector. Conjecture is your field of expertise, not mine.'

Sean took a long hard look at the body, noting the injuries he'd already observed when he'd first seen her lying in the woods – the split lip showing signs of healing, the grazing and bruising on her fingers and knee – none of which required Canning's skill to explain. But there were other bruises too, more clear now her flesh had been cleaned: small, round injuries that looked as if they had tiny burns at their centres.

'What are these?' he asked, his finger hovering over the strange marks. 'They look like bruises with burns in the centre.'

'I've been trying to fathom out what those are,' said Canning. 'Almost like cigarette burns surrounded by a cylindrical bruise. I'll have to run some simulation tests and see if I can reproduce the effect, find out what caused them.'

Sean pointed to a square-shaped bruise that also showed signs of burning. 'Any ideas what made that mark?'

'It's an older injury,' Canning explained, 'at least a week or so. I've seen it before, although not very often.'

'Then you know what it is?'

'That, Inspector, if I'm not mistaken, is an injury caused by a stun-gun.'

'Caused at the same time as she was abducted?'

'More or less – best as I can tell.'

'So that's how he incapacitates them: as soon as they open the door, he hits them with the stun-gun and then goes to the chloroform?'

'It's quite possible,' Canning agreed. 'Will that narrow the field for you? The sale and ownership of such an item in this country is highly restricted.'

'I doubt he obtained it legally – probably picked it up on the Continent and smuggled it into the country, but we'll check. Anything else for me, other than the superficial stuff? Anything I can use straight away?'

'Well . . .' Canning began, pricking Sean's interest, 'when I was swabbing the body I could smell traces of cosmetics. I took a closer look and, although it's too early to say, I believe she had recently applied both cream and perfume to her body. Looking at the general state of her, I would say she hasn't been allowed to bathe for several days, which is why the traces remain, but still, cosmetics of this type generally don't stick around for more than four or five days. I noticed the police report said she'd been missing for eight to nine days, which means—'

Sean cut across him, his head flooding with thoughts and images that made almost perfect sense, yet contradicted so much. 'Which means they were applied while she was being held captive. He made her put them on.'

'Or he put them on her,' Canning offered.

'No, I don't think so,' Sean dismissed the suggestion. 'Clearly she didn't have access to washing facilities for at least the last few days, but if the cream and perfume aren't fresh it could mean that round about the same time he stopped allowing her to wash he also stopped giving her them to use.'

Canning opened his mouth to speak but Sean raised a hand to silence him, his fickle brain dangling the answers tantalizingly close before snatching them away. He slowed his mind, relaxing and concentrating at the same time, clearing the fog of a thousand unrelated thoughts to allow the answers to come.

'He treated her well at first,' he began, 'gave her food and water, somewhere to wash. She was special to him, so special he gave her body cream and even perfume, as if she was his, his lover, but then something changed. Something changed and she became nothing to him, nothing more than a problem to be removed. He didn't feed her any more, or allow her to wash or even wear clothes, and there was no more pampering with cosmetics, just rape and torture. And when he couldn't stand the sight of her any more he took her into the woods and killed her like a farmer would kill an old sheep dog that couldn't earn its keep, without feeling or remorse. And then he left her cold and unclothed in the woods and went back to the woman he'd taken to replace her. He went back to Louise Russell and the cycle started all over again. But who did Karen Green replace? Or was she the one you coveted above all others, the one you fantasized about for years before taking her?' He froze for a few seconds, then turned back to Canning. 'The swabs you took from her body, with the cream and perfume samples – can I take them with me?'

'Why would you want to do that?' Canning asked, perplexed by the break with procedure.

'I need to know if she's the one that triggered his behaviour.'

'How will the swabs help you know if she was the one who caused him to behave in this extreme way?'

'Not caused,' Sean corrected him, 'triggered. The cause of his behaviour has its roots deep in his past. God only knows what's happened to him during his life to make him what he is now, to make an angry boy grow into a dangerous man. Maybe Karen Green showed him some kindness or affection that drew him to her, but he misinterpreted her, made more of it than there was and so she pushed him away. He couldn't handle the rejection, so he did something about it. He did this. If the swabs contain cream and perfume that we also find at her house, then I'll know they were hers and therefore that she could well be the one he's always coveted. But if they're not, then he made her use them because he was trying to make her someone else.'

Canning lifted several plastic phials from the portable table he kept his tools on and handed them to Sean. 'Here,' he said, 'take them, if you think it will help.'

'Thanks.' Sean slipped them carefully into his breast pocket. 'They will. I look forward to your report.'

'You should have it in a couple of days, but you already know the main findings.'

'Anything else? Anything at all?' Sean asked.

'Perhaps one last thing,' said Canning. 'I took scrapings from under her finger and toe nails, which of course contained soil and dirt, but at a first look under the microscope they appear to contain something rarer. I'll have to send them to the lab for a proper examination, but my guess would be coal dust. I'll know for sure after it's properly analysed.'

'Coal dust?' Sean's dancing eyes reflected his racing thoughts. 'Coal dust?' he repeated.

'At a first guess, yes.'

'He kept her underground. Before he killed her, he kept her underground – in an old cellar or coal bunker.'

'That's a logical suggestion,' Canning agreed.

Sean nodded, turned and headed for the exit, his mind already swimming with images of cold, stone dungeons underground.

Sally was pacing up and down in front of Karen Green's house, still waiting for forensics to arrive. She'd finished interviewing Terry and sent him on his way almost an hour ago, and was beginning to feel as if she was being deliberately isolated from the rest of the team and excluded from the main body of the investigation, but couldn't be sure if her feelings were manifestations of paranoia or real. One thing she knew that was real was that cops looked upon colleagues who were struggling mentally as if they had an infectious disease that could spread to them. It was like failure, always deserted, always an orphan – a mandatory sentence of solitary confinement. It reinforced her conviction to hide her troubles as best she could and mention them to no one. The phone she clutched in her palm made a noise like a small hungry animal and vibrated. She saw it was Sean. 'Guv'nor!'

'Have forensics got there yet?' he asked.

'No.'

'Good. Listen, I need you to go inside the house and gather up any moisturizers, creams, lotions and perfumes you can find. Check out the cabinet in the bathroom – that's where I remember seeing them when I took a look around this morning. Once it's all been bagged and tagged, bring them straight to the lab at Lambeth. I'll meet you there – understood?'

'Understood, but . . .' he hung up before she could ask for an explanation, doing little to lessen her paranoia.

Shrugging her doubts away, Sally looked at the two keys she held in her non-phone hand, turning and lifting them towards the locks. Anxiety rushed at her, paralysing her, refusing to let her move no matter how hard she tried. She surrendered and lowered the keys, despondent to have been seemingly defeated by a task she would have given little or no thought to before Sebastian Gibran attempted to tear her life away.

She managed to stop the tears before they grew too heavy and rolled from her eyes. She took a couple of deep breaths. 'Come on,' she whispered, 'just fucking do it.' Her hand began to rise, slowly, nervously, wary that at any second the anxiety could return and seize control of her body. She jiggled the mortise lock until she felt it smoothly slide from its secure position with a satisfying heavy click. Then she recovered the key and swapped it for the Yale key, again jiggling it into the precision-made slot, but with more difficulty this time, haunted by memories of the night when she'd fumbled with her own keys, at her own door, panicked by some sense of fear, some sense of being watched – and she'd been right, her primal instincts had been spot on, but she'd ignored them, with almost fatal consequences. As her memories threatened to incapacitate her, the door suddenly popped open and she found herself stepping inside, the silence and stillness within foreboding and oppressive. She thanked God it was daytime and closed the door behind her, looking along the simple, bright hallway with dread.

She didn't want to stay in Karen Green's house a second longer than she had to and had absolutely no intention of snooping around, something she wouldn't have been able to resist in the old days. Sean said she'd find the things she was looking for in the bathroom, so that's where she would go and nowhere else. Grab the things he wanted and get the bloody hell out of this mausoleum. She'd bag and tag them properly as evidence once she was safely back outside or in her car. Sally shivered, feeling accusing eyes watching her, asking her why she hadn't stopped the man who did this to her. She couldn't stand the silence any longer. 'Hello,' she called out, but her throat was dry, her voice coarse and quiet. 'I'm a police officer.' She waited for a reply she knew would never come.

After more than a minute of waiting she pushed herself forward, working hard to keep her legs striding one in front of the other. With each step her pace quickened, until she was at the foot of the stairs, then walking up them, looking straight ahead only, focusing on the space above. When she reached the top she was relieved to see the bathroom door was ajar, saving her from having to search around for it. She slowed down again, crossing the upstairs hallway inches at a time, resting the palm of her hand on the door and pushing it open gently and quietly, craning her neck to peer inside bit by bit, prepared for any would-be ambusher. Only once the door rested fully open did she accept she was alone and the room empty.

Stepping inside, she made her way to the cabinet Sean had mentioned, all the time thinking of the excuses she would give if she was disturbed while searching through a dead woman's cosmetics before forensics had examined them. She pulled on a pair of latex gloves, then opened the cabinet door – and was confronted by shelves crammed with bottles and jars. There were far more than she'd expected, and she immediately regretted not having brought a large evidence bag from her car. She began moving the contents to one side and was relieved to find what she was looking for – a scrunched-up plastic bag, the sort people saved to transport bottles that might leak when travelling. She shook the bag back in to shape and began to pluck items from the shelves and place them in it as carefully as she could. As the cabinet emptied the bag grew heavy until she was satisfied she'd taken anything that could pass as a cream, lotion, moisturizer or perfume.

She closed the cabinet door, anxious to flee the lifeless house before it shrank in on her even further, but the reflection of her own image in the mirror made her hesitate. Her face suddenly looked old and worn way beyond her thirty-four years, her eyes hollow and haunted – joyless. She tried to pull herself away from the troubling picture in the glass, but couldn't, her hand sliding inside her jacket and almost unconsciously unfastening a single button on her blouse, moving across soft, smooth skin, then suddenly recoiling as it touched the thick raised scar tissue of her upper wound before moving under the material again until it rested on the lower scar under her breast. She closed her eyes for a few seconds, her world suddenly merging with Karen Green's – two victims of violent men – one who survived and one who didn't. She felt Karen's fear and pain, her desperate wish to live another day, her willingness to do anything if he'd only let her live, just as she herself would have done anything for Sebastian Gibran if he'd promised to spare her. She had survived – Karen had not.

Sally pulled her hand from under her blouse and fastened the button self-consciously. Clutching the plastic bag of cosmetics she walked from the bathroom and then the house. She locked the front door and walked to her car without looking back.

Donnelly had remained at the scene where Karen Green had been found. Following the removal of the body the forensic team were busy in the woods, searching for evidence hidden between the trees and under the fallen foliage, gathering as much as they could before the weather turned against them.

They might be here for days, but Donnelly had no intention of sticking around that long. He yawned widely and decided to head back to the access road and his car for a smoke. As he sat on the bonnet he saw the familiar figure of DC Zukov walk towards him. 'All right, son?' Donnelly acknowledged him. 'What you doing here?'

'Thought I'd have a look for myself, see if there was anything I could help with.'

'You've got your actions to complete, haven't you, same as everyone else?'

'Yeah,' Zukov answered, barely disguising his contempt for the routine course of an investigation, the day-to-day mundane tasks that had to be completed, 'but the guv'nor's got me wasting my time doing personal inquiries for him, trying to trace the source of a tattoo on the victim's body that he now tells me isn't a tattoo after all, it's just a bloody transfer. What the fuck am I supposed to do with that?'

'What tattoo?' Donnelly kept his tone casual, hiding the concern he felt about not being kept informed about every aspect of the investigation.

'Like I said,' Zukov replied, 'the tattoo of a phoenix on the victim's arm, only now we know it's not a tattoo it's a—'

'A transfer,' Donnelly finished for him, 'yeah, yeah, you already told me that. But why's the boss interested in her tattoo, transfer, whatever the fuck it is?'

'I don't know. He didn't tell me.'

But Donnelly knew – Sean thought the killer put it there, and the fact it was a transfer and not a tattoo made that all the more likely.

'He's got me checking on scumbags with previous for using artifice too, particularly those with previous for sex offences and residential burglary.'

Donnelly had to admire Sean, he was an insightful bastard, always two steps ahead of the rest of them. He didn't like it, but he respected it. 'That makes sense,' he told Zukov. 'No forced entry into either victim's home, no reason to believe either knew their attacker. There's a better than fair chance our boy tricked his way in.'

'Maybe the guv'nor's trying to be too clever?' Zukov argued. 'Maybe whoever took them just knocked on their doors and they opened them? There's no artifice there.'

'Whatever,' Donnelly said dismissively. 'I'm off back to the office. You stay here and liaise with forensics, then you'd better get on with the inquiries the boss has given you, or you're going to be Mr Unpopular. And by the way, if and when you find out anything, any suspects flag-up, tell me first and I'll let the guv'nor know, understand?'

Zukov was on the verge of putting another question but decided against it. Best to keep his suspicions to himself. Instead he just said, 'Fair enough, guv.'

'Good,' said Donnelly, climbing into his car, the suspension creaking as he sat heavily in the seat. Zukov had to step clear as he pulled the door shut with a slam. The engine roared to life and he pulled away with a wheel spin along the last road Karen Green had ever seen.

It was almost three p.m. on Friday afternoon and Sean was in Lambeth, sitting in the second-floor Forensic Laboratory reception area, clutching his numbered ticket and the body swab samples he'd brought directly from the post-mortem. He glanced at his ticket, the kind they handed out at a supermarket delicatessen counter, and muttered an obscenity under his breath – if Sally didn't arrive soon he'd miss his turn and would have to take another ticket and start from the back of the queue all over again. Back in the days when the lab was run by the Home Office, it was manned by fellow public servants who were all too ready to impose harsh words and on-the-spot fines for any incorrectly labelled exhibits or ill-prepared laboratory submissions forms. Though he wasn't entirely in favour of the lab being placed in private sector hands, there was one big advantage from Sean's point of view. Its employees treated him as a paying customer, entitled to make demands that would previously have been met with howls of derision from the lowly paid scientists running the show.

His not so fond memories were wiped away the second he saw Sally step through the automatic double swing-doors, the items she'd grabbed from Karen Green's bathroom safe inside plastic evidence tubes that were in turn neatly sealed inside evidence bags. The number counter mounted on the wall clicked around to show 126 – the number on Sean's blue ticket. He took Sally by the arm and steered her towards the submissions counter. 'We're up,' he told her.

'It would be nice to know what the hell's going on,' she replied. 'Why you wanted the stuff from her bathroom, for example, and why I had to drop everything and rush to the lab with it.'

'Sorry, I didn't have time to explain, but you'll understand why once you've listened to me explaining it to the lab people.'

They completed the short walk from the waiting room to the exhibit reception desk, where a slim bespectacled man in his forties was waiting for them with a private sector smile.

'Afternoon,' he greeted them, 'and what have you got for us today?'

Sean didn't try to match his friendliness. 'Two sets of exhibits from two different scenes,' he said, pushing the swab tubes across the counter. 'These exhibits are marked with RC, the initials of the pathologist who took them during a post-mortem of a woman whose murder we're investigating.' The smile dropped from the receptionist's face like an Arctic sunset. 'They're swabs taken from her skin containing some type of cream and an unknown brand of perfume. These –' he took Sally's exhibits from her and pushed them across the counter, careful not to mix them with the others – 'are cosmetics and perfumes taken from the murdered woman's house. I'll keep this simple: I want you to compare the exhibits taken from the house with the exhibits taken from the body and see if any of them match. If they do, which ones? And if they don't, I need to know what brand the cream and perfume taken from her body are, and I need to know as a matter of urgency. Everything clear?'

'Perfectly,' said the receptionist, partially recovering his smile. 'But it'll take a few days to get the results, particularly if there's no match between the two sets of exhibits. Our library of cosmetics isn't vast. We might have to outsource it.'

'Do the best you can, but make sure the urgency of the situation is understood.'

The receptionist made some notes on the lab submission form and stamped it with a red marker that said urgent. He handed Sean a copy of the form by way of receipt. 'Good enough?' he asked.

'I hope so,' replied Sean, taking the form and heading for the exit.

Thomas Keller left work shortly after four p.m., passing through the gates of the sorting office still dressed in his uniform, walking fast with his head down, praying he would not be recognized or accosted by any malevolent colleagues who would unwittingly ruin what for him was about to become a very special day. A day he'd been planning for months. He knew her name and where she lived. He knew she lived alone. He knew the shape of her house and that the front door could not be seen from the quiet road. He knew that she banked with NatWest and worked as a nurse at St George's Hospital in Tooting. He knew she had electricity and gas from On Power, satellite television from Virgin, that her bins were collected on Thursdays, that she drove a red Honda Civic that she insured with the AA, that most months she was overdrawn, that she shopped at ASDA in Roehampton, that she'd been single for a long while but now had a boyfriend, that if she wasn't working she went out most weekends with some of her apparently many friends. Above all, he knew she was the one. They'd poisoned her mind and made her forget, but still she was the one and soon he'd rescue her from her state of ignorance and make her alive once again and then, then they could be together as they were always supposed to be: he and Sam together for ever.

The journey to Tooting Common passed in a blur, making no impression on his memory at all until he realized he'd arrived at the small car park near the swimming pool. Surrounded by trees, it was quiet at this time of day, most people choosing the morning to walk their dogs through the woods. He noted there were a few cars parked close by, but was sure they would either be gone by the time he returned or abandoned for the night by owners now too inebriated to drive them.

Making sure his car was locked, he headed for the pathway that would take him across the common, keeping an eye out for CCTV cameras he might have failed to spot on the many occasions he'd walked this route in preparation for today. Passers-by also came under scrutiny, in case they might be a cop in plain clothes looking for prostitutes or small-time drug dealers. It hadn't crossed his mind the police might be looking for him now.

It took him more than ten minutes to walk from the car park to the street – her street, Valleyfield Road. As he turned off the busy thoroughfares and into the narrower residential streets there were far fewer pedestrians around and the sounds of traffic fell away, the murmur of a big city mixing with the hypnotizing sound of the gentle, tentative spring breeze stirring virgin leaves on the largely barren trees.

He enjoyed the peaceful sounds and the warm air that surrounded him, still fresh from the cold of winter, unspoilt by the coming heat of a London summer. He breathed in deeply, reassured by the calmness he felt, his fears fading with every step. Occasionally he walked up to one of the houses that lined the street to post junk mail through the letterbox, just in case he was being watched by suspicious eyes. As he drew ever closer to number 6 he felt calm and in control, the experience of taking the other two helping him now as he began to mentally rehearse what would happen the minute he stepped inside the hallway of the newly built townhouse close to the end of the road.

Finally he reached the end of her driveway and paused, searching through his postal bag, apparently looking for the letters addressed to 6 Valleyfield Road. But his bag contained no such letters. The only contents were a squeezy bottle of chloroform, a clean fold of material to apply it to, a roll of masking tape and, most importantly, a stun-gun.

Deborah Thomson was tired after coming off a twelve-hour early shift at St George's, but her mood was buoyant. The rest of her day was full of things she was looking forward to. First she needed to change out of her uniform and go for a quick run across the common, then home for a long, hot shower. After that she'd take her time getting ready for a night out with friends in a local gastro-pub. No men tonight, just the girls. She was looking forward to telling them all about her new boyfriend, who she'd be seeing tomorrow. A whole Saturday with her new love, and the entire weekend off. It didn't get any better.

Humming to herself as she tugged off her sensible work shoes and tossed them to one side, she broke off when the sound of the doorbell ringing interrupted her preparations. 'Bollocks,' she swore, and set off downstairs vowing to be rid of the interloper as quickly as possible.

She bounced across the hallway to the front door, pausing to look through the spyhole. Having been brought up in New Cross, a south-east London neighbourhood where poverty went hand-in-hand with criminality, she never opened the door unthinkingly. There was a man in postman's uniform on the doorstep. He stepped back a little so she could see almost all of his body, and reached into his bag, pulling out a parcel the size of a small shoebox, too large to fit through the letter slot.

Deborah opened the front door, the smile returning to her face. 'Hi,' she chirped, expecting him to confirm her name and hand over the parcel, but he said nothing. Too late she sensed danger as the hand not holding the parcel whipped out of the bag at lightning speed clutching a strange-looking object. As it moved towards her, she reacted, slamming the door into his shoulder, but the stun-gun had already made it through the gap between door and frame and buried itself in her stomach. She flew backwards as if hurled by an invisible force, what little air she had left in her chest knocked out of her lungs as she lay convulsing on the hallway floor.

The man staggered and dropped to his knees alongside her, then reached into his bag. She stared from her frozen state of purgatory as he took a squeezy bottle and a fold of material, followed by a roll of black heavy-duty tape. She tried to speak, to beg him to leave her alone, not to hurt her, but could make only unintelligible guttural noises. He placed one finger to his lips.

'Ssssh,' he urged her. 'Everything's going to be all right now, Sam. I've come to take you home.'

Sean checked his watch as he pulled up outside the home of Douglas Levy, the Neighbourhood Watch coordinator for Louise Russell's street. For a moment he sat looking across the road at her house, seeing DC Cahill's car parked at the end of the drive. He knew he should look in on Cahill and John Russell, show his face and offer support and encouragement, but he couldn't find it in himself. He'd come here in the mood for harassment, not empathy.

Breathing the cool air through his nose, he approached Levy's front door and pressed the bell. He heard firm footsteps approaching from within, locks on the other side of the door turning and eventually the door opening, Levy standing tall and proud.

'Me again,' Sean announced before he could get a word in. 'I have a few more questions for you if that's OK.'

'Well, yes, but I wasn't expecting to have to speak to the police again.'

'This won't take long,' Sean assured him. 'May I come in?'

Levy hesitated for a second before stepping aside. 'Of course.'

'Thanks.' Sean stepped past him and walked briskly into the neat interior. He still couldn't sense a woman's presence inside and couldn't help wondering when and why Levy's wife had left him. He began to wander around the downstairs of the house, deliberately making Levy feel uncomfortable and challenged. Sean wanted him off-balance, flustered, answering questions without stopping to think; that way he would give true answers, not the ones he thought he should or the ones he thought Sean wanted to hear.

'It occurred to me,' Sean began, 'after the last time we talked, that whoever took her must have been here before, in this street. He would have wanted to watch, to study her movements so he could plan when and how to take her, don't you think?'

'Maybe,' Levy stumbled, 'I suppose so, I mean, I don't really know. Why are you telling me this?'

'I was just thinking about you being in all day, most days anyway, and how a man like you, Neighbourhood Watch coordinator and all that, would have noticed someone hanging around.'

'I would have, but I didn't,' Levy answered, the little patience he had failing, exactly as Sean had hoped. 'And I'm not in all day, every day.'

'No, of course not,' Sean patronized him, walking along the corridor to the lounge at the rear of the house, Levy pursuing him closely. 'I see your lounge is at the back of the house, not overlooking the street, so even if you were at home, you'd be in here all day watching telly and wouldn't have seen anything.'

'I'm a very busy man, Inspector. I can assure you I do not waste my time watching daytime TV. I have the Neighbourhood Watch to see to and I'm a local councillor too – and have been for many years.'

'So where do you work?' Sean asked. 'Where do you attend to all these important matters?'

'Here, of course. In my office upstairs.'

'Really?' Sean strode past him and up the stairs, searching for Levy's office and finding it – a converted bedroom that had an excellent view of the street outside. He entered the room and walked to the window, sensing Levy's presence close behind. 'Nice view,' he said, without turning away from the window.

'I don't work in here for the view,' Levy replied.

'No,' Sean agreed, 'but if someone was hanging around out there, someone you didn't know or recognize, you'd have noticed them, wouldn't you?' He turned to Levy and then back to the window to make the point. 'How could you not?'

'I don't spend all day spying on my neighbours.'

'I never said you did.'

'I mean I don't spend all day staring out of the window – I have work to do.'

'But if someone was out there, you'd sense the movement and look up, wouldn't you?'

'I suppose so, possibly, I don't really know.'

'But this is a Neighbourhood Watch area, isn't it? You know that better than anyone – you're the coordinator, after all. You did say you were the coordinator?'

'Yes, I did . . . I mean, I am.'

'Then you must be a vigilant man, yes? A more than vigilant man if you're responsible for the success or failure of the local Neighbourhood Watch. So you would have noticed a stranger in the street below. Maybe you would have even called the police, or at least made a note of it somewhere? Maybe you've just forgotten? Maybe you're embarrassed that you forgot to mention it to me last time we spoke?'

'No,' Levy protested. 'None of what you're implying happened.'

'So you've never seen anyone suspicious in the street? You're telling me you never looked out of this window and saw someone suspicious?'

'Well, yes, of course I—'

'And what did you do about it?'

'I can't remem—'

'You can't remember? The Neighbourhood Watch coordinator can't remember what he did when he saw someone suspicious in his own street?'

'Maybe I reported it to the police, I'm not sure.'

'When did you report it?'

'I don't know. I can't remember. You're confusing me.'

'Can you remember anything?'

'There's nothing wrong with my memory.'

'What does your local Home Beat Officer look like?'

'Excuse me?'

'What does your local Home Beat Officer look like?'

'Well, I . . .'

'What's his name?'

'It's . . . I have it written down somewhere.'

'When do the bins get collected?'

'Pardon?'

'When were there last roadworks in the street?'

'I'm not—'

'What does the guy who comes to read the meters dress like?'

'I . . .'

'What does the local postman look like?'

'He's, well he's—'

'Do you know anything, Mr Levy? These are the things you see every day, but you can't remember any of it.'

Levy looked crushed. 'Why are you doing this?' he pleaded. 'Why are you doing this to me?'

At Levy's words, Sean froze. For a moment he stood in a daze, as if only now returning to himself, bewildered and afraid of what his alter ego might have done in his absence, like a drunk waking the morning after, unable to recall the events of the previous night. What worried him most was the fact he'd enjoyed being cruel to Levy. Was that why he'd come back to interview him for a second time, so he could be cruel to him? Was that why he'd come alone, so no one would witness his cruelty or try to stop him? He decided both were probably true, and in the pit of his soul he knew why – he was drawing closer to the killer he would one day be face to face with. Across a street, across an interview-room table? He couldn't be sure where their confrontation would take place, but he knew it would happen soon. Already he was beginning to think like him and feel what he could feel.

At the same time, he'd felt sure Levy had some vital piece of the puzzle locked away in his uncooperative memory, something he needed to squeeze out of him, no matter what. Now he was less certain. He forced himself to speak: 'I'm sorry. I was just trying a new witness interview technique,' he lied. 'It's supposed to distract the witness by making them feel angry, allowing suppressed memories to be freed subconsciously.'

Levy studied him, deciding whether or not to believe him. 'Well,' he said, 'it doesn't seem to work, does it?'

'No,' Sean pretended to agree, still feeling numb. 'I'm sorry. I've wasted enough of your time.' He almost pushed past Levy in his haste to leave the neat little office and escape his house and all the pointlessness it stood for. He began to descend the stairs with Levy in close pursuit, hell-bent on haranguing him all the way to the front door.

'And just for the record, I do know what the local postman looks like, now I've had time to think about it.'

'What?' Sean snapped at him, interested. 'What does he look like?'

'Well, he's black for starters – which no doubt explains a thing or two – about fifty, short and stocky, with a beard and moustache.'

'I'll make a note of it,' Sean lied again. The age, colour and build of Levy's postman were all wrong. 'It may come in useful, thank you.' The front door glowed in front of him like a porthole to another, better world.

'I distinctly remember him because I had to complain about him a few days ago.'

'Really?' Sean's hand was reaching out for the door handle.

'I'd specifically asked the Post Office to stop putting junk mail through my letter box – damn stuff was filling my recycling bin. Miraculously, I thought they'd actually listened, but then the other day a bloody great pile was pushed through my door. So I phoned them and gave them a good dressing down. Anyway, it did the trick – no more junk mail.'

For the second time Levy's words made him freeze. 'Sorry. What did you just say?'

'Excuse me?' Levy replied, suspicious of Sean's interest in his petty complaint.

'Someone put junk mail through your letter box, although previously you'd stopped receiving it?'

'Yes,' Levy answered, confused. 'Because I'd told them to stop posting it, and for a while they did.'

'But it started again?' Sean asked, the fluttering in his chest and bright whiteness behind his eyes telling him he was close to something he needed, close to a key that would unlock the way to the man he had to find and stop.

'Yes, a few days ago.'

'How many times?'

'I told you, just once, because I phoned them and gave them a—'

'When?' he cut Levy dead.

'I . . . I'm not sure, a few days ago. Why?'

'I need to know when – exactly when.'

'I really couldn't say.'

'Morning? Afternoon?'

'Morning, definitely morning.'

'How can you be so sure? What were you doing?'

'I remember, I was walking down the stairs, I was dressed and ready to go out, so it must have been late morning. I saw the mail spilled over the floor as I walked downstairs.'

'And it made you angry?'

'I was annoyed, yes.'

'So you phoned the Post Office straight away?'

'No.'

'Why?'

'Because I needed to get away.'

'Get away for what?'

'I'm—'

'You put off calling the Post Office, so it must have been something important. What were you getting ready for?'

'Brunch,' Levy remembered, the weight lifting as soon as he said it. 'I was going out for brunch, at the garden centre in Beckenham.'

'What?' Sean snapped.

'It's half-price for pensioners on Tuesdays.'

'Tuesday – Jesus Christ,' Sean said to himself, 'he's dressing as a postman. That's how he gets the doors open, he dresses like a fucking postman.' The images played in his mind like a short film, the faceless man walking along Louise Russell's street, dressed in a postal uniform, Royal Mail bag over his shoulder, calm and relaxed, knowing exactly what he was doing, every so often casually walking to other front doors and dropping junk mail through letter boxes. The perfect urban disguise.

Levy chased the images away. 'What are you talking about, Inspector?'

'Nothing. I have to go.' He turned his back on Levy and pulled the front door open, leaving without another word, oblivious to Levy shaking his head in disapproval as he closed his front door. As he walked to his car he talked to the faceless man whose features were beginning to appear more distinct: 'I can feel you now, my friend. We'll be seeing each other soon.'

The car bumped wildly as Thomas Keller drove too quickly over the uneven surface of his driveway, rocking him violently in his seat. Hearing the loud banging from the boot as his precious cargo was tossed around, he frowned with concern. He didn't want her damaged. He needed her pristine if she was to be everything he wanted her to be.

By the time the car slid to a halt outside his ramshackle breezeblock cottage it was gone 5 p.m. Darkness would be closing in within another hour or two. Wanting to make sure everything was ready before night descended, he grabbed the keys from the ignition and jumped from his old Ford Mondeo, tripping and stumbling as he hurried to the front door.

Ignoring the squalor and filth, he ran through the house to the tiny spare bedroom, just big enough for a single bed – not that there was one. The room was in semi-darkness, its one window facing north, away from the sinking sun. He kicked aside piles of boxes and worn, tattered clothes until he uncovered what he was after: an old, thin, stained single mattress that was folded in two but sprang open as the weight was removed from on top of it. Taking hold of the mattress as best he could, he tried to shift it. But it was heavier than he'd remembered and he struggled to haul it through the confined space, cursing himself for not having moved it earlier. He'd planned everything so meticulously, weeks and weeks of making sure there would be no mistakes, yet somehow he'd failed to ensure things would be ready for her once he got her home.

Next time, he vowed to himself, he would be better prepared. The admission that there would be more, that his chosen one was already damned, was a paradox his consciousness did not dwell on.

He dragged the mattress from the room and along the narrow hallway, trying to suppress the anger and frustration welling within him as he battled with the inanimate foe. Passing through the narrow entrance to the kitchen, he scraped his knuckles on the door frame and let out a scream of pain. Throwing the mattress to the floor, he sucked on the blood that trickled through his broken skin. Then, as if trying to exorcise the rage from his body, he gave vent to his fury, stamping on the mattress and yelling abuse. Instead of receding, his anger grew; he tugged open a kitchen drawer and snatched a knife from inside, dropping to his knees on the offending mattress and plunging the blade deep into the foam, over and over again until fatigue weighed down his thin arms and calmed his frantic mind.

As his self-control gradually returned he loosened his grip on the knife and let it fall to the floor. He knocked it away, not looking as it slid across the old linoleum surface, his focus now on the damage to the mattress. There were two or three dozen stab marks, mostly in the centre, but fortunately it was made of foam and would still serve its purpose. Thomas crouched over it, waiting for his breathing to slow, feeling the sweat running down his back grow cold, making him shiver as it reached the base of his spine. He sniffed loose mucus from his nose and stood, then he took hold of the mattress once more and hauled it outside.

As he dragged it past his car he could hear knocking coming

from the boot, reminding him of the need to be quick – the boot wasn't air-tight, but she couldn't survive in there indefinitely. But despite his efforts the journey across his courtyard took for ever, the mattress snagging on every obstacle, forcing him to wrestle it this way and that to get it loose. Eventually he reached the cellar door and undid the padlock, pulled the door open and threw the mattress down the stairs. The one already down there was moving around in her cage, no doubt startled by the noisy arrival of her soon-to-be companion's makeshift bed. He descended the stairs slowly, brushing dust from his postman's uniform, feeling physically and mentally exhausted, but at the same time exuberant at having achieved what he set out to.

When he reached the bottom step he saw her cowering in the far corner of her cage, the duvet wrapped around her for protection as much as warmth. As he approached, she tried to retreat further, but there was nowhere for her to go. Producing another key from his trouser pocket, he unlocked her cage door and swung it slowly open, crouching down to peer in, but averting his eyes from her face, as if she were a Medusa with the power to turn him to stone merely by looking at him.

'Give me the quilt,' he demanded. She neither said nor did anything. 'Give me the fucking quilt,' he repeated, shouting now, but still avoiding her gaze.

His anger made her jump. Her face distorting in readiness for the tears that welled from her emerald green eyes, she unpeeled the duvet and pushed it towards him with her feet, her legs kicking it away quickly as if it were an intruding rat or spider. He grabbed it by the corner and pulled it off her and out of the cage in one movement, slamming the door shut and re-securing the padlock before moving to the other cage, dragging both the mattress and duvet with him. Stooping to pass through the entrance, he hauled the bedding inside, taking care to straighten out the mattress and lay the duvet on top of it so he could wrap her inside once she was in her safe place.

Happy with the arrangement, he left the cage and walked as quickly as his exhausted body would allow back to the car, looking up to the sky to ensure he still had plenty of daylight to play with, giving himself a few seconds to gather his composure before meeting her properly after all this time. When he was ready, he leaned into the front of the car and removed the bottle of chloroform and pad of material from his bag, stuffing them both into his jacket pocket. Then he pulled the lever that unlocked the boot and stepped away from the car. Breathing deeply, as if preparing himself to receive some life-changing news, he walked the few steps to the back of the car, coiled his fingers under the boot latch and pressed. The cover popped open, slowly and quietly rising with a pneumatic hiss.

Deborah Thomson blinked fast and hard against the punishing light that swarmed into the boot. She tried to speak, to call out for help or mercy, but her incoherent cries were prevented from escaping by the thick black tape fastened across her mouth. Before her eyes could adjust the light began to recede again and she felt a presence above her, the outline of someone leaning in. Despite the chill of fear running through her, she kicked her legs, trying to find purchase, her feet scraping and scuffing the interior surface of the boot.

The shape came closer and closer, her vision improving quickly, enabling her to make out the shape of a head and shoulders. More detail soon followed: his unkempt brown hair, strands of which had stuck to a forehead slick with a sheen of sweat; his crooked stained teeth glistened in the faint light; the writhing sinews of his thin arms, hands and neck, all latticed with swollen blood vessels. She saw his lips open and close and realized he was speaking, his words seeming to reach her seconds after he'd spoken them.

'Don't struggle,' he warned her, 'you could hurt yourself.

I'm taking you to your safe place now, but you'll still be a little woozy because of the chloroform. You'll have to let me help you walk, but first we need to get you out of this boot.'

Her eyes betrayed the horror she felt, the sheer disbelief that this could be happening to her. She struggled to recall the last thing she could remember before the darkness came, her mind awash with tentative images of being in her bedroom, being annoyed by someone unexpected calling at the front door . . . Then the nightmare overtook her, the feeling of being unable to move, unable to run from danger, followed by darkness and suffocation, confinement and the sensation of being buried alive. As his long, insect-like fingers reached for her, Deborah knew this nightmare was real. She felt his clammy hands touching her, one sliding under the back of her neck as the other coiled around her upper arm, gripping it tightly.

'Sit up,' he instructed, tugging roughly on her arm and neck, gritting his teeth with the effort. Instead of cooperating, she pushed against him, burrowing as deep as she could into the boot. He tightened his grip and pulled her, his face flitting between a thin, forced smile and a grimace of anger and effort. 'No, no,' he told her, 'don't do that. We have to get you out of here. It's not safe. They might be watching us. I can't do this on my own. I need you to help me.' He tugged her again, making her cry out with pain, but ignoring her muffled pleas he carried on pulling until he had forced her to bend at the waist into a sitting position. 'That's it. Almost there now,' he panted.

Her eyes left him, frantically searching for help or an opportunity to run or, if she had to, to fight back. But her vision was swimming in and out of focus, her mind and body too weak with shock and the remaining effects of the chloroform. She knew any attempt to escape or attack would be pointless.

Keeping one hand on her back, he used the other to scoop

her legs one at a time over the rim of the boot. Then he perched beside her, one arm snaking around her waist while the other cradled her bound forearms.

'Ready?' he asked. 'OK, let's do this together.' He pushed with his legs, thrusting them both to their feet, relieved she could support most of her own weight. 'Good,' he said, propelling her forward. 'Now we need to walk.'

Stumbling and staggering, they crossed the uneven courtyard. Sweat was pouring off him from the effort of supporting her, and his breathing was heavy and erratic. The smell of his sweet almond breath drifting into her face made her gag behind the tape that covered her mouth. Deborah tried to draw fresh air in through her nose to calm the nausea and clear her head of the drug-induced fog, instinct telling her that whatever she could learn now, whatever she could remember seeing as he dragged her across this cluttered wasteland, could yet prove to be the difference between living or dying.

Finally they reached a red-brick building, no bigger than an outside toilet, but as he led her through the door she realized it was merely the entrance to some type of underground shelter left over from the last war, or in readiness for the next. He steered her down the stairs and she watched him from the corners of her eyes, her hatred for him burning in her heart. The desire to attack him, to scratch at his eyes, knee him in his genitals was overwhelming, but she knew she wasn't yet strong enough and her bindings gave him too much of an advantage. She reassured herself that the time would come when they would face each other on more equal terms, and the thought of inflicting pain on him, of taking revenge, helped to quell the fear that could so easily have incapacitated her.

'Almost there,' he reassured her, as they stepped off the last stair together.

Deborah could see the outline of the cage he was leading

her to, the cage she knew would be her prison. She wanted to survive. On the most basic animal level she wanted to survive, and her instincts screamed at her not to go into the cage, warning her the cage was death.

She spun away from him and for a few confused seconds she was free, moving back towards the stairs. But her foot became entangled in an old screen and she toppled backwards, landing heavily on the unyielding stone floor, her hip bearing the brunt of the fall. Her eyes closed as she winced in pain, opening a second later as she remembered her perilous situation, searching frantically in the gloom for the madman she knew would come for her. It was then she saw it: another cage. Definitely not the one she was being led to but another cage, with someone inside it, cowering in the corner staring at her, eyes impossibly wide as they connected with hers in the twilight of the cellar.

She reached for the tape over her mouth and found its corner, ripping it away painfully, filling her lungs until they could expand no more in readiness to scream – not in pain, but in desperation, in fear that she would never awake from this nightmare. In the moment just before the scream was about to escape her mouth she was sure she could smell and taste perfume in the room, only for the unexpected pleasure to be replaced by the clinical smell of chloroform and the sensation of suffocating as damp material was pressed over her open mouth and nose. Her bound hands clutched at the unseen hands, clawing at them in an effort to pull them from her face so she could breathe air and not chemicals, but as the effects of the chloroform swept over her the kicking of her bare feet became nothing more than a slight twitching, her clawing fingers weakened, until finally she fell still, arms falling to her sides as her chest rose and fell gently.

When he felt her stillness he threw the chloroform-soaked pad to the far wall of the cellar. The effects of being so close to the escaping fumes had begun to make him feel a little dizzy and disorientated. He turned his face away from hers to avoid breathing the residual fumes coming from her skin and the inside of her mouth as she lay in his lap, mouth hanging wide open. He shook his head, trying to clear the fog, giving himself time to rest and regain his breath, readying himself for the tasks ahead. Her flawless, slightly olive skin, her short brown hair – shiny and straight, a few locks now fallen across her face – and her soft, wet red lips were enticing. He felt his groin tightening as the testicles swelled and twisted in his scrotum, telling him he needed to move her before the bad thoughts beat the real him away and took control of his actions.

Gently he cradled her head in his hands as he slipped her from his lap, positioning her head carefully on the hard floor, making sure it was pointing towards the cage before scuttling around so he could slide his hands under her armpits and drag her slowly across the room to the place where he knew she would be safe. Her body was now an uncooperative dead weight and he had difficulty manoeuvring her through the narrow entrance. Beads of sweat were forming under his hairline and down his spine, and once inside the cage it became even more difficult to move, but at last he managed to manoeuvre her into position on the mattress he'd prepared for her, arms by her side, legs together, slightly bent.

His unblinking eyes moved backward and forwards across her body, excitement and desire returning in waves that threatened to swamp his intentions to worship her tenderly until she decided it was right for them to be together in that way. He tried to fight the urge, clenching his fists tightly until he felt his nails cutting into his palms. He began to fumble at the small buttons that ran the full length of the front of her nurse's uniform, each one taking an age to unfasten, his sweaty hands making his task increasingly difficult as the anger stirred in his guts, flooding his body with adrenalin and testosterone. As the uniform began to fall open he could see her soft, warm skin, her pretty small breasts held closely together by a simple white lace bra. He let out an involuntary moan of pleasure as his hands and eyes brushed her breasts. Forcing himself to move to the next button, he tried to shake the bewildering sensations of pleasure from his consciousness, but each button he released revealed a new glimpse of things so beautiful he could only have imagined them before he'd begun to search for her. He brushed her unfastened uniform aside with the back of his hand, unable to resist the temptation to see more of what lay beneath, but regretting it as soon as the smooth skin of her belly became visible, desire making him again close his eyes as he struggled to control it.

Once her uniform was fully unfastened he had to twist and bend her elbows in order to free her arms from the ungiving material, until finally she lay on the filthy mattress naked but for her white bra and black knickers. His eyes gorged themselves on her beauty, the translucent skin pulled tight over the frame of her broad but feminine shoulders, as smooth as marble around her throat and neck, the rhythmic throbbing of her jugular's pulse hypnotizing. He watched helplessly as his hands reached out towards her, powerless to stop them as they fell around her throat, his fingers lying softly against her skin, so softly he could feel the steady beat of the valve in her blood vessel pumping the oxygen-hungry blood back towards her heart and lungs. He smiled joyfully as he spoke to himself. 'Yes. Yes, you're the one. I was right about you.'

His hands slipped under her back, searching for her bra's fastening, his fingers suddenly more assured and nimble as he undid the clip with little difficulty, easing the straps from her shoulders, his heart pounding as he so slowly eased the bra from breasts that moved only slightly when freed, her nipples becoming slightly erect as the cool air rushed over them. His mouth fell open at the sight of her, his tongue moving in circles around his lips, painting them with his saliva. He let the bra fall from his hands, directing his eyes further down her body, his tongue moving in ever-quickening circles as his hands once more reached out towards her spell-binding skin. Readjusting his body position so he was level with her knees, his face pointing towards hers, he hooked his fingers under the sides of her knickers and slowly rolled them from her hips, her pubic hair straightening, then curling again as it sprang free from the laced material, watched by his widening eyes. She moaned a little as he pulled them from her groin, making him pause, concerned she might be waking prematurely from the chloroform, but she settled quickly enough. He decided it must have been a moan of pleasure, that she was dreaming about him touching her there like he knew she wanted him to.

'Not yet,' he told her. 'It's not time yet. We have other things to do first.'

He continued slowly rolling the black panties from her body until they slipped from the ends of her toes.

Cowering in the other cage, Louise Russell watched his every move, waves of nausea washing over her each time he reached out to touch the other woman. She remembered how she had woken naked in the cage, opening her eyes to the sight of Karen Green. *Now you know*, Karen had told her. *Now you know what's going to happen to you.* Unless she could do something to stop him, Louise knew the fate he had in store for her. Somehow she would have to persuade this other woman to help her. Only if they acted together would they stand any chance of surviving.

Keller was still transfixed by Deborah Thomson. As he stared at her nakedness, her cut and bloodied feet seemed the only imperfection. He knew he should fold the duvet over her and leave, but he couldn't, not yet. His hands fell gently on her ankles and began to slide along her slim, smooth legs, his thumbs exploring her pubic hair and the cleft of her vagina before moving on to her soft belly and brushing over her ribs, coming to rest on her breasts, the pain of ecstasy suddenly too much for him to bear. He released the button of his trousers and undid the zip, thrusting his hand inside his underpants and gripping his fully erect penis. Moaning obscenely, he jerked his hand feverishly, and within seconds warm, sticky fluid was pumping into his hand and trousers, the relief of orgasm almost as sweet as the relief that he'd been too close to climax to have tried to enter her, his dark side threatening to spoil everything. He wiped his hand clean on the inside of his trousers and sheepishly gathered her clothes, carefully folding the duvet over her and leaning in to plant a gentle kiss on her forehead.

He crawled from her cage and stood fastening his trousers before securing the door. As he walked from the cellar he pulled the light cord, plunging the room into darkness, not once looking in Louise Russell's direction. Closing the metal door behind him, he walked to an old oil drum and threw Deborah Thomson's clothes inside. Then he lifted a can of petrol he kept next to the drum, unscrewed the lid and poured in more than was necessary, pulling a box of matches from his shirt pocket and lighting three bunched together. Taking a step back, he tossed the matches into the drum and watched as the orange flames leapt high before settling into the confines of the drum where her clothes shrivelled and charred.

'You don't need these any more,' he whispered. 'They can't make you pretend any more. You're home now, Sam. You're home.'

7

When Sean arrived back at the office it was approaching six thirty p.m., but the place was busier than usual for a Friday evening. Clearly a fair number of his team were still hoping to salvage some kind of a weekend, even if in their hearts they knew any real chance of spending time with friends or family had long since gone and they'd end up settling for a couple of hours in the local pub before beating their weary way home. He caught Donnelly's eye as he passed his desk. 'Guv'nor,' Donnelly acknowledged him.

'Looking forward to another relaxing weekend at home with the wife and kids?' Sean asked ironically.

Donnelly shrugged and gave a low laugh. 'At home with the wife and kids? I'd rather be here telling people what to do than be there being told what to do.'

Sean raised his eyebrows and kept walking until Sally stepped in front of him.

'There's someone in your office to see you,' she said quietly. 'Featherstone dropped her off a couple of hours ago.'

Sean looked towards his own office and saw the back of a woman's head. She was sitting in one of the chairs he kept for his frequent visitors.

'Who is she?'

'I don't know,' said Sally. 'I haven't spoken to her.'

'Does anyone know who she is?'

Sally shrugged and walked away, leaving Sean to look around the office accusingly at the faces turning from him and forming secretive huddles. Whoever she was, he sensed she was bad news. He strode towards his office, entering with far more of a performance than usual, throwing his raincoat across his desk and emptying his heavy pockets on to it, waiting for the woman to make the first move. Carefully placing the case report she'd been reading on the floor next to her chair, she got to her feet, hand outstretched.

'Anna Ravenni-Ceron. Detective Inspector Sean Corrigan, I presume.' He accepted her hand, holding it softly for a second before releasing it, studying her brown eyes, which were magnified by the small, heavy-framed designer glasses she wore. Her dark skin betrayed her Mediterranean origins as surely as her name, as did her almost black hair, which he suspected was long and curly, although she'd done her best to hide the fact by pinning it in a bundle on top of her head, leaving her fine-boned face clear. She wore a fitted blue cotton blouse, unbuttoned just enough to reveal her modest cleavage, and a slim-fitting grey knee-length skirt that showed her pleasantly wide hips as they tapered into a small waist. Temporarily disarmed by her attractiveness, he sat on the edge of his desk.

'If you're looking for DI Corrigan, then yes, you've found him. Please, have a seat.' He watched her smoothing her skirt out as she sat back down. 'So what can I do for you, Miss . . . sorry, I—'

'Anna Ravenni-Ceron and it's Mrs, but please, just call me Anna.'

'OK, Anna, what can I do for you?'

'It was my understanding that you would be expecting me. Superintendent Featherstone assured me he'd informed you that I would be assisting with the investigation.' Recognizing the blank expression on Sean's face, she added, 'I'm the criminal psychiatrist who's been assigned to help profile the man who kidnapped Louise Russell. I gather there's reason to believe he's also responsible for the murder of another woman.'

'Karen Green,' he said, the coolness returning to his voice now he understood who she was. Cops didn't like outsiders sticking their noses into police business. 'The woman he murdered – her name was Karen Green.'

'Yes, that was in the file.' She indicated the dossier she had been reading. 'A very interesting case, and I think I already have some suggestions about the suspect. I believe he . . .' Sean held his hand up to stop her.

'I'm sure you've got better things to do on a Friday night than sit around here with a bunch of grizzly old detectives. Please, take the file home with you and study it over the weekend, and then if you still think you can help, by all means pop back in on Monday and let me know what you've found.'

'Actually I'd rather make a start right away.'

'You don't have to do that,' said Sean. 'Monday will be fine.' A silence hung between them while she considered her next move.

'By then it could be too late,' she insisted. 'For Louise Russell and perhaps you too.'

'Don't waste your time worrying about me.'

'I'm not.'

'Then go home and study your file.'

'As I said, I'd rather stay here, close to the investigation, where I can be of most use.'

'Anna, I have two, three days, maybe less, before Louise Russell becomes his second victim. I'm sorry, but I don't have time to explain the ins and outs of a murder investigation to a layman.'

'I've studied many murder investigations, Inspector. I'm not a total layman.'

'Is that why you're here? So you can tell everyone you've got your hands dirty with a real murder investigation, instead of just studying one second-hand?'

'No.'

'Then why are you here?'

'To help.'

'To help how? How many murder investigations have you been involved with, exactly?'

'None. But I've conducted extensive interviews with many convicted murderers, including a study of some of Broadmoor's most troubled patients.'

'Really?' Sean asked, impressed despite himself. 'Like who?'

'Like Sebastian Gibran,' she answered. 'One of yours, I believe.'

'One of mine?' Sean repeated. 'I wouldn't call him that.'

'No,' she agreed. 'I was invited to examine him as part of his psychological assessment, to see if he was fit to stand trial.'

'And you decided he wasn't.'

'Yes.'

'You were wrong.'

'Sebastian was clearly suffering from a deep-rooted personality disorder, his psychopathic traits and complete inability to form meaningful relationships with people were obvious from the start. His marriage, relationships at work, even those with his parents and siblings were an act: he was merely portraying the person they wanted to him to be, while in fact he was living out an incredibly well-formed and detailed fantasy life from a very early age. He was clearly incapable of truly understanding his own trial, in the context of grasping the real-life implications it could have held for him.'

'He's bad,' Sean told her, 'not mad. He had every advantage in life, yet he chose to do what he did. He *chose* to do it.'

'If you mean he didn't have the typical background for a serial killer, then you're right. He doesn't appear to have been abused as a child or to have suffered any particularly traumatic incident that could have affected him adversely in later life. On the face of it, he was very successful and intelligent, but the fact remains he clearly has a psychotic social behavioural disorder.'

'He pulled the wool over your eyes,' Sean jeered. 'He did to you what he's spent his entire life doing – he told you what you wanted to hear and showed you only what he wanted you to see, made himself an interesting psychiatric case for the experts to pore over. What better way to keep himself out of prison? And now all he has to do is wait until he feels the time is right to pass all your blunt tests, leaving you with no choice but to declare him sane. Then what happens?'

'He'll stand trial for his crimes.'

'And use all the evidence you and your colleagues have amassed about his state of mind at the time to prove he can't be held accountable for his actions on the grounds of diminished responsibility. And then he walks free. True?'

'I don't know,' she answered truthfully, never looking away from him. 'I'm not an expert when it comes to the judicial system. My job is to provide clinical assessments. I don't get involved in the moral or legal judgements.'

'I wish I had that luxury.' Sean was silent for a moment before continuing: 'Listen, it's like this – I've never met a psychiatrist or read a psychiatric report about an offender that told me anything I wouldn't expect any of my detectives to be able to tell me.'

'I really believe I can help you.'

'I don't think so.'

'Well, at the end of the day it doesn't matter what you think, does it?'

'Meaning?'

She reached for the briefcase at the side of her chair and pulled an opened letter from inside, handing it to Sean.

'That's a letter from your assistant commissioner in charge of serious crime, instructing you to ensure that I have unrestricted access to all matters relating to this investigation, including forensic evidence and interviews with suspects. I will of course not be permitted knowledge of the use of existing covert human intelligent sources or the deployment of undercover officers, although any thoughts I have about how the undercover officer or officers may best infiltrate the offender or offenders would be expected to be fully explained to them, by you.'

Sean scanned the letter without reading it properly, sure everything she said was true. He folded it up, sighing and shaking his head slightly and handed it back to her. 'Fine,' he said. 'Just one thing.'

'What would that be?'

'Don't ask me questions I don't have time to answer. Keep your mouth shut and your eyes and ears open. Learn through observation not interrogation. You keep up or you get left behind – understand?'

'Yes. Thank you.'

'Thank you? Thank me for what?' Donnelly and Zukov appeared at his door before she could answer. Sean could tell by their faces they were excited. 'Something wrong?' he asked them.

'Paulo here's dug up a possible suspect you might want to take a look at,' Donnelly explained.

'Speak up, Paulo,' Sean encouraged.

'I did what you suggested, guv'nor, and searched the local intelligence records for anyone with previous for serious sexual offences and burglary artifice. You were right – it turns out to be a very unusual mix. I only got one hit: Jason Lawlor, male, IC1, forty-two years old, loads of previous for theft, assault, burglary, commercial and residential and serious sexual offences. But it was his previous convictions involving the use of artifice to gain entry that set him apart.'

'But has he ever used it to get into a house and then sexually assaulted the occupier?'

'Yeah,' Zukov answered, 'his last conviction. He did six years for burglary and sexual assault and was only released three months ago from Belmarsh, but he's failed to show up for his last two bail signing dates and he's also missed his last two Sexual Offenders' Register appointments. As of now, he's on the run.'

'Excuse me,' Ravenni-Ceron tentatively interrupted them. 'Sorry, it's just that the file on this case said the suspect apparently has no convictions, whereas this man has many.'

Zukov and Donnelly both looked at Sean.

'Don't make assumptions,' he told her. 'Funny things can happen to fingerprints – trust me, I know. And we also have to consider the possibility our suspect is not working alone. Perhaps this Lawlor character's made himself a friend who has no convictions. Maybe this friend does the grabbing and Lawlor does the rest.'

'I don't think so,' she argued. 'The psychological profile of the man we're after is already clearly indicating he's a loner, acting out some highly personal fantasy. It doesn't make sense that he could be working with a partner.'

'Truth is, we don't really know that – and nor will we until we arrest this Lawlor and drag him across the cobbles. Once we've done that we'll have a better understanding.'

'For the record, I disagree.'

'Noted,' said Sean, his feelings towards her a mixture of admiration for her courage in speaking up and irritation at her interference.

'And it doesn't seem to me you have any evidence to justify his arrest.'

'That won't be a problem,' Donnelly joined in. 'He's wanted for jumping bail. We can arrest him any time we like.'

'Do we have an address for him?' Sean asked.

'Only his bail address – 3 Canal Walk, Sydenham,' Zukov answered.

'That's a couple of miles from where Louise Russell was taken,' Sean pointed out.

'Same for Karen Green,' Donnelly added.

'Have the locals checked out the address?' Sean asked.

'No,' said Zukov. 'Apparently they're too busy to chase after bail offenders.'

'And sexual predators who fail to make their Sexual Register appointments?' Sean continued.

'They didn't have anything to say about that,' said Zukov.

'I bet they didn't,' Donnelly sneered. 'Fucking clowns.'

'I'm not interested in what they did or didn't do,' Sean put an end to the criticism. 'The fact is, if they haven't checked the address then there's a chance he may still be using it. What sort of place is it?' He looked at Zukov.

'A bedsit in a big old Victorian house. A number of the other bedsits are also used as bail addresses.'

'Bollocks.' Sean shook his head, thought for a moment. 'OK, we can't risk putting his door in, case he's not home. His bail house buddies will be straight on the phone to him and we'll never see him there again. So we plot it up and wait for him to show.'

'Do you want me to get hold of Featherstone and get some surveillance authorized?' Donnelly asked.

'No, we don't have time. Grab Sally and whoever else you can find. We'll do it ourselves. As soon as we see him, we'll take him out. Nothing fancy or complicated – nick him, spin his room and then back here to interview him. All right, let's go.'

Donnelly and Zukov headed for the main office while Sean started to pull his raincoat on and fill his pockets with phones, handcuffs, CS gas and anything else he thought he'd be needing. Then he looked up to see Anna imitating his actions. 'You're not actually thinking about coming with us?'

'As the letter from the assistant commissioner states, I'm to be given unrestricted access and assistance. If this is your man – although I personally don't believe it is – then I need to see how he reacts to being arrested. I need to see where and how he lives.'

Sean pursed his lips and let out a long sigh. 'Have it your own way. But, like I said – keep up or get left behind. I don't have time to wait for you. Understand?'

'Don't worry about me, Inspector. I'm a big girl.'

'Really? Well, I guess we'll find out soon enough, won't we, Anna. I just hope you have more of a clue about what you're letting yourself in for than I think you do.'

He was charging through the main office in the direction of the car park before she could answer.

Thomas Keller sat at his kitchen table and tried to stay calm, but he was too agitated. He got up and began to pace around the room looking for things to do, but it was no use, the excitement of having her so close overrode everything else. The memory of soft, warm skin made his entire body ripple and shiver with pleasure, but he cursed the ugly desires it stirred in his stomach and groin that threatened to destroy the beauty of the thing that existed between them. He had to go to the cellar, there was something he needed to do concerning the other woman, but he was afraid to go while the excitement gripped him, afraid of what it might make him do.

Suddenly the solution came to him. He hurried along the narrow corridor to his bedroom, coming to a halt in front of the cupboard where he kept his special treasures. Tentatively he reached for the handle, checking first to make sure that he was alone, that there were no intruders lurking in the shadows. He eased the drawer open carefully, savouring the moment, allowing the anticipation to rise slowly, the expectation making his muscles begin to tighten and coil, his eyes darting from side to side as the bundles of letters revealed themselves, each held together by an elastic band. His swelling penis grew uncomfortable in his trousers as he searched for the letters addressed to Deborah Thomson. Reverently he undid the bundle and laid each item neatly on his unmade bed. To him this mundane collection of invoices and bank statements held a significance that seemed almost mystical; just by running his fingers over the letters spelling out her name he felt he could absorb something of her, feel her life flowing into his own. While his left hand rested on the letters, moving from one to another, his right hand slid slowly to his trousers, its fingers fumbling awkwardly at the button and the zip, the urgency to release himself increasing with every passing second, until at last he felt his engorged penis fall into the palm of his hand. But as he began to stroke his hand back and forth, other thoughts began to invade his mind – thoughts of the other woman, the one who'd tried to fool him – the one who'd betrayed him, her face large and distorted as she laughed at him. Then more faces joined her, circling him, pointing and laughing: the face of Karen Green, taunting him for his stupidity, telling everyone how she'd fooled him into believing she was Sam; and the faces of the men from his sorting office, jeering, swearing at him, telling him he was a filthy queer. He felt his penis shrinking in his hand, withering to nothing.

'Leave me alone!' he screamed into the empty room. 'Go away. Just leave me alone.' But the faces wouldn't leave him. They kept spinning around him. Among them he could see the faces of his mother and the staff at the orphanage, the teachers who'd hated him and abused him. Self-consciously he struggled to zip up his trousers, but the faces were growing arms and hands which were pointing now at his pathetic, shrunken manhood. He tried to swat them away, but they danced out of his reach, their laughter reaching a crescendo as he used both arms to pull his precious letters close to his chest, protecting them from the phantoms.

Bitter tears stung his eyes and cheeks, the humiliation that had replaced desire giving way to rage. He'd make them sorry for laughing at him, for belittling him. He'd make them all pay, especially her. Abandoning the letters, he jumped to his feet and ran to the cupboard where he kept his stun-gun and the keys to the cellar. He threw open the back door and staggered out into the yard, swiping tears and mucus from his face, his teeth clenched in anger as he made his way to the cellar door. His movements became more fluid now that his purpose was clear, as if his fury were guiding him as he undid the lock and yanked the door open so hard it clattered into the wall and bounced closed. Again he pulled it open and stood for a moment at the top of the stairs, staring down into the semi-darkness, breathing hard. Then he moved down the stairs, steadily, purposefully, the tasks ahead clear to him. He rounded the bottom of the stairs and pulled the light cord, watching Louise Russell scuttle into the furthest corner of her cage, her red eyes wild with loathing and fear. He walked to her cage and opened the hatch on the side.

'Take the clothes off and put them through the hatch,' he ordered. 'Do it now.'

Louise crossed her arms across her chest, gripping the blouse and sweater, refusing to surrender these last remnants of decency. 'Please,' she begged him.

'You can keep the underwear,' he said, 'but I need everything else.'

'Please,' she repeated, 'I'll do whatever you want, but please, let me keep the clothes. You gave them to me, remember? You told me they were my real clothes, that I needed to wear them for you, for us.'

He held a hand up to stop her. 'Just give me the clothes.'

'Please. You don't want to do this, I know you don't.'

'Give me the fucking clothes,' he screamed. 'Give me the

fucking clothes, you lying whore.' She shook at the ferocity of his attack, pulling her knees up to her chest as if they were a shield, the hate in his eyes telling her he would not relent. Slowly she began to pull the sweater off, sobbing uncontrollably all the while. She passed it through the hatch to him, jumping back as soon as he took the item, unsure of what to remove next, the blouse or the skirt. 'Hurry up,' he demanded. She turned her back to him and began to undo the buttons of the blouse, her tears slowing as fear was replaced by humiliation and embarrassment, everyday emotions finding their way into her extraordinary situation. The blouse slipped from her shoulders and she passed it through the hatch, her left arm pressed across her chest, head bowed to avoid his leering face as she kneeled and unzipped the waist of her skirt, pulling it over her hips and down to her knees, adjusting herself into a sitting position before removing it completely and passing it through the hatch, his hands greedily grasping it, tugging it away.

As she hugged herself in the corner of her cage she looked up to see him moving around to the door of her prison, pulling the key from his pocket and easing it into the lock, opening the door and stooping into her space, the stun-gun held out in front of him as he inched towards her like a scorpion readying to strike. 'You shouldn't have betrayed me. That was a mistake. You're just a little whore trying to make me do things to you – dirty things, bad things. Well now you're going to get what you want, whore. I'm going to give you exactly what you want.'

Sally and Sean sat in the front of the unmarked car they'd concealed as best they could in a residents' parking area about forty metres from the house where Jason Lawlor was supposed to be living. If they parked any further away they wouldn't be able to recognize him when he arrived, but if they parked any closer he would almost certainly spot them and probably take flight. Several of the local low-lives had already paid them some unwanted attention. A small intelligence record photograph of Lawlor rested on Sean's thigh. Anna sat in the back of the silent car, while Donnelly and Zukov were close by in another, as were DCs Maggie O'Neil and Stan-the-man McGowan.

The dilapidated old house backed on to the railway lines, the sound of passing trains only adding to the sense of foreboding as they watched the streetlights flickering on in the dusk, making the surrounding trees appear quite black.

'He's going to be difficult to spot,' Sally stated, 'in this light, from this distance.'

'There's enough light around the entrance to the house,' Sean argued without looking away from the front door. 'If he turns up, I'll recognize him.'

Sally shrugged and the car returned to its silent vigil. After a few minutes Sally spoke again, to break the increasingly oppressive atmosphere as much as anything. 'You're Anna Ravenni-Ceron, aren't you?' she said, looking into the back of the car. 'I recognized you from the picture on your book cover.'

'Which book?' Anna asked with a smile.

'Your latest one, I think.'

'*Programmed to Kill*?'

'Yeah,' Sally answered. 'I thought it was good. You talked a lot of sense.'

Sean shifted uncomfortably in his seat and for a passing second considered telling Sally that the woman she was talking to was in part responsible for Gibran worming his way out of a trial for her attempted murder.

'Thank you,' said Anna. 'It's always good to get positive feedback from someone who actually deals with the sort of people I write about.'

'Until I read your book I hadn't realized most serial killers stay within their own ethnic group when selecting their victims.'

'I'm glad you could learn something new from it.'

Sean could listen to no more.

'Anna Ravenni-Ceron – is that your real name, or something you thought would help sell a few more copies?' he asked, only turning to look at her after he finished his question.

'I write books to try to educate people, not to make money.'

'So you give the profits to charity then?' he sneered, facing forward again. She didn't answer.

'Over there,' Sally suddenly said, 'other side of the street. It could be our man.'

Sean strained to see through the slightly misted windscreen. 'That's him.'

'How can you be so sure?' Sally asked.

'I just am. The way he moves, stands. The way he's looking around. It's him.'

'He knows we're here,' Sally said. 'He can sense us.'

'Wait, he's crossing the road. Let's do it.' Sean lifted the radio that had been hidden between his legs and spoke as clearly as he could into it. 'Suspect One's at the address, everybody move in, move in.' He started the engine and pulled away as quietly as he could, keeping the revs low as he closed the short distance to the man who had now crossed the road and was approaching the front door of the house. As they got nearer Sean suddenly accelerated then braked hard to stop directly outside the house. The other cars hadn't arrived yet. Sean jumped from the car, leaving the radio on his seat and pulling his warrant card from his jacket. Lawlor looked like a startled deer caught in the headlights of an approaching truck, his eyes frozen wide open and nostrils flared as he assessed the danger, his legs tense and ready to sprint.

'Police. Stay where you are!' Sean shouted, his warrant card held in front of him. Lawlor looked one way then the other, before suddenly jumping over the low wall at the side of the staircase that led to the door. He sprinted across the paved garden and leap-frogged another low wall, hitting the pavement running smoothly and powerfully. Sean reacted quickly, but not quickly enough to cut him off before he'd reached the open pavement. Both men tore off along the darkening, empty road, their legs and arms pumping, Sean desperately hoping their race would be no more than a short sprint before Lawlor gave in.

Sally and Anna got out of the car just in time to see the men disappear around the first corner and into an alleyway.

'Shit,' Sally shouted as the other two unmarked cars screeched to a stop next to her, the detectives spilling out. 'He's run, he's run,' she told them frantically. 'The guv'nor's gone after him, but he's got no radio.'

'Where?' Donnelly shouted.

'Down the alley.'

Donnelly turned to the younger, lighter detectives. 'Go on then. What you waiting for? Off you go.' Zukov and the two detectives broke into a hesitant run, staying close to each other as they jogged along the road and disappeared into the alley. He noticed Sally subconsciously clutching her chest. 'You all right?'

'Yes,' she replied, a little breathlessly. 'I should have gone after him. I should have stayed with the guv'nor.'

'And then the rest of us wouldn't have had any idea where you were or what had happened.'

'I would have taken a radio,' she argued.

'Don't worry,' he assured her. 'The others will catch up with him.'

'No they won't – and I don't think he wants them to.'

Sean's raincoat trailed behind him like broken wings as he burst from the alley. Lawlor was only a few metres ahead, never once looking over his shoulder – years of running from the police had taught him that could be a costly mistake. They ran straight across the emerging road, causing a passing car to judder to a stop, its horn blaring as the two figures disappeared into another alley and faded into the darkness.

Halfway along the alley Lawlor suddenly leapt to his side, hitting a six-foot fence and scrambling over it like a cat a second before Sean's hands could grasp his ankle. 'Bastard,' he muttered, launching himself at the fence, his upper-body strength dragging him over just in time to see Lawlor straddle the fence on the opposite side of the garden. Now that they'd left the roads and alleyways, Sean knew he was on his own; the chasing pack would have no idea where he'd gone. He felt his ankle almost give way as he landed on hard grass, relieved it was only a fleeting pain as he sprinted across the lawn and jumped at the fence, clearing it more smoothly than he had the last. Remembering to roll as he hit the grass on the other side, he sprang back to his feet in one motion, cursing the raincoat that continually threatened to trip him as he struggled to see clearly in the ever-increasing darkness. Lawlor had already cleared the next fence, using a garden bench to vault it, the distance between the two men remaining the same. Sean maintained his pace as his foot hit the bench while his left hand helped him clear it, but this time it wasn't grass that waited for him, it was paving slabs, slippery with winter moss and moisture from the cooling air. His right foot gave way under him and he hit the ground hard, his shoulder and hip taking the blow, his forehead connecting with the leg of a cast-iron table, forcing him to call out in pain as he pressed his hand to where he knew he'd been cut, feeling warm, slippery blood escaping from the wound.

'Come here,' he yelled after Lawlor, quickly back on his feet and moving across the garden, heaving himself over yet another fence, breathing hard and heavy now.

At first he could see nothing in the twilight, but where his eyes betrayed him his hearing came to the rescue: Lawlor had changed direction, heading for the end of the garden instead of traversing. Sean could hear the sound of feet scuffing against the higher fence as Lawlor struggled to pull himself over, fatigue beginning to override his fear and adrenalin. His own anger and the pain from his bleeding head and bruised shoulder drove him on, flooded his body with hormones that pushed him forward despite the burning in his brain and muscles. He hit the back fence just as Lawlor snaked across and landed on the other side with a thud, his footsteps heading away. Sean's hands grabbed the top of the fence as he jumped from a standing position, pulling and scrambling until he was able to hook a leg over and roll on to the other side, but the fall was much further than he'd expected as the ground fell away from the backs of the houses.

Suddenly he heard a tremendous noise screaming up behind him. As he turned to see what it was, a dazzling beam of light came bearing down on him like an exploding star. Shielding his eyes with one hand, he braced himself for the sound and light to send him to oblivion, stumbling backwards, tripping and falling, until he saw the train crashing past, its passengers oblivious to the drama only inches away as the whistle screamed in alarm. He rolled further from the tracks, pushing reflections of near death aside as he scrambled back to his feet and scanned the trackside for Lawlor. The lights of the train picked him out no more than twenty metres ahead and Sean took off after him with increasing determination, already looking forward to the moment when he'd be kneeling on Lawlor's back, twisting his shoulders and snapping on the quick-cuffs.

The train receded into the distance, leaving behind an eerie silence as Sean chased the shadow in front of him, concentrating on his running, maintaining a short powerful stride, arms pumping like pistons, occasionally flailing to the side when he slipped on the large pieces of loose gravel that ran alongside the tracks and between sleepers.

The darkness was almost total now, but then a spot of light appeared in the far distance, approaching slowly and silently at first. As it grew larger and louder, its speed seemed to increase tenfold and then tenfold more until it was a meteor hurtling towards them. Sean looked down at the darkness under his feet and assured himself that the approaching train would pass him safely by on the parallel set of tracks, but as it grew dangerously close he realized it had been disguising another sound, a rumbling and humming from the tracks he was running along. He glanced over his shoulder and saw a second light heading towards them, moving slower than the other, but still capable of bringing instant death to anyone who got in its way.

Sean knew he should stop, give up the chase and let Lawlor escape, hunt him down another day, but once he was after his man his police instincts took over, instincts that had been drummed into him since his first day on the force. To lose a suspect was the greatest of sins. So he resolved to keep going – keep going until he had Lawlor under his heel or lost him to the darkness of the night. He wouldn't give up the chase, no matter what.

The silhouette of Lawlor kept moving steadily forward, but Sean could see he was tiring as he kept losing his footing, teetering to one side and then the other, his arms jutting out to keep his balance or break his fall, and all the time the lights from in front and behind continued to converge on the two men. Soon Sean would be close enough to kick Lawlor's legs from under him and end the chase. But just as the train coming towards them was almost level with Lawlor, he burst across the tracks, his silhouette perfectly framed by the approaching light, and jumped clear less than a second before one hundred tons of metal moving at sixty miles per hour hurtled through the space he'd leapt from.

Despite the close proximity of the slower train behind him and the speed of the train in front of him, Sean could think of only one thing: unless he went now, Lawlor would be lost – and God knew when he'd surface again. Without looking over his shoulder, he crossed the first set of tracks, the reverberation vibrating the muscles in his legs, the lights so close they cast his shadow long and far, stretching it further with every fraction of a second, until he leapt to the second set of tracks, closing his eyes as he ran.

When he landed on the grass bank he was temporarily blinded and deafened by the noise and light of the train. Disorientated, almost confused to find himself still alive, he tried to work out which direction he was lying in. Along the tracks he saw a shadow stumbling down the grassy bank into the darkness below. He jumped to his feet and sprinted diagonally down the bank, closer and closer to his target until finally he threw himself headfirst across the remaining distance between them and brought Lawlor to the ground with a thud.

Sean pressed Lawlor's face into the wet grass and held him there while he got his breath back. 'I told you to stand still, didn't I?'

Lawlor twisted his head so he could talk and breathe, trying to spit out the pieces of grass that stuck to the saliva gluing his lips, his voice broken and disjointed. 'I . . . I didn't know . . . who, who you . . . were, guv'nor.'

'Bullshit,' Sean panted. 'You may not know who I am, but you know what I am.'

'I didn't, guv'nor, honest. I thought you was . . . vigilantes. I swear, if I'd known . . . you was Old Bill, I'd never have run.'

'Fucking bollocks. You ran for a reason!'

'No, guv'nor. I'm clean, I swear on my fucking eyes. I've been clean since I got out.'

'Then why d'you miss your bail signing?'

'What?'

'Your bailing signing and your Sex Offenders' Register appointment?' Sean repeated, seething with impatience, the excitement of the chase still pumping through his body.

'I was drunk. That's all. I went out and I got pissed and missed my bail signing. After that I knew I'd be wanted so I tried to keep out the way. That's all, I promise. I swear.'

'You're lying,' Sean spat at him. 'You missed them because you had better things to do, didn't you?'

'I don't know what you're talking about.'

'Don't lie to me. You were searching for them, weren't you, looking for the right ones?'

'I'm clean. I've done nothing.'

'And when you found them, you took them, didn't you? You took them, you raped them and you killed them?'

Lawlor looked as confused as he did scared, his head furiously shaking in disagreement with everything Sean was saying. 'I don't have a fucking clue what you're talking about. You're fucking crazy.'

'Are you working with someone else?' Sean persisted. 'Does he take them for you and then you do the rest? Don't you have the guts to take them yourself?' He pressed Lawlor's face hard into the grass, pulling one of his arms back and twisting it until he grimaced and groaned with pain while he looked all around the surrounding area, searching for any CCTV cameras British Transport Police might have deployed in an attempt to catch vandals and perverts. Once he decided there were none, he rolled Lawlor on to his back and gripped him around the neck one-handed, tightly enough to make him wheeze as he tried to draw breath. 'I asked you a question.'

'You're mad,' Lawlor struggled to say. 'You've got the wrong man.'

'Where do you keep them, once you've taken them? Where do you keep them?'

'Keep who?'

Sean looked at the silent, still darkness around them. They were alone. He squeezed Lawlor's neck harder and raised his other hand high and to the side. Resisting the temptation to turn his open hand into a clenched fist, he brought it down with a violent swipe into Lawlor's face, the sound of the slap echoing in the empty night. 'Answer my questions,' he hissed.

Lawlor struggled to escape, but Sean's powerful grip held him in place like a live fish waiting to be gutted. 'I don't know what you're talking about.' Another slap resounded along the grass bank. 'Who are you? What do you want?' Lawlor screamed as loud as he could through his constricted airway.

'Answers,' Sean told him.

'I don't have any.'

'Where's Louise Russell?'

'Who?' Another slap twisted his face.

'Who has her?'

'Please, wait.' Both men stopped for a few silent seconds as Lawlor searched for air and answers. 'You're talking about the man who's already killed one, right? It was on *Crimewatch*, yeah?'

'Yes.' Sean spoke through angry gritted teeth, his hand ready to strike Lawlor's sweating, reddening face. 'You know something. Tell me what you know.'

'That's the point – I don't know anything. Nobody knows anything.'

Sean's face contorted in confusion. '*Nobody* knows anything – what does that mean?'

'This one's working alone. Keeping himself to himself, saying nothing, sharing nothing. No Facebook, no Twitter, no YouTube. He doesn't want to share. This is just for him.'

'Who would he share with?'

'You're Old Bill, you know. We meet in prison, on the segregation wings. When we recognize each other, we share. But not this one. He gives us nothing and nobody recognizes his work. No one knows him, I swear. You're looking for someone who's never been caught.'

'Or someone who's only just started,' he said to himself, but Lawlor heard him.

'Yes,' Lawlor whispered excitedly. 'Yes. Someone new. Someone who's only just started. Of course. Of course. How did you know?'

'What?' Sean asked, distracted by his own thoughts.

'How did you know?'

'Shut the fuck up.' Sean felt his hand tightening around Lawlor's throat, the pain and panic spreading across his face, the power to kill or spare him totally within his control. It was a good feeling, potent and thrilling. Lawlor's hands clutched at his wrists, trying to release the grip on his throat, but it was too strong. His legs began to kick and splay, his body twisting and writhing, but Sean fell on his chest with one knee, sinking deep into his diaphragm.

Then sounds came, voices calling to each other from the grassy bank, torchlight stroking the gently swaying uncut grass, dark figures approaching. Lawlor's eyes darted between the descending shadows and Sean's black, lifeless eyes, as if trying to draw his attention to the only thing that could save him. Finally Sean's subconscious rage acknowledged the fact they had been disturbed by voices he recognized – Donnelly, Zukov and others too. His fingers began to loosen around Lawlor's thin neck, turning his lips from a whitish-blue to pale pink, flecks of spittle spiralling through the air as he coughed his lungs full, made silver by the light from the closing torches.

Sean rolled him over on to his stomach and pulled his arms behind his back, smoothly wrapping the handcuffs around his wrists. 'Get up,' he ordered and hoisted him to his feet.

Donnelly was the first to reach them, years of experience telling him something was wrong. He looked from Sean to Lawlor and back. 'Everything OK?'

'Everything's fine,' said Sean, shoving Lawlor towards him. 'Arrest him for the abduction and murder of Karen Green and the abduction and false imprisonment of Louise Russell.'

'Any evidence?'

'Yes,' Sean replied. 'He ran.'

'He's gone fucking mad,' Lawlor said, speaking loud enough to ensure everyone heard him. 'He tried to kill me – look at my fucking neck. He was gonna kill me.'

'Shut up and get moving,' growled Donnelly. 'You've only got yourself to blame. You know better than to run from the police.'

'But I ain't done nothing.'

'Well, well,' Donnelly said, 'an innocent man! And I thought I was the last of that dying breed.'

'Whatever,' Lawlor replied. 'Do what you got to do, just keep that maniac away from me. I'll tell you anything you want to know, but keep him away from me.'

Sally and Anna watched as Donnelly frogmarched Lawlor towards the waiting cars, flanked by DCs O'Neil and McGowan, Sean and Zukov walking behind them. The streetlights made them all look jaundiced. Donnelly manhandled Lawlor into the back of his car, pushing the top of his head down with his hand and slamming the door. Sally noticed the serious faces, the usual signs of relief and joviality after an arrest conspicuous by their absence.

'Everything all right?' she asked Donnelly.

'Aye,' he answered. 'We eventually found them on the other side of the railway embankment. Everyone's OK.'

'That's not what I meant.' Donnelly glanced towards Sean and rolled his eyes. She grabbed his forearm. 'I should have been there. I should have come with you, not stayed here hiding with the cars.'

'No, you shouldn't have,' he insisted. 'You're not ready yet. Don't try to rush it, you'll do more damage than good. Take your time. It'll come.'

'All the same—'

'Sally,' Sean interrupted her, 'I want you, Maggie and Stan

to spin his bedsit. If you find anything interesting, get hold of forensics and keep me informed. Dave, you and Paulo get this idiot back to Peckham and book him into custody. I'll interview him later.' Sally and Donnelly nodded their understanding.

'I'd like to come with you,' Anna said, appearing at his shoulder. 'To help you to prepare and do the interview.'

'Out of the question,' he replied. 'Go with Sally and search the bedsit if you want to be involved. Look through his things and see what you can learn.'

'But the letter from the assistant commissioner clearly states—' Sean held his hand up to stop her.

'I don't have time to discuss this with the committee,' he snapped. 'We can talk about it later.' He turned his back on her and walked to his car. She took a step after him, but Sally caught her arm and gently pulled her back, shaking her head.

'Let it go,' she said softly. 'Now is not the time to fight this battle.'

'Is he always this rude?'

'Only if he likes you,' Sally told her.

Deborah Thomson's eyes opened slowly before surrendering to the fog of chloroform and flickering shut, then bursting wide open again as her brain deciphered the hazy images it had been sent, recognizing danger and the need to fire the body alert. Her head and torso jerked in all directions, desperately trying to make sense of the near-darkness that surrounded her, her eyes growing increasingly accustomed to the gloom. She felt the mattress beneath her and the duvet on top of her rubbing against bare skin. She slid a hand tentatively under the duvet and confirmed her worst fears, that her clothes had been taken. Choking back tears of panic, she squinted into the darkness and cocked her head to one side, listening for a sound, any sound. A shuffling noise somewhere in the room made her freeze. She tried to focus on the source of the sound, but something was obscuring her view. Slowly and carefully she stretched out a hand, gently waving it from side to side, as if the thing she searched for was more ethereal than solid, its distance away impossible to judge in the poor light. Finally her fingers felt the unmistakeable cold of metal. Her fingers coiled around thin steel as her face came closer to investigate, hundreds of small squares spreading left and right, leading to more walls of squares and above her the same terrible pattern. The fingers of her other hand grabbed at the wire and gripped it hard as she realized what the squares were, that she was locked in a cage.

Suddenly she found it difficult to breathe, the enforced confinement inducing claustrophobia for the first time in her life. She began to shake the walls of her prison, praying the structure would collapse and free her, but all she did was prove to herself the solidity of her surrounds and the futility of attempting escape. She released the wire and retreated to the corner of the cage, pulling the duvet over her nakedness, giving in to tears of despair, until a voice turned her to stone.

'Don't be frightened,' it said, 'you're not alone.' It was the voice of a woman, quiet and gentle, unthreatening. 'My name's Louise. What's yours?' She couldn't answer, her fear now mixed with shock and bewilderment. 'It's OK,' the voice explained. 'He can't hear us, or at least I don't think he can. What's your name?'

'Deborah. My name's Deborah. Why are we here? Who is he?' Her breaths were coming fast and sharp as she tried to control her anxiety.

'I don't know,' Louise confessed, 'but he's dangerous. I think he may have . . .'

'May have what?'

'Nothing. It doesn't matter. The important thing is that our only hope of getting out of here is by working together.'

'How?' Deborah asked, barely able to comprehend the conversation she was having with a stranger she couldn't even see properly. Two women locked in animal cages planning their salvation.

'At first he'll treat you well.'

'You call this *well*?' she snapped.

Louise understood her anger and ignored her reaction. 'He'll let you out, to use the toilet and wash. After a few days he'll even give you clean clothes. Listen, when he comes down here, I think he leaves the door to wherever we are open. It leads outside, I'm sure it does. I've seen the sunlight and smelled the fresh air. When he gets you out of your cage—'

'This isn't *my* cage,' she snapped again, 'this is *his* cage. I'm locked in his cage.'

'I'm sorry. You're right. When he lets you out of his cage, that's when you have to do it.'

'Do what?'

'He's not very big or strong. He'll give you a tray with food on. Use that tray to attack him and then get the key to my cage from his tracksuit trouser pocket and let me out. Together we can overpower him and lock him in his own damn cage and escape – call the police and lead them straight to the bastard.'

Deborah shook her head involuntarily. 'You're mad. It'll never work and then it'll be worse for me.' She squinted as the other woman began to come into focus, her similarity to herself painfully obvious, as was the fact she wore only her underwear and had no mattress or covers. She looked like she had dark patches on her face.

'Listen to me,' Louise urged her. 'I'm sorry, but you need to know. There was another, before me. Her name was Karen Green. By the time he brought me here she already looked like I do now. I sat in this cage and I watched him beat her and rape her – and not just once. Then the night before he brought you, he took her away. She never came back.'

'Oh my God, no. I read something about her in the papers. They found her in the woods. She'd been strangled. He killed her. I have to get out of here. I have to get out of here now.'

'You can't,' Louise insisted, her voice raised above Deborah's increasing panic. 'Not yet. We have to work together.'

'No. I'll do what he wants. I'll make him think I like him,' she argued, 'and he'll let me out of here and then when I see a chance I'll get away from him. He's already killed somebody. If I attack him, he'll kill me too.'

'Look at me,' Louise insisted. 'I've tried all that, please believe me, I've tried, but it makes no difference. I am what you will become. Nothing you do can change that.'

'No.' Deborah refused to accept it. 'There must be a better way.'

'There isn't,' Louise answered, 'and unless you believe me, unless you do what I tell you, we're both going to die. He'll kill us both.'

Shortly after eleven p.m. Sean and Sally prepared to begin the interview of Jason Lawlor. Sean had wanted a woman present to try and make Lawlor as uncomfortable as possible, so that he could read the signs he would be unwittingly sending – guilt, remorse, excitement, ambivalence. Innocence? Sally's heart had dropped when he'd asked her, but she'd managed not to show it.

Sean pressed the red button on the twin-cassette machine that would record the interview. A loud, shrill buzzing sound filled the room for about five seconds, followed by silence. Sean cleared his throat and took a breath before he began: 'I am Detective Inspector Sean Corrigan and the other officer present is . . .'

Sally introduced herself. 'Detective Sergeant Sally Jones.'

'We are interviewing . . . could you state your name for the tape, please?'

Lawlor spoke without looking at the recording machine,

a sign he was a veteran of taped police interviews. 'Jason Lawlor,' he answered, sounding bored already.

'Jason,' Sean continued, 'I must remind you that you are still under caution and don't have to say anything unless you wish to do so, but if you fail to mention something that you later rely on in court, an inference can be drawn from that. Do you understand?'

Lawlor shrugged his shoulders.

'You need to tell me if you understand.'

'Yeah, I understand, OK?'

'You also have the right to free and independent legal advice. You have the right to consult with a solicitor before, during or after this interview, and this can be done in person or over the telephone, do you understand?'

'Yes.'

'So far you haven't asked to speak with a solicitor and you haven't consulted with one and there are none present in the interview. Are you sure you want to continue without one present?'

'I don't need a solicitor. I ain't done nothing.'

'Well, if you change your mind just let me know and I'll stop the interview and arrange it, OK?'

'Whatever.'

'Fine. The date is Friday the seventh of April and the time is eleven oh five p.m. I am now starting the interview. Jason, do you know why you're here?'

'Yeah, because you ain't got a clue who killed that woman so you thought you'd stitch me up for it.'

Sean looked down at the table and then straight into Lawlor's eyes. 'You're here because I believe you abducted Karen Green on the morning of Thursday the thirtieth of March, and then killed her one week later. I also believe you've abducted Louise Russell and that you're holding her against her will.'

'No you don't.'

'It's late and I'm tired,' Sean told him. 'I'm not here to play games, so why don't you just answer my questions, OK?'

'You know I've got nothing to do with this.'

Sean let the oppressive silence hang for a while, guessing it would intimidate Lawlor. 'You're a registered sex offender, aren't you, Jason?'

'What of it? I've done my time, paid my debt to society.' A sly smile spread across his lips.

'But you haven't been signing on, have you? You've missed your last two appointments.'

'So send me back to prison then. There's nothing for me outside anyway. You think anyone's gonna give me a job or rent me a decent place to live? Course they're fucking not. I'm better off inside.'

'Don't worry about that – you're going back inside. But right now I need to know where you were the Thursday before last.'

'Eight days ago? I can't remember eight days ago. I was probably pissed somewhere.'

'OK, try one day ago – last night, when Karen Green was taken into Three Halfpenny Wood and killed – strangled to death. Where were you then?'

'I was pissed, in some pub in Sydenham.'

'Is that going to be your answer to everything, that you were pissed and can't remember?'

'Probably.'

Sean leaned back in his chair, studying Lawlor, looking for a way in. 'The two women who have been taken look the same: white, late twenties, slim, short brown hair, attractive.' He saw a flicker of interest when he said attractive. 'They could have been sisters, twins even. Why is it important that they look the same? Why is that important to you?'

'To me?' Lawlor snapped. 'No, not to me. I told you, this ain't got nothing to do with me.'

'The woman we found, Karen Green, she'd been raped and sodomized. There was a significant amount of semen in her. Whoever raped her didn't use a condom.'

'If you've got his spunk then check it for DNA and you'll know it's not me.'

'That takes time. I haven't got time. You need to answer my questions now.'

'I am answering your questions, but I don't know nothing!'

'Your last rape conviction, I looked it up. You didn't use a condom.'

'So?'

'That's pretty unusual for a rapist.' He emphasized rapist.

'Maybe.'

'And you used artifice to get into the house. You tricked her, told her you were there to read her meter. We checked our records, Jason. You're the only one in this area with form for using artifice.'

'So somebody's copying me. Maybe I told someone how well it worked. No need to break in. No need to drag them into a car. I must have an admirer.'

'No use of a condom. Previous for using artifice to gain entry. Previous for rape. Can't account for your movements when either woman was taken or for when Karen Green's body was dumped. Failed to attend your registered sex offenders' appointments. Things don't look good for you, Jason.'

'Do the fucking DNA tests,' Lawlor almost shouted. 'Why are you pissing around with these stupid questions? It weren't me.'

'We will, Jason, don't worry. We'll do the tests and then you'll be dead in the water and all your lies will be shown to be exactly that.'

'What are you talking about?'

'The crime you were convicted for – not using a condom was a pretty stupid mistake, don't you think? Leaving us your DNA.'

'It wasn't a mistake, it was something I had to do.'

'What do you mean, "had to do"?'

'You're a man, you know what I mean.'

'No. No I don't.'

'Then what about you?' he asked Sally, who looked shocked at being suddenly involved in the interview, as if she'd been awoken from her daydreaming.

Sean intervened. 'You should stick to answering questions,' he told Lawlor, 'and let me ask them. So I'll ask you again: why was it something you had to do?'

'I needed to feel myself inside them. I needed to, you know, release myself inside of them. I needed to feel myself come inside of them. It's like it makes it last for days, you understand? If I use a Durex then I take myself with me when it's over, but if I come inside them then I can smell them on me for days. I can think about my come being still inside them days after and that helps me . . . helps me control my needs.'

Sally felt as if she was going to be sick. She couldn't bring herself to look into his face, her eyes wandering around the room, but never resting on Lawlor.

'And how does that make you feel?' Sean asked.

'It makes me feel good. It makes me feel really good.'

Sean could see Lawlor was reliving past experiences, his lips full and flushed red with blood, his eyes wide as if he was watching himself committing his own crimes with unbridled pleasure.

'Just good?' Sean wanted to pull him out of his trance, to keep him talking.

'No. Powerful. In control. It's like a drug from heaven – once you've had a taste, there's no going back, no stopping. When you're inside them, you're accepted, you understand? You're wanted. You're alive and you're loved, but . . .' His excitement seemed to fade as fast as it had grown.

'But?' Sean encouraged.

'But, when it's over, you feel ashamed and embarrassed.

You just want to tell them you're sorry and to run away, to get as far away as you can. And the fear, the fear is crushing, you know? It makes you feel weak, which is why the urges come back, which is why you know you're going to do it again, to not feel ashamed any more, to feel accepted and loved, even if it's only for a few minutes.'

'Is that why you've changed the way you operate? Is that why you keep them for days, so you can feel accepted for longer, loved for longer?'

'I've told you, I've got nothing to do with this. I would never kidnap anyone. That takes planning. I never mean to do what I do. I just see someone and the needs come back, I can't help myself. I follow them home, and if they're alone I try to trick my way inside and then I do bad things. But I didn't take these women – I've never taken any women – I never would.'

'Why?' Sally asked.

'I like doing it to them in their houses.' Somehow Sally managed to keep looking him in the eyes, despite her disgust.

Sean studied the man in front of him, a scared opportunistic offender, triggered by his surroundings, incapable of planning and forethought, the complete opposite of the man who killed Karen Green and the man who would undoubtedly kill Louise Russell, unless he could find him and stop him.

After a few seconds of silence Sean spoke. 'I've no more. Sally?'

She shook her head to clear her thoughts. 'No. No questions.'

'Is there anything you'd like to say, Jason, or to have me clarify for you?'

'No. Just make sure you get me back to Belmarsh in time for dinner tomorrow, will you? It's cod and chips on Saturdays. I don't want to miss that.'

'Don't worry,' said Sean, 'you'll be back in time for your

fish and chips. This interview is concluded.' He pressed the off button to stop the recording and leaned across the interview table putting his face close to Lawlor's. 'And I hope you fucking choke on them.'

He stomped out of the interview room, closely followed by Sally. The on-duty custody sergeant calling after them: 'What d'you want me to do with your prisoner?'

'Put him back in his cell for the night. He'll be recalled to prison in the morning.'

Once they were out of the busy custody area and in a quiet corridor, Sally grabbed his arm and stopped him walking away. He spun to face her, knowing he was about to be cross-examined himself.

'You knew he didn't do it, all along. As soon as Zukov told you about him you knew he wasn't our man.'

'I had some doubts.'

'No you didn't. You knew it wasn't him.'

'He looked a decent suspect. We had to at least arrest and interview him.'

'Why?' Sally persisted. 'When you knew it wasn't him. We've just wasted an entire evening chasing after the wrong man, and all the time you knew it.'

Sean pulled away from her as gently as he could and started walking. 'Jesus, Sally, leave it alone, will you.'

'I'm trying to understand what's going on.'

'He was an arrest, wasn't he? That's what the top brass want to see – that we're making arrests, progressing the investigation, that people are helping us with our inquiries.'

'Not if we're arresting the wrong people.'

'Give me a break, Sally. They don't care what's going on as long as they've got something to tell the media, as long as they've got something to build a load of bullshit around. So Lawlor wasn't our man – who cares? He served a purpose. By arresting him we've bought ourselves twenty-four hours of not being interfered with, maybe more.'

Sally struggled to keep pace with him as they strode along the corridor. Again she took hold of his arm to stop him, spinning him around and fixing eye contact. 'No, no, that's not it,' she insisted. 'There's more to it.' He said nothing as she searched in his eyes for answers. 'He gave you something, didn't he, something you were missing, something you needed, something you couldn't find in yourself?'

'I don't know what you're talking about.'

He tried to walk away, but Sally kept a firm grip on his arm. 'You're trying to think like him, aren't you? You're trying to think like the man we're after. You've been doing it since you agreed to take the missing persons case . . . But I still don't understand why you would go after someone like Lawlor.'

'Because I thought he could fill in the gaps, all right,' he finally confessed, knowing Sally wouldn't give in. 'I have to be able to think like him if we're going to find him quickly. I . . . I know so much about him already, but there were too many gaps. I needed to know why he's really doing this. Love? Hate? Anger? Power? Acceptance? Lawlor helped fill some of those gaps.'

Sally found herself nodding, both glad and afraid to be right. 'Are you sure it's a good idea to start thinking like he does? To have the likes of Lawlor going around inside your head?'

'I don't have a choice. If Louise Russell is to have any chance, then I don't have a choice. Anyway,' he tried to reassure her, 'I'll be fine.'

'I guess that depends on what's going on in your head already, doesn't it?'

Sean sighed, almost relieved to have someone to confide in, to share the burden of his innermost thoughts and fears. 'I'm just trying to think like him, not become him. I'll be fine, don't worry.' They started walking again.

'I hope you know what you're doing, guv'nor.'

'Yeah, well, me too.'

'And Lawlor – did you get what you want from him?'

'More or less.'

'Which was?'

'His motivation.'

'And now you know?'

'Not exactly, but I'm closer. I won't know exactly until all the pieces fall into place, that moment when everything suddenly makes sense. But Lawlor helped, for sure. I know that their actions are largely underpinned by the same need to feel powerful but at the same time to be accepted and loved. Lawlor achieved that by raping women in their own homes, women he'd stumbled across and made an instant decision to attack. Our man wants the same, but his primary way of getting what he wants is by keeping the women. The question is, why does he do that? Why does he have to keep them?'

'To make the experience last longer?' Sally guessed.

'That's what I thought, at first. Made good sense, but now I'm not so sure. I don't think he wants to make it last as long as he can, I think he wants to make it last a very specific period of time.'

'A week?'

'Give or take twelve hours, yes.'

'Why?'

'Acceptance and love.'

'I don't understand?'

'I think, and I'm only guessing, but I think he's reliving a relationship he had with someone, a relationship that might have lasted as little as a week or so, but one in which he was happy – accepted and loved. The two women he's taken look the same, remember?'

'An ex-girlfriend?'

Sean shrugged his shoulders. 'That would be my guess. Now all I have to do is work out how to use it to help me find the son-of-a-bitch before it's too late.' They'd almost reached the main office entrance. 'Do me a favour, Sally, keep this between the two of us, OK?'

'Sure. If that's what you want.'

'It is,' he told her and walked into the still busy main office.

Through the Perspex windows of his own office he could see Anna, waiting for him.

'How did the interview go?' said Donnelly. 'Did he cough for it?'

'No,' Sean answered dismissively. 'It's not him. We need to think again. What's she still doing here?' He jutted his chin towards his office.

Donnelly shrugged his shoulders. 'Said she wanted to wait for you.'

'Great.' Sean headed for his door, entering without speaking.

'How did the interview go?' she asked.

Sean exhaled as he sat heavily in his chair. 'It's not him, if that's what you mean.'

'But you knew that already, didn't you?'

'Bloody hell, not you as well.'

'It was clear from his previous crimes it wasn't him.'

'Wait a minute. You need to slow down a little. He could easily have been our man. His previous crimes had enough similarities to make him a viable suspect. Don't try and be too clever. That's a sure way of fucking things up. Anyway, are you planning on wasting the whole weekend here?'

'I wanted to hear about the interview.'

'And now you have.'

'I'd like to listen to it in full, if that's OK with you.'

'Why, given that Lawlor's not our man?'

'For research purposes. He's still a serial sex offender, even if he didn't commit these particular crimes. I'd like to listen to what he had to say.'

'How d'you know he said anything?'

'Let's just say I have faith in your powers of persuasion.'

Suddenly he was suspicious of her. Why had she been attached to the investigation? Was her brief to help him – or to study him? Whatever her motive, he was beginning to admire her persistence. Clearly she wasn't going to be shaken loose easily.

'Sure,' he said, and tossed her a working copy of the taped interview from his desktop. 'That's the only copy I have, so don't lose it. I'll need it for the unused material schedule.'

'Thank you.'

'Don't mention it.' He got up and put on his raincoat. 'I'm done. I'm going to go home and remind myself what my wife looks like. I recommend you do the same. Back here tomorrow, six a.m., if you can stomach it.'

'I'll be here,' she assured him.

'Yes,' he answered, 'I had a feeling you would be.'

Thomas Keller sat alone at his kitchen table scooping baked beans straight from the saucepan he'd heated them in, swallowing without chewing or tasting, eating to remove the distraction of hunger, not for pleasure, his mind needing to concentrate elsewhere – the cellar and the woman it held. He looked up at the clock hanging from the wall – it was almost midnight, too late to pay her a visit – that would be rude, not the right thing to do. Better to let her sleep and then see her in the morning, once she'd had time to rest and realize this was all for her own good. He smiled happily when his eyes alighted on the freshly washed women's garments drying on the clothes horse in the corner of the room, just as they had done a few days before, after he'd taken them from Karen Green. They were the only clothes he'd washed for weeks. He could hardly wait to see the joy in her face when he gave her the clothes that would by then be freshly pressed and ironed.

He grabbed the saucepan from the table and tossed it into

the already full sink, the sound of china breaking not registering in his thoughts as he took the last clean fork from his shambolic cutlery drawer and negotiated his way through the house to the back door. Picking up an economy-sized tin of cheap cat-food, he slowly and quietly opened the door and stepped into the cold night, searching the trees and hedges that surrounded the back of the single-storey house for the bright eyes that shone in the dark, waiting for him. He tapped the fork on the side of the tin, the sound penetrating deep into the woodland. He made a 'pssst, pssst,' sound as he dug out the solidifying food and slopped it into chipped, dirty bowls that littered the area at the back of the house. It wasn't long before he heard the faint rustling sounds in the hedges and saw the occasional blink of mirrored eyes as the stray cats examined him from a safe distance, sniffing the air scented with an easy meal.

'Come on,' he encouraged them softly. 'Pssst, pssst, pssst, come on. Come and get some supper, pssst, pssst, pssst.' But they kept their distance, circling him in the darkness, calling to each other, unwilling to show themselves to him, sensing something in him they feared. He grew impatient waiting for them to approach. 'Don't you want this food? Not good enough for you? Ungrateful demons is what you are. Fine – have it your way.'

He threw the tin into the bushes, the noise of scattering paws and catcalls echoing off the walls as he went from bowl to bowl, kicking them in all directions, the feeling of rejection crashing over him like a foaming tidal wave.

As he stormed back inside, slamming the door, the feelings stirred memories of the last time he had seen the mother who abandoned him, almost eight years ago, just before he'd turned twenty. Emily Keller had made contact with him through the Internet, telling him she was proud that he was now a man and that he'd got himself a job with the Post Office. She'd told him how sorry she was that she'd abandoned him and betrayed him, but she had been so young. She had changed since then – could they meet and start again? He'd agreed to meet her in a café in Forest Hill.

On the morning he'd arranged to see her he'd been glad to wake with a developing cold, his throat sore and the mucus building in his nasal passages. He remembered showering and dressing, taking his time to make himself look as presentable as he could, combing his hair and dressing in his best clothes, his one and only suit that he'd last worn three years earlier for his interview with the Post Office. He'd walked along the busy morning streets, oblivious to the people he passed, ignoring their looks of surprise as he occasionally bumped shoulders, until he reached the café they'd arranged to meet in, the type that has photographs of the food on the glossy but sticky menus.

He recognized her from the pictures she'd attached to her emails: still relatively young, in her mid-thirties, slim with long dark hair that framed her pretty face. She sat at a window table, nervously toying with a steaming cup of tea, looking up as he entered, recognition sparking in her eyes, despite not having seen him since he was four years old, when she handed him over to Social Services for voluntary adoption before sinking into a life of drugs and petty crime – although she'd promised him those days were long gone. He hadn't sent her a picture of himself, but clearly she knew the young man who had just walked into the café was her abandoned son. A smile spread across her lips and her eyes sparkled with happiness as she rose from the table and smoothed her clothes, wanting to look her best, wanting to make a good impression. He walked towards her without smiling, drawing the mucus down from his nasal cavity and into the back of his throat before contracting the muscles in his neck to push the green ball of secretion into his mouth, rolling it around and tasting the years of bitterness it represented, all the painful memories she'd caused and all the hate he felt for her. When he was close enough to kiss her he filled his lungs as full as he could and spat the phlegm directly into her face, her smile replaced with a look of shock and repulsion. He turned and walked out of the café without saying a word. As the door closed behind him he could hear her screams of revulsion and rejection. He never saw or spoke to her again.

8

Saturday morning, four thirty a.m., and the iPhone's alarm chirped quietly on the bedside cabinet, barely enough noise to wake any living creature, but it was sufficient to stir Sean from his shallow sleep, his constantly whirring mind never allowing real rest to come. He grabbed the phone on the second chirp and turned it off, quickly checking to make sure it hadn't woken Kate. The initial shock of awakening soon gave way to a feeling of dreadful tiredness that threatened to drag him down into unconsciousness. He'd been here a hundred times before and would probably be here a hundred more times before he could ever dream of returning to anything like normal sleep patterns. He knew he had to move now or risk falling into the sort of sleep he wished he'd managed during the night, pulling the warm duvet from his body, exposing its near-nakedness to the cold air of the room. He sat on the edge of his bed rubbing the back of his neck, the muscles in his torso flexing and twitching to life, the lines of his conditioned body as prominent as those of any middle-weight boxer.

Once his mind had caught up with where he was and why he was awake so early, he stood unsteadily and headed for the bathroom, flipping up the toilet seat and waiting to urinate, but it took a long time to come and only lasted a few seconds, warning him of his own dehydration and reminding him of the shortness of his sleep. He decided against flushing and risking waking Kate or the girls and headed for the shower, setting the temperature at lukewarm and stepping in straight away, the cold water bringing him back to life. He washed and dressed quickly and went downstairs feeling passably human. He was aware that the feeling would only last a few hours and then the rest of the day would be a struggle to hold mind and body together and he'd have to push through the pain barrier more than once.

As he sat in the quiet kitchen, sipping black coffee and pushing a barely touched slice of toast around the plate he sensed Kate's presence approaching long before he heard or saw her. A few seconds later she drifted into the room wrapped in his old dressing gown and sat down opposite him, her swollen eyes and puffy cheeks hiding her natural attractiveness. Sean smiled in spite of his tiredness and slid his coffee across the table.

She lifted it and took a mouthful, murmured, 'Thanks.'

'My pleasure,' he said. 'What you doing up so early?'

'Seeing you.'

'I'm flattered.'

'You should be. How's the case going?'

'It's not,' he answered, prompting her to look up from the coffee that used to be his, recognizing the traces of stress in his voice.

'Oh,' she said. 'How come?'

'I don't know. I can't seem to get inside this one's head.'

'Doesn't sound like a good place to be anyway.'

'Yeah, well it's the best place to be if I'm going to find him quickly.'

They were quiet for a while, then Kate spoke again.

'You look really tired.'

'I am really tired.'

Determined to hide the fear and anxiety she felt every time he walked out the front door, she kept her tone neutral as she asked, 'Will you catch him soon?'

'I'll have him within a week.'

'You must be confident.'

'I'm close,' he confided, 'I just need to figure out his motivation . . . I mean his primary motivation. I'm nearly there, but the answer keeps slipping out of reach. It'll all come together soon though, and then I'll find him.'

'What part of his motivation don't you understand?'

'Why he keeps them.' He ran a hand through his hair. 'I have theories and ideas, but I don't know for sure and I can't afford to guess. If you pushed me, I'd say he keeps them to remind himself of an old girlfriend, probably one he had a serious relationship with. That's the best I've got so far, but it doesn't feel completely right and I don't know why.'

'Because it's not right,' she said matter-of-factly.

'Why's that?'

'Women keep things to remind them of what they once had or what they once were: photographs, old dresses, their kids' old clothes, their husband's old dressing gowns.' She tugged the gown she was wearing for extra emphasis. 'Men don't. Men collect things to remind them of what they want but can't have: models of aeroplanes, badges of old sports cars, pictures of Page Three girls,' she added with a grin, but Sean wasn't smiling any more. He knew he'd been handed an important piece of the jigsaw. Now all he needed was to find out where it fitted.

Sean closed his eyes, his head slumping backwards. 'Jesus Christ, of course. Of course.'

'You OK?' Kate asked.

'You're right,' Sean told her. 'You're right. He's trying to create something he never had but always wanted – maybe even believed he had, but didn't. I have to go.' He grabbed his coat, its pockets already loaded with the things he'd need for the day, and headed for the front door. 'I'll call you later,' he promised.

'No you won't,' she whispered when he was gone, a familiar fluttering feeling returning to her chest. 'You never do.'

Donnelly arrived in the office shortly after five thirty a.m. It was deserted except for the regular cleaner, who dragged a noisy hoover around behind him, emptying wastepaper bins into his white bin-liner as and when he found them. Donnelly gave him nod and a smile, hiding his frustration at not being totally alone. He sat at his desk and pretended to be reading while he waited for the cleaner to reach the far end of the office and disappear through the swing doors. 'And I thought I had a shit job,' he muttered to himself as he pushed his weight off the worn-out wooden chair, its green cloth torn and frayed, what little padding it ever had long since flattened. Furtively he wandered around the office, examining each and every desk, flicking through his colleagues' in and out trays, reading any memos left on desks and flicking through diaries that hadn't been locked away, not moving from a desktop until he was happy he knew what that detective was up to: how much work they had on, whether they'd been keeping up with their actions and CPS memos and, most importantly of all, whether they were holding anything back from him, business or personal. As far as he was concerned this was his Murder Investigation Team every bit as much as it was Sean's and it was his absolute duty to keep abreast of everything that was happening within its borders. Any detective sergeant worth his salt would do the same.

Eventually he came to Sally's desk. It at least appeared neat and organized, but he was well aware she'd been far from herself since the incident with Sebastian Gibran and as her only fellow DS on the team it was his responsibility to make sure she was coping. All it needed was one person to make a serious mistake and the whole investigation could go down the pan. He thumbed through her diary first, the standard four-by-three-inch black Metropolitan Police Friendly Society diary everyone seemed to receive each year. What he saw was page after page of emptiness – no notes, no meetings, no appointments, nothing. Technology had moved on, but detectives were creatures of habit and had been using these little diaries to scribble notes in for decades. They were still faster and easier to use than any mobile phone or tablet, so an empty diary suggested troubled waters. Her in and out trays were the same, just a few old memos and CPS requests that appeared to have been largely ignored, nothing current or apparently important. Clearly Sean had been keeping her away from too much work or responsibility, trying to protect her, buy her some time to fully recover. He was disappointed that she hadn't felt able to confide in him, but shrugged it off, promising himself that he'd keep an even closer eye on her in future, for her sake and everybody else's. Making sure her diary was back exactly where she'd left it, he headed for Sean's open door.

Donnelly slipped into Sean's office and began to search through the piles of papers that were beginning to form on his two desks, but they contained little of interest and told him nothing he didn't already know. Sean was too long in the tooth to leave anything sensitive or interesting on public view. He pulled at Sean's top drawer, one of three hiding under his desk, the same wooden set that everyone in the office would have, but it was locked, as he'd expected. He tried the others and found them locked too. 'No problem,' he announced to the empty room, and pulled a set of keys from his trouser pocket, fanning them out in his hand until he located the master key that fitted each and every wooden drawer under each and every desk in the Met. Whistling to himself, he jiggled the long, thin piece of metal into the small slot of the top drawer. After a few seconds he was able to rotate the key through one-hundred-eighty degrees signifying the drawer was open. There would be no need to check the other drawers, he already knew they contained little more than stationery and reference books.

He slid the top drawer open and was relieved to see his prize waiting for him – Sean's leather-bound journal, the type of thing you buy someone for Christmas when you can't think of anything else. But Sean had put his to good use and Donnelly knew it. 'And what secrets will you reveal today, my old friend?' he asked the book in his hands as he placed it on the desk and began to flick through the pages, skipping past things he'd already read, until he found scribbles and text he didn't recognize. 'Well hello and what do we have here?' It was as if he was partially entering Sean's mind, a conduit straight to his secret theories and innermost thoughts about this and other investigations. A baffling array of circled names, others crossed out, words of varying sizes, written in different styles as if a dozen people had contributed to the journal, strong, emotive words scrawled in different-coloured pens: love, anger, hate, jealousy, greed, possession, passion, fear, some circled and joined together with lines that snaked across the pages.

'You're either a madman or a genius,' Donnelly spoke to the absent Sean while turning the pages, finding the names of the victims, Louise Russell and Karen Green, one dead, one still missing, Green's name circled in a mixture of blue and red ink, Russell's circled in blue only. A myriad of words and colours, names and places squeezed themselves into every millimetre of the pages, almost completely indecipherable. Short questions covered other pages: *Why six/seven days? Why keep them? Why rape? Why violence? Why victs look same? Why same houses? Why kills? Why dump bodies naked? Why no remorse or compassion? Why woods? Why wooded car parks? Comfortable in woods? Lives in woods? Staying in comfort zone? Failed relationship? Covets them? Loves them? Motivation? Motivation? Motivation?*

'Jesus,' he said to himself, flicking through pages and pages of the rambling notes of an obsessed man on the edge. It crossed his mind Sean might be laying the groundwork for manufacturing early retirement on the grounds of a stress-related illness, but he knew the man better than that and he'd seen his manic scribbles in the past, usually just before he led the team to the man they were after. But they'd never been this frantic, this desperate.

A noise coming from the corridor on the other side of the double swing doors startled him. Hurriedly he replaced the journal in the drawer and slid it silently shut, turning the master key and locking it, then ghosting from the room back into the main office.

He managed to be a few steps clear as the double doors swung open and Anna walked in looking unreasonably fresh and alert, considering she could have had no more than three or four hours' sleep. He welcomed her with a broad smile, his moustache bending up at the ends. 'Good morning. Nice to have another early bird on the team.'

'I've always liked this time of day,' she said. 'It's quiet and peaceful – gives me the time and space I need to think.'

'And I thought it was because you were trying to impress me.'

'Maybe I am,' she answered with a falsely suggestive smile.

'Or maybe it's someone else you're trying to impress? Someone a little higher in rank?' She didn't answer. 'So,' he continued, 'you're a what . . . a criminal psychiatrist?'

'I certainly hope not,' she answered, 'and I'm sure you'd arrest me if I was.'

'You know what I mean.'

'No, I'm a psychiatrist and a criminologist, specializing in offender profiling. The FBI have been doing it for years, but it's relatively new to the police here. They've been somewhat resistant to the idea.'

'That sounds like us,' Donnelly teased her. 'So away you

go then: impress me – tell me all about the man we're looking for.'

'It's too soon to be accurate. I need more information, more time to study the case and previous case histories before I'd be willing to commit to a profile.'

'Come on,' Donnelly encouraged, 'it'll be between the two of us, nothing official.'

'OK,' she agreed with a sigh. 'Based on what we know so far, I believe he's white, probably small or slight – that's based on the fact he uses drugs to subdue his victims, which suggests he's not physically confident. He has a troubled past and was almost certainly abused or abandoned as a child, possibly both. I understand he appears to have no previous convictions, but I'm convinced he would have committed residential burglaries and other serious sexual assaults; perhaps he's just never been caught.'

'It's possible,' Donnelly partially agreed.

'This type of offender usually takes trophies from victims, but I believe that in this case the women themselves are his trophies, albeit perishable ones, ones he tires of and then disposes of with no regrets, pity or remorse – by then they are just objects to him.

'I imagine him to be a bit of a social misfit who lives alone. I can't see him forming any lasting relationships or tolerating an invasion into his private life, and his lack of confidence means he'll very much stay in his comfort zone, which in turn means he's almost certainly local. He knows these areas well. He sees them every day. They are his world and he's not going to start operating outside of that world.

'The fact the victims look very similar is interesting. I think they remind him of somebody, somebody he has genuine hatred for, possibly his mother, possibly because she failed to stop whatever abuse was happening to him – maybe it was his father who abused him or the mother's boyfriend.'

'Why doesn't he project his hatred directly to the abuser? Why the mother?' Donnelly asked.

'Transferred hatred or blame is not uncommon. He probably loved his mother, but had no relationship outside of the abuse with his abuser. To him, hating the person who actually abused him would be as pointless as you or I hating the wasp that stung us – there's no emotional attachment there. Love and hate are dangerously close to each other.

'There is of course a sexual element to his attacks, that I believe he displays all the common traits of those who commit such acts, in as much as it makes him feel powerful and in control, something he rarely is in the real world. His normal everyday life is a bit of a struggle for him. Not one of life's winners, you might say.'

Donnelly mimed applause. 'Very impressive. It's amazing what you can learn from books these days.'

'Actually most of my observations are based on my own clinical studies of serious offenders. Interviews with sexual predators and murderers. Some sane, some not.'

'Funnily enough, I've had a bit of experience of that myself.'

Their conversation was interrupted by Sean clattering through the double doors, a look of surprise and disappointment that he wasn't the first to arrive etched on his face.

'You two are early. Trying to impress someone?'

Donnelly and Anna almost laughed. The doors clattered again, kicked open by Sally, her hands full of bags and a tray of coffee in polystyrene cups. She dropped her bags on the floor and slid the tray on to the desk closest to their gathering.

'I didn't know who would be here yet so I bought a few,' she said, slumping into a chair.

'Nice one, Sally,' Donnelly said.

'Thank you,' Anna added.

'You look a little rough around the edges there, Sally,' Donnelly told her.

'Thanks. I love you too.'

'Just saying.'

'We're all going to look a lot worse by the time this is over, so put your collective vanities to one side if you can,' Sean rescued Sally. He helped himself to a coffee off the tray, unconcerned whether it was black, white, sweetened or otherwise, and took a swig. 'OK, while everybody's here who matters, we might as well catch up on where we are.'

'That'd be nice,' Donnelly chipped in.

'The way I see it, we have two, maybe three days before Louise Russell will be killed.' The coldness of the fact made even Sean uncomfortable with what he was saying. 'And when she dies I think it will only be a matter of days before he takes another.'

'A replacement?' Anna asked.

'I think so. We already know he's kept two hostages at the same time. It seems to be part of his modus operandi. It's reasonable to suppose he will want to again.'

'That would make some sort of sense,' agreed Anna.

'Hold on a minute,' Sally interrupted. 'If he replaces the ones he kills, then why hasn't he taken someone to replace Karen Green? She was killed almost thirty-six hours ago now.'

'He might have,' Sean confessed. 'All surrounding stations have been asked to report any missing persons of similar descriptions straight to us. If he's already taken someone and they get reported missing, we'll soon know about it.'

'And if no one reports them missing?' Donnelly asked.

'We wait for a body,' Sean answered – more cold truths. 'In the meantime, we're drawing on all the resources that can be spared. Featherstone's arranged for extra detectives to be assigned door-to-door inquiries over an expanded area and uniform are carrying out roadblocks close to both abduction locations and the body drop site, checking for suspects and witnesses. We've even got India 99 up and about looking for whatever it is helicopters look for. Plus there are uniform patrols, both foot and vehicles, searching for the sort of locations our man could be keeping the victims at, old smallholdings, abandoned factories and particularly anything underground – coal bunkers, cellars, bomb shelters, anywhere remote or concealed, but within a few miles of the crime scenes – our boy doesn't travel far.'

'You think he keeps them underground?' Anna asked, causing all eyes to fall on Sean.

'Yes. Dr Canning discovered what appears to be coal dust under the victim's finger and toe nails.'

'Oh, how I would like a few minutes alone with this bastard,' muttered Donnelly.

'Save the tough talk for when we've found him,' said Sean. 'Everybody happy?'

'Yeah, sure,' Sally answered tiredly.

'Sounds like a plan,' Donnelly acknowledged. Anna said nothing.

'One more thing,' Sean continued hesitantly, afraid of too many awkward questions about how he came by the information, remembering his ruthless breaking down of Douglas Levy. 'I think he's disguising himself as a postie. That's how he gets the doors open.'

'I've not seen anything to suggest that,' Sally argued.

'A new witness,' said Sean. 'He mentioned something that suggested it.'

'What?' Sally persisted.

'It's a long and very uninteresting story. Just take my word for it, he's pretending to be a postman, but let's keep that between us for the time being – I don't want to risk a detail like that leaking to the press, and let's not forget we still have the forensics from five different crime scenes to chase and then we have to cross-reference DNA and fingerprints from all scenes to be sure that this is indeed the same man at each.'

'It's the same man,' Anna said a little too loudly.

'Of course it is,' Sean said impatiently, 'but courts are a real pain in the arse about something called evidence. Theories are fine in the classroom, but not out here.'

Donnelly and Sally looked away, leaving Anna to her own private humiliation.

Sean continued: 'While we're all here I might as well say it – this investigation is turning into a monster. We've got the world and his wife out there looking for Louise Russell, but it won't feel like it to us. We'll be the ones stuck here till all hours, fighting through piles of reports, making phone calls, chasing up forensics, pestering potential witnesses, reading fucking useless intelligence reports and trying to fend off every unsolved murder in the last decade the powers-that-be try to dump on us. But be mindful, and make sure everybody on the team is mindful, that this investigation will be under the national microscope. Which means everybody needs to be on their best, please – no smoking at the crime scenes, no laughing and joking when the cameras are around and be damn careful what you say when you're talking on your mobiles – if we can eavesdrop on phone conversations, you can be sure the media can. If a conversation you had with the lab turns up in your favourite Sunday redtop, you'll know where it's come from. Everybody understand?' His audience of three nodded and grunted their understanding. 'Good.'

He was about to head for his office when Sally stopped him.

'What's this one about? Why's he doing it?'

'It's about acceptance,' he answered without hesitation. 'About finally having what he's always wanted, but until now could never have. It's about love – loving them and being loved by them.'

'Love!' Donnelly interrupted loudly and abruptly. 'This doesn't look like love to me – taking her out to the middle of some godforsaken wood in the middle of the night and squeezing the life out of her, then leaving the poor wee cow's body lying naked for a fucking dog to find. Which bit of that sounds like love to you?'

'I didn't say he was rational,' Sean explained. 'His perception of love and what it means is completely different from yours, but it's still ultimately about love. It's the one thing he covets more than anything else and it's the one thing he's never had.'

'Are we supposed to feel sorry for him?' sneered Donnelly. 'He's just another sick pervert who needs to be locked up with the general prison population for a few nights before they stick him in segregation. The other prisoners will soon make sure he gets justice.'

'Not sorry for what he is,' Sean answered, 'but maybe we should consider what may have happened to him to make him what he is now.'

'How do we know anything happened to him?' Donnelly persisted. 'Perhaps he just enjoys it?'

'This one's no Sebastian Gibran,' Sean spilled out, immediately glancing apologetically at Sally. 'He's a product of circumstance, not nature.'

'Aye, maybe, but all this love nonsense, I don't believe it and neither does she,' said Donnelly, indicating Anna.

'Really,' Sean said. 'Care to enlighten me?'

Anna cleared her throat. 'At this time it would be correct to say that I don't see any particular signs of love from offender to victims. I see transferred expressions of revenge and the need to feel powerful, hence the acts of sexual aggression and abuse. But no signs of empathy or affection.'

'What about the moisturizing cream and traces of perfume on the body? They were too fresh to have been applied before she was taken,' Sean argued.

'We don't know that they weren't the victim's own cosmetics,' Donnelly reminded him.

'Even if they were the victim's own, he still gave them to her or allowed her to have them. At the very least that shows a degree of empathy,' Sean explained.

'I don't think they are the victim's own cosmetics,' Anna said. 'I believe they'll turn out to be the brands used by whoever it is he has this hatred for.'

'Like his mother?' Donnelly suggested.

'Possibly his mother,' Anna agreed.

'You're wrong,' Sean snapped at them. 'Strands of what you're saying are probably true, but you don't understand him – you don't understand what motivates him, why he has to do what he does.' A tense atmosphere hung in the room until Sally broke the silence.

'So what's our next move?'

'Chase forensics and the door-to-door and wait for the tidal wave of information that's about to come our way,' said Sean. 'Speaking of which, I'll be in my office if anyone needs me.' He regathered his coat and headed for his small, partitioned room. Donnelly shook his head before burying it in a pile of information reports.

'I can't stand drinking from these things,' Sally told Anna, looking accusingly at her polystyrene cup. 'Come on, let's sneak off to the canteen and I'll treat you to a decent cup.'

Anna shrugged her shoulders. 'Why not?'

They made sure they were well clear of the inquiry office before speaking again, talking as they walked.

'So,' Sally asked, 'what do you make of Sean then? Intense, isn't he?'

'I was thinking more along the lines of arrogant and rude,' Anna replied.

'He doesn't do it on purpose,' Sally assured her. 'He can't help himself, not when he's absorbed in an investigation.' They walked in silence for a while as they passed a steady flow of uniform officers heading away from the canteen. 'He doesn't approach investigations in a way I've ever seen before

– he doesn't rely totally on the tangible evidence laid on a plate for him. He's more instinctive, intuitive.' They entered the already busy canteen and found a couple of seats at the end of a long table, where Anna sat alone, feeling self-conscious until Sally returned from the counter with two porcelain mugs of coffee. 'Where were we?'

'You were telling me about Sean.'

'Oh yeah,' Sally remembered, 'DI Corrigan.'

'Do you like working with him?' Anna asked.

'Like isn't necessarily the right word. It's more a case of being interesting, I suppose.'

'Because of his intuitions?'

'He can think like them, you know,' Sally blurted out. 'Not just how and when and where, but really think like them, in every detail. He seems to be able to understand why they do whatever it is they're doing. It can be a little unnerving at times, but he's able to control it, to turn it off and on.'

'Where is he, when he *turns on* this intuition? Can he be anywhere, or does he do it more often in certain places?'

'I think he can do it anywhere, but mainly at the crime scenes. He seems to get a lot of information from scenes that nobody else notices. Like I said – details.'

'Does he talk to himself when he's examining a scene?'

'That I haven't seen, but if you're there with him he'll tell you what he's seeing or feeling, like a kind of commentary.'

'Feeling?'

'What he believes the killer was feeling.'

'That's interesting.'

'Is that what all the questions are about, you find him interesting?'

'I suppose so.'

'Interesting or attractive?'

'Interesting from a clinical perspective. Anyway, I'm married and so is he.'

'Married, not dead,' Sally teased. 'And he is a good-looking man. Fit too, keeps himself in good shape. Don't tell me you haven't noticed, because I won't believe you.'

'He's not my type. I don't do men who have mood swings.'

'I know what you mean,' Sally agreed. 'Although there was a time when I had a bit of a crush on him, I have to admit. I found his intensity very attractive.'

Anna wasn't interested in the subject. 'Has he had a traumatic experience recently, perhaps a serious injury while on duty or something in his private life?'

Sally's smile fell away fast. 'No,' she said. 'Not as far as I know.'

'I'm surprised.'

'If it's injuries and post-traumatic stress you're looking for, then I'm your girl.'

'Excuse me?' said Anna, her face changing as the meaning sank in. 'Oh, I'm sorry, of course. I heard about what happened to you. It must have been terrible.' She didn't tell Sally about her role in assessing Sebastian Gibran, knowing it would destroy any trust there was between them. 'How are you coping?'

'I'm pretty much healed. Still get a little short of breath now and then, but I'll get there.'

'That's not what I meant.'

'I know it isn't,' said Sally, lowering her voice and looking around to ensure she wasn't being watched or overheard.

'Have you had any counselling?'

'No.'

'Why not?'

'Because I'm a cop. We don't do counselling, it's a sign of not coping and not coping's a sign you're not up to the job and that means failure. We don't do failure. Most of the people I work with are men, and the women I work with have been working with them so long they think like men. I guess I did a bit too, until . . . well, you know.'

'Nobody would judge you if you wanted help.'

'They wouldn't understand. If I was a man I'd probably think my scars were cool, showing them off every chance I got, on the beach, in the pool – you know how stupid men can be. They wouldn't need help, they'd be the talk of the office, a proper hero, and they'd love it. It's not like that for a woman. These scars make me ugly. They mark me as a victim.'

'You're neither ugly nor a vic—'

'Yes, I am,' Sally answered coldly. 'I'm both.'

Anna studied her for a while before trying to reach her. 'You really need to speak to someone, Sally. And I would like to be that someone. Just take it slowly, move at your own speed. I'm a good listener.'

'I'll think about it,' said Sally, standing up to leave. 'I need to get back to the office.' She gathered her belongings from the table and headed for the door.

Anna stared into her drink as if she might see answers swirling in the cup. It appeared she now had two new cases instead of one.

Alone in his office, Sean was oblivious to the noisy mixture of banter and business beyond his door as the rest of the team arrived for work. Already his eyes were red and tired from staring at the computer screen, reading through every crime report of stalking complaints recorded on the Crime Reporting Input System over the last two years.

He didn't look up as Donnelly entered with a stack of information reports, peering over his shoulder at the monitor. 'CRIS reports?' he enquired. 'Hoping to find something?'

'What?' said Sean, drifting out of his trance.

Donnelly indicated the screen. 'I was wondering what you were looking for.'

'Just an idea,' he answered. 'A possible angle.'

'Care to share?'

'If I'm right about him using the victims as substitutes for something he wants but can't have, then the thing he wants has to be a woman.'

'Naturally.'

'And if she's that important to him, he must have watched her, maybe even tried to approach her, made a bit of a pest of himself.'

'You mean stalked her?'

'It's a possibility. A good possibility. And maybe she became aware of it, got sick of him and reported it . . .'

'How far you going back?'

'A couple of years. If I use roughly the same description as our victims, I shouldn't hit too many. I can't use an exact description in case she's changed her appearance at some point.'

'Young, attractive women who've been stalked.' Donnelly raised an eyebrow. 'You're going to be a busy man.'

'Still, I reckon it's worth trying.'

'Say you're right,' Donnelly continued, 'about him wanting these women as replacements for someone else, for someone he . . .'

'Wants, but can't have,' Sean finished for him.

'Aye, that. What I don't get is why he doesn't just take the one he wants – do to her what he's done to the others.'

Sean looked confused. It seemed incomprehensible to him that Donnelly didn't understand. 'Because she's his god,' he said, as if stating the obvious. 'You don't kill your gods.'

'Aye.' Unconvinced, Donnelly nevertheless pretended it made sense to him. 'I'd best let you get on with it then.'

Sean didn't reply, his mind already elsewhere as he watched Donnelly leave. His fingers hovered above the keypad for a few seconds while he cleared his thoughts. When he was ready, he began to type the information for the search criteria into the machine. He pressed the key marked search, leaned back in his chair and waited, a tangible sense of excitement crawling up his spine, spreading through his stomach and chest, making his heart skip along like a flat stone skimmed over a still pond. After a few seconds the screen changed, the number in the top right-hand corner telling him during the last three years there had been over 250 reported cases of harassment, more commonly referred to as stalking, involving women of the description he'd entered. He felt the excitement rush from his torso, leaving the emptiness of disappointment.

'Too many,' he said to himself, knowing it could take him days to read all the reports properly and make phone calls to victims, witnesses, investigating officers – days he didn't have. He needed to narrow the search fields, but the fear of missing the one vital report momentarily paralysed him, his own reflection in the computer screen melting away and then reforming as that of Karen Green, her eyes open and staring, contrasting with the pale skin of her dead face, her image fading and being re-born on the screen as Louise Russell, her eyes pleading with him to find her. As her image solidified he could see it was already too late, her skin turning pale, dark, wet strands of hair sticking to her skin as brown leaves gently blew across her face.

'Their eyes,' he said to himself as the image of Louise Russell sank into the blackness of the screen and disappeared. 'You both have green eyes. He wouldn't change that, not the eyes.'

He added the eye colour to the descriptive search page and ran the inquiry again, the excitement mounting within him. Eyes nervously fixed in the top right-hand corner, he waited until the screen blinked once indicating that the search had been completed. The number of hits had been reduced to forty-three. It was still more than he'd bargained for, but manageable. He brought up the first crime report and began to read.

* * *

Thomas Keller stood at the top of the flight of stairs that led down into the darkness of the cellar. Barely able to control his excitement, he paused in the open doorway, listening for signs of danger, watching for a threatening shadow moving across the floor that could mean one of them was out of their cage and waiting for him. They were both strong, athletic young women – if they caught him by surprise they could do him serious harm, and he knew it – he feared it. Satisfied all was well, he began his descent, carefully balancing the food and drink on its tray, clean pressed clothes draped over his free forearm.

As he stepped into the room he only had eyes for the cage that held Deborah Thomson, a happy smile spread across his lips as he peered through the gloom at the shaking figure cowering under the filthy duvet he'd left for her. But he didn't see her terror, he saw Sam, safe now, safe in his care.

Sliding the tray on to the table behind the screen that he used to hang her new clothes over, he greeted her. 'Good morning. Do you mind if I put the light on?' She didn't answer. 'Good,' he continued, 'I can't really see what I'm doing without it.'

He reached out and pulled the cord, flooding the cellar with weak yellow light. Then he walked slowly towards Deborah, his hand held out in front of him, palm up to convince her he was no threat, and crouched next to her cage, still smiling as she pushed herself into the furthest corner, the duvet pulled up to her chin, her eyes wide open with incomprehension, like a deer just before the car that's going to kill it hits.

'Did you have a good sleep?' he asked. 'I hope the chloroform didn't make you feel too sick. I'm sorry I had to use it, but it was the only way to get you safely and quickly out of there. I know you'll forgive me, in time.' He rubbed his hands together nervously. 'Anyway, you'll probably want to clean yourself up and maybe try to eat something. You'll feel better if you can manage it. OK? Let's have you out of there then.'

He spoke as if they were on an awkward first date, but his words made her recoil, her feet desperately trying to push her further away, the wire of her prison imprinting a pattern of squares in her back.

'It's OK, it's OK,' he tried to soothe her, 'you won't have to stay in here too long, I promise. It's only to keep you safe until you're stronger, until you understand. We have to be careful because they'll be looking for you, trying to take you back, make you believe you're someone you're not. In time you'll understand what I've done for you – for us.'

Deborah's throat fluttered and pulsed as she repeatedly tried to swallow non-existent saliva, fear and nausea straining every muscle taut to the point where it felt as if they would snap, shock drawing the blood away from her non-vital organs, redirecting it to her brain in an effort to keep her conscious, turning her lips almost white and her skin grey.

Oblivious to her terror, he unlocked the cage door, swinging it open carefully so as not to alarm her. His face reddened slightly with excitement and anticipation, his lips swelling plump and purple as his eyes moved over the shape under the duvet, the familiar tightness returning to his groin as he remembered her shape and warmth – the soft skin of the woman under the bedding. Without thinking he found himself moving into the cage, his eyes growing larger and larger as the tightening in his trousers grew more and more uncomfortable, suddenly snapping out of his trance as instinct kicked in, warning him he was being reckless, putting himself in danger. He checked his hands and realized he was unarmed.

In a panic he stumbled backwards out of the cage, tugging at the stun-gun that was tangled in the pocket of his tracksuit, ripping the material as he finally pulled it free, panting and smiling with relief, looking back into the cage, seeing the recognition of what he was holding in her eyes. The feeling in his groin had faded away and again he felt in control of the woman and himself. He looked down at the stun-gun and back to her. 'Don't be afraid of this,' he said. 'It's not to hurt you, it's to keep you safe.'

'I don't want you to keep me safe. I want you to let me go.'

He hadn't been expecting her to speak and her words momentarily shocked him into silence, the smile still fixed on his face like a painted doll's. 'You shouldn't say things like that, Sam. I'm here to look after you.'

'I don't need anyone to look after me,' she answered, the aggression and bitterness in her voice obvious. 'All I need is for you to let me out of here and stop calling me Sam – my name is Deborah, Deborah Thomson.'

'No,' he insisted, trying to restrain his anger, 'that's what they want you to believe, but it's all lies. Your name is Sam. Don't you remember? It's me, Tommy. I told you I'd come back for you. So that we could be together, like we're supposed to be.'

'I don't know you,' she yelled, tears of anger and fear bursting through her frustration. 'My name is Deborah Thomson and I want to go home.'

'Shut up!' Face twisted in rage, he advanced towards her holding the stun-gun in front of him. 'Shut the fuck up! That's just their lies. You have to clean yourself of their lies and then you'll remember.'

Louise Russell watched from her cage, eyes darting between the two unevenly matched combatants, praying that Deborah would do as she had asked, knowing that his anger would be redirected to her, the way it had been when Karen Green was occupying the other cage. She remembered unwittingly playing a dangerous game with Karen's safety, and now Deborah was doing the same thing, pushing him ever closer to venting his anger on Louise. She prayed for Deborah to stop, her eyes never leaving him while her heart punched against her ribs, the sound echoing deafeningly loud in her head. 'Please stop, please be quiet,' she silently pleaded with Deborah, unaware that she was mouthing the words as she said them over and over again, waiting for Deborah to respond to his accusations. After a few seconds she realized Deborah had fallen silent, the relief causing her body to slump as she drew in a long, staggered breath. She listened to the silence, her eyes once again darting between the two of them, as something like calm spread through the cellar.

Finally he spoke. 'I'm sorry,' he told Deborah. 'I forgot: you've been through a lot. You must be tired.' He walked to the screen, his eyes never leaving her, and picked up the tray in his free hand, taking it back to the cage and sliding it in through the open door, then returning to the screen and, as carefully as he could, pulling her clothes from the metal frame, carrying them back across the room and placing them on the floor just inside the entrance to her wire prison before closing and locking the door. 'It's probably better if you get cleaned up a bit later, but you can wear the clothes – they're yours, after all. Your real clothes, not the ones they made you wear.' He searched her face for some sign of approval, but she merely stared back at him with unblinking bright green eyes. 'I'll leave you to get some rest.'

He hesitated at the entrance to her cage, expecting her to thank him or tell him she looked forward to seeing him again, but to his disappointment she said nothing.

'OK, well . . .' he said, to cover his embarrassment, 'I'll see you later.'

Turning the main light off, he scampered up the stairs, slamming and locking the door behind him.

Neither woman said anything. They waited, listening to the quiet sounds of the cellar, praying he wouldn't return. Louise knew his habits well by now – if he didn't come back immediately, he would be gone for hours. When she felt it was safe she exhaled a long slow breath, stale air she'd been holding in her lungs for what seemed like hours finally escaping.

'Deborah . . . Deborah you need to listen to me.'

'He's a fucking lunatic,' Deborah whispered.

'Yes, he is,' Louise agreed. 'He's a lunatic who's going to kill us both if we don't help each other escape.'

'You've said all this already. You want me to attack him when he lets me out of his fucking cage and grab his key and let you out. Overpower him together, right?'

'Yes. It's our only chance. You have to believe me.'

'It won't work. And then it'll be worse for me.'

Louise fell silent, thinking of a way to cut through Deborah's self-preservation instincts.

'I was you,' she said. 'Just a day or so ago – I was you. He gave me a mattress and a duvet, he let me clean myself and gave me food and drink. He gave me those clothes, Deborah. Those same clothes he's given you – he made me wear them.'

Deborah looked at the clothes on the floor of her cage. 'These?' she asked.

'Yes.'

Deborah picked up the pile of laundered items and threw them against the wire, kicking them away with her feet. 'I won't be part of this sick fucker's fantasy,' she said loudly, unconcerned who heard her, her South London accent as thick as her anger.

'No!' Louise tried to calm her. 'No, don't do that. We need the clothes, you have to wear them.'

'No fucking way.'

'We have to play along with him, make him think everything is exactly how he wants it to be. That's the only way he'll relax, so we can catch him by surprise.'

'You mean long enough for *me* to catch him by surprise and risk *my* neck.'

'We have no choice.'

'Yes, we do,' said Deborah, and looked away, signifying an end to the discussion.

There was another silence, then Louise spoke again.

'Soon he's going to start coming down here, Deborah, he's going to start coming down here and he'll come into my cage and he'll beat me and rape me – and you're going to have to watch, you're going to have to listen to me scream while he holds me down and . . . Soon after that he'll come and take me away, and you'll have to listen to me beg him not to take me, beg him not to kill me. And when I don't come back, you'll know what's happened. Then, soon after I disappear, he'll come down here and he'll come to you, Deb—'

'Stop it!' Deborah pleaded. 'I don't want to—'

'He'll come to you and he'll take those clothes off you and he'll take your duvet and your mattress. And then, when he brings another woman down here and puts her in this cage, you will become me, Deborah. You will become me.'

Louise could hear sobbing coming from the other cage. Knowing that the next words had to come from Deborah, she waited.

'All right,' Deborah finally said. 'What do we do?'

Louise felt a flutter of nervous excitement for the first time since he'd taken her, the chance to regain control of her own destiny suddenly thrilling, giving her hope that she would escape the darkness and find her way back to the light that was home and her husband and their plans for an unremarkable, happy life with each other and the children they were yet to have. 'Next time he comes, he'll let you out to have a wash. You'll need to wear the clothes or he could get angry and not allow you out. He'll bring you a tray of food and drink that he'll leave behind the screen. After you've washed he'll tell you to carry the tray yourself and that's when you have to do it.'

'Do what?' Deborah asked.

'Throw whatever's on the tray in his face, in his eyes. Then, as many times as you can, as hard as you can, hit him with the tray, scratch his eyes – if he has the stun-gun, grab it and use it on him. While he's disorientated, get the key. He always seems to keep it in his trouser pocket – the left one, I think. If he starts to fight back before you have the key, kick and punch him, keep kicking him, keep punching. You can do this, I know you can.'

'I went to school in New Cross,' said Deborah. 'I know how to kick and punch, believe me.'

'Good,' said Louise. 'Once you've got the key, slide it along the floor towards my cage and I'll let myself out – I can get my hand through the wire and reach the lock, I've already tried it. Once I'm out, I'll join you and we'll kick the bastard to till he's almost dead, agreed?'

'Agreed.'

'Then we drag him into one of these stinking cages and lock him in.'

'As easy as that,' Deborah mocked.

'No,' Louise answered. 'But if I'm going to die, if I'm never going to see my husband again, when the truth of what's happened here comes out, I want him to know that I tried, I fought back, I wasn't meekly slaughtered like some farmyard animal. I want him to be proud of me. I want him to know.'

'OK,' Deborah agreed. 'So once we've got him locked in a cage, then what?'

'We leave him,' said Louise. 'We leave him there. For ever. Let the bastard starve to death.'

'But the police – what about the police?'

'We tell them nothing about this place. We tell them he kept us in a dark place somewhere we didn't know. Then he blindfolded us and drove us back to our homes and let us go. We can't help them find him, we don't know anything about him. And all the while he's down here, rotting in this cellar, screaming for help that never comes.'

'I'm not sure,' said Deborah. 'We should tell the police.'

'So he can be locked up in some cushy prison for a few years and then they let him go? No, he deserves more than that.'

'Then we'd be murderers.'

'No. We're not going to kill him, we're just not going to keep him alive.'

'It won't work. Someone will miss him, his work – his family. They'll find him before he dies and no one will know what he's done. He'll be free. He knows where I live. He'll come after me – and you too.'

Louise thought for a while, refusing to abandon her revenge. 'No, you're right. We can't leave it to chance.'

'What do you mean?'

'When he took your clothes, soon after I could smell fire.'

'Huh?'

'I think he burned your clothes, somewhere close by.'

'So?'

'So he must have petrol or something.'

Neither woman spoke for a while, each alone in their own thoughts of fire and screaming, the smell of burning flesh and acrid smoke swirling around in their dark dreaming.

'I can't do that,' Deborah shuddered.

'You won't have to,' said Louise. 'I'll do it. I want to do it. I want to hear him scream. I'll make sure the fire's burning well and then I'll close the door. If the fire doesn't kill him, the smoke will.'

'And when they find him?'

'We tell the police he said he was going to kill himself. When he let us go, he told us he was going to punish himself, take his own life. That's why he was locked in the cage, to punish himself. He was looking for redemption.'

'They won't believe it.'

'He's a rapist and a murderer. D'you think they'll give a damn what happened, what really happened?'

'I don't know.'

'They won't. And we'll never have to think about him again; never have to worry about him waiting for us every time we step outside. We won't wake up every night thinking about him, seeing his face every time we close our eyes. We'll be able to move on, live our lives the way we wanted to before this fucking bastard decided it was up to him how we lived and how and when we died.'

'There'll be so many questions though,' Deborah argued. 'Maybe we should just tell the police?'

'No!' Louise barked at her. 'I won't be a victim. I've been stuck down here for God knows how many days and I've had plenty of time to think and I know one thing – I won't be a victim, I won't have people feeling sorry for me, patronizing me, always checking on me, asking me if I'm all right, cops and journalists hanging around my home, having to stand up in court and tell the whole world what happened while he sits smugly in the dock reliving his sick fantasies through my testimony. And what if he gets off? What do we do then? No, I can't let that happen. I'd rather watch him burn. I want to see him burn.'

Silence hung in the room. Louise's fingers curled around the wire of the cage, her head cocked to one side as she listened for Deborah's answer.

'OK. OK, I'll do it. I'll try. It'll be like fighting my brothers when we were growing up . . . But I won't help you burn him. If things work, if somehow they work, I'll help you get him into the cage. I'll even help you lock him in. But I can't help you start the fire. I can't do that.'

'You don't have to,' Louise assured her.

'And once we're out of here, we go our separate ways. We never see each other again and we never speak about what happened. We stick to the story and never change it, no matter what anyone says or tells us they know, we stick to the story – he killed himself, just like he told us he was going to. Agreed?'

'Agreed,' said Louise, releasing her grip on the wire of her cage and sitting on the stone floor. After a while she began to laugh quietly to herself, the alien noise disrupting the bleak atmosphere of the cellar, disturbing Deborah, making her feel uneasy and suspicious.

'Are you all right?' she asked.

'Yes.' Louise struggled to suppress the laughter. 'I'm sorry, I was just thinking, I've just had the most important conversation of my life with a total stranger in a lightless cellar, sitting in a bloody locked cage. It seemed so ridiculous, it made me laugh.'

A new sense of fear gripped Deborah; not the rush of terror and panic that he brought with him every time he pulled open the metal door, but a trickle of anxiety and concern that the only other person in the world who could help her was slowly sinking into a form of temporary insanity that would render her useless to both of them. 'Are you sure you're OK, Louise?' She waited longer than she'd hoped for an answer.

'I'm not mad, if that's what you mean.'

'Of course you're not. It's just . . . you've been down here for days. You've been through so much. The things that bastard did to the other—'

'Karen. Her name was Karen.'

'Sorry, the things he did to Karen. The things you saw him do. It must be difficult to keep it all together. I don't think I could have.'

'If it doesn't work out,' Louise told her coldly, 'you'll find out. But now, now you need to put the clothes on, or he'll know something's wrong.'

Deborah didn't answer, but she leaned forward and tentatively took hold of the pile of clothes he'd stripped from Louise, the very act of touching them making her feel complicit in his abuse of her fellow captive. She pulled them towards her and slowly, reluctantly, she began to dress.

9

Sean's universe was a room, inhabited only by himself, an out-dated computer system and the forty-three crime reports of people who rightly or wrongly believed they'd been stalked. At that moment nothing else existed: no family, no friends, no past, no future, just the reports and him. Most he'd been able to dispel quickly enough: ex-husbands, ex-boyfriends intent on giving their old partners as hard a time as possible, many had form for other types of petty crime and were not what he was looking for, not the one he was waiting for – not the one he expected to jump from the screen and solve the puzzle for him in one moment of perfect realization. Others, but only a few, had drawn him in further, made his heart skip a beat and his eyes narrow: men who had started with flattery, then flowers, moving quickly to over-familiar love letters, too many unannounced visits to the women's homes and places of work, devoted affection turning to vile threats and desperate pleas for love and acceptance once the inevitable rejection of their advances occurred. The majority of these had been easily scared off by a visit from the police, although a handful had gone on to stalk new victims, victims who looked nothing like Karen Green or Louise Russell.

Sean read through the last of the reports, but soon realized it was petering out to nothing, just like all the others. The man he was looking for wasn't here. 'Fuck it,' he muttered under his breath. He was sure Karen Green's killer would have pursued the woman he was now trying to replace with substitutes. But the reports said otherwise. He stared at the screen, waiting for answers and ideas, considering the possibility that the killer might have recently moved to South London from further afield, but he doubted it. He was sure the killer was local, staying in his comfort zone. So what was he missing?

'Christ,' he muttered, rubbing his hair in frustration, tapping his knuckles on the desk, feeling as if he already knew the answer, that it was inside him somewhere, but he just couldn't dig it out. He slumped in his chair and spread his arms, talking to himself, theorizing where he might be going wrong. 'Maybe she never reported it? Maybe she didn't even know he existed, that he was watching her, always thinking about her.'

The ringing of his phone slowly pulled him back into the wider world. He wearily picked up the receiver. 'DI Corrigan.'

'Hi, I'm Rebecca Owen, calling from the lab.'

'Go on.'

'You submitted samples of moisturizer and perfume, some from a house and some from a murder victim's body?'

'I'm listening.'

'The samples from the body swabs don't match any of the cosmetic items taken from the house. They're not the same.'

So Karen Green wasn't the woman he sought replacements for, she was herself a replacement.

'Do you know what the samples from the body are?' Sean asked.

'Yes. They're significantly more exotic and expensive than anything submitted from the house, although still not unique or handcrafted, so you won't be able to narrow them down to a single retail source.'

'I understand, but can you tell me the brands?'

'Of course. The moisturizer is Elemis body cream and the perfume is Black Orchid by Tom Ford.'

'How long have these products been available?'

'The cream's been around for a good few years, but the perfume's only been on the market for a couple.'

Sean looked back at his computer. The last of the stalker reports still flickered on the screen. His search had gone back three years, yet the perfume only two, so his timelines were right.

'You sure the perfume's only been out for two years?' he asked.

'Certain,' came the reply. 'We'll dispatch the report to you straight away.'

He hung up, his mind already analysing the information from the lab, the names of the cosmetics etching themselves into his consciousness. He eased his eyes closed, allowing the images of the hooded man without a face to form behind the lids, going to the woman he'd taken, gently spraying the expensive perfume into the air close to her neck, the microscopic droplets drifting until they came to rest on the soft, taut skin of her throat. He saw the faceless man unscrewing the lid from the jar of Elemis body cream, thin fingers carefully scooping the moisturizer from within, spreading it over warm, olive skin, gently at first, then more firmly as the cream soaked in, his fingers and thumbs forming dimples and valleys as his hands moved across her body. Sean felt an awakening in his own sexuality and tried to remember the last time he'd made love to his wife, but couldn't. His eyes opened as he chastised himself for allowing a physical want to break his concentration. Once the sexual desires had faded away he closed his eyes again and waited for the scene to return; he didn't have to wait long, the woman with short brown hair lying on her back submitting to his touch as he massaged the Elemis into her body.

His eyes snapped open as he spoke to himself. 'No. That's wrong.' He steadied his breathing and readied himself to try again, his eyes slowly closing, the image of the faceless man returning, but now not touching the woman, not using his own hands to apply the cream or holding the bottle of perfume close enough to spray her himself. This time he left the cosmetics for them to apply it to themselves. 'Yes,' he said to himself, 'that's what you did.' A knock at his open door made him jump.

'Not disturbing anything, am I?' Anna asked.

'Yes, but that's never bothered anyone round here.'

'Do you want me to leave?'

'Only if you want to.'

She took it as an invitation and stepped into his office, taking a seat. 'Working on anything specific?'

'Just trying to get inside this one's head.'

'Yes. I've been told that's what you do.'

'Oh? Someone been speaking out of school?'

She moved the conversation on without answering. 'Is that how you're able to catch them, by thinking like them?'

He shrugged, suspicious. 'I suppose so. I don't really know.'

'How do you do it? How do you project your imagination so you see what they see?'

'Who says I do?'

'No one,' she lied. 'It's something I've noticed from my own observations.'

'You're not going to start telling me I'm psychic, are you, because I can work a few things out other people can't?'

'No,' she laughed. 'I've seen a lot of weird things and interviewed a lot of interesting people with *unusual* gifts, but I've never come across anything that could be described as psychic, or even anything to support the possibility of it. I have however come across people with abilities similar to yours – able to turn their imagination into a tool they can control, almost as if they can just press a play button in their minds and see a scene exactly as it happened, despite not having witnessed it themselves. You often find it in talented filmmakers or writers.'

'Well, let me tell you something, Anna. A lot of shit's been said about my imagination – and most of it's wrong.'

'Who else has been asking about your imagination?'

He ignored her question, but wouldn't forget she'd asked it. 'Why are you really here?' he demanded.

'To help.'

'And what is it you think you can help me with?'

'Well, what is it you're working on at this moment?'

He looked her up and down, uncertain whether he should let her into his world. But the opportunity to show her he was right and she was wrong was powerfully seductive. 'OK, I've just heard back from the lab – the cosmetics found on Karen Green's body don't match any of the cosmetics we took from her house.'

'Meaning he's using them to make her more like the person he wants her to be,' she pre-empted him.

'Yes. That part's straightforward enough. The point is, he didn't apply the cosmetics to her body himself, although he would desperately have wanted to. So the question is why? Why deny himself that moment, a pleasure like that?'

It was her turn to shrug her shoulders.

'Because he's afraid of them,' Sean continued. 'To put the cream and perfume on them himself, he'd have to get close to them. He'd have to expose himself to possible danger, be close enough to have his eyes scratched out, to get a kick in the bollocks, even if they were tied up. Remember, he uses chloroform to dominate them. He's not confident in his physical ability. But in that case, why doesn't he use chloroform? Put them under and take his time, massaging the cream into their skin, watching the perfume make their skin shine. Why didn't he just use the chloroform again?'

Anna shook her head. 'You're talking as if all this is fact, but it's conjecture. For all you know, maybe he did use chloroform. Or maybe they were bound. At this stage—'

'No,' he snapped. 'You're missing the point. The question is why didn't he just use chloroform?'

'Why is it so important for you to understand his reason for *not* doing something?'

'Because I need to understand him. Everything about him. What he does isn't enough. I need to know why.'

'OK, then why didn't he use the chloroform?'

Sean pressed his knuckles into his temples and pressed until he could almost feel bone grinding against bone. 'I don't know,' he said, pressing harder and harder, the same question banging in his mind over and over again, making him forget he was not alone. Then suddenly the answer jumped into his head – an answer so simple he couldn't believe he'd almost missed it.

'He couldn't use the chloroform because that would ruin everything. If he'd used it, he wouldn't have been able to smell the cream, the perfume. The chloroform would have over-powered all other scents – and he couldn't bear that. It's not enough for them to look like her, they have to smell like her, taste like her. My God, it must have been heaven for him, watching her spreading the cream across her skin, the scent of her mixing with the perfume – and all the time he's standing there, watching her, smelling her.' The smile suddenly fell from his lips. 'But how does he do that, if he's afraid to be too close to them unless they're drugged?'

Anna watched him without speaking, not wanting to break the spell he was under, analysing him as he worked, unwilling and unable to enter the world he'd retreated to. She resisted the temptation to make notes of what she saw, instead trying to memorize everything he did.

'How did he watch them? He had to watch them. How did he get close enough to smell that sweet perfume?' He stared into space, temporarily bewildered by his own question. 'He can't keep them locked in a cellar, because when he's in there with them he'd be at risk, Our guy needs to stay in control, which means he must have them in chains or tied up. But then how would they apply the cream to themselves? When he first takes them, he adores them, he worships them. He wouldn't want them in chains or bondage, so how does he manage them? How does he get close enough to have their scent make him feel alive, properly alive, wanted and accepted?' He felt like slapping his own face, as if the pain would draw the answer. 'Does the cellar have a window, so he can safely watch them, through it? In the door maybe? No. That wouldn't be enough for him, because he's more than just visually driven. Looking's not going to do it for him, he needs it all – smell, touch . . . Does he speak to them as well? Of course he does. But how does he do all these things and stay safe?' He put his hands together, the fingers touching his lips as if he was praying. 'So he needs a barrier between them and him, but it can't be solid, can't be something that . . . that isolates them from him, so if it's not a damn window or a wall then it has to be . . .'

His hands slowly fell from his mouth as he remembered the case of the estate agent from Birmingham, abducted and held captive inside a wooden cage inside a garage. A prison within a prison . . . 'A cage! He keeps them in a cage, the cruel son-of-a-bitch. A cage inside a cellar or bunker somewhere. Any time he wants to feel alive he can just walk into that room and stroll around their cage in complete safety, watching them, inhaling their scent and dreaming about the day he'll be with them. But when his illusions fall apart and he needs to punish them, to force himself on them, he has to go into the cage. He can't use chloroform, not straight away, because he'd have to get too close, so what does he do?'

He thought back to the post-mortem, trying to recall the marks he'd seen on Karen Green's sad, broken body, the multitude of superficial injuries, too many bruises to count. And then there were those strange little circular bruises, each with what looked like a burn mark at the centre. He chewed his bottom lip while Anna looked on, fascinated, aware that he had forgotten she was there and that he was now talking solely to himself, unpicking lock after lock, each answer leading to another question, his combination of logic and imagination leading him through the maze.

Sean's middle finger rhythmically tapped on the desk, subconsciously keeping pace with his own heartbeat, waiting for the answer. 'He used something to suppress them, something that meant he could keep his distance and still control them, something that left those marks.' His finger continued to tap away on the desk, every implement of wounding, death and torture he'd ever seen moving through his mind on an imaginary conveyer-belt. 'I need to know what made those marks.'

Anna broke his trance. 'What marks?'

Sean turned to her, looking at her as if he was seeing a figure from a dream, something he didn't believe was really there at all. He snatched the phone off his desk before she could say anything else and called Dr Canning's office number. He got the answer machine.

'Doctor, it's Sean Corrigan. The circular bruises left on Karen Green's body – I need to know what caused them sooner rather than later. Run the tests as a matter of priority and keep me posted.' He hung up without further explanation, ideas rushing at him now he'd opened Pandora's box. 'Whatever he's using in the cage, we know how he took them from their houses. They opened the door because they saw a postman, but as soon as they opened the door he hit them with his stun-gun and paralysed them. Then he took his time preparing them – that's when he used the chloroform, when they were beginning to recover. He used it to put them under, so they couldn't fight, because he's not strong enough to carry or drag them into the boot of their own car. He's weak and he's a coward and I'm going to fucking find you.' The phone ringing broke through his swelling rage. He grabbed it, hoping it would be Canning.

'Mr Corrigan, it's Sergeant Roddis.'

'I'm listening.'

'The unidentified prints found at the Green house and the Russell house definitely came from the same man. Given that they were both recovered from the inside door handles we can assume they belong to the killer. They also match the prints we took from both victims' cars. I took them to Fingerprints myself and supervised the search. I'm afraid I can confirm they don't match any on file. Your killer has no previous convictions, not in this country anyway. I've sent a copy to Interpol, but even for a murder it's going to take days if not weeks before they get back to us.'

'What about DNA?' Sean asked.

'It'll take a few more days to prepare a full profile, but if he doesn't have any previous convictions it's still not going to help you find him. It'll convict him, as will the fingerprints, but it won't identify him.'

'I know, I know.' Sean couldn't contain his frustration. 'Anything else comes up, let me know.'

'Of course.'

Sean hung up, dissecting the importance of what he'd just learned, not simply dismissing the lack of previous convictions as a dead end, but cross-examining it, interrogating it for information and relevance, using it to connect him to the heart and mind of the man he hunted, thinking silently.

So this one doesn't care about leaving his prints and DNA, because he knows it can't help us identify him from police records, or because he just doesn't care? He must know he's leaving enough evidence to convict himself ten times over, so why be careless?

He suddenly reverted to talking quietly to himself, as if Anna wasn't there. 'He's working to a plan that makes his identification irrelevant. He knows that sooner or later we'll find him, but he doesn't care. He's not even comprehending being caught . . . He takes the women and keeps them for a week, or close to, then he takes them from their cage to a place he knows and kills them. He worships them at first, then he hates them. The same cycle over and over again, from love to hate, from acceptance to rejection. But he wasn't just rejected by one person, he was rejected by everyone. He hates everyone?'

His eyes moved from side to side as he began to realize what he was saying. 'These women are a snapshot of his anger and rejection, even if he doesn't know it himself yet. When he feels me closing in, what will he do? Walk into a high street, a shopping centre, a school . . . and what will he use, a knife, home-made pipe bombs, a gun? That's why he doesn't care about leaving his prints, his DNA – subconsciously he's already planned for that day, haven't you? You're not going to let anyone take you alive. You're going to send yourself to hell and drag as many others with you as—'

A knock at his door made him spin around, angry at the interruption. If Featherstone had heard him talking to himself he didn't show it.

'Morning, Sean. Anna.'

'Boss,' Sean addressed him.

'Alan,' said Anna.

Sean's eyebrows rose at the sound of Featherstone's never-used Christian name. Clearly they were more familiar than he'd realized.

'I'm doing another TV appeal for assistance. Do you have anything new I could use, either of you? The telly people always like to have new stuff for the paying public.'

Sean looked at his computer screen, his latest CRIS inquiry still displayed. He considered telling Featherstone about his stalker theory, asking him to appeal to anyone who had been harassed in the last two or three years to come forward, but some instinct and the negative results of his search told him not to.

'Nothing that you'd want to put in a TV appeal,' he said. 'We need to focus our search efforts on decent-sized properties, or isolated plots of land within a twenty-mile radius of where the women were taken. It's possible he keeps them somewhere other than his home – a disused factory or an abandoned smallholding. Other than that, I don't have anything. Just do the usual, appeal to family, friends and colleagues who may have noticed anyone behaving strangely lately, keeping odd hours, disappearing without explanation, not turning up for work. You never know your luck.'

'No problem,' Featherstone assured him.

'Actually,' Sean suddenly remembered, 'there is one thing.'

'Go on.'

'I'm pretty sure he dresses like a postman. That's how he gets the doors open. Maybe we could ask the public whether anyone's noticed a postman behaving strangely, someone who's not their regular postie hanging around an area longer than usual, putting junk mail through their doors when they'd already asked the Post Office not to.'

Featherstone sucked in a long breath, shaking his head like a mechanic about to give an estimate for a car repair. 'Sorry, Sean, no can do. I'd have to get prior approval from the Post Office before releasing that, and they'd have to get prior authority from their members' union – and it's unlikely they'll be given it. Look, it's a pain in the arse, but if we put it out there that this nutter's going around dressed like a postie, by this time tomorrow we'll probably have half a dozen postal workers in hospital, stabbed or kicked to shit by vigilantes or nervous husbands, not to mention the several dozen that'll be blocking up every casualty in South London waiting to have the CS gas washed out of their eyes after paranoid women – no offence meant, Anna – have sprayed them. The postie release is a no-go.'

'I think it's important,' Sean pushed. 'It could stir something in a witness that they haven't even considered.'

'Sorry, Sean, but it can't happen. Anything else? Anna?'

'I'm absolutely certain he's a local man, or at least someone who knows the area well or visits it regularly, so I recommend you continue with the roadblocks and door-to-door inquiries. Also, I agree with DI Corrigan that he needs somewhere relatively secluded to keep them, so concentrate your searches around farms, wasteland, derelict buildings, anywhere he could conceal the women, particularly anything underground.'

'Round here or Central London that wouldn't take long,' Featherstone replied, 'but once you start getting into Bromley and the Kent borders, near where the women were taken from, there's bloody thousands of places he could keep them. They don't call it "the sticks" for nothing.'

'Publicize what you're doing,' Anna continued. 'It may panic him into moving the victim, increasing the chances he'll make a mistake or that someone will see them and call the police.'

'If you reckon it's worth trying,' Featherstone agreed before turning to Sean. 'What about this suspect I hear you arrested? Judging by the fact you haven't mentioned it to me, I take it you don't think he's our man?'

'No,' Sean answered quickly, 'he's nothing to do with this. We won't be looking at him any further.'

'Shame,' Featherstone said. 'Well, must get on. The telly people want to film me standing outside Scotland Yard, next to that bloody rotating sign. Call me if anything new comes up.' And then he was gone, leaving them sitting in an uncomfortable silence until Anna spoke.

'You didn't tell him that you never considered Lawlor responsible.'

'How d'you know I didn't?'

'I've watched you work, Sean. If I could tell he wasn't our

guy, then so could you. The question, is why did you go after him, knowing that?'

'Because he filled some gaps,' Sean confessed, 'allowed me to see some things I was struggling to understand.'

'To understand or . . .?

'To feel.'

'What did he help you feel?'

'Things that were already in me, but buried too deep to use.'

'And he unburied those feelings?'

'No,' Sean answered. 'He just helped me bring them to the surface. Gave me the taste for what he feels when he's doing what he does.'

'What does he feel? What do you feel?'

'Right now I feel hungry.' He glanced at his watch. 'Grab your coat and I'll take you for brunch. There's a half-decent café not too far away. We'll walk there. The air will do us both good. Just promise me one thing . . .'

'Of course.'

'Don't try and analyse me,' he warned her. 'If I want your help, I'll ask for it. Understood?'

'Sorry. Occupational hazard.'

'Fair enough. Now, let's go get something to eat.'

The silence in the kitchen was becoming oppressive, allowing his mind too much room to wander to old, bitter memories of his childhood, the faces of people he hated, past and present, refusing to let him be at peace, even for a second. He hurriedly searched through the shambolic kitchen drawer that held, amongst other things, the CD of a rock band with his favourite song on it. He remembered the first time he'd heard it, years before and how the lyrics seemed like they must have been written for him, giving him hope that somebody understood him – understood what he would eventually do. But unlike the words of the song, the hope faded and died. Fumbling the disc from its scratched and cracked cover, he loaded it into the portable CD player he'd bought himself as a Christmas present, back in the days when he was still trying to cling on to the belief he could one day live as others did.

Selecting the track he needed to hear, Thomas Keller sat back and waited for the music to carry him away, the vocals kicking in soon after the intro, his eyes closing as the beautiful images raced through his mind, a feeling of indestructible power tightening his every muscle while his heart pumped to the beat of the song, the singer telling the tale of a boy despised by his mother and rejected by his father – ignored and ridiculed by the other children at school and detested by the teachers – just as he had been. He began to lose himself in the song, seeing himself walking through his old school cutting down all who'd humiliated him – reaping the sweetest and cruellest revenge as the dead mounted at his feet. He smiled gently as he mouthed along to the words of the song until a sudden noise from outside startled him from his dreaming: a car's wheels moving across the rough gravel, towards his house. He searched for the off switch to stop the music, accidentally hitting the volume control in his panic, his favourite song betraying his presence to anyone close enough to hear. He covered his ears with his hands in a childlike attempt to pretend it wasn't happening before yanking the plug from the socket. The silence that followed felt more deafening than the music had been.

He listened, senses alert like a trapped rabbit listening to the fox scratching around the entrance to its burrow, at first sure he'd been mistaken. But as the ringing and buzzing cleared from his ears the sound of the approaching car returned, prompting him to cross the kitchen and carefully peek through the curtainless window, just able to make out the markings on the police car through the grease and dirt on the glass. 'Fuck,' he shouted, immediately clamping his own treacherous mouth shut with his hand, the fear in his belly making his eyes fill with water. This can't be happening, he told himself. It's too soon. Not yet. I'm not ready. He crawled across the floor of his kitchen like a lizard, reaching into the cupboard for the sawn-off double-barrelled shotgun, snapping it open at the breach, breathing deeply with relief when he saw it was already loaded with twelve-gauge rounds – if there were two of them in the car he could kill them both before they even opened their lying pig mouths.

He walked in a crouch back across the kitchen, rising to glance at the police car that pulled to a halt some twenty feet from his front door, the two uniformed figures stepping simultaneously from the vehicle and beginning to search the area with their eyes without moving from the car. 'Fuck,' he swore again as he ducked away from the window, whispering to himself repeatedly. 'What do I do? What do I do? What do they know? Maybe they don't know anything. Fuck. Fuck. Fuck.' He exhaled and tried to steady himself, calm down enough to be able to think. After a few seconds he crept to his front door and propped the shotgun up against the inside wall, within reaching distance of the entrance. He took a breath and opened the door, the two police officers immediately turning towards him, apparently unconcerned.

'Can I help you?' Keller managed to ask without stuttering or blurting.

The officers looked at each other before answering, the taller, slimmer one speaking first.

'Nothing to worry about,' he said, 'we're just checking on some reports that a prowler was seen around here earlier this morning. Have you noticed anything yourself, sir?'

'No,' Keller answered, a little too quickly and surely, while trying to work out if the policeman was lying. He thought he was but couldn't be sure. Not sure enough to reach for the shotgun only inches away.

'You haven't seen or heard anything?'

'Not around here, no.'

'Is this your place?' the shorter, more heavily muscled one asked.

'Yes.'

'Does anyone else live here?'

'No. I live alone.' He watched the taller one surveying the grounds, noting the outbuildings and debris, nodding to himself as he did so while the heavier one began to approach him. Panic rising in his stomach with every step the policeman took, Keller stepped from his house and walked towards him.

'You've got a lot of land here,' the heavier one remarked. 'Must have cost a fair bit, eh?'

'Not really. It was land the council repossessed. Nobody else seemed to want it. I got it quite cheaply.'

'You should sell it to a developer – make a fortune.'

'Maybe,' Keller answered awkwardly, unused to small talk.

'Do you mind if I take your name, sir?'

'Why do you want to know my name?'

'Just so we can have a record that we've spoken to you about the prowler.'

Keller's eyes darted around, spooked by the thought of giving his name to the police, suspicious they knew more than they were telling him, trying to convince himself that, if that was the case, they would have sent a small army, not two uniformed policemen. 'My name? My name is Thomas Keller.'

'Do you have any ID?' the heavier one asked.

'ID? Why do you need that? I'm not the prowler – this is my land.'

'Of course you're not,' the policeman agreed. 'It's routine when we're doing an inquiry like this to ask for ID from anyone we've spoken to. It's just procedure. Nothing to worry about.'

'OK,' Keller told him. 'Wait there.' He turned and walked back into the house, his hand momentarily resting on the stock of the shotgun. The desire to lift it, walk out into the courtyard and blow their heads off was almost overpowering, but he managed to pull his hand away and step further inside the kitchen, where he began to rifle through another cluttered drawer until he found his driving licence. He moved quickly, desperate to stop the police getting too close to the house or wandering off, sticking their noses into places he couldn't let them see. As he stepped outside, fear squeezed the air from his chest when he realized the taller one was no longer standing by the car. His head twisted in all directions as he searched for the missing policeman, finally seeing him casually wandering towards the abandoned battery chicken shed, peering inside then ducking out, moving deeper into the courtyard and its derelict buildings.

Keller glanced over his shoulder at the cottage entrance; the shotgun was close, but too far away to grab and point in a single motion. Besides, the policemen were now too far apart. By the time he'd shot one, the other would have escaped into the surrounding woods to radio for help, then it would be over for him. Even if he managed to chase the cop down and shoot him like a dog, the world would know.

'Are you looking for something?' he called to the policeman in the courtyard.

'The prowler, remember? You don't mind if I have a look around, do you? There's a lot of places a man could hide out here.'

'No,' Keller managed to lie. 'Look all you want. Can I get you a drink?' he asked, trying to imagine what would be a normal thing to say. 'I could make some tea, if you like.'

'We're fine thanks,' the heavier one dismissed him. 'Do you have any underground buildings on the land, sir? Any bomb shelters or coal cellars?'

Keller swallowed hard before lying. 'No. No I don't.'

'Probably best,' the heavier uniform replied. 'Those old shelters can be dangerous – especially for kids.'

'I suppose so,' Keller managed to answer, forcing himself

to step away from the door of his cottage and walk to the cop asking the questions, handing him his driving licence. 'Will this do?'

The policeman studied it for a few seconds then handed it back. 'That's fine, sir.'

They stood next to each other, silently watching the taller policeman as he crossed the courtyard heading for the shed-like construction that concealed the staircase leading to the cellar. In his anxiety and terror Keller had a moment of clarity, a vision of exactly what he would do if the tall one reached the padlocked door, if he asked for the key to the lock. He would tell him the key was inside and that he'd fetch it. Once in the cottage he would retrieve the shotgun and slowly walk back into the courtyard. He'd kill the heavier one, but he'd let the other one go, let him tell the world what he'd found. It wouldn't matter any more. He'd do what he had to do to the women in the cellar and then he'd go on to take care of the other business he needed to attend to.

The taller one was only feet away from the cellar door now, and the calmness of resignation swept over Keller, making him feel more at peace in that moment than he'd felt in years, maybe in his entire life. Suddenly a disembodied voice cut through the silence and shattered his tranquillity and certainty. 'All unit response please. Police officer requires urgent assistance in Keston High Street. Repeat, urgent assistance Keston High Street.' Their radios sounded in stereo, the distance the policemen stood apart producing a slight echo effect. They looked at each other, the heavier one nodding to his colleague to confirm he understood their telepathic message. He pressed the transmit switch on his radio and spoke.

'Kilo Kilo Two-Two will take that. We're only a couple of minutes away.'

'Thank you, Kilo Kilo Two-Two, we'll show you running.'

The taller one was already moving quickly back to the car

as the heavier one began to climb into the passenger seat. 'Looks like we're on our way,' he said, 'but thanks for your help. Remember, if you see anything suspicious, let us know.'

'I will,' Keller lied, his heart almost exploding inside his chest as he waited for them to leave, the thrill of seeing them drive away instantly replaced by utter terror and rage at the thought they might know who he really was, that they might just be playing games with him. He ran inside and grabbed the shotgun without breaking stride, pacing across the kitchen to the main cupboard, filling his pockets with as many cartridges as he could find before storming from the house and heading towards the cellar and the woman who'd somehow managed to betray him to the police, his plans for what he must do running through his darkening mind as he walked. He saw himself raising the shotgun, aiming it at the treacherous bitch's face, his finger smoothly pulling the trigger, the bitch's brains and pieces of skull exploding from the back of her head.

Then would come the hard part, the thing he had to do more than wanted to, but he wouldn't leave Sam for them to take again, to fill with their poisonous lies. He would get close enough to shoot her through the chest, leaving her face untouched. He prayed she wouldn't move as he pulled the trigger, unable to stand the thought of her screaming, wounded and in agony. Better for her if she doesn't move, if she understands why he has to do it for her.

Then he would get in his car and drive to work where he would hunt down his tormentors one by one, dragging them from their hiding places and blowing them all to hell. But he'd have to keep moving, stay ahead of the police, make sure he still had enough time to reach his old school, and then the children's home before paying his mother a final visit, at the place where he'd discovered she worked, saving the last cartridge for her, shooting her through her hateful face. And then all he'd have to do is sit down and wait for the police with guns to arrive, wait for them to call to him, demand he throw the gun out and walk towards them with his arms raised. But he wouldn't do that. He'd walk out with his shotgun pointed straight at them, and then it would be over and everybody would know his name.

As he neared the cellar his pace began to slow and with it his mind and the dark thoughts of revenge against those who'd wronged him. The idea of having to kill Sam just as they were growing closer to the time when they would be together, when she would love him and accept him, was unbearable. Maybe he was being too hasty, assuming they knew much more than they did. He stopped and stood in the middle of the courtyard, listening for unfamiliar sounds, his body turning through three hundred and sixty degrees as he searched the surrounding trees and scrubland for signs of the police closing in on him. He could see nothing, hear nothing. He exhaled, expelling stale air and the anger that had almost driven him too far, and headed back to his house, calm and in control, assuring himself he wouldn't be panicked into attacking before he was ready. It was fate that the police had left without finding the cellar, a clear sign that things would happen as he'd seen they would – as he'd planned they would. He, and only he, would decide when everything would end.

As the patrol car bumped along the drive, PC Ingram glanced in the wing mirror at Thomas Keller returning to his derelict property. 'I can't believe anyone could actually live in a dump like that,' he said.

'If it was me, I'd build a couple of houses on it and make a few quid,' agreed PC Adams.

'He was a bit jumpy though, wasn't he?'

'Maybe, but he seemed harmless enough. Didn't come charging at us with an axe in one hand and his cock in the other.'

'No, he didn't do that,' Ingram agreed, 'but maybe we should have checked the other buildings?'

'That wasn't our brief,' Adams reminded him. 'They just want us to find possible locations this woman could be at and pass the information on to CID. If they want to, they can get a warrant and search it properly.'

'I know,' said Ingram, 'but I would have liked a look around all the same.'

'We've got another dozen places to check before lunch, on top of this urgent assist. You won't be so keen to go sniffing around them after we've done that lot and filled in the reports.'

'Maybe not.'

'Like I said, let CID sort it out.'

'I didn't realize Peckham had places like this,' Anna remarked as she surveyed the tasteful café that sold decent coffee and reasonable food.

'Probably not what you're used to, but I like it well enough.'

'No, I mean it. It's very nice.'

'It doesn't bother me what you think. It's not like I own the place.'

'Good to know my opinion means so much to you.'

'I'll be honest with you, Anna, the only opinion that really matters to me is my own.'

'Such as, in your opinion the man who took these women is slowly but surely spiralling out of control?'

'Something like that.'

'I noticed you didn't share that opinion with Superintendent Featherstone.'

'He wouldn't understand.'

'Don't you think you should have tried?'

'He's a good enough cop, but he's two-dimensional. He only deals with what's in front of him. He wouldn't understand.'

'I can't say I understand your theory myself. I see no evidence he'll turn from micro-dramas and personalized victim selection and abuse to something more expressive and grandiose. Also I don't see him as self-destructive.'

'He's not – yet,' said Sean. 'But he's turning that way. When he feels me around the corner he'll blow up. I promise you.'

'I suppose we'll have to agree to disagree. All the same, I find your insights very interesting. Have you ever studied psychology?'

He almost choked on a mouthful of coffee and pastry, coughing drily for several seconds before he was able to answer.

'I don't have time for other people's theories,' he said. 'Everything I know, I've learned out here, in the real world, dealing with lunatics like Sebastian Gibran. Trust me, when you're chasing down these people, you learn fast – and you'd better be right or there'll be hell to pay. There's no time to sit around for weeks writing theses for other academics to argue the toss over. No offence, but if you get it wrong, who cares? I get it wrong, at best I'll end up spending the rest of my career in the back of beyond. At worst I'm on Sky News in the evening and on trial for God knows what a few months later.'

'Surely not?'

'You don't believe me? Listen, it's always the police's fault. At the end of the day, no matter what, we'll get the blame. We're an easy scapegoat. Stephen Lawrence is murdered by a gang of racist thugs – it's our fault. A bunch of anarchists smash up the West End – it's our fault because we were too soft. A student gets badly injured on a protest march – it's our fault because we were too heavy-handed. The *News of the World* hacks into the phones of publicity-hungry celebrities who probably love the attention – guess what, it's our fault for not investigating it sooner. We don't catch this psychopath before he kills again – it'll be my fault.'

He took an angry bite from his pastry, eyes fixed on Anna as if challenging her to refute his claims. When she remained silent, he continued, 'Have you any idea what it's like, working day after day with practically no sleep, forcing yourself to keep going and going, having to tell your wife and your children you won't be seeing them till God knows when. And then, when you finally get the job done and the baddy's locked up nice and tight, when you finally get to go home you turn the TV on and what's the first thing you see? Politicians telling the world it was the police's fault, that heads will roll. They never mention the good stuff we do, the personal risks we take for the sake of total strangers, the thousands of seriously nasty bastards we take off the streets every year. Sometimes it makes you want to chuck it all in, walk away.'

'I'd never thought about like that,' Anna confessed. 'It can't be easy.'

'No. No it's not.'

'How do you feel when you see the news coverage of murder cases?'

'You're not trying to analyse me again, are you?'

'No. Just interested in a police perspective.'

'They make me angry,' he said. 'They treat it like a reality show, titillation for the masses. If they'd ever been inside a real murder scene, on their own, before it had been cleaned up, they wouldn't sound so excited. You can tell they've never had the taste of death in their mouths. It lingers for days, no matter how many times you brush your teeth or rinse with mouthwash. But then again, how many people have? Have you?'

'I want to ask you a question, Sean, and obviously you don't have to answer it if you don't want to.'

'I can't stop you asking it.'

'Did something happen to you, when you were younger?'

'No,' he lied.

'Some trauma perhaps, a serious injury or critical situation you encountered while doing your job?'

'Plenty, but no one thing. Why?'

'Sometimes you display the traits of someone suffering from a type of post-traumatic-stress syndrome.'

'I don't think so.'

'It's as if your insights are driven more by memory than imagination.'

She was getting too close and he didn't like it. 'You want to know if I can think like the people I spend my life trying to catch? The answer is yes,' he told her. 'But if you want to know how I do it, then I'm sorry, the answer is I don't know. Am I comfortable with it? No – but if I can use it to save lives and lock up some very bad people then I'll use it, no matter how uncomfortable it is.'

'That kind of self-sacrifice can be damaging. Who looks after you while you're looking after everybody else?'

'My wife. My children. Myself.'

'Sounds a little insular.'

'To you maybe. Not to me.'

'You don't like talking about yourself, do you?'

'No, I don't, so let's not. Besides, I've found a way you can finally be useful to me.' He didn't stop to think how that sounded.

'Wow, thanks.'

'You've spoken to DS Jones?'

'Sally? Yes.'

'You know what happened to her. You read the report, before you interviewed Gibran.'

'I did, but anything Sally may have told me would be subject to patient confidentiality. I can't discuss it with anyone.'

'Appreciated, but all I want to know is whether there's a serious problem there. Am I doing the right thing by letting her come to work, or should I re-think things?'

'Isolation won't help her, but I can't say anything else. Understand?'

'Understood. Loud and clear.'

'Just don't put her in harm's way or expect too much from her.'

'I won't, but don't underestimate her.' He glanced at his watch. 'Listen, I appreciate the time out and the heads-up about Sally, but as you know, I'm standing in the middle of a storm here.'

'And you need to get back to work.'

'Sorry.' He stood to leave, then paused, remembering the thing that had been playing on his mind since they'd first met. 'I almost forgot – there's something I've been meaning to ask you.'

'I'm intrigued.'

'Did Sebastian Gibran ever discuss James Hellier with you? His real name was Stefan Korsakov, but Gibran would have known him as Hellier.'

'He did. Hellier was the one he blamed his crimes on – said he'd set him up, that he'd obviously spent years studying him so the police would think it was him and not Hellier who was the killer. Hellier seemed to be the focal point of his paranoid delusions.'

'Clever bastard,' Sean told her. 'He switched the truth around. It was him who was using Hellier.'

'So the police reports said.'

'You mean what *my* report said?' She didn't answer. 'He was an interesting character, James Hellier. I bet you would have liked to have had a chance to interview that one. You could have written a whole book about him.'

'Why don't you tell me about him?'

'I can tell you that when I first met him I hated him. Then I was scared of him. But ultimately he saved my life . . .' As if realizing he had let down his guard and come close to confiding, he broke off. When he spoke again, it was in his usual clipped, businesslike tone. 'Truth is, I don't really know how I feel about him. Time to go.' He stretched out a hand to pick up the bill from its china plate, but Anna made a grab for it.

'I'll get this,' she insisted, their fingers touching as they reached the plate at the same time, their eyes simultaneously flashing towards each other. Sean remained expressionless despite the sudden excitement he felt stirring inside him. He pulled his hand away, taking the bill with it.

'My treat,' he told her.

As Thomas Keller descended the stone stairs the syringe containing the alfentanil rolled from side to side on the tray. Keeping his thumb pressed on the precious transfer to prevent it from slipping away, he gave Louise Russell's cage little more than a cursory glance as he crossed the room and crouched down beside Deborah Thomson. 'I think it's time, Sam,' he said. 'We've both been patient long enough.' He placed the tray on the floor and picked up the transfer of the phoenix, showing it to her, anticipation and excitement coursing through him, and pride, pride at having rescued her from all the liars and manipulators. 'This is for you,' he continued, rolling up his sleeve to show her his identical tattoo, shaking the paper the transfer was stuck to, ensuring she was looking at it. 'This isn't a permanent one – you can have that done later, but this will do for now. Once you have this, we can be together, properly together.'

Her eyes moved from the ugly transfer to the syringe containing the clear liquid. Louise had told her he might use some type of anaesthetic on her. And then he'd apply the transfer to her arm, and then he'd come into her cage and he'd do things to her, things that horrified her, just as Louise had told her he would. She looked at the amount of liquid in the syringe, her nursing experience telling her it was almost certainly not enough to fully anaesthetize her, meaning he wanted her conscious. She forced herself to speak. 'I need to get washed first,' she said. 'If we're going to be together, then I want to be clean, for you.'

His eyes dilated fully before shrinking to black holes, his

body shaking, almost unable to deal with her sudden acceptance of him. He frantically scratched at his forehead with the fingernails of his right hand, biting his bottom lip hard enough to draw a little blood that seeped into the tiny lines of the thin skin. 'OK,' he agreed. 'Of course, but forgive me, I need to make you safe first, for your own protection, you understand.'

'What do you mean?' she asked. 'What are you going to do to me?'

'I'm going to protect you,' he said, a confused look on his face, as if he couldn't understand why she sounded so concerned and afraid. 'I would never hurt you, Sam.' She accidentally looked past him towards Louise, and his head whipped around to catch what she was looking at. Louise quickly looked away, hoping he hadn't noticed the silent communication between them. 'What's she been saying?' he asked Deborah, his lips pale, eyes burning with hatred. 'She's been poisoning you against me, hasn't she? Fucking with your head, filling it with her lies.'

'No,' Deborah told him, 'she hasn't said anything and I wouldn't believe her anyway. This is about us, not her. Forget her, please.'

'I know how to punish dirty little whores like her.' His words made Louise shrink into the furthest corner of her cage, her lips beginning to tremble as he moved towards her, fumbling in his tracksuit trousers for his stun-gun.

'Forget her,' Deborah called to him. 'It's me you want to be with and I want to be with you. She's nothing to us.' He stopped and turned back towards her, the fire of anger dampened by the expression of affection and desire.

'You're right,' he said. 'She's nothing.'

'Good,' Deborah encouraged him like an obedient dog. 'You were going to let me out, remember, so I can wash.'

'Yes. Yes, of course.' He took the key from his pocket, moved to her cage door and began to unlock it, then stopped short, years of self-preservation kicking in, saving him. 'I'm sorry. I almost forgot. Before I let you out I need you to do one thing for me.'

'What?' she asked nervously, too many horrifying images flashing through her mind to focus on one in particular. She swallowed the vomit rising in her mouth.

'I need you to put your hands through the hatch.'

'Why?'

'You have to trust me, Sam. You have to learn to trust me.' He opened the hatch and waited for her to obey him. She knew she had to do it, or soon she would become Louise and then she would become Karen Green – nothing but a memory to those who loved her. Tears rolled from the corners of her eyes, but she managed to stifle her sobbing and hide her fear of him as she slid her hands through the hatch. She fought the desperate desire to look away, instead staring into his eyes, trying to push her mouth into a smile. He smiled back as he took a length of nylon wire from the pocket of his tracksuit top. She watched as he wound the wire around and around her wrists, tightly enough so she could feel the blood welling in her hands, but not so painful as to make her struggle and betray herself. Once the wire was wrapped around her wrists several times he twisted the loose ends as if he was securing a freezer bag. 'There,' he announced. 'Not too tight is it?'

'No,' she forced herself to say. 'It's fine. Thank you.'

He wiped the sweat from his hands on to the back of his trousers and moved slowly to the cage door, turning the key that he'd left in the lock and swinging it open, one hand lifting the tray from the floor while the other snaked inside, offering her assistance. She placed her hands on his and let him guide her from the cage, praying that Louise was watching and ready as she allowed him to lead her across the room. She followed him behind the screen to the sink, his hand uncoiling from hers, placing the tray with the syringe on the little table as he stepped back, but only a few feet, watching her, licking the drying blood from his swelling lips. She looked away from him and turned the tap on, the screeching of the old metal soon replaced by the sound of running water. 'I don't want to get my clothes wet,' she said.

He looked confused. 'Don't worry. Just wash your face for now.'

'But I want to be properly clean for you,' she insisted, calculating how best to play him. 'I want to be as pure as I can for you. If you untie me I can take these clothes off, then I can wash everywhere.'

He felt his testicles begin to coil and tighten. The thought of watching her willingly undress and bathe in front of him, the water running down her slim body, following her curves, made him forget his caution. He stepped forward to untie her. But as he held her wrists he stopped, looking from Deborah to the pitiful figure crouched in the corner of the other cage, then back to Deborah. She sensed him hesitate. 'You can watch,' she told him. 'You can watch me wash myself. I don't mind.'

'No,' he said, stepping back. 'It's not safe for you yet. Some of their poison may still be in you.'

Deborah knew her face betrayed her disappointment and only hoped he misinterpreted it, that his sick mind actually thought she was saddened by his physical rejection. 'You're right,' she lied. 'Let's be careful.' She began to cup water in her bound hands, bringing it up to wash her face, trying to sense his position. Carefully she dabbed her fingers on to the bar of soap and pretended to massage it into her face. 'Ow,' she suddenly winced.

'Are you OK?' he asked. 'Is something wrong?'

'My eyes,' she complained. 'I've got soap in my eyes. It really stings. I can't see.' He felt anxiety begin to creep up his spine, thin strands reaching through the bone and wrapping themselves around his spinal cord, transmitting the sense of panic to every sinew in his being, freezing him where he stood, smelling a trap, but unable to overcome his instinct to help the woman he loved. 'Please,' she implored him, 'I need a towel. My eyes are really burning.' Tears of frustration and sorrow blurred his vision and he moved towards her, snatching the towel from the screen and handing it to her searching fingers, smiling as she rubbed the cloth into her eyes, the pain clearly easing.

'Is that better?' he asked.

'Yes. Thank—' Deborah broke off mid-sentence, slamming her right knee into his groin. It connected with his testicles, bending him double. Memories of childhood fights with her brothers flooded back to her. Only this time she wouldn't be pulling any punches – not when her life depended on winning. She drew her knee back again and launched it towards his face, aiming for the bridge of his nose. He saw it coming and moved just in time, but the knee still connected powerfully with the side of his face, splitting the inside of his cheek wide open and loosening several teeth. He coughed on the blood that ran down his throat and struggled to keep his bearings, feeling nails gouging and scratching at his eyes. By the time he realized the onslaught had stopped it was too late, the searing pain in the side of his neck replaced everything else, making him moan and whimper like a wounded animal. His hand shook as it moved to the source of his agony.

Deborah released the syringe, leaving it embedded in the side of his neck. She'd aimed for his jugular but missed, although she'd still forced the liquid into his body, praying that if it was an anaesthetic it would at least slow him down, even if she hadn't pumped it straight into his bloodstream. The sight of him bloodied and wounded, pawing at the syringe that hung from his neck was both appalling and terrifying. Her will to survive was screaming at her to run before the tide turned, before his rage made him rise again with the strength of a madman, adrenalin driving him forward through his pain.

A woman's voice cried out from behind her: 'Get the key, Deborah. Get the key!' Louise was clawing the wire of her cage door, trying to shake it open with what little strength she had left in her body after days without food or water. Deborah looked from the woman to the wounded beast crawling on the floor, still trying to pull the syringe from its neck. The muscles had constricted around the needle, making it difficult to budge. The smell of fresh air drifted down the stairs and into her face, fuelling the urge to run. 'Hit him again and get me out of here. Deborah. Deborah,' Louise screamed, sensing the other woman's intentions.

'I'm sorry,' Deborah mouthed at her. 'I'm so sorry . . .' And then she ran. She ran past the wretch on the floor, who made a grab for her ankle, the touch of his damp skin making her squeal more than scream. But his grip was weak and he couldn't stop her. When she got to the stairs, she tried to climb them three at a time, but her bound hands threw her off balance and she fell forward, both shins crashing into the harsh edge of a stone stair, the pain making her call out as she dragged herself back to her feet, running up the stairs again, trying to be more careful. Fear of what was behind her made her reckless and uncoordinated as she grew closer and closer to the oblong of light above, its brightness making the tears sting her eyes so painfully she had to close them. And all the while Louise's voice screamed after her:

'You fucking bitch. Don't leave me. You can't leave me here. I hope you die, you fucking bitch. I hope he fucking kills you. I hope he fucking kills you.'

The staircase felt like an unconquerable mountain as she stumbled up the last few stairs, slipping again, smashing her kneecap, the pain as it fractured punching the remaining breath from her chest. Gripping the knee in both hands, she tried to squeeze the pain from it. Movement in her peripheral vision drew her eyes down into the darkness: a shape was emerging from the gloom below and beginning to climb the stairs, lolling from side to side, arms outstretched, feeling for the walls either side of the staircase as if drunk or blind, his head too heavy to lift. She didn't have the strength to scream, the only sound that escaped her mouth was an exhausted whimper as she pulled herself to her feet, the injured knee rendering one leg little more than useless as she tried to run.

Deborah burst into the light, temporarily blinded by the bright sunshine, unable to see the sharp stones beneath her bare feet that cut through her thin skin. She staggered forward, her broken knee suddenly collapsing, her outstretched hands breaking the fall. As her vision returned she searched the door for a lock, but found only a flapping latch, the padlock that locked it missing, still down there, in the darkness with him, the darkness where she had abandoned Louise Russell to her fate. She slammed the door shut anyway and tried to run across the littered courtyard, unfamiliar objects making her trip and stumble. A jagged lump of concrete protruding from the ground caught the foot of her injured leg, sending a jolt of pain up through her bones and into the knee, dropping her to the floor. Barely able to see for tears, she searched the ground for a makeshift weapon or a crutch. Finding neither, she looked back to the cellar door. Despite all the pain and effort, she'd travelled less than twenty feet. Her scream shattered the quiet of the spring morning as the door burst open and her captor fell into the light, the syringe still obscenely protruding from his neck as he shook his head violently from side to side, trying to dispel the effects of the anaesthetic.

Squinting against the effects of the alfentanil and the sunlight, Keller steadied himself, his eyes drawn by the sudden movement of Deborah scrambling to her feet. He lunged towards her, swaying from side to side as he used the oil drums to steady himself, his prey little more than a hazy figure that seemed to his confused mind to be moving in slow motion, as if they were both trapped in a nightmare where they were running through treacle or glue.

But the gap between them was shrinking. Deborah's injured knee couldn't support her weight, so she hobbled, dragging it after her, on feet that were cut and bleeding from the stones and broken glass that littered the yard. Her eyes were frantically scanning the area for help, but there was no road with passing traffic, no neighbouring houses, just an ugly cottage that she instinctively knew was his home. She decided her only hope was to carry on along the uneven dirt road and hope that it would lead her away from this hell, but he was gaining on her, his unsteady footsteps louder. Still she kept moving, tears streaming from her eyes, until finally she sensed he was right behind her, fingers like tendrils reaching out to grab her.

Filling her lungs, Deborah readied herself for one desperate scream, but the searing pain that ripped into the base of her spine stole the last of her resistance and sent her crashing to the stony ground, the electricity from the stun-gun reverberating through every sinew of her body.

Hands clutched at her clothes and pulled her over on to her back. Her unblinking eyes fixed on the face hovering above her, contorted in a grimace of agony as he tugged at the syringe, the skin of his neck stretching until at last the metal spike came free. He threw it as far as he could, the momentum of his swinging arm throwing him off balance as the alfentanil continued to impede his motor-skills. He screamed a primeval yell into the bright, clear sky and dropped to his knees next to her, resting his head on her chest, his hand gently stroking her hair as he sobbed. 'You shouldn't have done that, Sam,' he whispered. 'You shouldn't listen to their lies. I'm the only one who really loves you. I'm the only one who really knows you. This is your home.'

The convulsions of the body underneath him gradually slowed, her arms and legs beginning to bend and move slightly as they came back to life, but her muscles were exhausted. She tried to push him off her, but her weak limbs made it seem more like an embrace. He lifted his head from her chest and moved towards her face. He wiped her tears and mucus away with his thumbs and began to kiss her face softly, each kiss lingering on her skin as if it would be the last kiss he ever gave, the salt of her sweat and tears making his bloodied lips sting and effervesce exquisitely, a sensation he'd never experienced before, except with her, except with Sam, so long ago he'd almost forgotten.

Pushing himself away, he slipped a hand under her and draped her arm over his shoulder, hauling her to her feet, but he had to bear most of her weight along with his own, dragging her back towards the cellar, her injured leg trailing behind them as they walked like two injured soldiers, one helping the other. 'Come on,' he said, 'before anyone sees you. Hold on to me. I won't let you go. I promise I'll never let you go.' She wanted to push him away, to knock him to the floor and cave his skull in with the nearest brick or rock, but she couldn't; her body was too weak from her injuries and the after-effects of the brutal electric shock, her adrenalin spent.

As they moved closer to the cellar door Deborah felt her numb body gradually coming back to life. Though still weak and slow to respond, her muscles were beginning to heed the commands of her mind. And while she was growing stronger, he was weakening, drained by the effort of dragging her. But if her recovery continued at its current pace she was afraid it would be too late to save her; she could picture the cage door slamming shut just as she felt strong enough to overpower him. As the doorway loomed in front of them, her jaw unfroze enough for her to mumble, 'No,' her free hand stretching out, fingers grasping and holding the door frame, jolting them both to a halt once the slack in her arm had been fully extended. 'No,' she repeated, her words becoming clearer. 'Not down there, please.' He pulled at her arm, but she wouldn't let go, fear lending her strength.

Realizing he was running out of time and strength, but reluctant to use the stun-gun on her again and leave himself with a dead weight to carry down the stairs, Keller lashed out in blind panic, sinking his teeth into the fingers that were clutching the door frame. He bit hard and deep into her knuckles, the serrated ends of his sharp teeth gnawing at her skin and bones, the coppery taste of warm blood seeping across his tongue. The primal brutality of his actions seemed to fire life and strength into Keller. The louder she screamed, the harder he bit, his teeth struggling to find purchase on the slippery bones of her fingers, his throat pulsing as he swallowed the blood welling in his mouth.

Unable to hold on any longer, Deborah released her grip on the door frame, sending them both plunging through the doorway and down the first few stairs, their limbs tangled together like two erotic dancers, neither making a sound, neither calling out in pain as their bodies jarred and bounced off the hard steps that battered and bruised them as they fell. When they finally came to a stop, he was lying on top of her, his face millimetres from hers, their breath mixing together to make one sickly-sweet scent. For a second their eyes met, each as terrified as the other, an understanding between them that they were engaged in a fight for their lives.

Her blows came in a torrent, her legs and knees trapped under his, bucking and kicking as hard as they could, her weakly clenched fists pummelling the top and sides of his head, intermittently turning into scratching talons searching for his eyes. His skin burned with the searing pain of broken, jagged nails tearing at the soft flesh of his face. He squealed and screeched in pain, peering through the thin slits of his eyes, trying to catch her flailing arms by the wrists.

He hadn't wanted to hurt her, not his beloved Sam, but she was clearly still full of their poison and her attempted escape and her renewed violence towards him had all but pushed his compassion away. It retreated into the depths of his soul, replaced by the anger that had always simmered so close to the surface. His fury gave him a new-found strength, his squeals turning into a roar as he gripped the hair on top of her head and dragged her mercilessly down the stairs, backwards and head first, her backbone and ribs crunching into the edge of each step until at last the ground beneath her flattened out. Tightening his grip on her hair, he hauled her across the cellar floor, her good leg desperately trying to find purchase, to resist their progress. Her struggling jerked his shoulder, the pain increasing his anger. He pulled his foot back as far as he could without overbalancing and kicked her in the spine halfway down her back, the agony making her entire body arch. Inch by inch he dragged her closer to the cage that she'd escaped from only minutes earlier.

Words spluttered from her mouth, minute flecks of her blood and spit leaving a treasure trove of forensic evidence on his skin, clothes and hair, evidence that might one day bury her executioner, but meaningless to her now. 'Please, you fucking animal, let me go, please. I won't tell anyone, please. I'll kill you, let me go or I swear I'll kill you. Let me fucking go.'

Breaking his own rules of self-preservation, he backed into the cage first. Too tired to pull her in one fluid motion, he tried to do it bit by bit, yanking her by the hair, as if he was shifting an old trunk that was too heavy for him, ignoring the sounds of her scalp beginning to tear away from her skull. As he pulled her across the threshold of the wire cell and collapsed into a sitting position, her hands suddenly flew out and gripped the sides of the cage's entrance, her eyes clenched tight shut against the agonizing pain in her scalp.

'I won't go in there! I won't!' she screamed, her pitch so high her words were barely intelligible, her knuckles turning white she gripped the frame. 'No. No,' she cried as he jerked at her hair, the intense pain only strengthening her grip on the frame of the cage's door, fear of sinking into the abyss driving her determination to survive.

His strength was beginning to fail when he remembered that the stun-gun was still in his tracksuit pocket. Making sure that she was halfway inside the prison, he untangled his fingers from her hair and felt himself immediately being pulled towards the entrance, the woman's strength surpassing his own now, inching them both back through the cage door. His hand thrust into his pocket and quickly found the small plastic box, euphoria and panic breaking over him in equal waves. There was no need to consider his next act. He knew this was his only chance. He pulled the stun-gun from his pocket and stabbed it into the side of her neck, pressing the dual control switches to fire the current into her body, forcing it against her skin far longer than he needed to subdue her as he watched her straight, stiff body convulse and writhe. Finally he stopped the flow of electricity and pulled the stun-gun away, thrusting it back in his pocket, no time to waste, letting go of her hair and grabbing her by the clothing around her shoulders. With one last effort he heaved her into the cage.

He slumped against the wire and wiped the sweat from his brow with his shirt sleeve, smiling and quietly laughing to himself. As he studied the woman lying in front of him, the laughter turned to sobs. Blinking away heavy tears, he reached out to touch her convulsing body. Gently stroking her hair, he murmured 'Look what they made you do.' Then, as the stinging pain in his face reminded him of his own injuries: 'Look what they made you do to me – trying to turn us against each other, just like they did before. Just like they'll always try and do, Sam. But I won't let them take you. I'll never let them take you.' She mumbled a reply, but he couldn't understand the obscenities she tried to spit at him. 'Rest,' he told her. 'You should rest now.'

He crawled from the cage and locked it behind him, pulling himself upright, heaving in lungfuls of air to feed his exhausted muscles before staggering to the stairs and beginning his ascent to the daylight, each step a mountain, until finally the cool spring air revived him sufficiently that he was able to snap the padlock into place and walk slowly, carefully across the courtyard.

Submerged in a tide of sorrow and loss, he couldn't hold back the tears. When he made it to his ugly little cottage, he fell to his knees and crawled across the floor to the cabinet. He took out the shotgun and thrust the barrels between his teeth, resting his thumb across the double triggers, teeth clanking against the metal as he tried to control the terrible sound coming from deep within him. He bit down hard on the barrels and tried to force his thumb to press the triggers, but it refused to move. He screamed into the room, his words turned to an incoherent babble by the cold metal tubes obscuring the movement of his tongue, the meaning clear only inside his mind: *'Please. I can't do this any more. I want to end this,'* he pleaded with himself. *'Just fucking do it, you fucking coward!'*

But he couldn't, not yet. As much as he thought he wanted to take his own life, deep inside his tortured soul he wasn't ready. He wouldn't end it until they had suffered more, until they knew he had the power to shatter their lives, to make them pay for all the years he'd had to survive alone in the jungle of children's homes and vast, anonymous London state schools, preyed upon by the strong, ostracized by the other children who treated him like a leper.

His thumb eased off the triggers as he slowly slid the barrels from his mouth, their ends wet and shiny from his saliva and tears. He uncocked the gun's hammers with the barrels still pointing towards his face and threw it across the vinyl floor where it slid to rest under his kitchen table. He buried his face in his hands and keeled over on to his side, lying on the floor sobbing like an infant, overwhelmed by emotions he could neither understand nor control. In the midst of this self-loathing he drew a hand away from his face and down his shivering body, fingers working their way under his waistband and inside his underwear, his shrivelled member slowly swelling as his hand gripped it and began to stroke up and down, faster and faster, images of the women from the cages flashing in his mind, their lips, skin, breasts and pubic triangles – their scent. His snivelling turning to moans of pleasure as their images mixed with other scenes playing in his head, pictures inspired by his favourite song: the story of one boy's bloody revenge.

10

Sean sat in his office poring over information reports gathered from roadblocks, open-ground searches and every other aspect of the investigation. Anna sat to his side having insisted on reading each piece of paper his eyes passed over, her presence tolerated only because she worked quickly and quietly, never interrupting him and thus derailing a train of thought. Instead it was the phone ringing loudly on his desk that made him jump and scramble back to the real world. Annoyed at the disturbance, he snatched it up and barked his name into the receiver. 'Sean Corrigan. What is it?' The voice on the other end didn't seem to have taken offence.

'Sir, DC Croucher speaking – Paul Croucher from Lambeth Borough CID.' The name meant nothing to Sean. 'I understand you're interested in missing persons?'

'Only of a particular type,' Sean pointed out.

'How does white, female, about five foot six, twenty-seven years old, slim build, shortish brown hair, green eyes sound?'

'I'm listening.'

'Deborah Thomson, a nurse at St George's Hospital in Tooting, home address 6 Valley Road, Streatham. She left work some time after 2 p.m. yesterday, hasn't been seen since. She failed to turn up for an evening out with friends and this morning she failed to turn up for breakfast with her new boyfriend. He's the one who reported her missing after he got no reply on her home and mobile numbers. No answer at her home address either and her car's gone. He called around her friends and found out she'd stood them up too, which is when he came down to the nick and reported it. Interested?'

'Do you have a photograph of her?'

'We do.'

'Can you email it to me?'

'No problem.'

'Stay on the line while you do it,' said Sean. 'I need to see her face before I make a decision.' But the sick, tightening feeling in his stomach already told him his worst fears had been realized.

'I'm sending it now,' DC Croucher confirmed. Sean pulled up his emails on the screen and waited for the message to appear in his inbox. A few seconds later it jumped straight to the top of his unread list. As quickly as he could, he directed the arrow to the New Mail and double-clicked. There was no text, simply an attached document. He double-clicked again and waited for his antiquated hard drive to produce a picture on the screen. After what seemed like minutes the image of a young, attractive woman jumped on to his monitor. The similarities between her and the other victims were striking. As he stared into her green eyes he had no doubt she had been taken and that Louise Russell was now rapidly running out of time.

There was a sharp intake of breath from Anna when she saw the likeness. 'Trouble?' she asked.

Sean's response was a curt shake of the head. It would take too long to brief her. She'd have to pick up the pieces as they went along.

'We're taking over this Missing Persons inquiry,' he informed DC Croucher. 'I need you to get round her home and check it out yourself, just to make sure she's not lying in bed with flu. Force entry if you have to, but preserve the scene for a full forensic examination. Understand?'

'It'll be done.'

'Phone me as soon as you find anything.'

Sean hung up, immediately leaping to his feet and striding into the main office, one hand raised to warn the occupants he wanted their full and immediate attention. Donnelly saw him first and quickly made his way to Sean's side. 'Where's Sally?' Sean asked.

'Chasing down some dead-end leads from Featherstone's TV appeal. Why? What's going on?'

Ignoring the question, Sean called out: 'All right everybody, listen up.'

Donnelly decided he hadn't shouted loudly enough. 'Whatever you're doing,' he boomed, 'stop doing it and start listening.'

The office fell silent as all heads turned towards Sean.

'Thanks,' he told Donnelly before addressing the rest of the room. 'As soon as this briefing's over I'll be emailing you all a photograph of a woman called Deborah Thomson. She just became our third victim.' The room filled with disgruntled murmurs of disbelief. 'Last time anyone saw her alive and well was when she left work sometime shortly after 2 p.m. yesterday. She failed to meet friends for a night out and didn't turn up this morning to meet her boyfriend for breakfast. She's not answering her phones and there's no answer at her home address and her car is missing. When you see her photograph and read her physical description you'll understand why I believe the man we're after has taken her. Her abduction means more crime scenes to examine, more door-to-door, more roadblocks, more witnesses to trace, more everything – so call your wives, your husbands, girlfriends, boyfriends, whoever and let them know they won't be seeing much of you for a while, not until we find this prick and bury him.

Eat as and when you can, sleep where and when you can, but do it on the hoof. Our chances of finding Louise Russell alive are shrinking by the hour, so you're all going to have to push yourselves to the limit. Any of you feel you're beginning to unravel, speak to me or Dave and we'll see what we can do. Paulo –' Sean turned towards Zukov.

'Yes, guv'nor.'

'How are you getting on with the transfer found on Karen Green?'

'I'm speaking with the companies that make that sort of thing, but so far it means nothing to them. They've promised to check through their back catalogues, but it's going to take time.'

'Well, keep on them. I want to know everything about it as soon as possible.'

'Why's it so important?' Zukov challenged. 'It's a mass-produced transfer, nothing unique, so why waste our time on it?'

'Keep looking,' Sean snapped back. 'I'll decide what is and isn't important. Understand?'

Zukov knew when to wind his neck in. 'Yes, boss.'

'Everybody needs to keep pushing,' Sean reminded them. 'Get your actions from Dave and Sally and do them immediately. As soon as they're complete, come back for more – and there will be more. Keep on the move, you don't have to come back here to tell me what's going on: use your mobiles, email me – tweet me, if you have to, but keep on the move. Make something happen, don't just wait for it to. Fiona?'

DC Cahill straightened. 'Yes, guv'nor?'

'Get hold of Sergeant Roddis and tell him the good news about our new scene.' She nodded her understanding. 'And everybody needs to be aware our man could be disguising himself as a postman. I think that's how he gets the front doors open.'

'Where's that information come from?' one of the weary detectives asked.

'A witness I spoke to,' Sean replied, keen to avoid details. 'I also think he could be posting junk mail in the streets he's taking the women from, so he blends in better. When you're doing your door-to-doors, ask the occupants if they've had any junk mail in the last couple of days. If they have and they've kept it, seize it and preserve it for forensics. Everybody clear?'

The response was a mix of mumbled agreement and softly spoken questions.

'Just one more thing –' Sean looked around the room, meeting their eyes, making sure the message hit home – 'the pub's off limits until this one's in the bag. I can't afford to lose a single soul, especially not to hangovers.'

The mumbling grew louder. Sean ignored it and headed back into his office, closely followed by Donnelly.

Sean slumped into a chair and waited for the inevitable cross-examination.

'Disguised as a postie, eh? Interesting idea,' Donnelly began.

'One of Louise Russell's neighbours had junk-mail deliveries stopped, but round about the time she was taken he got a pile through the door. He was not a happy man.'

'That's it? One neighbour and a bit of junk mail?'

'It makes sense. That's how he gets the doors open without anyone thinking too much about it. It's probably how he researches the woman as well. Who's going to pay attention to a postie walking along the street? Which sorting office covers the venues?'

'Sorting office?' said Donnelly. 'Hang about, I thought you were looking for someone *disguising* themselves as a postie. Why the interest in sorting offices?'

'I have to consider the possibility our man's a real postman.'

'Consider it, or believe it?'

'The more I think about it, the more it makes sense that

he could be a real postman. Everything he needed to know he could have found out by reading their mail. Where they work, whether they were married or had a partner, whether they had children. He could even have found out when Karen Green was due to leave for Australia. Everything he needs to know comes straight to him through the mail. If he was just disguising himself as a postman he'd have to watch them for weeks and hours at a time – constantly having to re-visit them to make sure nothing's changed. But if he's a real postman . . .'

'He only needs to monitor the mail.' Donnelly gave a low whistle. 'A fucking postie. Why didn't you tell the rest of the team?'

'Featherstone gave me the gypsy's warning about openly mentioning the postman theory. Doesn't want posties getting the shit kicked out of them all over south-east London, so keep it on a need-to-know basis for the time being.'

'Fair enough,' Donnelly agreed. 'And it's South Norwood – the sorting office that covers our venues.'

'All three?'

Donnelly scrunched his eyes as he tried to recall previous inquiries that had involved checking mail coverage zones. 'Aye, I'm pretty sure it covers all three.'

'OK,' Sean sighed. 'Let's go there.' He jumped from his chair and started gathering his belongings.

'The sorting office?' Donnelly checked.

'Why not?'

'Surely the scene's more important?'

'No,' Sean disagreed, looking for Sally's number in his iPhone. She answered it within a few rings.

'Sally, we've had another abduction.'

'I know. Paulo texted me.'

'I need you to check out the victim's home address. Fiona will meet you there. I'll get her to send you the address. As soon as you find anything, let me know.' He hung up before she could protest, stalking through the main office until he found DC Cahill at her desk on the phone.

'Just a second,' she told the person on the other end, covered the mouthpiece with her hand and looked at Sean.

'Fiona, I need you to text the victim's address to DS Jones and then get down to the scene and meet her there.'

'OK,' Cahill agreed without question.

'Any luck with Roddis?'

'I'm on the phone to them now.'

'Good. Have the informant meet you at the address. Find out everything you can from him.'

'Her boyfriend?'

'Yes,' confirmed Sean. 'And get the details of her missing car. If our man's following his normal pattern, he would have taken it and dumped it in a park or woods. We need to find and preserve it.'

'I'll make sure it's done,' she assured him.

'Good,' Sean replied, suddenly sensing Anna close behind him.

'Is it OK if I go with Fiona to the scene?' she asked. Sean studied her for a few seconds before answering, trying to work out her intentions. She felt his wariness. 'I'd like to see the scene from the suspect's perspective, see if I can't learn something more about him.'

'OK, fine,' Sean finally agreed, turning to Donnelly and nodding towards the main office door. 'Keep me updated, everyone,' he called, striding from the room without a backward glance. 'As soon as anyone finds anything, I want to know about it.' He waved his iPhone above his head to make his point and disappeared through the swing doors.

As Sally pulled up outside Deborah Thomson's home she was immediately struck by the similarities between it and the homes of the other women who'd been taken. Another uninspiring, featureless, modern townhouse with a private drive and garage and a concealed front door. She almost called Sean straight away, but decided it could wait a little longer. DC Cahill was already standing outside the address with a short but muscular man in his early thirties, well groomed and well dressed. For the boyfriend of a missing woman he looked remarkably calm. Sally decided not to judge him until she had some more facts. She gave herself a few seconds to get into character before climbing from her car and walking towards them.

DC Cahill did the introductions. 'Sam, this is DS Jones. DS Jones, this is Sam Ewart, Deborah's boyfriend and our informant about her disappearance.'

Sally held out her hand. Underneath his slicked-back hair and tan Sally could see fear in his eyes, but what had aroused that fear – concern for Deborah or the prospect of being found out? Working on the assumption that DC Cahill had already done the softly-softly bit, she decided to jump in with the serious questioning and find out what Sam Ewart was really all about.

'What makes you think she's missing, Mr Ewart? Maybe she just doesn't want to see you?'

'No,' Ewart replied, sounding sad and anxious. 'She was supposed to meet me for breakfast – she was looking forward to it, I know she was, and so was I.'

'How long have you been together?'

'Only a few weeks.' Sally looked him up and down, the reason for his appearance becoming clear to her now – he was still trying to impress Deborah, keep the fledgling relationship on course. 'Listen,' he said, 'I know about the other two women. The women that went missing. I saw it on the news. He's already killed one. He's taken her, hasn't he? That's why you're here, because you think he's taken Deborah?'

'We don't know anything for sure yet. Let's try not to get too far ahead of ourselves, eh? Sometimes people take off, you know. They need a little time alone. That might be all—'

'Not Deborah,' Ewart snapped. 'He's taken her. I'm certain of it.' He was shaking as he tried to hold back his tears of frustration.

'Do you have keys for the house?' Sally asked.

'Yes.' He fumbled in his pocket and handed her two keys, one for the mortise and one for the Yale locks.

'Have you been inside?'

'No.'

'Why not?'

'I only got the keys an hour ago. I don't have a set for her house. A friend of hers from the hospital had these. By the time she gave them to me, the police had already told me not to go inside.' Sally nodded her understanding. She considered delegating the task to DC Cahill, but felt more afraid of being left alone with Ewart, his sorrow and fear, than she did about entering the house by herself.

'I need to take a look inside,' she told DC Cahill. 'You wait here with Mr Ewart.'

'Shouldn't we wait for forensics to arrive?' queried Cahill.

'Guv'nor wants me to take a look first. Besides, we haven't checked the address for any signs of the victim.' Immediately regretting referring to Deborah Thomson as a victim in Ewart's presence, she almost apologized, but then decided it would only amplify her mistake. 'I'll be a few minutes,' she said.

Unlocking first the mortise and then the Yale, she pushed the door ajar and peered into the small house, the warmth from the blaring central heating washing over her as it rushed into the chill of outside. 'Hello,' she called weakly into the silent interior, her voice choked by her constricted, dry throat. She coughed her airway open wider. 'Hello. Police. Is anyone at home?' No answer.

Sally stepped inside, pulling the door to behind her, making sure it was left slightly ajar and unlocked. If she needed to get out fast she didn't want to be struggling with locks and latches. As she moved away from the entrance she noticed her hands were trembling and gripped them together to control the shaking. She pushed herself further into the innards of Deborah Thomson's once-safe haven, now the scene of the first of many crimes that would be committed against her.

She moved slowly forward, occasionally glancing at her feet to ensure she wasn't trampling over obvious evidence left by the madness that had come into Deborah Thomson's life, training and experience kicking in as if she'd switched to autopilot, guiding her through the scene without her having to consciously think about what she was doing or where she was.

Noticing a burglar alarm control panel on the side of the hallway wall, she moved in closer to examine it. The alarm was unarmed, its light blinking green. Had the other houses been alarmed? She thought back to the time she'd spent in Karen Green's house, to the reports of the findings from both the previous scenes. She couldn't be sure, but she seemed to remember both homes had alarms, although neither had been activated. Clearly the madman wasn't comfortable with alarms and lacked the expertise or knowledge to deactivate them – another reason why he used artifice to gain entry and risked abducting the women during daylight.

The kitchen was straight ahead, but first she needed to check the room immediately to her right, the door to which was half-closed. As she peered through the crack she prayed the room was empty, knowing she would be unable to deal with a dead body – or even a hung-over Deborah Thomson, sleeping through the phone calls and Sally's noisy progress through her house. Even if it meant the swift, uncomplicated, safe conclusion of the search for the missing woman, Sally could do without any surprises.

She eased the door open slowly, pushing with the back of her hand, ready to take flight the second she sensed danger, pausing while she unclipped her extendable baton, known as an ASP, from the holder strapped to her belt. The heavy metal in her hand made her feel a little more in control as she swung the door fully open and stared inside at what was clearly the living room. The modern inexpensive furniture made her suspect the house was only rented and that the fake leather suite, along with pretty much everything else, came included in the rent. It was impersonal and slightly scruffy – half-read magazines lying on the sofa and floor, prints of Monet and Cezanne in plastic frames adorning the walls. A heavy grey box with a small screen made do for a television, the digital conversion box perched precariously on top. Sally remembered the missing woman was a nurse. Clearly the rent was swallowing most of her income – even her collection of CDs and DVDs was far from impressive. 'Or maybe you just have more of a life than I do?' she whispered to herself. A shiver ran through her whole body as she backed out of the room, returning the door to half-open position, careful not to leave her fingerprints on it.

She covered the few steps to the wide open kitchen door and looked inside, her eyes searching every angle and corner, the smells of Deborah Thomson's last meals still clinging to the walls and work surfaces, magnified by the heat in the room and the windows that had been sealed shut since the first signs of winter the preceding year. Once inside the room she immediately noticed a functional brown handbag perched on the kitchen table. Next to it lay a simple mobile phone that occasionally vibrated to warn the owner they had missed calls or text messages still waiting to be read. The thought that Deborah Thomson might never read those messages or listen to the voicemails flashed through her mind. She shook it away, but could do nothing about the bitter taste of bile seeping into her mouth.

Sally crossed the kitchen and tried to look into the handbag without touching it, but it was no use. Cursing herself for not having a pair of rubber gloves with her, she took a pen from her jacket pocket and began to poke around inside the bag. After a few minutes of searching as best she could without emptying the contents out, she was satisfied that what she was looking for was indeed missing. Deborah's bag was still here and so was her mobile phone, but both her house and car keys were nowhere to be seen. For Sally it was the final confirmation that Deborah Thomson been taken by the man they were hunting. She needed to phone Sean, but as she searched for his number a voice calling from the door startled her, making her almost drop her phone. It was Anna. 'Sally. You in there?'

'Don't come in,' Sally commanded, but Anna ignored her and stepped into the hallway. 'This is a crime scene. You shouldn't be in here.'

'Sorry, but I was worried about you. I don't think you should be in here alone, not yet.'

'I'm fine,' Sally lied. 'What are you doing here anyway?'

'I came with DC Cahill.'

'I didn't see you when I arrived,' Sally accused.

'No. I was checking the rest of the street.'

'What for?'

'Trying to see things as he would have seen them.'

Sally rolled her eyes and muttered under her breath. 'Not you as well.'

'Sorry?'

'Nothing, but if you're coming in, at least stick to the sides of the hallway.'

'I know the procedure at a crime scene,' said Anna, walking to meet Sally in the kitchen. 'Find anything?'

'Her bag and mobile are here, but her keys are missing.'

'It's him then?' Sally didn't answer. 'I really don't think you're ready for this,' Anna persisted. 'You need to move more slowly, tell Sean you need to ease yourself back to what you did before.'

'You don't understand,' Sally whispered. 'If I tell Sean, I'm finished. He'll have to refer me for psychiatric help, then I'm finished in the CID, finished in the police. I'm a cop. We're not allowed to need help. We're expected to deal with it, no matter what. Once we can't, we're no use to anyone. Sean's a good man, but the second he thinks I'm a liability to him or the team he'll get rid of me just as fast as anyone else would.'

'I think you're underestimating him.'

'He's a cop,' said Sally. 'He won't be able to help himself.'

'Then come and see me privately. I guarantee I'll keep it totally confidential – no feedback to the police. We all need someone to talk to, Sally, especially after a life-changing event.'

'Maybe,' Sally answered without commitment. A loud angry voice at the front door ended their conversation.

'What the bloody hell are you two doing in my crime scene?' an angry DS Roddis shouted. 'Right, neither of you are going anywhere until I've had a look at your shoes. If you're lucky, I might let you keep your clothes.'

Sean and Donnelly entered the large, chaotic building that served as the South Norwood sorting office unannounced. Sean finished talking to Sally on his mobile and stuffed the phone into the pocket of his raincoat.

'Well?' Donnelly asked.

'Sally, from the latest scene. Everything seems to indicate our boy has taken her.'

'This is getting seriously out of hand,' Donnelly warned. 'A third victim – the media are gonna go crazy.'

'Best we end it then, and quickly.' Sean was preoccupied, looking around the inside of the cavernous building. The high ceilings and exposed pipework made it look more like the bowels of a giant ship than a place where mail was sorted. People in Royal Mail uniforms mingled with people dressed normally, adding to the feeling of disorganization.

There seemed to be an absence of leadership or direction; although many of the workers had watched them suspiciously, no one had yet queried their presence. Losing patience with being ignored, Sean grabbed the next person who walked past. 'I need to speak with a supervisor or a manager,' he demanded.

'Upstairs,' the man stammered. 'F-first floor.' Sean followed the man's eyes across the room to a wide metal staircase. 'There's signs,' he added, unwilling to help further, aware of unfriendly eyes watching his every move.

'Thanks,' said Sean, holding on to the man's arm a few seconds before releasing him. The man scuttled away, glancing over his shoulder.

The detectives crossed the room, staring hard at everyone they passed, hoping they might get lucky and spook someone into running. As soon as he'd chased the runaway down, Sean knew it would only take one look into his eyes to tell him whether it was their man.

Their shoes clanked loudly on the metal steps. 'These stairs are murder on my old knees,' Donnelly quipped. Sean ignored him, his mind already turned towards the supervisor they were yet to meet – the questions he would ask him; the threats and promises he would make to get the information he needed. He paused at the top of the stairs and looked around, breathing the stale air in deeply, listening to the sounds of the living building.

Donnelly walked on a few steps before he realized Sean had stopped. 'Problem?'

Sean raised his hand to stop him saying more. 'He works here.' He was nodding to himself. 'Our guy's a real postman and he works here, in this sorting office.'

'Maybe.'

'No. Definitely,' Sean insisted.

'How do you know? We haven't even confirmed this office covers all the abduction sites.'

'It feels right. Everything about it feels right. I can feel him here. Can't you?'

'Let's just say if it turns out he does work here I won't exactly fall off my chair,' said Donnelly. 'But for now perhaps we should concentrate on getting hold of a supervisor – see if we can't find some evidence to go with your gut feeling.'

'What?' Sean asked, his semi-trance broken. 'Yeah, sure. Lead the way.'

The man Sean had accosted had been right about the signs – they were everywhere. They found one marked *Supervisor* and walked in the direction the arrow indicated, along narrow, gloomily lit corridors, passing cheap wooden doors adorned with white plastic name plates. It was Saturday and most of the side rooms were abandoned for the weekend. The detectives moved deeper into the upper floor of the building, searching for signs of life.

'Fuck me, guv'nor, this place makes your average police station look positively cheery,' Donnelly announced.

'Not exactly big on security either,' Sean agreed.

They kept walking until they finally found a room that had someone inside. The name plate said *Supervisors Only.* Sean knocked on the open door and waited for the man to turn around, but he carried on sitting with his back to them.

'If it's overtime you're after, there's plenty of it. If you want to change routes, you'll have to fill in the forms,' the man said without looking.

'I'll bear that in mind,' Donnelly couldn't resist saying, but at least it made the man turn around.

'Who are you and what do you want?' the supervisor asked in a slight West Indian accent.

Sean studied him for a few seconds before speaking. He had receding grey hair and a beard to match, spectacles perched on the bridge of his nose, a brown cardigan draped over his tall, slim torso, casual grey slacks flowing down to shoes that were more like slippers. He looked as if he should be at home in front of his ancient electric bar heater rather than at work. Retirement wasn't far away, but he'd obviously decided to start practising already. Sean flipped his warrant card open and held it out.

'DI Sean Corrigan, and this is DS Donnelly. We have a few questions I think you can help us with.'

'If you're here to arrest a member of staff you need to speak to the Post Office investigation team. I don't want to get involved in any of that. If I do, their union will string me up and hang me out to dry, you understand?'

'We're not interested in any member of staff who may have been nicking credit cards or cash sent in the post by Grannie Whoever. There's no need to get the Post Office investigation people involved,' Donnelly told him.

'Then why are you here?'

'Watched much telly lately? Read any newspapers, Mr . . .?' Donnelly continued.

'Leonard Trewsbury, supervisor here, and if you're asking whether I know what's happening in the world then the answer is yes.'

Sean sensed an intelligence in the man's eyes and an integrity in the way he held himself. 'Then you're probably aware that a couple of women were abducted last week. One of whom was subsequently found murdered?'

'I saw it,' Trewsbury answered. 'A terrible thing, but terrible things happen in this world, don't they? You gentlemen would know that better than most, I suppose.'

Sean found himself liking the man, his planned approach changing from aggression and threats to one of cooperation. 'I need your help with something – something that could save a life, maybe two.'

'Two?' Trewsbury asked. 'Then by the very nature of what you've just said, the man you are looking for must have abducted another woman?'

'Unfortunately, yes,' Sean confirmed.

'What do you need from me?'

'Access to your work records, employee details, unexplained absenteeism.'

'I can't show you that without a Production Order, and even then I'd have to speak to the Board of Directors. I can't just give you access to that kind of information.'

'I don't have time to go through the proper channels,' Sean told him. 'One of the women he's holding probably has less than forty-eight hours to live unless we find her. Her name is Louise Russell and she doesn't deserve to die because of bureaucracy.' The three men stared silently at each other for several seconds before Sean spoke again. 'Anything you tell us will be off the record. It'll never come out that we even spoke to you. Tell us what we need to know and we'll find a way to make it look like the information came from someplace else, I promise. But I can't walk out of here without information that could save lives, just because I don't have a piece of paper with a judge's signature on it. I can't do that.'

Trewsbury considered this for a moment. 'No, I don't suppose you can. So, what do you want to know?'

Sean handed him a piece of paper pulled from his coat's inside pocket. 'These are the addresses the women were taken from. I need to find out who works those routes.'

'Hold on a second,' said Trewsbury. 'I'll need to log on to the system to find that out.' He tapped the postcodes into the keyboard on his desk and waited a few seconds. 'These addresses are on different routes, covered by three different guys: Mathew Bright, Mike Plant and Arif Saddique.'

'Have you had problems with any of them?' Sean asked.

'No. They're all good workers, keep themselves to themselves.'

'Have they ever covered each other's routes – say, if one of them was sick or on holiday, for instance?'

'That information's not going to be in the system, I'm afraid. There would be a paper trail, but it could take days to trace and cross-reference. I'll do it for you if you still want to know, but I can't do it straight away.'

'I haven't got that sort of time.' Sean rubbed his temples with his middle fingers. 'What about yesterday? Who covered the address in Streatham?'

'Mathew Bright,' Trewsbury answered unhesitatingly. 'Same as he always does.'

'How can you be so sure?' queried Donnelly.

'I was here yesterday and so were these three guys. No one covered for any of them.'

'But this would have been in the afternoon,' Sean told him, 'some time after 2 p.m. That's a bit late for post to be delivered.'

'Not here it's not,' Trewsbury said. 'We've got such a backlog we're permanently paying guys overtime so they can catch up on deliveries, and yesterday was no different. Mathew was working all the way up to six o'clock.'

'Tell me about him,' said Sean. 'Tell me about Mathew Bright.'

'He's not the man you're looking for,' Trewsbury insisted. 'I've known him for years. He's a straightforward family man who likes a pint with the boys every now and then. He's as predictable as he is unintelligent.'

'What does he look like?' Sean asked.

'He's white, in his forties, a big man . . .'

'It's not him,' Sean stopped him. 'What about the other two? What do they look like?'

'Plant is white and Saddique is obviously Asian, both in their fifties . . .'

Sean cut him off again. 'In their fifties?'

'I would say so.'

'Then it's not them either.'

'Anything else you want me to try?' offered Trewsbury.

'Is there anyone who works here who's given you cause for real concern – strange behaviour, violent outbursts, reclusive, secretive?' Sean asked.

'Hundreds of people work here, some for years, others only last a few days. Full-time employees, casual workers – we have them all. There are plenty who aren't exactly angels, but no one's ever given me real trouble, nothing I can't handle. There's a group think they run the place, give the other workers a hard time now and again, but they're just shop-floor bullies, all bark and no bite. Nobody here strikes me as the type to do what you're talking about. I'd like to think that if there was, I'd be able to tell.'

'Not always that easy,' Sean told him. 'Do you have photographs of the men that work here?'

'Yes.'

'Can I see them?'

'I want to help, Inspector, but I can't let you do that. If I start pulling up employee records, someone somewhere is going to work out it was me that gave you unauthorized and frankly illegal access. I'm sorry, but I just can't do it.'

'OK, but if it was something more subtle would you help me? Something no one could trace. Something off the computer system.'

'I'm listening.'

'I'm looking for someone who's worked all three of those routes at one time or another during the last twelve months or so. Maybe they were his routes or maybe he was just filling in. There'd be a paper trail of that, right?'

'There would.'

'Can you do that for me? Will you check the paper trail?'

'It'll take a couple of days.'

'I know, but will you do it?'

Trewsbury paused a few seconds, exhaling before speaking. 'I'll do it, but if anyone says I did, I'll deny it.'

'Fair enough.'

'Well, if there's nothing else, gentlemen, it appears I have a lot of work to get through.'

'I can't tell you how much I appreciate this,' Sean assured

him, handing him his business card. 'Give me a ring on the mobile number as soon as you find anything, no matter what time of day.'

'I will,' Trewsbury promised.

'Thanks for your time,' said Sean, heading for the door. 'Oh, one more thing.' He turned back to the supervisor.

'Go on.'

'Have there been any reports or allegations of unusual thefts here in the last few months? Drugs or medical supplies?'

'Why do you ask?'

'I can't tell you. If I could, I would, but I need to know.'

Trewsbury slowly nodded his head, the belief that he might be working alongside a man who had killed a young woman troubling him deeply. 'A few months ago there was an incident,' he confessed.

'Go on,' Sean encouraged.

'A consignment of alfentanil went missing. Our investigation team looked into it, but whoever took it was never found.'

'You have controlled drugs passing through this sorting office?' Donnelly asked disbelievingly.

'Of course,' Trewsbury answered, 'particularly smaller consignments going abroad, often for relief agencies working in the subcontinent. We're still the cheapest way to get small packages overseas, despite what you may hear.'

'I assume you keep them in a secure location?' Sean asked.

'Yes. We lock them in our strong room, but someone got in and out without being seen and took the alfentanil.'

'CCTV?' Sean queried.

'No. Unions won't allow it – quoted the European Commission on Human Rights, no less.'

'A very unfortunate piece of legislation.' Donnelly shook his head mournfully.

'Fair enough,' Sean conceded. 'If you find anything, call me straight away.'

'I will,' Trewsbury promised. 'Wait a minute.' He scribbled something on a notepad, ripped the top sheet off and handed it to Sean. 'My mobile number, in case I'm not on duty when you need to speak. I probably shouldn't be doing this, but what the hell.'

Sean took the note and slipped it in his inside jacket pocket. 'Appreciated,' he told Trewsbury.

As Trewsbury watched the detectives walk from his office back into the gloom of the corridor he chewed the soft end of a pen and considered Sean for a while. He'd met dozens of Donnellys in his time with the Post Office, but he sensed a difference in Sean, a rare intensity and determination. He would do what he could to help him.

As the detectives headed for the exit, Sean could think of nothing other than the man he hunted, seeing him everywhere he turned in the giant building, imagining him standing by a bank of pigeonholes organizing his daily drop; climbing the same staircase he and Donnelly had as he headed for the canteen or even Trewsbury's office, hands gripping the same rail, feet stepping on the same flooring tiles. He breathed the air in deeply, hoping to somehow pick up on the scent of his prey, seeing himself walking up behind the faceless man, resting a hand on his shoulder and slowly turning him around, confident that as soon as he looked into his eyes he would know he had found the killer he hunted.

His thoughts were broken like shattering glass by Donnelly's gruff voice, a mixture of Glaswegian and Cockney, his throat rubbed raw by the thirty cigarettes he'd consumed every day for the last twenty-five years. Donnelly couldn't wait to be free of the ubiquitous *No Smoking* signs so he could fill his lungs with warm, nicotine-laced smoke. 'So, what do we do next?'

'He works here,' Sean told him. 'It all makes sense. I should have been on to it quicker.'

'You need to slow down, guv'nor, not speed up. Don't get

me wrong – in theory what you're saying makes sense. But hard evidence – we don't have a thing. One witness saying a postie put junk mail through his door even though he told the Post Office not to, that's really all you've got. The rest is in your—'

'In my what?' Sean barked. Donnelly didn't answer. 'We need to take DNA off everybody who works here. Within a few days we'll match it to samples from Karen Green and he'll be dead in the water. Fucking game over.'

'That's gonna take some time to organize,' Donnelly reminded him. 'Today's Saturday which means tomorrow is Sunday. This place won't even be open and nobody at the Yard's gonna authorize a mass DNA screening until it's been discussed to death by the powers that be, so maybe we get it authorized by what . . . Tuesday at the earliest? Start testing on Wednesday or Thursday?'

'That's too slow. We need to start now.' Sean sounded desperate, almost irrational, ignoring the very real legal obstacles that meant it was impossible to do what he wanted when he wanted.

'Guv'nor, we can't. It isn't going to happen.'

'So what do you suggest, Dave?'

'I don't know, but we had better pray we don't have to rely on a mass DNA screening to find Louise Russell. Because if we do, then she's fucked and so are we.'

Sean recoiled from Donnelly's crass assessment of their hopeless situation. 'Then we'll have to think of something else,' he said.

'Listen, guv'nor, I've seen you pull a rabbit from the hat more than once, but we can't always rely on that. I mean, walking around here, chasing leads and witnesses, we shouldn't be doing this – the DCs and the uniforms should be. We should be back in the office checking through everything that everybody brings to us. The devil will be in the detail, that's how we'll find this bastard.'

'I know,' Sean agreed reluctantly, calming down, 'but I needed to come here, I needed to see the scenes. If I don't, then all the information reports and the witness statements mean nothing to me, d'you understand? I might as well be looking at blank bits of paper. I have to feel him. We will do what you want, but not just yet. I'm not ready yet.'

'Well, don't take too long,' Donnelly warned him. 'For all our sakes.'

Thomas Keller stood naked in front of the smeared cabinet mirror bolted to the wall of his dingy bathroom. The place reeked of damp from the black mould growing up the walls, the once pristine white seal inside the shower had long since rotted away to nothing. Cold water sprayed from the shower head behind him as he inspected the damage Deborah Thomson had done to his face. He poked and picked at the gouged scratches around his eyes and down his cheeks, their stinging pain and gaping, bloodless ugliness making him wince and moan. Maybe she wasn't the one after all? Maybe she wasn't the real Sam, just another imposter sent to try and destroy him? The wounds to his face told him it was something he had to consider.

He lifted a cotton-wool pad from the antiseptic it had been soaking in, took a deep breath and pressed it into the first of the cuts, waiting for the burning pain to come, screaming into the mirror when it did. Over and over he soaked the pad and applied it to his wounds, each time bawling like a child, the noise of the running shower distorting his agony.

When he was finally finished he surveyed his work, happy he'd removed the risk of infection. But it was obvious the scratches would take a while to fade and would probably leave him scarred. He thanked the God who had already forsaken him that today was Saturday and he didn't have to go back to work until Monday. By then the injuries should have calmed down a little and he would have had time to think of an excuse for how they came to be. For the time being all he could do was force himself into the waiting cold shower to ward off the lingering effects of the anaesthetic. He stepped into the freezing water and felt it sweep his breath away, the pressurized drops like the pricks of thousands of sharp needles on his skin. His mouth gaped open as he struggled to draw breath, his diaphragm refusing to relax and let him breathe. As he slowly grew accustomed to the temperature, the cleansing water had a revitalizing effect on his mind and body and he began to feel better.

He rolled his head on his shoulders and closed his eyes, allowing his mind to drift, hoping it would take him to a happy memory, back when he was with Sam or maybe the times spent in the cages with the women. But he had so few happy memories and so many nightmares. Suddenly he was a boy again, thirteen or fourteen, he couldn't remember. Small for his age and sexually immature, he would cower in a corner of the communal shower in the large, open changing room at the comprehensive school, hoping the other boys wouldn't notice him, but all too often they did. He felt someone kick his legs away, knocking him to the floor as the shower head above sprayed blinding water into his eyes, rendering his attackers almost invisible. He heard the squeaking of the tap as one of his tormentors turned the water from warm to cold and then up to scalding while kicks and punches battered his slim body. When the blows stopped, the whipping with damp towels began, their *whip-crack* mixing with the sounds of high-pitched hysterical laughter, the merciless attackers spurred on by the sight of violent red welts erupting all over his body, his thin white skin threatening to tear apart, the torture only ceasing when commanded to by the booming voice of a man.

'That's enough of that, boys. Turn off the showers, get dried, put your towels in the used towel basket and get dressed. If I hear any of you were late for your next class you'll be in detention.' The boys' laughter turned to moans and protests as they begrudgingly did as they were told.

Thomas Keller waited for the boys to leave the shower before pulling himself to his feet and heading for the exit, but as he reached the gap that led to the changing room, the teacher's arm stretched across his escape and blocked his path.

'Not you, Keller,' said a low voice. 'You're not dry yet.'

He looked up at the man in front of him. One of the much feared PE teachers, dressed in a green tracksuit, whistle around his neck on a ribbon, stared back at him with the same look in his eyes as he'd seen in the past, when others had made him do things he didn't want to do. 'Hurry up, you lot,' the teacher shouted over his shoulder to the rest of the boys. 'I want you all out of here in two minutes flat.'

Thomas stood in front of the man, shivering, one arm across his chest and the hand of the other cupping his undeveloped genitals. 'Please, sir, I'm cold. Can I get dressed?'

'Of course, Thomas,' the teacher agreed, but he stepped in front of the boy before he could pass. 'First, there's something I want you to do for me.'

'I don't understand,' he lied, all too familiar with the lascivious look in the man's eyes and what it meant.

The teacher stretched out a hand, making the boy take a step back.

'Don't worry, Tommy,' he reassured him. 'I won't hurt you. I'm here to protect you, to keep the other boys away from you – you'd like that, wouldn't you, to have someone to look after you?'

'Please, sir,' the boy pleaded, 'I'll be late for my next class.'

'Don't worry about that. I'll make sure you don't get in trouble.' Again he stretched his hand out, but this time the boy didn't move away, even though all his instincts told him to run. The promise of having someone to protect him, an adult to trust, overwhelmed his instinct to survive the moment. The teacher gently stroked his hair before allowing his hand to drift downwards, caressing the side of the boy's face. 'But first there's something I want you to do for me. You understand, don't you?'

Thomas shook his head. 'No, sir. What do you want me to do?'

The teacher's hand followed the curve of the boy's slim shoulders and slid down his arm, taking Thomas's hand in his own and pulling it towards the elasticated waistband of his tracksuit.

'Take it out,' the teacher ordered.

'I don't know what you want me to do,' the boy pretended.

'Yes you do,' said the teacher, still smiling, still holding the boy's hand. 'If you want me to help you, you'll have to do this for me first.' He let go of the boy's hand and rested both of his own on the boy's shoulders. 'Now do it.'

Tears of self-loathing began to sting the boy's eyes as he reached inside the teacher's tracksuit bottoms, feeling the warmth, the coiled pubic hairs scratching and itching his hand as his fingers found the teacher's rapidly swelling penis. 'Take it out,' he commanded, and the boy did as he was told. 'Move your hand up and down,' said the teacher between moans of pleasure, his head lolling backwards as his eyes began to close. The boy continued almost frantically pulling at his abuser's penis, experience telling him that the faster he did it, the sooner his humiliation and degradation would be over. 'Too fast,' the teacher managed to say. 'Do it slowly.' The boy obeyed. 'Good. Good. That's better. You know what to do next.'

'No,' the boy pleaded. 'I don't know how to do that.'

'Don't lie to me,' snarled the teacher. 'You don't think I know? You'd better do as you're told, you little slut, or I'll have to tell the children's home how I caught you stealing from the other boys' bags – then you'll be fucked, won't you, you little slut. When the grown-ups come on visiting days, when they come to find someone to adopt and take back to a proper home, they won't take you, will they? Not after the staff let them know you're a thief. Now, do as you're told.'

The boy felt sick, constricting convulsions in his chest and throat making him gag, but he knew he had no choice. If he ever wanted to be loved again, accepted again, he had no choice. He shuffled forward on his knees and did what the teacher wanted, the man's ecstatic moans drowning out the sound of his weak sobs. 'Yessss,' the teacher hissed, 'yessss, that's good, oh you little slut – you little fucking whore. You fucking whore, yes.'

Keller's body suddenly remembered it hadn't breathed for minutes, not since the memory returned to haunt and torture him. He breathed in as if he'd just broken through the surface of water he'd been trapped beneath, held under by an invisible force trying to drown him, his eyes springing wide open, the water from the shower washing over his eyelashes like tiny waterfalls. He buried his face in his hands and began to cry like he'd cried when he was thirteen or fourteen years old, alone in the shower with a man who'd promised to look after him. But the man hadn't protected him, he'd used him over and over again until he grew bored of him, his eyes turning to other vulnerable boys – boys living in care, boys whose parents couldn't cope with another mouth that needed feeding – and then he'd given Thomas to other men, all of whom had the same special name for him – *The little whore.* He slid down the wall of the shower and cowered on the floor, mumbling as the water filled his mouth. 'Mummy. Mummy, why did you leave me? You said you'd come back for me, but you didn't, you fucking bitch. Why did you leave me?' He curled into a tight ball and waited for the other boys to start kicking and punching him – to start tearing at his skin with their whip-like towels.

Sean and Donnelly pulled up outside Deborah Thomson's home, finding a parking space squeezed between the gathering forensic vehicles, little white car-vans fully loaded with everything Roddis and his team would need to sweep the scene clean. They walked towards the cordoned-off area and ducked under the blue-and-white police tape, flashing their warrant cards at one of the uniformed officers Roddis had drafted in to guard his precious exclusion zone. As they approached the house, Sean saw Sally standing at the end of the drive talking with Anna. Roddis was close to the front door with two of his team, already resplendent in their dark-blue paper forensic suits, preparing plastic and brown paper bags to receive their anticipated exhibits from inside the house. Sean acknowledged Sally and Anna, but kept walking towards Roddis.

'Mr Corrigan,' Roddis greeted him. 'I hope you don't expect to be allowed in the house dressed like that? You shouldn't even be inside the cordon.'

'My apologies,' Sean answered. 'And no, I don't need to go inside, not this time.' He scanned the house in front of him, a near identical property to the other two scenes. 'Anything for me yet?' He made no apologies for his impatience.

'We've had a poke around. There are traces of chloroform on the hallway floor and a couple of full ident fingerprints on the inside door handle which appear to be the same as the ones we took from the other two abduction sites.'

'How do you know they're the same?' Sean quizzed him. 'They haven't been to Fingerprints yet.'

'I keep my own copies on the laptop – the digital age is a wonderful thing. To my untrained eye, I'd say they were a match, but I imagine you already knew it was the same man, yes?'

Sean didn't answer. 'I need you to liaise with the door-to-door teams,' he said. 'If anyone in the street's had junk mail pushed through their front doors in the last couple of days, I want them to seize it and hand it all over to you for finger-printing. I'm assuming you've worked out why?'

'Probably,' Roddis confirmed. 'So you think your man's been posting stuff through other doors, no doubt trying to blend in while he scouted the area?'

'I do.' Sean's iPhone vibrated in his coat pocket. He wrestled it free of the resisting material and touched his finger on the screen to answer. 'Sean Corrigan.'

'Inspector Corrigan. How are you this fine day?' He recognized Dr Canning's voice immediately.

'I've been better.'

'Never mind. Thought you'd like to know that I've released Karen Green's body into the care of the Coroner's Officer. The family are due to formally identify her at 2 p.m.' Sean glanced at his watch – it was already 1 p.m. 'Her body has been moved to the chapel of rest. Better for the family to see her there. We'll make her look as presentable as we can.'

'Good,' said Sean, 'and thank you.'

'Don't mention it. By the way, I've also identified what made the rather mysterious circular bruises we found all over her body.'

'I'm listening,' Sean encouraged, unaware that he'd stopped breathing while he waited for what could be the breakthrough piece of the puzzle he'd been searching for.

'He used an electric cattle prod. We tested a fair few instruments of torture, but only the prod gave us an exact match.'

Sean breathed again. 'Son of a bitch. Question now is, where the hell did he get it from?'

'A farm,' Canning offered. 'Maybe he keeps his victims on a farm?'

'Not many farms in south-east London.'

'Perhaps he lives further afield than you thought?'

'No,' Sean dismissed the suggestion. 'He's no farmer coming up from the sticks to snatch his victims. This one likes to stay close to what he knows.'

'Well, I know better than to argue with you.'

Sean had already moved on. 'I need you to do something else for me.'

'Such as?'

'Run a full screening for toxins in her blood.'

'No doubt you're going to ask me if she has traces of anything that could be used as an anaesthetic or a pre-anaesthetic, something that would make a person compliant but not technically unconscious?'

Sean's eyes darted from side to side, uncomfortable with having anybody one step ahead of him, even Dr Canning, a man he trusted more than most. He suddenly realized what must have happened. 'You've already run the tests, haven't you?'

'Of course,' Canning answered, the satisfaction in his voice barely concealed.

'And you found traces of alfentanil.'

The satisfaction in Canning's voice turned to disbelief. 'How did you know?'

'I'll tell you later,' Sean promised. 'Could you inform the Coroner's Officer that I'll be there to meet the family at the identification.'

'Of course,' said Canning.

Sean hung up and turned to Sally. 'The formal identification of Karen Green will be at Guy's at two. I could do with you there.'

Sally's mouth fell open, but no words came out.

'I'll go,' Anna jumped in. 'I'd like to go. I want to go.'

'This won't be fun,' Sean assured her. 'Sally has experience with this. You don't. Sally?' She looked at the floor rather than answer. He saw she wasn't ready yet.

'Besides,' Anna continued, 'if I see the victim's body and meet with some of her family, it may help me with profiling the offender. And there'll be a Family Liaison Officer with them too, correct?'

'There will be,' Sean agreed. 'DC Jesson.'

'Then I can't see a problem.'

Recognizing her noble intent, Sean decided that if it gave Sally an easy out then he'd take it. 'OK, but follow my lead and don't say a damn thing without checking with me first. Understood?'

'Understood,' she promised. Sean began to walk towards his car, continually shaking his head. He realized Anna wasn't following and turned back.

'Well, you coming or what?'

She rested a hand on Sally's shoulder and rolled her eyes before walking after him.

'Women,' Sean muttered to himself. 'The one thing I'll never understand.'

The two women sat together but alone under the dull, jaundicing light of the low-powered bulb that hung above their heads, the sound of water trickling somewhere in the cellar as deafening in the silence as it was maddening. Deborah Thomson clutched her damaged knee and rocked backwards and forwards on the floor of her hellish prison. Her body was drained of adrenalin and she sobbed quietly from the pain and the fear, her last chance of escape and survival surely gone. She was going to die in this dark, damp cellar – or somewhere worse. He would eventually come to take her life. She saw his hands slipping around her throat, squeezing, pushing his fingers into her trachea until it was crushed, the pressure halting the flow of blood through her carotid arteries to her brain, unconsciousness and death soon following.

Her rocking became increasingly frantic and her breathing on the verge of hyperventilation. She looked across the room to Louise Russell, lying silent and motionless but for her constant shivering, her near naked body coiled on the floor, her back towards her, the bones of her spine already becoming more prominent after just a few days without water or food. Deborah knew Louise was growing weaker and weaker – if he didn't kill her she would probably be dead from hypothermia soon anyway.

A trembling voice made Deborah jump with fright. 'How could you leave me?' the weak voice asked. 'How could you do that?'

It was a while before she could answer, the words stuck in her shrunken throat as if his fingers were already coiled around it.

'I panicked,' she managed to say. 'I was scared, so scared. I saw the light and could smell the air from outside and I just . . . I just had to get away. I had to get away from here. I couldn't think of anything else. My mind went blank . . . and I ran. I'm sorry. I'm so sorry.' Her tears ran into the mucus trickling from her nose, making her face shiny and slippery as she tried to rub it away with the backs of her hands. She inhaled deeply to clear her nose and control her crying. 'If I get another chance I won't leave you, I promise. I won't panic.'

'There won't be another chance,' Louise whispered calmly, as if she'd already accepted her fate. 'You've killed us both.' She rolled over slowly so she was facing Deborah, her eyes wide open and sparkling with life despite her exhaustion. 'You've killed us both.'

'Don't say that,' Deborah told her sharply. 'You don't know that.' Louise didn't answer, her green eyes staring in accusation.

'We'd already picked names for them,' she said.

'Sorry?' Deborah asked. 'I don't understand. Names for who?'

'Our children. The children we were going to have. We'd already picked their names. If we had three boys we were going to call them John, Simon and David. If they were girls we were going to call them Rosie, Sara and Elizabeth.'

'What if you had a mixture?' Deborah asked, wishing she hadn't.

'We never talked about that. Somehow I knew we'd have three boys or three girls, so we never discussed it. Silly really.' Deborah said nothing. Louise continued, her voice growing a little stronger as her mind temporarily freed her body from her hell. 'I like the boys' names – strong and simple, like my husband. He's called John too.'

'I remember,' said Deborah.

'His name suits him. Honest and strong. Not the most handsome, not the funniest or cleverest, but good and reliable. I don't know how he's going to be when he finds out what's happened to me. I'm worried he'll never forgive himself for not being there to stop it, for not being able to save me.'

'You shouldn't think like that,' Deborah said, more because it was torture for her, having to listen to it, than out of any wish to help Louise.

'I miss him so much,' Louise continued. 'I even miss the children – isn't that ridiculous? I miss the children we haven't even had. We talked about them so often I can see their faces, the shades of their hair, their freckles. I can smell them – somehow I can feel them, yet they don't exist, and now they never will.'

'Because of me,' Deborah snapped. 'That's what you're saying, isn't it? They won't exist because of me.'

'No,' Louise answered, her dry, shrunken lips forming a tiny smile. 'No matter what you did, you didn't bring me here. He's the one that did that.'

'Listen,' Deborah sighed, 'I was brought up in New Cross, you know it?'

'A little.'

'Then you know what it's like. I was the only girl with three older brothers and I had to fight for everything. Sometimes I even had to fight my brothers for food or go hungry. I had to fight the other kids at school or forever be picked on. Whatever I got, I got it myself. Where I grew up, there was only one rule – look after number one, because nobody else would. So when I saw my chance I took it, and I was wrong. I should have got the keys and let you out. I should have given you the same chance I had, but I didn't. I'm ashamed of my instinct, but if your life had been like mine you'd have run too, no matter what you think you'd have done. I promise you, you would have run.'

Neither spoke for a long while. Then Louise broke the silent tension.

'Are you loved?' she asked. 'Like I'm loved by John. Does anyone love you like that?'

'I don't know . . . my mum, brothers.'

'No, not like that. A man – a man who's your soul mate. Or a woman?'

'Maybe there's a man. His name's Sam. I haven't known him long.'

'Sam – that's a good name.'

'I think he's a good man, but I don't miss him the way you miss John. I'm alone down here. You have John and your imagined children, but I'm alone. I can't escape this hell, not even for a second.' There was another lengthy silence between them. 'I still keep thinking this has to be a nightmare – that I'll wake up soon. But it's been going on too long to be a nightmare, hasn't it? And the pain, you don't feel pain like this in nightmares, so I know it's real, but I still can't believe it.'

'We're here, aren't we? And we're real. Out there, people we've never met or known will be watching the news, following our story, looking at photographs of us, listening to our families appealing to this bastard to let us go unharmed. But you're right, we won't be real to them. They'll feel nothing for us. To them, we're light entertainment. We're only real to the people who love us. No one else cares. Once we're dead, so is the story and we'll be forgotten by everyone but those who love us.'

'Then those who love us won't give up on us and we shouldn't give up on them. And the police, they won't give up on us. They'll keep looking for us. They won't stop. They can't.'

'The police? How could they possibly find us down here? What could lead them to . . . him. You've heard him, you've seen him. He's completely insane. The police like things to make sense – a motive they can understand. Who could ever understand this lunatic?' Louise laughed quietly and cynically, the effort making her cough. 'What policeman on the face of God's earth could ever understand this madman enough to find him? If there is such a man, then may God pity his soul.'

11

Sean and Anna entered the mortuary area in Guy's Hospital and went straight to the chapel that was attached to the complex. He'd been tempted to enter via the autopsy area, to show his face to Dr Canning and to see how Anna would react to being in the company of the dead, but had decided her reaction to seeing Karen Green's lifeless body would be enough. Inside the chapel was quiet and peaceful, feeling more like a church than a hospital, the walls painted a tranquil dark purple. Someone had even gone to the lengths of hanging long red curtains either side of the door the relatives would soon be brought through, despite the fact there were no windows. A crucifix bearing the body of Christ overlooked the scene below. A coffin-shaped, padded casket lay at the centre of the room on a low table that had been draped in red cloth that spread to the floor. Karen Green's body lay within.

Sean crossed the floor and looked into the long box. She'd been prepared well, as all murder victims were here, by Dr Canning's assistant and a little technical help from a local undertakers. A purple satin sheet covered her body, leaving only her face on show. Canning's team had worked miracles on her facial injuries and had even taken time to prepare her hair as best they could, brushing it neatly to one side so as not to obscure any of her once pretty face. He fought hard not to reach out and touch her face, as if somehow feeling her cold skin would connect him to the man who had ripped her young life away. Anna's voice close behind him dragged him back.

'I wasn't expecting it to be like this.'

'What were you expecting?'

'I don't know. Just . . . not this.'

'Did you think we were going to take her family into the main mortuary and slide her out of the freezer, pull back the green sheet and ask "Is this her?"'

'I don't know.'

'You've been watching too many TV cop shows.'

'Maybe.'

'How many dead bodies have you seen?' he asked, suspecting he already knew the answer.

'None,' she answered quickly and truthfully. He said nothing, but nodded his head knowingly.

Anna could sense his slight hostility and disapproval, as if she hadn't earned the right to be there in the same room as Karen Green or to be part of a murder investigation. He'd spent most of his adult life dealing with the unthinkable while she'd been cocooned in universities, giving lectures and writing books. She stepped forward and looked at Karen Green, her crystal green eyes now covered with dead eyelids. 'She looks peaceful, despite everything she must have been through.'

Sean looked away from the body to Anna, whose eyes were still fixed on Karen Green. He looked her up and down while she wasn't watching, judging her before responding to what she'd said. 'She didn't when she was lying in the woods. She didn't look peaceful then. They never do. They look . . . broken, like their souls have been torn away against their will. Death brings no peace.'

She looked at him from the corner of her eyes, feeling his cold blue stare. He was waiting for a reaction – a chance to study her the way she was used to studying others. The sound of his phone ringing made him look away.

'Hello.'

'Guv'nor, it's Sally. Uniform have found Deborah Thomson's car abandoned on Tooting Common, close to the outdoor swimming pool.' He didn't know the area, but the picture in his mind was vivid: a dirt-road leading to a secluded parking area, leafless trees bending slightly in the breeze as if reaching out for the car.

'Shit,' he cursed. 'Have we got anyone left who can cover the scene?'

'I don't think so,' Sally told him. 'That last box of soldiers you opened is just about empty. We're running out of people faster than we can replace them. This guy is getting ahead of us, Sean.'

'No he's not. I'll cover the scene myself. You stay with Roddis at her house and see what you can milk out of him. Call me if you find anything.' Without waiting for an answer, he hung up.

'Trouble?' said Anna.

'We've found Deborah Thomson's car. Abandoned. Tooting Common. I need to take a look. You can come, if you want.'

She nodded that she would. 'Don't you want to wait to see the family first?'

'No time for that now,' he told her, hoping she couldn't see the relief in his eyes at not having to face them. 'I need to check out the place her car was found as soon as possible.' He glanced over at the body of Karen Green. 'There's nothing more I can do for her now other than catch her killer. Her family will have to wait.'

Donnelly repeatedly cursed under his breath as he waded through the piles of information reports on his desk – door-to-door forms, each detailing the description of the person spoken to. Where were they at the time of the relevant abduction? Had they seen or heard anything? There were thousands of these statements, and all needed to be checked and cross-referenced, as did the information reports from the dozens of roadblocks carried out and drivers spoken to, ditto the reports back from officers checking possible venues where the women could be being kept, including the report from PC Ingram and PC Adams, following their brief search of Thomas Keller's land and buildings. Eventually all the information would be fed into the Home Office Large Major Enquiry System – HOLMES for short. Introduced in the early eighties, this lumbering dinosaur of a database was intended to allow relatively rapid and accurate cross-referencing of every type of document a murder investigation could generate. The intention was to prevent the sort of mistakes that had allowed the likes of Peter Sutcliffe, aka the Yorkshire Ripper, to kill as many women as he did, when simple cross-referencing would have brought his killing spree to a halt after two or three victims. For the most part, it worked well, but it still relied on the killer making a mistake.

Donnelly blew hard and made his lips and moustache vibrate as he pondered yet another useless door-to-door report before tossing it into the pile he'd designated *Not of interest.* The pile was growing monstrously high, while the pile designated *Of interest* remained worryingly small, but Donnelly knew exactly what he was doing, even if he never confided it in anyone else, cutting the reports down to a manageable size so that when Sean eventually read through them he wouldn't be swamped. The less crap Sean had to sift through, the freer he would be to think, to turn his unquestionable instinct to best use, to pick the diamond from the diamantes and eventually lead them to the man they so desperately needed to find.

Sensing a presence behind him, Donnelly peered over his shoulder. He had a fair instinct of his own and knew who it was without looking. 'What d'you fucking want, Paulo?'

'How d'you know it was me?' Zukov asked with a mischievous smile.

'I used my detective's intuition – you should try it sometime. Now, unlike you, I'm very busy, so what the fuck you want?'

'I was looking for the guv'nor, actually.'

'Why?' Donnelly asked, his patience beginning to fail him.

'It's about that transfer he had me researching, the one of the phoenix that was found on Karen Green's body.'

'Well, go on,' Donnelly encouraged an increasingly suspicious Zukov. 'You can tell me. I'll make sure the information gets passed on to the boss. Or have you discovered some vital clue that's going to solve the entire case and you want to be the one who tells the guv'nor yourself? Get all the credit?'

'Not exactly.'

'Well then, stop pissing about and tell me.'

'It's from a box of Rice Krispies.'

'What?' Donnelly asked incredulously, a broad, sarcastic smile spreading across his red face. 'That's it? That's the ground-breaking piece of information, is it? So we now know what the victim liked to eat for breakfast – Rice fucking Krispies. And how long did you waste finding this out, eh? Two days? Three days?'

'I dunno – three or four.'

'Oh Jesus Christ.' Donnelly shook his head in disapproval. 'What am I going to do with you, Paulo? What am I going to do with you?'

'Yeah, well you can take the piss all you like, but it might be important. The guv'nor seemed to think so, anyway. Besides, it doesn't tell us what she liked for breakfast, at least not now. Might tell us what she liked for breakfast sixteen years ago.'

'What are you on about?'

'The transfer was a free gift in boxes of Rice Krispies sixteen years ago. The manufacturers only did the one run of them, so either Karen Green hasn't had a bath or shower for sixteen years or for some reason she'd kept it safe for all that time and decided to use it just before travelling to Australia.'

'Is that the information report there?' Donnelly asked, pointing to the cardboard folder Zukov was holding.

'Yes,' Zukov answered.

'I'll take that,' Donnelly insisted, relieving the unhappy Zukov of his prize. 'It's probably nothing. I can't see its relevance, but all the same I'll pass it on to the boss, see what he makes of it. As for you, it's about time you got down to some proper police work.'

The aggrieved Zukov sloped away, leaving Donnelly to flick through the report. Zukov was right, the phoenix transfer was indeed sixteen years old.

'Weird,' he declared and tossed the report on to the pile designated *Of interest.*

A deeply disturbing sense of déjà-vu swept over Sean as he and Anna drove to the edge of the police cordon on Tooting Common. A one-time haunt of London's lowest class of prostitute, the area had changed significantly over the preceding ten years as the soaring house prices in Putney, Barnes and Sheen forced the wealthy and educated to seek new residential areas to colonize, pushing the not so fortunate ever further south or out of London altogether.

The blue-and-white police tape whistled in the breeze as it surrounded the entire car park. Sean parked quickly and headed for one of only two uniformed officers who were desperately trying to stop dog walkers and joggers from entering the scene to recover their cars. Anna struggled to keep pace with him as he closed on the policeman and flashed his warrant card. 'DI Corrigan. This is Dr Ravenni-Ceron. She's with me.' He ducked under the tape and held it up for Anna to follow. 'Have you touched the car?' Sean asked the young cop, looking across the car park at Deborah Thomson's abandoned red Honda Civic.

'No, sir,' he answered too quickly. 'Only to see if it was open.'

'I take it the car was locked,' said Sean.

'No, sir. It's open. The keys are still in the ignition.'

Sean stopped walking for a second, a little confused and surprised. 'The keys are still in it?'

'Yes, sir.'

'He's changed his method,' he told Anna, although he could barely believe what he was saying. 'I didn't see that coming.'

'It's a minor detail,' Anna replied. 'It doesn't necessarily mean anything.'

Sean stormed across the car park, talking as he walked. 'It has to mean something. With this one everything means something. If he's changed his method, then he's done it for a reason.' He stopped when he reached the car, filling his lungs with cool air before he began his cursory examination – an examination that he knew would draw him into another world.

'Maybe someone disturbed him?' Anna offered. 'Made him panic and leave the keys in the ignition.'

'No.' Sean snapped on a pair of rubber gloves. 'If he'd been disturbed we'd have known about it by now. Uniform would have come poking around and found the car. No. He left the keys behind because he's beginning to lose control, lose patience. He knows where all this is leading – maybe only subconsciously, but he knows.'

'You still think he's going to blow up?'

'Yes,' said Sean grimly, pulling the handle on the passenger's side door and slowly easing it open a couple of inches, his body tense as he prepared for the onslaught of scents that were about to rush from the car. The fragrance of a pine air freshener washed over him first, quickly followed by traces of perfume and make-up. He tried to remember the smell of Black Orchid and was as sure as he could be that this was not the same. What did that mean? Confirmation the killer made his victims wear the perfume of his choice? He tried to pick up a trace of Elemis body cream, but could not. He eased the door open wider and pushed his head into the space, recoiling at a smell he recognized – the same animalistic, musky scent he'd detected on other killers, other criminals he'd dealt with in the past – a smell of fear and desperation, guilt and excitement, a smell all good cops knew meant they had the right man. A scent he often feared oozed from his own skin pores. The madman had been here less than a day ago. His presence remained strong, almost as if he was still there inside the car.

Sean found himself staring at the driver's seat, unmoving, unblinking, watching as the shape of a man formed in his imagination, a dark hooded top covering his head. As he concentrated, the head slowly began to turn towards him, but the spectre had no face, just darkness where it should have been. In an instant the spectre faded, a solid image turning to gas before disappearing completely.

With a sigh Sean pulled himself out of the car and walked around to the boot, popping the hatch open, giving the door an initial pull, then allowing the pneumatics to do the rest. Once the hatch was fully open he placed his face as close as he dared to the carpeted floor of the boot and inhaled deeply. Anna saw how pale he looked.

'What is it?' she asked.

'Chloroform. He took her all right.' He looked around at the trees hissing conspiratorially in the wind, unspeaking witnesses to the beginning of Deborah Thomson's nightmare. Did the man he hunted see the trees as his allies, hiding him from the people who chased him – hiding him from Sean? 'Always the woods,' he said to himself.

'Sorry?' said Anna.

'Always the woods. Always the trees. It's the city he knows, but it's the woods where he's most comfortable. Wherever he lives will be surrounded by trees.'

'That doesn't narrow it down much.'

'No. No, it doesn't,' he admitted and started walking back to his own car. Anna rolled her eyes and followed him, feeling like a lost dog following its adopted owner, half-expecting Sean to try and chase her away at any time. 'Wait here until forensics arrive,' he instructed one of the uniformed officers as he walked briskly past them. The officer nodded his reply.

As they reached the car, Anna managed to slow Sean down by taking hold of his arm. 'I need to talk to you.'

'I've told you, I don't want to talk about me,' his eyes moved to the hand wrapped around his forearm and she released her grip.

'Nor do I.' He looked at her in surprise. 'I need to talk to you about Sally.'

'What about Sally?'

'She needs help. She needs counselling. I'd like to help her and I think she wants me to, but she could use a push from someone she trusts.'

'Meaning me?' Anna shrugged her shoulders. 'I can't do that. Sally's a cop, she wouldn't want anyone to know, including me. If she thought for a second anyone on the team knew she was getting counselling, she'd be destroyed.'

'Why?'

'Like I said, she's a cop.'

'I think Sally may be above the stereotypical macho image of a police officer.'

'Because she's a woman? Trust me, she's a cop before she's a woman, and that means she knows the score.'

'What on earth does—'

'We don't admit to needing help, even when we do. Being physically broken is fine, but mentally . . .? No one would work with her again.'

'That's pathetic.'

'I didn't say it was right, I just said that's the way it is. If you can persuade her to see you, fine, but for Christ's sake don't let anyone else know.'

'Jesus, you're a strange bunch. Cops, I'm beginning to think you're all crazy.'

'We're crazy – what about you? One minute you're helping the man who almost killed her, next you want to help her. Do you really know what happened to Sally? That night when Gibran broke into her home?'

'Of course. I read the reports before interviewing Sebastian.'

'The reports? And what did the reports say?'

'That she was attacked in her own home and seriously injured by two knife wounds to the chest.'

'That's nice and neat. Doesn't tell you how he stood over her while she was bleeding to death on her own living-room floor. Doesn't tell you about how she watched him searching through her kitchen knives for one to finish her off with. Doesn't tell you about the four different surgeries she had to keep her alive. Doesn't tell you about months of breathing, eating and drinking through plastic tubes. Doesn't tell you about the nightmares.'

'She told you all of this?'

'Christ, she didn't have to tell me, I saw it.' Neither spoke for a while. 'Listen, Anna, I like you, but you'll only ever be an outsider to us. You'll never be a cop. You stick around long enough, you'll learn more than most, but you'll never be one of us. You'll never really see what we do.'

'I know,' she admitted, 'and frankly I wouldn't want to be. Working with almost no sleep day after day, hardly eating or drinking, trying to think straight when your mind and body are exhausted . . . I admire you. I didn't think I would, but I do. And I admit it, I had no idea it would be like this.'

'You get used to it. I'll keep going, without sleep or rest if necessary, until I find this bastard and bury him. You never know, I might get lucky – he may blow up and top himself.'

'But not before he kills the women he's taken. And

according to your theory, not before he goes on a spree, settles a few old scores, real or imagined.'

'He's heading that way,' said Sean. 'Leaving the car open, with the keys inside – his control is slipping. Soon the women won't be enough.'

'I disagree,' said Anna. 'You're reading too much into the keys. If you want to catch him quickly you need to stick with local criminals, ones with juvenile convictions for residential burglaries, particularly ones with a history of defecating inside the houses they broke into. As they grew older there'll have been a progression to minor sexual offences, gradually becoming more serious. Possibly even rape.'

'No,' Sean snapped. 'He's beyond that. Besides, he's got no previous convictions, remember?'

'Then the police have missed something or the offender is incredibly lucky. Either way, he's showing all the signs of a sexual predator progressing from burglary to rape and murder. His crimes are a classic expression of power and anger, probably brought on by some cataclysmic rejection. The actual women mean little or nothing to him. The similarities in their appearance is due to the fact they remind him of the person who rejected him, most likely his mother or even grandmother, yet despite her rejection he still loves her and wants to be with her, hence he takes the women who remind him of her.'

'No,' Sean argued, his voice raised in frustration. 'He hates his mother, his grandmother, everyone who betrayed him, and that means everyone in the world. Everyone except for one woman – the one who showed him kindness and acceptance, at least initially. But it didn't last. Again he was rejected, but he still loves her; despite the rejection, he still loves her.' As he spoke he began to drift away from her, melting into the shadow-land, a land inhabited by just two people: Sean and the man he hunted. A land of thousands of questions and almost no answers, but still it was where he needed to go, to keep walking through the fog. His mind stretched out as if trying to see the path ahead before he tripped and fell on unseen hazards. 'Everybody who's ever rejected him, he hates. He despises them. Dreams about the day when he'll have his revenge. Yet in her case, even after she rejected him, he's gone on loving her. He covets her, craves her, wants to keep the time they had together alive. Why doesn't he hate her too?' He sensed Anna was about to speak and thrust an upturned palm towards her to stop her. 'It doesn't make sense – she does to him what everyone else has done to him, yet he still loves her – I mean *really* loves her. Why is she so different?' It felt as though he was reading a burning letter – the answer smouldering in gentle orange flames, turning to ashes before he could read it to the end.

Anna was more than just watching him now – she was studying him, his eye movements, how often he closed his eyes, his hand gestures, the movement of his constantly clenching and releasing fingers, the way he occasionally cocked his head to one side as if to hear some whisper only he could detect, the way he rotated on the spot where he stood, turning fully three hundred and sixty degrees one way then back the other. She'd seen this level of projected imagination in some of the killers she'd interviewed, but never so strong in someone *sane,* and always their imaginations would only satisfy them for so long before their fantasies had to become reality. She continued to study him, even when he suddenly froze, eyes staring at nothing.

'Fuck it,' he swore. 'It's gone.'

'What's gone?' Anna asked, hoping he would be able to return to his conscious trance.

'Nothing. It doesn't matter.'

'Sean, I have to say, I think this theory of yours about some mythical woman he's looking to replace is a red herring that will lead—'

'No,' Sean broke in. 'It's the key to finding him. Find her, we find him.'

'What you believe would indicate he is an Expressive killer, killing as a release of anger and frustration, using the victims as replacements for someone known to him, but I see no sign of that here. His crimes are classically Instrumental: planned, cold, unemotional, an expression of some other as yet unknown desire.'

'Clinical terms,' Sean barked, his temper rising, swelling painfully in his chest. 'Instrumental, Expressive – just clever clinical terms. They don't belong out here. This is the real world.'

'Yes, but these studies can be applied to the real world.'

'Why are you here?' he demanded, stunning Anna into silence. 'Why are you really here? You can't help me, not out here. What, are you trying to give yourself credibility, so the next time you meet your fellow psychiatrists at some convention you can impress them with an account of a real murder investigation? Are you going to tell them all how you helped the clueless police solve the case? No, no, wait, I know why you're here – it's for your next book, isn't it? So you can enthral your readers with tales of horror and bad men who might come for them in the night. That should sell a few thousand copies.'

She wouldn't be his victim any longer. 'Why don't you just tell me what you're really afraid of, Sean, instead of hiding behind your anger?'

'I'll tell you what I'm afraid of, I'm afraid of the fact that I'm running out of ideas and time and so is Louise Russell and so is Deborah Thomson. I'm afraid because the answer to this riddle is buried under ten thousand information and intelligence reports. I'm afraid because the name of the man I'm after is locked in the fucking Post Office sorting depot in South Norwood, but I can't go look for it because I need a Production Order, and even if I had one I couldn't use it until Monday, and then only if the powers that be manage to get the union's agreement. So yes, I am very fucking afraid.'

'Then let me help you. Use what I know.'

'No.'

'What is your problem?'

'I'll tell you what my problem is,' he said rounding on her, 'twenty years ago I was a rookie cop, barely out of uniform on the Crime Squad at Plumstead, when suddenly I find myself attached to the Parkside Rapist inquiry team. Someone was attacking and raping young women in and around south-east London parks popular with walkers, similar to Putney Heath – mean anything yet?'

Anna shrugged her shoulders without commitment.

'That's the first time I met Detective Chief Superintendent Charlie Bannan. He was the most brilliant detective I've ever seen, let alone worked with. Every now and then he'd pull a young cop like me aside and run something past them – you know, just to test their mettle, their *instincts*. One day he drops a photograph of Rebecca Fordham in front of me and tells me he thinks the Parkside Rapist and Rebecca's murderer are one and the same man, and he asks me what I think. I look at the crime scene photographs, the victims' descriptions, the excessive use of violence, apparent weapon used, the wounds he'd inflicted and the strong sexual element to the crime. But there's one glaring difference between this scene and the Parkside Rapist's scenes – Rebecca had been murdered inside, in her flat, whereas the Parkside Rapist always struck outside, or so it seemed. But I took the file with the crime scene photographs back to where she'd lived, in a flat just off Putney Heath – a mixture of open common land and woods – just like the areas the Parkside Rapist was using. So I checked back further into the files and discovered she'd been walking in the woods earlier in the afternoon on the day she was murdered. And that wasn't all I found: she'd been walking with her son – her seven-year-old son – but unknown to her killer she dropped him off at a neighbour's in the same building before going home. Apparently she had a lot of work to catch up on so the neighbour had agreed to look after him for a few hours.'

'What's the relevance of the son being with her?' Anna asked.

'Because everyone always assumed that the children were irrelevant – that when Richards attacked women who were with their children he did so in spite of them being there.'

'But not you?' Anna questioned.

'No. Not me. I always believed it was his *preference* to attack women because they were with their children, not that he simply wasn't put off by the fact they were present.'

'But as you said, Rebecca Fordham's son wasn't with her when she was attacked.'

'Yes, but he didn't know that. All he knew was that he failed to attack her while she was in the woods, but now he'd managed to follow her home, and all he had to do was stay out of sight, hiding in the trees, and wait for her to make a mistake.'

'And she did.'

'Yes. Her flat was on the ground floor – it was summer. How was she to know there was a monster like Richards watching her – waiting? She left a kitchen window open and eventually he built up the courage and he slipped inside and he killed her. He killed her then he mutilated and sexually abused her dead body – cleaned up as best he could and left. But there was something else in the photographs that stood out for me, something that only Charlie Bannan had also seen and considered.'

'What was it?'

'A doll.'

'A doll?'

'Larger than normal, right in the middle of the crime scene, sitting on the chair opposite the couch where Rebecca was butchered.'

'And you thought he'd used it as a replacement for the child who wasn't there?' Anna caught on. 'You thought he took the doll from somewhere inside the flat and placed it as if it was watching him rape and murder the mother?'

'Yes,' he told her coldly. 'But blood spray patterns on the doll indicated that it hadn't been present when she'd had her throat cut, but had been present when the other wounds had been inflicted.'

'So he inflicted an incapacitating and ultimately fatal blow and as she lay bleeding to death he went looking for the child, to make him watch the rest, only he couldn't find him, so he replaced him with the doll before finishing his...'

'His performance,' Sean finished for her. 'And yes, that's what I believed happened. It had to be the same man. Only trouble was, the Rebecca Fordham team had already charged Ian McCaig, who'd killed himself while on remand waiting for his trial. McCaig was clearly unstable from the outset, but he was no killer. The media frenzy around his arrest and the public hatred drove him over the edge. He just couldn't take it. Everyone took his suicide as his admission of guilt.'

'But not you?'

'No and not Charlie Bannan either. As far as we were concerned, the Parkside Rapist was still on the loose and therefore so was Rebecca's killer. It just couldn't be McCaig – he was all wrong for it. So why had they charged him in the first place? I'll tell you why, because some fucking historical criminologist reckoned he could be the one. But there's no way he could have been. McCaig's only conviction was for indecent exposure, a crime of self-degradation. Rebecca's killer was all about the degradation of others. Two traits that can never exist in the same offender. They're opposite ends of the spectrum – night and day, light and darkness. But the team investigating Rebecca's murder wouldn't entertain the idea they had the wrong man. Bannan had pleaded with them to listen, but they wouldn't. So we met with the criminologist ourselves and asked her to consider a possible link between Rebecca's murder and the Parkside rapes.'

'And?'

'She agreed they appeared to be linked.'

'So she admitted she could have been wrong?'

'She said she'd never told the Fordham Team McCaig was guilty, just that he fitted elements of the profile. But the damage had already been done. The investigating team had allowed themselves to be influenced by an outsider and it had led to a catastrophic mistake. Anyway, a few weeks later we found Lindsey Harter and her four-year-old daughter raped and murdered in their own home. The brutality of the attack left us in no doubt it was the same man who had killed Rebecca. The same man who was committing the Parkside rapes. When we looked at the blood spray patterns around the area where the mother had been killed it became apparent that something had been removed from the scene after she'd been killed – something or *someone* who'd been sitting in the chair opposite. So we had the daughter's body and clothes examined for traces of her mother's blood and Christ, we found plenty. The blood spray patterns confirmed it – the killer had made the daughter sit and watch him sexually and physically mutilate her own mother before leading her to her own bedroom and killing her too.'

'Just like the doll,' Anna said, pulling her coat tight against the cold of the day and the chill of what she was being told.

'Yeah. Just like the doll. Later we arrested and charged Christopher Richards with the murder of Lindsey and her daughter Izzy. He admitted his guilt. But when we asked about Rebecca's murder, he denied having anything to do with it. The criminologist continued to deny her involvement in the conviction of McCaig. Maybe she'd been misunderstood – maybe she was just scared of her reputation being destroyed. I don't suppose we'll ever know.

'It took until 2007 for DNA tests to finally prove that it was Richards who murdered Rebecca. He pleaded guilty to Manslaughter on grounds of diminished responsibility. We'd been right, Charlie Bannan and I – we'd been right all along. A young mother and her four-year-old child, both raped and murdered unnecessarily. Dozens of other women raped by Richards after he'd killed Rebecca – all because the investigation team stopped listening to their own instincts – allowed the world of academic theories and clinical papers into their world – the real world. My world. These things don't belong in my world.'

'We've improved since then,' Anna pleaded, all too aware of the cases to which he referred. 'We've learned from our mistakes, we know so much more now.'

'Why don't you save what you know for the next time you're in court, so you can use it to help some other bastard like Gibran get away with murder.'

Anna's mouth hung slightly open for a few seconds. 'I don't deserve that,' she said.

He closed his eyes and rubbed his temples, letting the anger and bitterness sink back into the dark places that littered his corrupted soul. 'I'm sorry. I didn't . . .'

'I think we should just go.'

'Fine,' he agreed. They both climbed into the unmarked car and prepared for a long, silent journey back to Peckham.

Thomas Keller lay on the stained and soiled mattress, a filthy duvet pulled up to his chest. It was early evening outside and still light enough to see without turning the overhead light on. Underneath the duvet he wore his tracksuit bottoms and an unwashed T-shirt. He could see her, see her so clearly, as if she was lying in the bed with him – the only person he ever really loved. The only person who ever really loved him.

They were alone together, a long time ago when he was only twelve years old, in her garden, bathed in August sunshine, warm and strong, early in the summer's evening, the smell of freshly cut grass from the surrounding gardens filling their heads. Alone where no one could see them, away from prying eyes that would try and stop them if they could see them together. He stroked her long brown hair, occasionally glancing at the transfer of a phoenix on his forearm while she hummed and made a daisy chain, her identical transfer vivid in the bright light – transfers they'd put on each other, a symbol of their never-ending love. She turned to him, smiling. 'What you thinking about, Tommy?' she asked, her gentle, kind voice like an angel speaking to him, his one and only escape from the harshness of his reality.

'I was thinking of you.'

'Why, do you love me?' she giggled.

'Yes,' he said, not afraid to tell her – not afraid to tell her anything.

'Enough to stay with me for ever?'

'Yes.'

'Don't be silly – we've only been friends for a week.'

'But I've known you for a lot longer than that,' he protested.

'No you haven't,' she insisted. 'Not properly.'

'I've watched you for a long time. Watched you with the others. But I knew you weren't like them. I knew you were different.'

'They're OK,' she said unconvincingly.

'To you maybe, but not to me.'

'They just don't understand you, Tommy. They think you think you're too good for them or something.'

'Is that what they told you?'

'Not exactly, but I know what they say to each other.' Thomas Keller didn't respond. 'You should just ignore them when they're being mean to you.'

'I do, mostly, but one day I'll show them all what I can do. Then they'll be sorry they picked on me.'

'What do you mean?' Sam asked, looking up from her daisy chain, peering into his brown, almost black eyes.

'Nothing.' He suddenly leaned forward, his lips pursed, but she bent away from him.

'What are you doing?' she said, still smiling, but more anxiously now.

'I wanted to kiss you. That's all.'

She watched him as he looked away and stared at the ground, a sense of pity and friendship overwhelming her resistance. She knew what the other children at school did to him, physically and emotionally tormenting him whenever a teacher wasn't there to stop them or sometimes even when there was, but she had never joined in. By befriending him she had risked her position as one of the popular kids, one of the in-crowd; her friendship had been enough to confer on him a degree of protective cover. All the same, his attitude towards her did concern her a little. From the very first time she had spoken to him, just a week ago, when she had intervened to stop a group of boys from tearing his school books to pieces, his intensity towards her had seemed . . . unnatural. She'd told herself it wasn't surprising – clearly she was the only friend he'd ever had. Her parents and older relatives had always been amused and charmed by her natural instinct to protect the innocent, embarrassing her with tales of when she would rescue writhing caterpillars from attacking ants or free moths from the spider's web, and now she had Tommy – another insect to be saved from the ants. She leaned close to him and quickly kissed him on the cheek.

He looked up, joy and fear etched on his face, confusion and excitement, his lips swelling with the blood of embarrassment and desire. He'd never felt quite like this before – a stirring in the very pit of his stomach; a tightening feeling in his groin. He knew what to do next. Some of the older boys at the children's home had made him watch their secret DVDs. He knew what men were supposed to do to women – especially when they loved them – the older boys had made that very clear. He leaned towards her and kissed her on the cheek. To his pleasure and surprise she didn't pull away, so he kissed her again and again, moving across her cheek to her beautiful red lips, the taste and warmth of her skin firing through his entire body like electricity, making his heart pound out of control, his breathing reduced to tiny gasps.

She giggled nervously, placing a hand on his chest as his lips searched for hers, probing and slipping on the side of her face. She tried to twist away, but felt his hands slip under her armpits and begin to hold her in place, pulling her closer to him. She pushed hard at his chest again with both hands, the increasingly fraught struggle making them over-balance and fall sideways on to the grass, his lips never ceasing their search for hers.

'No, Tommy,' she managed to say. 'Stop it, please. Stop it, Tommy, you're hurting me.' She felt a hand slide under her top and grope her chest for breasts she didn't have yet, his jagged fingernails clawing at her soft skin. And then he was on top of her, his hand pulling and tugging at the buttons and zip of her jeans, her hand pulling at his wrist, tears beginning to seep from her green eyes as she fought to free herself from him. But the madness had made him too strong and she felt his powerful thin fingers push themselves into her knickers pressing hard on her crotch. 'Stop, Tommy. Please, you have to stop.' But he didn't, a single finger pushing its way inside her, the pain and shock electrifying her body, making her do the only thing she could think of doing.

Her shrill scream ripped through him like a bullet, freezing time as he became totally still, his eyes wide and round, misty with sexual desire that he knew now would never be fulfilled. For that second nothing in the world existed except the two of them, locked in their grotesque embrace. He felt her lungs filling with air, watched her mouth spread wide open, every muscle in her body tense as she prepared to shatter the very air around them with another scream. The horror of the situation punched him in the chest and shocked him to action before the scream could leave her mouth, his hand clamping over the opening in her face that threatened to destroy him once and for all.

She blinked mechanically as she realized what was

happening, the tears being pushed from her eyes and rolling down her temples and disappearing into her hairline. 'You shouldn't have done that,' he told her. 'You shouldn't have done that. I . . . I . . . only wanted to prove to you that I love you. You want me to show you that don't you?' She tried to shake her head, to show him she didn't, that she just wanted him to go and never speak of this again to anyone, but it was too late – too late for both of them.

The silhouette loomed up behind him, the sun glaring into her eyes making it impossible to see who it could be, but suddenly the weight of Tommy's body was no longer on her as he appeared to be flying backwards through the air, the angry voice of an adult breaking through her hypnotic nightmare – the voice of her father. 'Get the fuck off my daughter, you little bastard. What the fuck d'you think you're doing?' She watched her father raise his hand to strike the boy and despite the horror of a few seconds before she couldn't let him.

'No. Don't hit him.' Her father looked at her silently, the rage in his heart making her words sound distorted and unclear, but her pleading eyes told him what she was saying, begging him to spare the boy who had tried to violate her. 'Please,' she asked. Her father lowered his hand and stared at Tommy as if he was filth, stared at him the way he was used to being stared at. Then he dragged him from the garden and through the gate that led to his car, her voice following them all the way. 'Please don't hurt him, Daddy. He didn't mean to hurt me,' as she tried to defend him through her confusion and shock, despite her feelings of revulsion.

Her father spun on her, his finger raised to her face. 'You wait here till I get back.' He grabbed Tommy by the back of his neck and pointed his face back at his daughter's. 'Take a good look at her, son, because it's the last time you'll ever see her. Understand?'

The boy said nothing as he was pushed into the boot of

her father's car, the slamming of the lid bringing darkness and fear as they drove the short distance to the children's home. Then light rushed into the boot, blinding light, as strong arms pulled him from the car and pushed him along the path to the entrance. Her father made sure all the staff and children knew what he'd done, that he didn't want to press charges, so long as the boy stayed away from his daughter. No need to get the police involved, the staff at the home could deal with it – just so long as the boy stayed away.

But Thomas Keller couldn't stay away, no matter how hard he tried, because he loved her and knew she loved him too. Every chance he had, he watched her, followed her home from school, hiding in the darkness. But he was young and clumsy and her treacherous parents saw him. This time the police were involved. They came to the children's home and spoke to him – warned him that a Crime Report had been created and that he was shown as the suspect for the harassment of one Samantha Shaw, but that he was lucky this once, the parents just wanted him warned off. If he stayed away, they'd say no more about it. He would have to change schools of course, but that could be arranged easily enough.

He suddenly sat bolt upright in his filthy bed as he remembered agreeing to stay away from her. But he hadn't stayed away – how could he? She was his religion. His god. How could he stay away?

And so he'd learned to be more careful – to make the shadows and darkness his allies. He'd learnt to blend into his surroundings, like an urban chameleon. And he watched her – he went on watching her for years.

Keller rolled out of bed and stepped across the bedroom to the drawer where he kept the bundles of letters. Quickly he searched through the detritus until he found what he was looking for – a bottle of Black Orchid perfume and a jar of Elemis body cream. Lifting the perfume carefully from the drawer, as if it was so delicate his mere touch might shatter it, he sprayed a tiny amount on to the back of his hand, breathing in the drops of fine vapour as they travelled through the air. His eyes rolled back into their sockets with pleasure, exposing blood-vessel-streaked whites. When his pupils returned he slowly unscrewed the lid from the Elemis cream, savouring the anticipation of what was to come, the smell of it, the feel of it. Only when he was truly ready did he push his index finger into the cream, its oily coolness making him sigh with delight, his eyes flickering, overcome by such rare sensations of absolute joy. Slowly he pulled his finger from the whiteness and carefully wiped the excess on the side of the jar, gently, painstakingly massaging what was left into the back of his hand, releasing the scent of the Elemis to mix with the perfume, the combination once more carrying him back in time – back to the day only weeks ago when he'd let himself into her house, while she and the man she lived with were at work. The man who pretended to be her lover, but who he knew was one of *them*, sent to watch over her, sent to keep her from him.

The kitchen window had been easy enough to open and the house wasn't even alarmed. He'd slipped the blade of his flick-knife between the upper and lower sash and snapped the latch. The window slid open silently and easily, the scent of her life rushing at him all at once, almost knocking him back out of the window as he snaked into the house, his agile, wiry body ideally suited for climbing through tight spaces. Doing his best to ignore the assault on his senses, he jumped down to the kitchen floor, landing like an alert cat alive to any changes in sound or shade; to even the tiniest deviation to the atmosphere of the interior. Once he was satisfied he was alone, he explored the small house, always taking care that he could not be seen from the windows, searching drawers and cupboards, picking up anything and everything that belonged to her, carefully replacing items in exactly the same place he'd taken them from. He drank in as much of her life as he could without over-gorging and losing control, overloading his starved senses with her essence.

Eventually he reached her bedroom and slipped through the barely open door, the indentations left by her body still visible on the unmade bed, her pillow flattened in the centre and puffed at the sides. But what should have been a magical moment had been ruined by the smell of the man and the deeper mould his heavy body had left in *her* bed. Trying to block out everything else, he had knelt next to where she had laid, his hands tracing the shape of her body and head, the faintest trace of her warmth still detectable. He rested his hands on the bed until the warmth had completely gone. Then he began to move inch by inch around the room, absorbing every detail, until he came to her dressing table, littered with make-up and things only women had, things that were strange and exotic to him, things that had never had a place in his life.

His eyes searched the chaotic surface, finally coming to rest on two of the larger, more eye-catching items: a black bottle with a gold label, and a heavy glass jar with a chrome seal containing something white. He lifted the black bottle and read the words embossed on the label: Black Orchid Eau de Parfum. He sniffed at the top of the bottle, nervous and suspicious of the contents, surprised at the beauty of the odour, glancing from side to side as if he was being watched, then quickly stuffing it into his trouser pocket, its weight and size awkward, but worth it for the prize. Next he lifted the heavy glass jar and read the unfamiliar words written around its body – Elemis body cream. He unscrewed the lid and let the subtle, pleasant vapours drift up and into his face. Unable to resist, he pushed his finger into the cream. That had been the first time he'd enjoyed its cool oiliness, but there had been many occasions since. He rubbed the cream into his face, closing his eyes to allow images of Sam massaging the cream into her skin – all of her skin. This was not how he remembered her scent, but he knew it was how she must smell now – now the girl had become a woman.

A sudden noise in the distance outside startled him, brought him back to where he was and what he was doing. He screwed the top back on the Elemis, tucked it into his other pocket and left the bedroom and then the house, slipping out of the same window and closing it behind him.

The memory was a sweet one, but now he was alone again in his own bedroom, the opened jar of Elemis in his hand. He noted that the jar was half-full – enough to last a long time yet, provided he wasn't wasteful, provided he only used it on those who really could be *her*. He would have to be more selective in the future, but even so, he had enough for many more women – for many more Sams. He screwed the lid back on the cream and carefully replaced it in the drawer.

Close to midnight and Sean sat alone in his office with the overhead lights turned off to lessen the chances of being ambushed by a migraine, a desktop lamp the only lighting in the room, although the strip lights in the main office still washed the place with harsh, white light. There were a few people floating around, including Donnelly and Sally. Most were typing up their reports of the day's findings, others making apologetic phone calls to husbands, wives and partners. His tired eyes searched the office, subconsciously processing who was there and who was missing. He noticed Sally and Anna hunched over Sally's desk, whispering conspiratorially, no doubt discussing his harsh words at the scene of Deborah Thomson's car, or perhaps Anna was still trying to persuade Sally to let her help. If that was the case, he wished her luck.

He was still considering the possibilities when he saw Donnelly stretch, stand up and head his way. The lack of urgency in his manner told Sean not to expect any groundbreaking news.

Donnelly stepped into his office and sat without being invited. 'Guv'nor.'

'Dave,' Sean replied.

'Anything happening?'

'You tell me.'

'Anything in the information reports prick your interest, from the roadblocks . . . door-to-door?'

'Not yet,' Sean answered, 'although, as you can see, I still have plenty to get through.' He gestured to the pile of A4 sheets on his desk.

'Aye,' Donnelly sympathized. 'I've cut the wheat from the chaff as much as I could, but you know what it's like with an investigation of this profile: every Tom, Dick and Harry wants to get their little piece of information in so they can spend the rest of their careers in the canteen boring anyone who'll listen that they were the one who discovered the key that broke the case and caught a murderer.'

'I know,' Sean agreed, 'but the answer will be in there, somewhere. It's just a matter of whether I can find it.'

'You will,' Donnelly told him.

'Not until I get that Production Order for the Post Office employee files, and you and I both know there isn't a judge in the land who's going to give me an Order on all I've got so far – one wobbly witness who's had a bit of junk mail stuffed through his door.'

'We keep digging, we'll find more. Hopefully enough to get the Order by Monday.'

'Maybe,' Sean answered. 'Anyway, not much else you can do here tonight. Why don't you go home for a bit or go for a drink?'

Donnelly glanced at his watch. 'Too late for the pub,' he sighed.

'You don't actually expect me to believe that Dave Donnelly doesn't know where to get an after-hours drink from, do you?'

'Aye, well,' Donnelly stuttered, embarrassed and delighted at his infamy.

'And do me a favour,' Sean added, 'take Sally and Anna with you, will you? Just keep your phones handy. I'll call if anything breaks.'

'Fair enough,' Donnelly cheerfully agreed and swept from his office back into the main incident room, gathering up Sally and Anna despite their protests and ushering them towards the swing-door exit and away.

Somehow their leaving made Sean breathe easier, as if he'd been relieved of a burden he hadn't even known he'd been carrying. He rubbed his eyes hard, waiting for the mist to clear before staring at the small mountain of papers and reports he had to plough through. He couldn't let go of the feeling that he already knew the answer, so why had his search of the Crime Reporting Investigation System drawn a blank? Could he really be so wrong? 'No,' he whispered to himself. 'I'm right, I know I am.' He pulled the pile of reports towards him and began to read, at first without enthusiasm, sheet after sheet of pointless bits of information, but as he sank deeper into the ocean of intelligence he forgot what he was doing and where he was, drifting away on a tide of possibilities. Every so often, he read something that stabbed excitedly at his chest. But there were still too many possibles, too many people stopped and questioned whom the interviewing officer had thought a little strange or uncooperative. Too many men who'd appeared keen to avoid telling the police of their whereabouts at the times of the crimes. Too many disused factories and smallholdings to allow any one thing to stand out. He needed something to cross-reference itself – a nervous postman stopped at a roadblock or living on an abandoned farm. If he could find that in amongst the deluge of information, if he could find that one report, he knew he would find his quarry.

The next time he looked up and into the main office it was empty and in as much darkness as any police room ever is. He quickly looked at his watch and then his phone, suddenly remembering he hadn't called Kate all day. Now it was two a.m. and too late to do anything other than drop himself in it even more. If he didn't phone he faced a few frosty hours next time he saw her, but if he did and woke the kids, it wouldn't improve his popularity. He considered sending a text, but decided it was too late to try anything.

He looked away from the phone and back to the slowly diminishing pile of reports on his desk, resisting the urge to go home and grab a few hours' sleep before everything started all over again the next morning. Lifting another piece of paper to read, he promised himself that after this one he would pack it in for the night. One more report, then he'd head home to the short fitful sleep full of nightmares that waited for him – Louise Russell's near-naked body lying in woods, her accusing eyes pleading with him for the answer – why? Why hadn't he been able to find her in time?

He looked at the paper in his hands, his eyes so tired he could hardly focus, the sick feeling in his stomach and the pounding in his head reminding him he had forgotten to drink or eat since brunch with Anna. His eyes flickered until the words settled and formed. It was an information report submitted by two uniformed officers checking possible locations where the abducted women could be being kept. Their names – PCs Ingram and Adams. They'd visited a disused poultry factory out in Keston, on the Kent–London border. The report said the land was poorly maintained and hazardous, but that it contained a small abode and numerous outhouses. The man living on the land gave the name Thomas Keller, twenty-eight years old, five foot nine inches tall, slim, white, identification checked out OK and nothing particularly suspicious or untoward noted. Sean frantically scanned the report for Keller's occupation, but none was shown. 'Damn it,' he cursed quietly. 'Fuck.' He began to move his index finger backwards and forwards under the name Thomas Keller, backwards and forwards, until finally he tossed it back on to his desk before cursing again.

'Christ, I'm fucking losing it,' he accused himself, convinced the tiredness was close to making him hallucinate. 'Go home,' he told himself. 'For Christ's sake, just go home.' He hauled himself from the chair he'd been stuck in for more hours than he could remember, pulled on his coat, filling the pockets with the trappings of his life and headed towards the exit. By the time he reached the swing doors the name Thomas Keller had all but been wiped from his mind – just another name on another information report. One of hundreds.

He lay in his bed tossing and turning until he could take no more of the hellish images that tore around inside his head. Demons that always came in the night, dancing behind his closed eyelids, never allowing him to escape his cursed life – not even in sleep. Tonight had been worse than usual, somehow more intense and vivid, as if he was reaching the climax of his very existence. Finally, maybe the end was near. The end of this life and the beginning of the next. He threw the soiled duvet off his overly slim, ugly body and stood in the darkness, the moonlight from outside the only illumination, blue and cold.

Almost without thinking, as if he was unaware of his own intentions, he tugged his tatty underpants down past his hips and let them fall to the floor, stepping out of them and grabbing the tracksuit bottoms from the bedpost and pulling them over his hairless, vein-ridden legs before recovering his hooded top from the floor and struggling into it, searching in the faint light for his training shoes and pushing his neglected feet into them. He grabbed the cellar keys from the chest of drawers where he kept so many special things and walked through the cramped, dingy house to the bathroom, taking a phial of alfentanil and a syringe from the cabinet, drawing fifty-millilitres into it before replacing the safety cap over the needle and marching to what served as the front door, stopping only once more to recover the cattle prod from the same kitchen cupboard where he kept his shotgun. For a moment he considered also taking the stun-gun as he would have normally, but tonight, for some reason he didn't. The cattle prod and alfentanil would be enough.

He stepped out into the bitter night, the clear skies allowing the temperature to drop dramatically, the freezing, still air catching him by surprise, causing his breath to shallow until his lungs adjusted to the cold mixture he forced into them. As he strode through the night across the derelict yard, great plumes of breath burst from his mouth, clouds of condensation reflecting the moonlight before dying to nothing. He unlocked the padlock and pulled the metal door to the cellar open, its scraping and screeching turning him to a statue as he listened to the darkness for signs of danger, only daring to move once the resonating sounds of the door had faded. Slowly he began to descend into the faintest yellow light below, the underground cavern significantly warmer than the world outside. He reached the bottom of the stairs and stepped into the cellar, not speaking, waiting in the gloom, listening for the women, allowing his eyes to adjust to the man-made light, feeling calmer than usual, more in control, more instinctive, as if whatever was going to happen was somehow by his unconscious design – clear and unstoppable. Fate. His and theirs.

After a few minutes he walked purposefully to the cage in which Louise Russell cowered in the corner, her eyes wide with terror and suspicion, unblinking, following his every slightest move, waiting for him to speak. But he just stood next to her cage, staring in at her through the wire and faint light, until finally he turned his back on her and walked mechanically to the string that hung from the ceiling and acted as a light switch. He pulled the string and washed the room with the weak light. She could see the cattle prod clearly now, the memories of how he'd used it to torture Karen Green still painfully fresh – how he'd used it to make her compliant the night he had taken her from her cage and led her to the stairs, half helping her, half dragging her, ignoring her pleas and promises to do whatever he wanted her to, just so long as he let her stay. Life in the cage was better than no life at all.

Panic spread through Louise's body as she realized why he had come in the dead of night. She scuttled around inside her cage like an animal sensing it's about to be put down, looking for an escape she knew didn't exist, a weakness in the metal wire she knew she wouldn't find – watching him with horror as he strode back to her cage, moving around to the small hatch and unlocking it, placing the prod on top of the cage while he took the syringe from his tracksuit bottoms and removed the safety cap.

'Give me your arm,' he demanded, his voice strong, but cold and lifeless. She wrapped her arms around her in a futile attempt to save them from the inevitable. 'Give me your arm or you know what'll happen,' he warned, resting his free hand on the cattle prod as a reminder of Karen Green's fate.

'No,' she pleaded. 'I can't. Please. I can't.' Tears streaked down her dirty face leaving clean tracks through the thin layer of dust that had settled on her skin over the last few days during which she hadn't been allowed to wash. He stood and watched her for a while, then closed the hatch, replacing the safety cap on the syringe and returning it to his pocket, recovering the prod and moving around to the main door of the cage. Louise's terrified eyes followed him every inch of the way, watching as he held the prod under his armpit while he fumbled for the padlock key in his pocket. Her heart pounded uncontrollably as she watched him slot the key into the lock and jiggle the padlock free, her eyes darting from side to side. She felt her bowels and bladder loosen as he slowly eased the door open, a trickle of urine running down the inside of her legs.

Now he was in the cage with her, the cattle prod once more held firmly in his hands, pointing straight towards her. She felt close to fainting as she remembered Karen's body twisting and contorting each time he'd stabbed the prod into her bare flesh, her screams of agony. She couldn't let that happen to her. Her mind suddenly flashed with false hope, that maybe he had let Karen go free – had taken her into the woods or city and released her, that the drug he had given her was purely so she wouldn't remember where she'd been kept, that Deborah had been wrong about her body being found, or that it had been the body of someone else. 'Please,' she begged him, unfolding her arms and offering both to him, each upturned and ready to be injected. 'I'm sorry. I'll do as you say. I'll do anything you say.' He was so close, moving slowly towards her, his mouth slightly open, revealing his crooked, stained teeth, his eyes narrow and cruel.

'Too late for that,' he hissed at her. 'I know what you are, you little whore.'

She was about to speak, but the electricity that the cattle prod poured into her body jammed her jaw shut as she fell on to her side, every muscle wracked in spasm, the pain etching itself into her brain. The convulsion lasted a matter of seconds, unlike the longer-lasting effects of the stun-gun, and she felt her body begin to relax only to be punished again by another shot from the prod and then another and another, in her spine, her stomach and thighs, until she lay exhausted and motionless.

He stood over her, watching for signs that she was still capable of resisting him, the deep scratches in his face reminding him to be cautious, even of fallen prey. He kicked her without venom several times in her ribcage, causing her to moan slightly, but barely stir. Satisfied, he knelt beside her, resting the cattle prod on the floor and removing the syringe from his pocket, taking her arm in his other hand and searching for a useable artery, but her dehydration made it impossible to find one. He clasped the syringe in his teeth and began to slap the crook of her arm, trying to raise the blood vessels, until finally he saw the traces of a blue line running beneath her skin. Quickly he clamped her arm just above the elbow with his fingers and waited for the blood to dam and make the artery more prominent, watching without emotion as it swelled to an almost normal size. He took the syringe from his teeth and laid the needle across the blue line in her arm before bringing it to a shallow angle and pushing its sharp point through her thin, pale skin, sinking it deeply into the blood vessel, drawing the miniature plunger backwards first, pulling a few millilitres of her own blood into the syringe, the red liquid swirling and mixing with the alfentanil already inside. Then he remorselessly pushed both blood and drug into her arm, the beat of her own heart rushing it to the far reaches of her body. He pulled the needle from her artery and waited, listening for the sigh he knew would ease from her mouth, a sigh that would mean the anaesthetic had worked and she would now be unable to resist his will. After a few seconds he heard what he was waiting to hear.

Looking down on Louise Russell's prostrate body he watched her chest gently rise and fall as her half-shut eyes flickered, quiet moans coming from her mouth, her arms lying behind her, above her head. He watched as her breasts rose and fell, her lips opening and closing, as if she was speaking silent words that only he could hear, telling him she wanted him, needed him, making his already stiff penis harder than he could bear. 'I know you do, you little whore. I know you desire me.' Hurriedly he pushed her legs apart and kneeled between them, pulling his tracksuit trousers halfway down to his thighs and releasing himself, swollen and grotesque. 'Look what you've done,' he chastised her. 'You've made me as disgusting as you are. As weak as you are. You're nothing to me now,' he told her, his face twisted with contempt.

Deborah had been looking on, transfixed in horror, but knowing what was coming she could watch and listen no more.

She squeezed her eyes tightly shut, clamped her hands over her ears, but she couldn't block out the sound of him grunting and whining, she couldn't block out the involuntary cries and moans of his victim. Humming to herself as loudly as she dared, she waited until the terrible sounds of Louise's torture relented before summoning the courage to look back at the other cage, watching as Keller pulled up his trousers. He knew she was looking but he seemed unable to meet her eyes, panting and breathing heavily after the effort of his assault.

'See what you made me do,' he asked Louise. 'Well, you've tricked me for the last time. You won't cheapen me again. You're the little whore now, not me.' His voice was flat and mechanical, devoid of emotion. 'It's time for you to go. I don't want you here any more.'

He hauled Louise to her feet and hauled her from her cage. Deborah tried to speak, to scream at him to stop, to leave Louise alone, but no words came from her open mouth, the terror of knowing what was going to happen to Louise striking her dumb. She looked on in silence as he half-dragged and half-assisted the partially anaesthetized woman across the cellar floor, pulling the string that returned the cellar to near darkness as he passed it. Still Deborah couldn't speak as she listened to him leading Louise around the corner to the stairs, the sound of their shuffling, unsteady feet more awful than anything she'd ever heard.

The metallic clang of the door being closed and locked was followed by silence, broken only by the sound of running water. For the first time since he'd taken her, Deborah was alone. But for how long?

Louise's terribly prophesy had come true. It was her turn now – her turn to become Louise Russell. To become Karen Green.

Deborah sank to the floor of her cage and hugged herself, rocking and crying in the twilight of the cellar. Alone.

12

Sean drove through the virtually deserted streets of south-east London to his modest terraced home in Dulwich, the empty roads making the short journey a fast one. He enjoyed the peaceful eeriness of the streets at dawn, a nether-world that few other than emergency service workers ever saw, at least while they were sober. It reminded him of his early days in the police, a young uniformed officer driving home after a night-shift, tired but content, watching all the bleary-eyed commuters driving in the other direction. It made him feel different – unique. He parked as close as he could to his house and walked the short distance to the front door, his footsteps heavier than he would have wished in the quiet of the night, although thankfully a gusting wind disguised his approach. As he unlocked the door he was pleased to see Kate had followed his often repeated instructions and had used the dead-lock as well, not just relying on the far more easily opened latch-lock. He eased the door open and stepped into his home, the warmth and comforting scent of his family temporarily chasing away the daytime demons. Kate had left a small lamp on for him, her own experiences of arriving home in the dead of night making her appreciate a little illumination when first stepping inside your own house, while at the same time not wanting to turn the more powerful overhead lights on and risk disturbing the rest of the family while they slept. Police and doctors, firemen and nurses – eternal teenagers who would never be allowed to grow out of sneaking into their own homes in the middle of the night, forever fearful of capture.

He closed the door behind him even more carefully than he'd opened it, slipped his shoes off and tiptoed to the kitchen, where he turned on the lights of the overhead extractor-hood to help him navigate his way around. Next he emptied his pockets on to a newspaper on the kitchen table, its density nullifying the sound of his phone, keys, wallet, warrant card and assorted coins as they hit the surface. He hung his raincoat and jacket over a chair, loosened his tie even more than it already was and headed for the cupboard where he knew he'd find a bottle of Jack Daniel's and a short, fat glass. He poured himself what he thought he could get away with and still be able to drag himself out of his bed in little more than three hours' time and sat at the table, sighing loudly as he felt the pain in all his joints at once.

Three hours' sleep wasn't going to be anywhere near enough to allow his body and mind to regroup. He tried to work out how many hours he'd been awake for, but exhaustion made the problem almost impossible to solve and he soon gave up. The clock hanging on the kitchen wall warned him it was nearly 2.30 a.m. He gave another sigh and stared into the drink in his hand, the bourbon the only thing he could think of that was going to slow his thoughts enough to allow any sort of sleep to come. He drank it in one go, burning his throat and chest as it headed for his empty stomach, the lack of food making the effects of the alcohol instant and satisfying.

He heaved himself out of the chair, left the kitchen and climbed the stairs. As he passed his daughters' bedroom, he tried to resist peeking in through the gap in the door but failed, the faint blue light from their night lamps somehow making them look even more alive than they did in natural light, although he could barely remember the last time he'd seen them in daylight. Two little girls who before he knew it would become young women – just like the young women the madman had taken. His eldest daughter even had the same name – Louise.

Sean chased the thoughts away as quickly as they'd come – they had no place in his home. He eased his head back through the gap and sneaked into his bedroom, Kate's shape clear underneath the duvet, still and silent. He undressed in the dark, draping his clothes over the only chair in the room, and slipped into bed, the bourbon acting like an anaesthetic, like the chloroform the madman used on his victims. Again he chased the thoughts away, thoughts that had no place in his bed as he lay next to his wife.

Kate's voice startled him – not the voice of someone who had been asleep and then woken, but the voice of someone who hadn't been able to sleep – the voice of someone who had been waiting for him. 'If you're home, then I assume you haven't caught him yet. You haven't found the women.'

'No.' His heart was still racing from the surprise. 'Not yet, but it won't be long. I'm sure of it. We're coming to the end. I'll be meeting him soon.'

'How d'you know? Have you found something?'

'No,' he answered, 'but I will. The answer's there, just waiting for me to see it.'

'I know what you mean,' she said, giving him an idea.

'Kate.'

'Uhhhm.'

'What do you do when you've got a patient who is critically ill, one you've tried everything on, done everything to try and save them, everything that should have helped them recover, yet their condition goes on getting worse and worse? What would you do?'

She thought in silence for a while before answering. 'In that scenario I would assume I'd missed something. I'd go back over everything I'd done and double-check I hadn't missed anything.'

'And if you hadn't?' he asked. 'What then?'

Kate rolled over to look at him, her face little more than a silhouette. 'If that was the case,' she said, 'then the patient would die and we'd all feel really bad, even though there was nothing we could have done.'

She kissed him on the cheek and rolled over to sleep, leaving him to stare at the ceiling in the darkness. Alone.

She stumbled through the trees, arms wrapped around her torso in a futile effort to keep out the cold, her only clothing the same soiled underwear he'd given her days before – how many days she couldn't be sure of any more. Her bare feet stepped on sharp stones and thorns as she stumbled, her arms untwisting from her body as she tried to steady himself, her head occasionally turning to look at the hooded figure who followed close behind, a stumpy baseball bat in one hand and the cattle prod in the other. Whenever she slowed too much she felt the bat being jabbed into her spine, driving her on to a fate he had decided for her, the alfentanil's effects making her too weak and uncoordinated to either run or fight. All she could do was beg for her life.

'Please,' she sobbed. 'You don't have to do this.' Her words were slurred but clear enough. 'I won't tell anyone. I promise.' Another stab in the back propelled her on, the cold breeze feeling like a gale on her exposed skin. She stumbled again, gathering more lacerations to her feet and body, as if the trees were his accomplices, cruelly bending to lash her with their thin branches. 'I have a husband,' she pleaded. 'My children need me,' she lied, desperate to try and reach the man trapped inside the monster.

'Liar,' he said. 'You don't have children. You shouldn't lie about things like that. If you do, I'll know.'

'You were watching me,' she accused him. 'You've been watching me for weeks.' She stopped and turned to face him, expecting the stab of the bat in her spine, but it didn't come.

'I thought you were the one,' he told her. 'I thought you were her, but I was wrong. I have no need of you now. You were a mistake.'

'No,' she tried to reach him. 'Maybe I am her? You need to help me be her. I can be her. I know I can – for you.'

'No,' he barked. 'It's too late. Keep moving.'

'I can't,' she pleaded, leaning with her back to a tree. 'No more, please. No more.'

'Just a little further and you can go,' he promised. 'I'm not going to kill you. Just a little further and you can go.'

She knew the hope he had given her was a false hope, but it was all she had and she clung to it. 'You'll let me go?' she asked breathlessly. He nodded in the moonlight. 'You promise?'

'Just a little further.' He pointed deeper into the woods with the bat.

Louise pushed herself from the tree, brushing the thin branches away from her face with her outstretched arms, closing her eyes in silent prayer, feeling her way through the trees until she sensed she was in a clearing, the ground softer under her feet where invading sunlight had allowed grass to grow and all around her an eerie flapping sound, as if hundreds of birds were trapped in the surrounding trees, unable to escape, not matter how hard they beat their wings. She opened her eyes and walked into the open space, looking for the source of the strange sound, but couldn't see it in the darkness, feeling him behind her, getting closer, and she knew, she knew this would be where he killed her. If he was going to let her go, he would have melted back into the woods by now, a ghost disappearing into the waiting shadows, but he hadn't. He'd known this clearing was here and he'd known this was where he was going to bring her. This would be the place where she took her last breath.

Panic and the animal will to survive swept away most of the effects of the anaesthetic, her body becoming aware and alert. She sprang forward into the clearing, her bare feet pushing off the soft ground strongly, but he was ready, as if he'd anticipated she would try to run. Within four strides she felt her legs kicked from under her, sending her unsupported body flying through the air until it crashed hard into the ground, knocking the wind and fight from her, leaving her disorientated and confused. She gave herself a few seconds then rose to her knees, looking around, trying to get her bearings, a new direction to run in, but before she could do either the dark figure stepped in front of her, each hand still clutching a weapon. She gazed up at him, blinking, trying to focus on the blackness inside the hood where his face should have been. 'Please,' she pleaded. 'Please.' He tossed the bat to one side and slipped the cattle prod inside his trouser pocket, still standing above her, staring down.

Millimetre by millimetre his hands moved from his sides, stretching out towards her, reaching for her throat as she watched through her tears, her own hands slowly rising to meet his, her fingers curling around his wrists, but barely able to resist at all, as if she was guiding his hands to her, strong, thin fingers coiling around her neck as his thumbs sank into her throat, slowly crushing her trachea. The blood supply to and from her brain fell to nothing, her eyes bulging under the pressure and her swollen tongue protruding from her mouth searching for oxygen. For a brief second she thought she could see her husband, hear his voice, see the children she'd so often imagined having, their presence encouraging her to frantically claw and scratch at the hands clamping her throat, but she had grown too weak and he too strong. Finally her resisting fingers slowed and slipped away from his, her arms becoming too heavy to hold up any more as they fell limp at her side, and an ugly hiss leaked from her mouth – the last sound she would ever make.

He kept his hands wrapped tightly around her neck, staring at the dead creature he held kneeling in front of him, glad he hadn't knocked her semi-unconscious with the baseball bat before squeezing the life from her. The sudden overwhelming desire to see her slip from this world to the next had been impossible to resist, to see her full life-force leave her body, not just the remains after he'd partially caved her head in as he had with Karen Green. This had been so much more *rewarding*.

He held her for a long time, watching until her dead staring eyes began to mist over, then he released his grip and allowed her to slump to the ground, falling in an almost foetal position, except for her arms, one of which was trapped under her body while the other had fallen behind her back in a pose only the dead could bear. Still he stood over her, wondering why it felt different to the last time. Then he realized that the difference was he had actually felt something this time – something calm and powerful.

The freezing breeze blowing into his face slowly drew him back to the real world, the dead woman at his feet inconsequential. It was time for him to leave. He crouched next to the body and awkwardly removed her underwear and bra, rolling them together and pushing them into the pocket of his hooded top before returning her limbs to almost exactly the same position she had fallen in without knowing or considering why. He looked at Louise Russell one last time then turned, striding back into the trees heading towards his car and home. Tomorrow was Sunday. He would rest for a day – get things ready – clean the cage and her clothes, once he'd taken them off the woman who was wearing them now. Then on Monday, after work, he'd rescue her. He already knew where she lived and how she lived. He'd been watching her a long time, just like he had the others, but this time he was sure she was the one, even if she didn't know it herself.

13

It was barely six thirty a.m. Sunday morning and Anna was already awake and showered, sitting on the edge of her bed unrolling a pair of tights along her legs as her husband looked on through tired, sleepy eyes. He hadn't seen her look so exhausted in years, if ever. 'I'll be glad when this is all over,' he mumbled. 'Half-past six on a Sunday – what's the matter with these people? Don't they know this is supposed to be a day of rest?'

'I don't suppose they have much choice, do they?' she reprimanded him, feeling a little bit like a cop for the first time, living by different rules and values to everyone around her, but not always liking it.

'Do you have to go?'

'Sorry, Charlie.' She stood to straighten her skirt. 'Duty calls.'

'Try and get home a little earlier today,' he insisted. 'It would be nice to actually see you sometime this weekend.'

'I can't promise anything at the moment,' she warned him. 'I'll be back when I'm back.'

Charles Temple propped himself up against his pillow and reached for the packet of cigarettes by his bedside, tapping one from the box and lighting it with a gold-plated Zippo.

'Fuck's sake, Charlie,' Anna moaned. 'Do you have to smoke in bed? In fact, do you have to smoke in the house at all? Now I'm going to stink of fags.'

'Then you'll probably smell like the rest of them,' he teased. 'Like a proper cop. A proper detective.'

'What's that supposed to mean?' she snapped.

'Nothing,' he answered with a smirk. 'Anyway, I only smoke at the weekends.'

'You shouldn't smoke at all – you're a bloody surgeon,' she reminded him. He merely shrugged his shoulders.

'I must say, you seem quite smitten with your little police buddies. Something must have pricked your interest to have you running off to Peckham, of all places, on a Sunday morning.'

'I'm working, remember?' she reminded him.

'Really?' he asked with mock suspicion.

'Yes, really. What is it you're implying?'

'Just thought you might've fallen for this DI's animalistic charms. A bit of rough, and all that.'

'His name's Sean Corrigan and he's neither rough or charming.'

'Like him, though, don't you?'

'No really,' she laughed. 'Besides, he's work. Or rather, it's work.'

Bored with his little game, he gave a dismissive wave of his cigarette. 'Whatever. Just hurry up and help the cops catch this sicko so we can return to a normal life.'

'Is that what you think I'm there to do?' she demanded, suddenly serious, annoyed by his ignorance as much as she was by her own feelings of deceit and treachery. 'You think I'm there to help the police find this offender?'

'Aren't you?' he questioned, puzzled.

'Partly,' she admitted, 'but it's not as simple as that. Never mind. I need to get going.'

'Try not to let it get to you,' he warned her, without really caring. 'Be like the cops, blank it all out.'

'You think it has no effect on them – seeing young lives torn away, dealing with the families of the victims? You think they just carry on, business as usual, and forget about it? Forget about everything?'

'Don't tell me you're going native on me, Detective Chief Inspector Ravenni-Ceron.'

'No,' she answered. 'I could never be one of them. Even if I worked with them for ten years, I'd never be one of them. For that to happen I'd have to become a police officer. They're a closed shop to outsiders, it's just the way they operate.'

'But you admire them, don't you?' he seemed to accuse her, as if admiration was a betrayal of their own preconceived self-importance.

'Of course I do,' she snapped back. 'If you saw what they had to do and how they had to do it, the hours they have to work, the lack of sleep or rest – and still they keep going, never asking for or expecting anyone's gratitude, always expecting to be kicked when they're down and blamed for everything that goes wrong in the world, but doing what they have to do anyway – if you saw that the way I've seen it, you'd admire them too.'

'Don't get too hooked on your new friends, Anna,' he warned. 'They're only temporary, remember? It's like you said, you can never be one of them.'

'If you think I'm hooked, you must be delusional,' she told him. 'I want this over as much as you do, but not until I find out what I'm there to find out.'

'And what would that be?'

'I'm not sure,' she answered as she pulled her suit jacket on. 'Not any more.'

Sean pushed through the swing doors into the main incident room and found it deserted. He checked his watch – just gone half-past six in the morning. The office looked like a tip: dirty plates left on desks, mugs stained with half-drunk coffee dumped on every conceivable surface, rubbish bins overflowing with polystyrene cups, plastic sandwich boxes and screwed-up balls of paper that should have been shredded and placed in the confidential waste sacks, but people were getting too tired to care. He remembered it was Sunday, so the cleaners wouldn't be through the office until the following morning. Things would get a lot worse before they got better. He couldn't help but draw comparisons between the state of the office and the state of the investigation. Sundays – he always felt something bad was about to happen on Sunday and this was no different. Sundays as a child meant his father would be around more than usual, drinking, leading him by the hand to the upstairs bedroom, away from the rest of his family and his mother. Blind eyes turned.

He pushed the memories aside as he crossed the room and slunk into his office, throwing the contents of his pockets across his cluttered desk and hanging his raincoat on one of the metal hooks on the back of his door that served as a coat-rack. He considered sitting on the uncomfortable chair waiting for him behind his desk, but knew he needed to keep moving for a while, or at least standing. The few hours' sleep and a hot shower had revived him somewhat, but if he sat in the chair now, as uncomfortable as it was, the tiredness would sweep back over him and beg him to allow his body and mind to sleep. He couldn't let that happen. He was already feeling guilty about going home when the killer was still out there, the lives of two women Sean had never met hanging on his ability to find them.

It was too early for the local cafés, or even the station canteen, to be open, so the caffeine he both craved and needed would have to come from something other than his usual black coffee. Still standing he rummaged through the desk drawers for his caffeine tablets, pushing aside packets of ibuprofen, paracetamol and indigestion tablets until he found what he was looking for, popping two from the silver foil and swallowing them without water, then taking another without checking the dosage instructions. 'I'm getting too old for this,' he muttered to himself as he began to push papers around his desk, waiting for the tablets to stimulate his brain enough for him to begin reading through the seemingly endless reports, the memory of last night's fitful sleep fading to nothing – the dreams of trees in the dark, the constant hissing of the leaves in the breeze, the faceless man in the hooded top standing over a semi-naked Louise Russell giving way to the images that would plague him during the day to come.

As he looked around his office his attention was drawn to an enlarged photograph of Louise Russell's face stuck to his whiteboard, her green eyes staring at him, pleading with him to find her – to save her. Involuntarily his hand came from his side and reached out to her, his index finger tracing the outline of her face. He stepped back with a jolt as an image of her yet-to-be crime-scene photographs flashed in his mind. The green eyes were still staring out at him, only now they were lifeless, no longer pleading but accusing – damning him.

When the image cleared he stepped forward and studied her picture again. 'Are you still alive?' he asked her. 'Am I too late?'

The sound of Sally barging through the swing doors helped him look away from the photograph. They nodded hellos at a distance as he watched her go through the same routine of emptying her coat pockets on to her desk as he had just minutes earlier. He moved to the door frame of his office entrance. 'How's it going?' he asked without enthusiasm.

'Well, it's barely seven o'clock in the morning, my eyes are sore and so are my feet, it's Sunday and I'm at work . . . Other than that, I'm great. How about you?'

'The same,' he answered without smiling.

'Any news on Louise Russell?'

Sean knew what she meant – had a body been discovered

overnight or was there still a chance? 'No one's called me, so I'm assuming things remain the same.'

'It's Sunday, remember,' she warned him. 'People walk their dogs later on a Sunday morning. My guess is we won't be in the clear until about nine-ish.'

'We should have one more day,' he argued, 'provided he keeps to his seven-day cycle.' He spoke more in hope than belief, the fear that the killer was spiralling towards an end game – an orgy of unrelenting violence – marred his faint optimism.

'Let's hope he does,' Sally muttered, looking away distractedly, searching through the notes and memos on her desk, mumbling to herself more than to him. 'What time's that bloody canteen open on a Sunday? Their coffee's foul, but it's better than nothing.'

Sean didn't answer, sliding back into his office and shuffling paper around on his desk only to look up and see the big, white-faced clock hanging on his wall. Sally was right – they had to survive past nine o'clock. Louise Russell had to survive past nine o'clock. If her body hadn't been found by then, she might still be alive and maybe he had as much as another twenty-four hours to find her before . . . But even that wouldn't give him enough time to get a Production Order, serve it and then gain access to the employee records at the sorting office. He needed something to break today – something to fall into place – something that would tear down the brick wall between the madman and him.

In sudden desperation he grabbed a chair and pulled it up to his computer desk, sitting astride it as his fingers began to nimbly type on the keyboard. He called up the CRIS system and punched in the instructions for the same search he'd already carried out with a negative result. 'I know you stalked the woman they're replacements for, you must have. You must have watched her and you must have known her and she you. She couldn't have been some stranger you obsessed over – she accepted you, but then something happened and she was taken away from you, but what and how? I know I'm right,' he reassured himself. 'I have to be.'

He typed in the details of the crime he was searching for, the description of a young woman matching that of the three women he'd taken. He pressed the key to run the search and pushed himself away from the desk while he waited for the result, his heart hammering inside his ribcage. 'I have to be right,' he told himself, 'I must have missed something.' After a few seconds the screen blinked and changed to the results page. The search had returned *no results*. 'Fuck,' he called out loudly enough to make Sally look up. Last night's conversation with Kate began to play over and over in his mind.

. . . I would assume I'd missed something. I'd go back over everything I'd done and double-check I hadn't missed anything.

And if you hadn't? What then?

Then the patient would die . . .

He pulled himself and the chair back to the computer and began again, this time expanding the age group of the victim by a few years either way – *no results*. He tried changing the length of the victim's hair; maybe she'd had it cut since he knew her – *no results*. He tried changing the height of the victim a few inches either way – *no results*. He tried removing the specific eye colour – *no results*. Over and over he tried, but it was always the same – *no results*.

The sound of a phone ringing in the main office somehow cut through his concentration when other distractions had not. His head spun to look at the big clock – it was almost eight o'clock. Christ, he'd been fruitlessly searching the CRIS database for more than an hour without even noticing the detectives who'd been slowly arriving and filling the office with chatter and noise, including Donnelly – but the phone ringing, its shrill electronic chirping, was something he'd been unable to block out. Why? Once again his heart started kicking and punching his chest walls. He felt his throat grow tight as he watched Sally lift the corded phone from its receiver and hold it to the side of her face as if everything was happening in slow motion, but only to him. He watched her listen to the caller, lip-reading as she responded, *Where?* She wrote something on a piece of paper, hung up and got to her feet, turning towards his office, head down, eyes cast to the floor.

Silently he cursed her for walking towards him with the piece of paper in her hand. He cursed her for answering the damn phone and he cursed her for what she was about to tell him. She reached his door and looked up into his eyes without stepping inside. 'I'm sorry,' was all she said.

He felt the life force flowing out of him, as if he'd been shot in the chest at point-blank range, the realization of what he was being told stabbing at his fragile self-belief. He'd failed – failed to solve the puzzle in time – and now she was dead. The madman had killed Louise Russell, but her blood would be for ever on Sean's hands. Her lifeless staring green eyes would for ever haunt his dreams.

It had been a long night and he hadn't got to bed until the early hours of the morning, the night's events leaving him excited but calm, for the time being at any rate. But as the light penetrated through the thin sheets tacked over the windows of his home, his sleep grew increasingly restless – the deep sleep of oblivion replaced by the shallow sleep that allowed the nightmares to come.

He was young, only seven or eight, and already a veteran of the children's home in Penge, south-east London. Other children had come and gone, but he remained. It was Sunday – the day when the grown-ups came to look at them, to talk to them and take them out for the day and buy them sweets and ice cream, maybe even take them home – just for a day visit at first, then for a night or two, and then, who knows, maybe take them home for ever. The youngest children were usually snapped up quite quickly, especially if they didn't have siblings, but the older children, the teenagers, rarely left. They used to tell him that if you were still there when you were ten, then you'd stay there for ever.

There had been no day trips for Thomas Keller for a while, no ice cream or visits to *normal* homes – not since his last trip. There had been suspicions even before that – *incidents*. At first nobody could be certain he was responsible. Nobody wanted to consider the consequences if he had been responsible – what that would signify, what that would mean he was. At first it was a case of things going missing, toys belonging to the other children in the family he was visiting. Nobody wanted to make a fuss, after all it was understandable, the other children had so much and he had so little. Nobody wanted him to get into trouble, but they didn't want him to visit again either, if that was OK with the staff at the children's home. But then it wasn't just any toys, it was the special toys – the treasured teddy bears and dollies the children of the host family had had since they were babies. Some turned up, some didn't, but the ones they found were always the same – slashed open with something sharp, the stuffing pulled out and the limbs removed. Still nobody wanted to make a fuss; he was angry and jealous, it was understandable given what had happened to him – they just didn't want him to visit again. But it didn't stop there.

As he grew older and bolder, the family pets became his targets: the tropical fish killed by someone pouring bleach into their tank; the mice and hamsters and gerbils that went missing from their cages and were later found buried in the garden. Again, nobody could be a hundred per cent certain he was responsible. But suspicions had grown stronger when a family's cat disappeared, only to be found hanging from a tree with a wire cord bound around its neck, swinging gently in the wind, eyes bulging, tongue protruding. They'd gone in search of Thomas then and discovered him, alone in a neighbour's garden, withdrawn and silent, eyes staring madly with telltale scratches covering his hands and wrists – the cat had marked its killer.

Some at the children's home had said enough was enough, he should never be placed with a family again. Others argued that they had a duty to try, but that families who had animals, any animals, must be avoided – at least until they could overcome his cruelty towards them. Reluctantly, the doubters agreed.

A few weeks later he had gone on a day visit to the home of a Christian family who believed that between God and themselves any child could be saved. They'd been watching him closely, as they'd been warned to do, but somehow he'd managed to sneak away. There was concern, but no panic – or at least there wasn't until they realized their five-year-old daughter was also missing. She'd been playing alone in her bedroom with her dolls, and now she was *missing*. The mother had been hysterical and wanted to call the police immediately, but the father had urged her to wait, saying he would go and find them. There was no sign of them in the house, nor in the garden, nor the garage. So he began to search the alley that ran behind the back gardens. And that was where he found them – in a shed in a neighbour's back garden, his five-year-old daughter standing naked, tears rolling down her face as Thomas Keller stood in front of her, his trousers and underpants pulled to his knees, a tiny erection gripped between the fingers and thumb of one hand while the other pointed the blade of a penknife at the stricken girl.

The Christian father charged in and swatted Thomas to the floor with an open hand. 'You sick little bastard! I'm going to teach you a lesson you'll never forget,' he told him. Then he proceeded to slip the leather belt from his waistband, gripping the buckle and letting the rest uncoil like a whip. Thomas had watched as the man's big hand eased the shed door closed, raising the belt above his head.

What followed had indeed taught him a lesson, one he never would forget – he was alone and always would be. Totally alone.

After that day there were no more visits for Thomas Keller.

Sean and Sally bumped along the dirt road through Elmstead Woods on the Kent–London border. They'd hardly spoken the entire length of the journey from Peckham. Sean saw two marked police cars and knew they were in the right place. A long strip of blue-and-white police tape closed off the road ahead of where the cars were parked. Sean pulled in behind them and he and Sally climbed from the car in what looked a synchronized movement. One of the uniformed cops who'd been sheltering from the morning chill jumped out of his car and approached them.

Sean held up his warrant card: 'DI Corrigan' – he nodded towards Sally – 'and DS Jones. Why have you taped the road off?' The woods to his side he expected to be cordoned off, but not necessarily the road.

'Tyre tracks,' explained the uniform. 'Looks like he pulled up on the side of the road, where the ground's softer. Left some pretty good tyre marks – and footprints too. Two people, by the look of it, one wearing trainers, the other—'

Sean cut him off: 'The other barefoot.' He saw the confusion in the officer's face. 'The last victim – she was barefoot too.'

The uniform didn't speak, but his face said everything.

As Sean looked around, breathing in the atmosphere of the woods – he felt the madman's presence. The place stank of him. They could have been back in the woods where they'd found Karen Green; the two places were so similar he could hardly tell one from the other. 'Who found her?' he asked. 'A dog walker?'

'No,' the uniformed cop replied. 'It was too early for most dog walkers round here on a Sunday. She was found by a birdwatcher looking for pied wagtails, or so he tells me. Good time of year for it, apparently.'

'I wouldn't know,' said Sean distractedly. 'Anything suspicious about your birdwatcher?'

'You're asking the wrong person, sir. I didn't meet him. That was another local unit – they took him back to the nick before we got here.'

'I see,' Sean answered, still not interested in what he was being told – merely going through the question-and-answer routine the uniformed cops would expect. He knew the man he hunted wouldn't have reported the body to the police in some self-destructive game of risk. He'd be back in whatever hovel he'd crawled from, dreaming of his night's work and fantasizing about more good times ahead.

Sean looked at the ground on the edge of the forest where he could make out the tyre-tracks the uniformed cop had mentioned and the accompanying footprints, both of which disappeared into the grass as they headed deeper into the trees. Beyond the treeline his eyes could see nothing, but his mind could see everything – the madman walking close behind Louise Russell as he marched her towards her death, occasionally shoving her in the back to encourage her to keep walking.

'Guv'nor . . .' Sally asked without being heard. Then, louder: 'Sean.'

'Sorry. What is it?'

'You OK?'

'I'm fine,' he lied. 'What about you?'

She shrugged, but he could see the tension and fear in her face. This would be the first time she'd been to a crime scene where the body was still in situ since she'd almost become a murder victim herself. Sean knew that when she saw Louise Russell's body she would be seeing herself. 'You don't have to do this,' he told her. 'I can go alone. You can wait here or search the perimeter for something that might have been missed.'

Sally breathed in deeply through her nose, desperately wishing she still smoked. 'No,' she said. 'I think I need to do this.'

'OK,' he agreed, turning back to the cop guarding his crime scene. 'Do you have an alternative route to the victim?'

'Sure – duck under the tape across the road there and keep going for a few metres. You'll come to some more tape leading into the woods. Just follow that tape all the way and it'll take you straight to her.'

He sounded as if he was giving a lost motorist directions, but Sean admired his professionalism – using crime-scene cordon tape to mark a forensically safe path to the victim was a sound idea.

Sean took one last look at the soft ground where the training shoe prints led both into and out of the wood, but the barefoot prints led only in – so the killer had probably exited the same way he'd entered, leaving them with one route to concentrate on. It also meant the killer had chosen the path of least resistance, both before and after he'd killed her. Clearly convenience was still more important to him than concealing forensic evidence.

Sean walked past the parked police cars and ducked under the tape, holding it higher for Sally to follow, like a trainer helping his boxer enter the ring. Without speaking they followed the treeline until they found the trampled ground and tape that snaked into the woods, like Hansel and Gretel's trail of breadcrumbs. They began to stumble deeper into the wood, their city footwear and clothing hindering their progress – long coats catching on branches that seemed to reach out and search for them, their smooth-soled shoes constantly slipping on the damp grass and moss, the air surrounding them both heavy and fresh, the strong breeze encouraging Sally to button her coat as they walked ever closer to Louise Russell's body. 'D'you think it's much further?' she asked, more out of a need to say something than curiosity, the constant eerie rustling sound from the trees, like waves breaking on a deserted pebble beach, increasingly spooking her.

'I don't know,' he answered truthfully, wishing he could have walked the same path the killer and Louise Russell had, but knowing he couldn't. He reminded himself that their journey into the woods would have been almost exactly the same as his and Sally's, but somehow not stepping in the killer's footsteps was stopping him feeling how he would have felt – stopping him seeing what he would have seen. He pushed a branch away from his face, but it sprang loose and whipped back, an unseen sharpness cutting him along his cheekbone, just under his left eye. 'Bastard,' he cried out, putting the back of his hand to the wound, seeing the blood when he took it away.

'You all right?' Sally asked.

He kept walking. 'I'm fine.'

'I don't know how Roddis and his forensic team are gonna hump their gear through this.'

'They might have to wake someone up at the council – get a few blokes down here with chainsaws to cut a decent path. If that's what we have to do, then that's what we have to do.'

'Roddis won't like it,' Sally warned, 'letting civilians that close to his crime scene.'

'Yeah, well, that's his problem, not ours,' muttered Sean, tired of the small talk that was clouding his mind. He pushed ahead more quickly, not caring if the branches of trees punished his recklessness further, subconsciously hoping he would leave Sally behind, temporarily lost in the woods, allowing him to be alone with Louise Russell and any remaining traces of the man he hunted – be they physical or otherwise. But Sally kept pace with him, the fear of being abandoned in the woods driving her on.

'Nice of the uniforms to warn us about the route they'd

chosen. If I'd known I was gonna get my tights laddered I'd've stayed with the car.'

Sean saw through her bravado – trying to be flippant and jokey to conceal her anxiety. But at least it was a sign of the old Sally breaking through. Perhaps she did need this – needed to go through it before she could start truly healing.

'They did the right thing,' he said, pushing deeper into the woods. 'Choosing the path of most resistance is exactly what our man would never do.'

'You know that, do you?'

He stopped and looked at her for a moment. 'Yes,' was all he said. They locked eyes, not speaking, until he turned away and carried on walking.

Sally waited a few seconds then followed, watching him ahead of her, pushing through branches that closed behind him, obscuring her view, as if he and the trees were conspiring to isolate her. For the first time since they'd entered the woods she became aware of the sound of birds all around them – the shrill alarm whistles of blackbirds warning the dwellers of the forest of their approach mixing with the mocking laughter of magpies. She was sure Sean was unaware of the avian eyes observing their intrusion. He was going to another place, forcing himself to enter into the mind of the murderer – a place where she didn't belong, where she wasn't wanted. She allowed Sean the distance he needed.

Every step he took towards Louise Russell was a step closer to the madman, and with every step he took he changed a little more, his thoughts and those of the killer beginning to merge. He was close now and Sean could feel him, see through his eyes: the woods at night with nothing other than the moon to light the way, the sharp branches grabbing and scratching at her bare skin, catching and pulling at his loose clothes, feeling calm and in control, almost for the first time in his life, accepting what he had to do with no trace of doubt or guilt.

Suddenly the sound of the woods seemed to change, the hissing of the leaves replaced with a strange alien sound, like the flapping of thousands of tiny man-made wings or hundreds of broken kites. He kept following the length of blue-and-white tape that appeared to be leading him directly to the source of the mysterious noise. What must she have been thinking, he wondered – alone in the dark woods with the madman, not knowing what beast, man or animal was making the terrible flapping sound? Suddenly he stepped into a clearing, instinctively thrusting out his arm behind him until he was sure that the source of the sound represented no danger to them.

As he looked around the clearing he saw what was making the hellish noise – dozens of empty plastic bags trapped on the barbs of the bramble-bushes, blown here from God knows where, inflating and flapping in the breeze like obscene Christmas decorations, tattered and haunting. In the moonlight Louise Russell would not have been able to see the innocent, harmless things that serenaded her death.

'Christ,' he said out loud. 'What were you thinking when you heard that sound?'

Another voice reminded him he was not alone.

'Sean?' called Sally. 'Is everything OK?'

'Everything's fine,' he answered. 'Just give me a few seconds.'

He forced his eyes from the bramble-bushes and scanned the clearing, until there, almost dead centre, about twenty feet away he saw her, partially covered in brown leaves swept over her by the wind, piled up against her in the direction the breeze had been travelling. Even from this distance he could see she was lying on her side, her knees apparently folded in a near foetal position. Her pale skin contrasted somehow beautifully with the rich brown of the leaves and the green of the moss that provided her soft deathbed. His eyes followed the outskirts of the clearing until he saw the place where both killer and victim would have entered – a break in the trees, where the wood wasn't so dense – the path of least resistance. A trail of flattened grass and moss led from the same place to where Louise Russell's body was lying. Another path stretched out directly in front of him, made by the first officers on scene who confirmed the birdwatcher's fears – he had indeed stumbled across a dead body lying in the woods.

Sean wondered which direction the birdwatcher would have approached from and decided it was most likely the same one as the killer. He might have entered the woods at a different point, but at some point the paths they'd used had joined. The birdwatcher was about to lose his favourite walking boots to Roddis.

Finally he lowered his hand, signalling it was safe for Sally to move forward. After a few seconds he felt her by his side. He gave her as long as she needed, waiting for her to speak first. Eventually he heard her voice.

'I suppose we should take a closer look,' she almost whispered, as if she didn't really want to say what she just had – afraid he would agree. He answered with movement, carefully stepping into the clearing, scrutinizing the forest floor in front of him before each next step, looking for the slightest sign the ground could have been disturbed by someone other than the police who initially attended the scene, trying to step inside the footmarks they'd already left. Sally followed gingerly behind him. Once he was no more than seven or eight feet away from the body he squatted as low as he could to the ground and looked across at the face of the dead woman – short hazel hair fallen over her temples and brow, eyes half-closed, mouth open with her tongue sticking slightly out between her blue lips, gripped by her upper and lower teeth. She was completely naked, the cuts and bruises on her body too numerous to count, but even from this distance he could see the same telltale circular marks the cattle prod had left on Karen Green – confirmation of what he already knew: it was the same man.

'Is it her?' Sally asked sombrely, expecting only one answer.

Sean looked over his shoulder at her. 'It's her – Louise Russell. We're too late. Nothing we can do now.'

She sensed the self-accusation in his voice. 'It's not your fault, Sean.'

'Yes it is,' he snapped back. 'I missed something. We're here because I missed something.'

She knew there were no words that would change his mind. 'We should go,' she said. 'There's nothing more we can do here other than mess up the crime scene.'

'Not yet,' he argued. 'I need to check something out first.'

'Roddis won't be happy,' she warned, still standing at the edge of the clearing, not wanting to step inside the circle.

'It won't take long,' he assured her as he began to move towards Louise Russell's lifeless body. The closer he got, the more the world around him ceased to exist – the sounds of the birds and trees replaced by a thundering humming in his mind, like the sound of rushing water. He tugged a pair of rubber gloves over his hands and reached out for her head, gently gripping her chin and forehead. The bruising and reddening around her neck and throat told him she'd been strangled, but he needed to know what else had happened.

'What are you doing?' Sally whispered as loudly as she could, but her words fell on deaf ears as Sean carefully tilted Louise Russell's head, the onset of rigor-mortis making her muscles stiff and difficult to manoeuvre. Eventually he was able to see the back of her skull. He held her head just above the ground in one hand while the fingers of the other gently moved her hair aside, looking for a wound – a wound like the one he'd found on Karen Green. But he could find no sticky, hair-matted patch of blood. He laid her head back, exactly as he'd found it, the rushing sound in his mind growing ever louder as he crouched, staring into the earth at his feet.

Again Sally called from the edge of the clearing, louder this time. 'What is it?' He didn't hear her. 'What is it?' she repeated. Sean looked up at her, unspeaking, as if in a daze. 'Did you find something?'

'There's no head wound,' he said, sounding confused, 'and he's at least a day early. He shouldn't have killed her yet.'

'What does that mean?'

'It means he's changing. His cycle is speeding up. But not just that, something else too . . .'

'Go on,' she encouraged him.

'When he killed Karen Green it was functional – it meant nothing – the actual killing. Everything that went before the killing was intensely personal, but when it came to her murder, it was a simple case of disposing of something that had no value to him. He was more worried about self-preservation than the experience of taking a life – that's why he all but killed her with a blow to the head before he strangled her, or . . . or at least that's what he told himself. He was trying to convince himself that he wasn't killing for the thrill of it, because that would have . . . what? Affected his self-image? But what image do you have of yourself? What do you think you are?'

He broke off the questions and pictures in his head. 'Fuck's sake,' he swore at himself for not being able to solve the puzzle instantly, then continued: 'This time there's no head wound . . . because . . . he wanted to feel her life drain away. Not just what was left of it, but all of it.' He studied the position of the body for a few seconds, then went on: 'He stood in front of her. She was already kneeling on the ground because she'd tried to run away, but in her bare feet, in the dark, she had no chance and she fell or he tripped her, so she was on the floor when he came to her, standing above her, looking down into her eyes. He took his time, reaching out towards her, his fingers sliding around her neck, his thumbs pressing into her throat. She tried to fight, but he was too strong and it felt so good – her struggling, her life ebbing away as he held her tight, it felt good. Even after she was dead he kept hold of her, looking down into her dead face, until eventually he released her and watched her fall to the ground in exactly the same position she's in now. And then he watched her some more. The cold night air must have felt so good and once you've admitted to yourself that the killing feels good too, you're not going to stop until you're stopped, are you? Not until I stop you.'

'Sean?' Sally called. 'Sean – who're you talking to?'

He turned his head quickly towards her, suddenly aware of what he must have done. 'You,' he lied. 'I was talking to you.'

They stood in silence for a moment, then Sally spoke. 'I think we should go now.'

'Just one more thing I need to check,' he promised.

'Fine. Do what you have to do and let's get out of here before forensics show up.'

Still crouching next to the body, he looked over her torso at the arm that lay partially concealed under her. He saw scratches and bruises, but nothing else.

'What are you looking for?' Sally asked nervously, desperate to get as far away from the crime scene and body of Louise Russell as she could – to distance herself from her own memories and thoughts of what she'd almost become – a lifeless *thing* to be pored over and photographed before being removed to a mortuary to be dissected in the search for evidence. Not a person any more, just a case-file.

Sean ignored her as he reached for Louise Russell's other arm, the one that hung behind her back. As gently as he could, he took hold of her wrist and twisted it to reveal the underside of her forearm – the sight of the garish phoenix making him feel dizzy, exhilarated and confused all at the same time. He almost dropped her arm and toppled over, but managed to catch himself and lower the arm back to its previous position before standing bolt upright, his eyes never leaving the body.

'What?' Sally called, keeping her distance. 'What have you found?'

'The key,' he told her. 'The key to everything. Now I just need to find the lock it fits.'

'I still don't understand,' she admitted as Sean walked back towards her, pulling his phone from his coat pocket, searching for the number he knew would be in his contacts. After a few rings he heard Donnelly's voice answer.

'Dave? Don't say anything, just listen. This is important and I don't have much time. That transfer I asked Paulo to look into – the phoenix – did anything come of it? Did he find anything?'

'Oh God – that useless thing. Yeah, he gave me a report about it. Last I remember I put it on your desk, with the other information reports. I thought you would have put that through the shredder by now. How you getting on at the crime scene?'

'Listen,' said Sean, the tone of his voice pricking Donnelly's ears, 'Louise Russell has the same transfer in the same place as the one we found on Karen Green.'

Donnelly thought for a second. 'No way. It's not possible. The only way they could have the same fake tattoo would be if . . . oh Jesus Christ,' he blasphemed as the reality of the situation dawned over him.

'And if he put the transfers on them, it must be important to him. Important because *she* had a tattoo of a phoenix – the woman he's taking them to replace. Either he got lucky and found a transfer that matched her tattoo – which I doubt – or he had them made for him by some specialist company that produces custom-made transfers. Had them made specifically because it made the women seem more like her

– like the one he's coveted for months if not years. Where are you now?'

'I'm in the office.'

'Good. Go through my in-tray and find the report Zukov gave you – maybe it's got the name of the company that made the transfers. They should be able to tell us who they made them for.'

'This isn't possible.'

'Trust me,' Sean pleaded, 'it's possible. Now dig out the report and read what it says to me.'

'No, no,' Donnelly replied, 'you don't understand. I've read Zukov's report. The transfer on Karen Green was sixteen years old. They were mass-produced for some cereal company who gave them away in packets of cornflakes or Rice Krispies or fuck knows what.' Sean listened in stunned silence. 'That's why I reckoned it was a dead end,' Donnelly explained. 'How the hell could a sixteen-year-old transfer from a cornflake packet be relevant to our case? But if you're telling me it is, then the man we're looking for has been keeping those transfers for the last sixteen years.'

Sean stood wide-eyed, trembling with excitement and apprehension, terrified that the answer to the puzzle would slip from his mind before he could ensnare it and make it his permanent captive. 'Get in front of a CRIS machine,' he ordered.

'One minute,' said Donnelly, striding to the nearest computer and logging into CRIS. 'OK, I'm in. What next?'

'Run an inquiry for any allegations of harassment – female victim. The year I'm looking for is 1996 and the age of the victim will be between ten and twelve. D'you understand?' he asked, his heart pounding in his chest as his belief that he was right, that he was close to finding the madman, grew within him.

'I'm with you,' Donnelly assured him as he punched the details into CRIS, waiting for the relevant screens to roll past.

'The harassment would have been reported by the parents,' Sean continued.

After a few seconds Donnelly spoke: 'OK, I have seven reports of young girls being harassed. What now?'

'Our man has no convictions, remember? Which means he probably wasn't charged, meaning the parents just wanted us to warn him off. Does that match anything you have?'

The silence on the other end of the phone told him it did.

'Victim's name is Samantha Shaw,' Donnelly said. 'Suspect's name is Thomas Keller, who was also twelve at the time of the offence. His address is shown as a children's home in Penge, so he won't be there any more.'

'No, but she might still live with her parents.'

'At the same address? It's unlikely,' Donnelly warned.

'Even if they've moved, we have enough details to locate them,' Sean reminded him. 'See if you can't find an address for this Thomas Keller, and track down the Shaws – we need to know where Samantha is now – right now.'

'No problem. And while I'm doing that, what will you be doing?'

'I'm going to meet our friendly supervisor from the sorting depot.'

'On a Sunday?' Donnelly queried.

'I have his mobile number, remember,' Sean reminded him. 'He'll meet me. Deborah Thomson's still alive – I know she is. If necessary I'll give him no choice. I won't let there be a third murder – no matter what.'

Superintendent Featherstone drove through the light mid-morning traffic towards Peckham police station, having decided that location offered the best chance of intercepting Sean and getting an update on the second body, as well as showing his face to the rank and file. After that he might yet make it home for the Sunday roast his wife was in the process of preparing. Anything else he was fairly confident he could deal with over the phone, at least until the real shit-storm got underway on Monday morning. Besides, Corrigan knew what he was doing, even if he was a little *unconventional.*

The very phone he'd just been thinking of began to chirp and vibrate in the centre console. He grabbed it with his non-steering hand and checked the caller ID, but the number was withheld – never a good sign on a cop's mobile phone. For a brief second he considered not answering, but decided he'd rather deal with whatever the call brought than fret about who it might have been for the rest of the morning.

'Hello,' he answered guardedly.

'Good morning, Alan,' said a voice he recognized. 'Assistant Commissioner Addis here,' he added unnecessarily.

'Good morning, sir,' Featherstone forced himself to respond, inwardly cursing himself for answering the damn phone.

'I hear your DI Corrigan has a second victim on his hands.'

'Bad news travels fast.'

'Like I told you, certain people have taken an interest in DI Corrigan. The progress of any case he's involved in finds its way to my ears quicker than you might imagine.'

'Indeed,' was Featherstone's only reply.

'And what of our mutual friend?' Addis continued. 'Has she submitted her report to you yet, or informed you of any interesting observations she may have made?'

'No,' said Featherstone. 'Not yet.'

'Uhhm, I was thinking – on reflection, it's probably better if she reports to me directly. There's no need to create unnecessary . . . bureaucracy. Don't you agree?'

'I understand.'

'Good. One last thing . . .' Addis said. 'Does he suspect anything?'

'I don't think so.'

'Excellent,' said Addis. 'Make sure it stays that way.'

Featherstone heard the line go dead and found himself staring at his phone. For a second he considered calling Sean and warning him to tread carefully, but he knew he couldn't trust his own phone not to betray him, not now Addis and his *people* were involved.

With a shrug of his shoulders he tossed the phone on to the passenger seat. Maybe he'd still make it home in time for his Sunday roast.

Sean and Sally drew closer to the sorting office in South Norwood where they had arranged to meet Leonard Trewsbury, the depot supervisor. They'd travelled in almost complete silence, Sally driving while Sean spent most of his time nervously cradling his phone, waiting for Donnelly to call back. It had rung several times during the journey, making them both jump, but he'd answered only once, when the caller ID showed it was DS Roddis from the forensic team. Sally wondered who the other calls were from.

'Something bothering you?' she asked. 'Aside from the usual.'

'That CRIS search I had Dave run,' he told her. 'I did the same search myself, several times, only I never thought about changing the dates of the offence by more than a couple of years. If I'd only changed the dates, moved them back further, then Louise Russell would be alive.'

'Fuck sake, Sean – how could you possibly have known to move the date back *sixteen* years? How could anyone have known to do that?'

'I should have,' he snapped. 'As soon as I saw that tattoo, as soon as we discovered it was only a transfer, I should have checked back further – much further.'

'Hey, give yourself a break. We don't even know if this guy Thomas Keller has got anything to do with these murders.'

'It's him,' Sean assured her. 'I know it's him. He's coveted her for sixteen years – planned this for sixteen years – and now at last, finally he's making it all come true. When we meet Trewsbury, he'll confirm that Keller works from the

Norwood sorting office and then there'll be no doubt he's our man. Then this'll be over.'

'There's something else,' Sally probed. 'Something you're not telling me.'

'It's that name – Thomas Keller. I've heard it before somewhere, or dealt with him in the past. Christ, I don't know, maybe I nicked him when I was still in uniform or interviewed him someplace, sometime. Ever since Dave said his name it's been driving me mad trying to remember – where have I heard that name?'

'You're knackered,' Sally reminded him. 'It's probably just déjà-vu. By the time your tired brain processes a new piece of information your memory has already logged it, hence the information appears strangely familiar to you. It's a case of the memory overtaking the conscious thought process.'

Sean looked at her with eyebrows raised. 'I know what déjà-vu is.'

'Sorry,' she apologized. 'Of course you do.'

Sean's phone rang again. He checked the caller ID and answered. 'Dave. What have you got for me?'

'First off, we drew a blank on Thomas Keller. No address, no intelligence, no nothing. Anything created as a result of the sexual assault and subsequent stalking has been deleted from our intelligence records a long time ago and it appears he's kept himself clean since. The Shaws still live at the same address, but Samantha flew the nest a few years back and now lives with her boyfriend at 16 Sangley Road, Catford. I'll text you the address and her phone number, unless you want me to call her?'

'No,' Sean insisted. 'No phone calls. I need to see her face to face. I have to know how she feels about him.'

Donnelly didn't argue. 'Fair enough. Is there anything else you want me to do?'

'No,' Sean answered. 'Hold fire with the team until I get an address for Keller. I'll call as soon as I have it.' He hung up.

'You're not going to call him are you?' Sally said. 'If we get an address for Keller – you're not going to call anyone.'

Sean ignored her and pointed to the side of the road next to the sorting office. 'Pull over here. That's our man.' He almost jumped out of the car while it was still moving, desperate to quiz Leonard Trewsbury, desperate for confirmation.

The two men had already shaken hands by the time Sally joined them. Sean didn't bother introducing her. 'Thanks for meeting us,' he said.

'You didn't give me much choice, Inspector,' Trewsbury replied. 'Another young woman found murdered – what could I say? I'll probably lose my job and most of my pension too, but at least I'll be able to look myself in the mirror.'

'If there'd been any other way, I wouldn't have asked,' Sean assured him. 'I had no alternative, not while there's still a chance to save another.'

'The third woman he took?' Trewsbury asked, his eyes narrowing.

'There's no reason to believe he'll treat her any differently,' Sean warned him.

'So what is it you want from me that you couldn't ask over the phone?'

'Thomas Keller – does that name mean anything to you?'

Trewsbury's lips went a strange shade of grey. 'Tommy, yeah, sure, he works here, but he couldn't be involved in this – he wouldn't say boo to a goose. He's a good kid, you know, hard worker, keeps himself to himself. He gets hassled by the other guys sometimes, but never caused me no trouble.'

He was unaware he was describing exactly the sort of man Sean was looking for, causing his heart to flutter as all his theories began to fall into place. How the killer had been able to walk around residential areas without drawing attention to himself, dressed in the urban camouflage of his Post Office uniform, selecting his victims, intercepting their mail to learn about their lives, tricking them into opening their front doors and snatching them from their own homes – it was all coming true.

'I need his address,' he told Trewsbury without trying to justify why he suspected Thomas Keller.

'I don't have it,' Trewsbury answered.

'I know. That's why I wanted to meet you here, so we can check the employment records. You said it yourself, Leonard, two young women already murdered and one missing, presumed alive – for the time being.'

'But Tommy . . .' Trewsbury struggled. 'I don't suppose you have a Production Order?'

'No,' said Sean. 'By the time I get one, it'll be too late for Deborah Thomson. I'm sorry, Leonard, but it's him, I know it's him and I need his address now.'

14

Thomas Keller awoke from his nightmares shortly before 11 a.m., his clothes and bedding soaked with sweat, his eyes instantly wide open and bloodshot. He rolled out of bed as if he was escaping a torture rack and landed hard on the floor, scrambling and crawling to the corner of the littered room, eyes darting from side to side looking for danger – children from the home, colleagues from work, the police. Finally he remembered where he was, in time and place, and allowed his tensed body to relax, his shoulders falling away from his neck as he slowly exhaled, the bright sunlight pouring through his improvised curtains and making him blink repeatedly. He stayed sitting in the corner for almost fifteen minutes, trying to fully orientate himself with the world around him, a million confused messages and ideas swirling inside his head, each telling him to do a different thing – kill the woman in his cellar and then himself. Kill himself and spare the woman. Find his mother and kill her. Kill his mother and run. Kill his work colleagues and himself. Go to the children's home and kill everyone there – his old school, all the potential adoptive parents who'd rejected him, everyone who'd ever rejected him – not accepted him. Kill as many as he could – kill them all.

'No!' he screamed at himself, at the ugly thoughts taking

over his mind – the thoughts that reminded him of last night – how good it felt to squeeze the life from *the whore's* neck. 'That was different,' he yelled. 'She betrayed me.'

He jumped to his feet and stumbled to the drawer where he kept his precious letters, pulling it open and searching frantically through the bundles until he found the one he was looking for – a thick roll of envelopes addressed to Hannah O'Brien. Yanking the elastic band away, he let the letters fall over the surface of the chest of drawers and began to spread them around so he could see as many of them as possible at the same time. Without even realizing it, his hand had slipped inside his tracksuit bottoms and gripped himself. Yes, he told himself, the others had all been mistakes, but at last he'd found the real Sam. He would rescue her and then she would save him from the ugly thoughts. It was how it was meant to be. Once he'd rescued her, he'd pile the other letters into one of the oil drums and burn them and with them all the ugly thoughts. But what if she didn't understand what he'd had to do – the *sacrifices* he'd had to make? No, no, he reassured himself – she'd understand, she wouldn't judge him – she never had.

First, however, there was still one more mistake he had to deal with. He took his hand away from the letters and headed slowly towards his bathroom.

Sally parked their car a good fifty metres from the address that Trewsbury had illegally given them. If Keller was at home, they didn't want to spook him by screeching up outside his front door. They climbed from the car and began to walk along the neglected street of three-storey Victorian terraced houses, most of which had been converted into flats. Sean was already beginning to suspect that Keller had given the Post Office a false address or, more likely, had moved and not bothered to tell them. He was a Post Office employee, so discreetly having his mail re-directed wouldn't have been too difficult.

As they closed on the address Sally became increasingly concerned about their course of action.

'Maybe we should get TSG to hit the address? Go in hard and shake him up,' she suggested.

'No,' said Sean, assessing the house. Even if Keller was still here, it was clear that Deborah Thomson would not be. 'Let's check it out first, see how the land lies, then we can consider using the TSG.'

'Perhaps we should put him under surveillance,' suggested Sally, 'see if he leads us to Deborah Thomson. If we grab him now he may never talk. He could leave her to starve to death in some hole in the ground.'

'Time,' he reminded her, 'it's all about time we don't have. Karen Green abducted – found dead seven days later. Louise Russell abducted – found dead five days later.' He stopped and turned to face her. 'He's speeding up, Sally. The interval between the abduction and the killing is shrinking. How many days does Deborah Thomson have? Four? Three? Less?'

He started walking again, Sally trailing behind, almost breaking into a run to keep up until they reached the three shallow steps that led to the front door and a panel of doorbells mounted on the side of the door frame. Six bells meant six separate flats. The peeling paint on the front door and lack of names next to the intercom buttons told Sean the flats were probably occupied by the transient – London's throngs of the unsettled and unwanted. He rang the only buzzer that had a readable name beside it and waited. After a few seconds that felt like minutes the intercom crackled and a voice leaked out of it.

'Yes?'

'Police,' Sean said into the machine as quietly as he could without sounding like anything but a cop. 'Can I have a word?'

More silent seconds. 'What's it about?'

'Open the door and I'll tell you,' Sean promised.

'Hold on a minute. I'll come to the front door.' They waited, listening to the sounds of doors opening and closing, locks being turned, shuffling footsteps growing nearer and a chain being attached to the door before finally it opened by four inches and the plump, pink face of a woman in her fifties peered through the gap, her small crooked teeth revealing the brown stains of years of cigarette smoking when she spoke.

'Yeah?' she asked them suspiciously in a thick South London accent. Sean couldn't help but look her up and down, noting her ancient slippers and cardigan, her wild grey hair and swollen limbs.

'DI Corrigan,' he announced, holding his warrant card out.

The woman looked to Sally, who realized she wasn't going to be satisfied with seeing just one warrant card. She sighed, pulling hers from her coat pocket and thrusting it towards the suspicious old woman who immediately looked back to Sean.

'We need to find out if a certain person lives here. Can we come in?'

The woman's eyes darted between them before she finally relented – more time wasted. 'I suppose so,' she muttered, releasing the chain and allowing Sean to push the door fully open and step past her into the building. Sally followed suit, closing the door behind her. The poky hallway felt very crowded with three of them in it.

'Would you like a drink – a cup of tea or something?' The image of foul-tasting tea served in a filthy cup flashed through Sean's mind.

'No, thanks, we're in a hurry.'

'It's no bother. I was about to put the kettle on.'

Sean talked over the top of her. 'Mrs . . .?'

'Miss, actually. Miss Rose Vickery.'

'Miss Vickery, does—'

'But you can call me Rose.'

'Rose. Does the name Thomas Keller mean anything to you? Does anyone by that name live in this house?'

'People come and go from here all the time,' she said.

'Nobody stays long, except me. I've been here almost twenty years, back when you used to know your neighbours. Ain't got a clue who lives here now – people coming and going all hours, but I never see nobody – just keep meself to meself.'

'Do you rent your flat?'

'Yeah, of course I do. All the flats in here are rented by the same landlord – Mr Williams.'

Sean was about to ask for Williams's telephone number when Sally interrupted. 'Guv'nor.' He turned and saw her holding a bundle of mail, most of which looked like junk. She took a couple of letters from the pile and handed them to him. He read the name – *Thomas Keller, Flat 4, 184 Ravenscroft Road, Penge*. Sean passed the letters to Rose.

'This is 184 Ravenscroft Road, right?'

'Yes.' She sounded nervous.

'And this is the name of the man I just asked you about – Thomas Keller.'

'Yes, but I don't read other people's mail,' she protested. 'Besides, there's mail still comes here for people who are long gone.'

'Come on,' said Sean. 'You must see the names on the letters, when you're searching for your own mail?'

'What you trying to say?'

'I'm saying you know who lives here and who doesn't. So you need to tell me, does Thomas Keller live in flat 4? Now!' he demanded, raising his voice and making Rose flinch.

'I don't know,' she insisted, pulling her cardigan tightly around herself.

Sean thought for a second. 'He's a postman. Maybe you remember seeing him in his Post Office uniform.'

'Oh,' Rose declared, almost smiling with relief, 'him. The postie, yeah, he used to live here, but he don't no more – ain't lived here for a few years. He pops back every now and then to pick up his mail. I suppose he kept his key for the front door – most of the old residents do, you know. I saw him a few weeks ago, actually. I remember it because I said to him, you'd think he'd be able to get his mail sent to the right address, seeing how he's a postie and all.'

Sean and Sally looked at each other – they needed to go.

'I don't suppose you have a forwarding address for him?' Sean asked, more in blind hope than anticipation.

'No, love,' Rose answered.

'What now?' said Sally.

Sean stared down at the letter in his hand and jabbed at the name. 'I know this name,' he said, 'but how and where?' He shook his head as if clearing it of a foolish idea. 'Samantha Shaw,' he finally said. 'We need to see her, maybe she knows where he lives.'

'Shall I tell him you're looking for him?' said Rose. 'You know, the postie. If I see him, shall I tell him to get in touch?'

'No,' Sean told her. 'Don't worry about it, Rose. I'll be seeing him soon enough.'

Anna had been at Peckham when she'd received the phone call summoning her to New Scotland Yard, but no one had noticed her slip away. The light Sunday traffic made the journey from one side of the Thames to the other reasonably short and the pavements around New Scotland Yard that were usually swarming with human traffic were deserted. She passed the armed guards clutching their sub-machine guns overtly in a manner that would have been unthinkable on the streets of London little more than a decade ago, flashing her security pass to the private guards manning the metal detectors just inside the entrance and then walking along the long corridor to the back of the building where the main lifts were. She ascended to the penultimate floor where she knew Assistant Chief Constable Robert Addis, Serious and Organized Crime Directorate, awaited.

She entered the reception area expecting to see the ever-present secretary who guarded Addis's office like a rabid

Rottweiler sitting at her desk, scowling at anyone who dared request an audience with the deity next door. But the reception was empty. As she walked deeper into the room she could hear the faint shuffling of paper coming from the adjoining office and began to move slowly towards it, the sudden sound of a man's voice, loud and bold, making her jump.

'Anna – glad you could make it. Come in and sit down.'

She took a seat on the other side of the large wooden desk to the smiling Addis, who sat with his hands together as if praying. 'How did you know it was me?' she asked. 'You must get a lot of visitors.'

'Not on a Sunday,' he said. 'Even the great police of the metropolis slow down on the Sabbath. If I was ever going to commit a serious crime I'd commit it on a Sunday.'

'I didn't know assistant commissioners were expected to work on Sundays,' Anna continued. 'Aren't you supposed to be at home with your family?'

'My family understand,' Addis assured her, the smile falling from his lips. 'Besides, I'm not expected to work on Sundays – I prefer to. I've always found it an excellent day to deal with some of the . . . shall we say, more sensitive policing matters, when there aren't so many people around who could accidently overhear something they weren't supposed to.'

'Like your secretary?'

The smile jumped back on to Addis's face. 'Did you bring it? The report?'

'I have it,' she confirmed. 'It's as complete as it can be, given the time and circumstances it was prepared under and taking into account the non-cooperation of the subject.'

'But it's informative – yes?'

'I believe so, but I'm having some serious concerns about possible client confidentiality. This doesn't feel entirely ethically correct.'

'Client confidentiality?' Addis mused, his praying fingers tapping against each other. 'But my dear Anna, I am the client, remember? I hired you to prepare a psychological profile and in exchange you were given access to areas and information others in your trade could only dream about. A mutually beneficial arrangement – I'm sure you'll agree.'

'But what about his basic human rights – freedom of information and his right to know?'

'Anna, Anna, Anna – he's a police officer. I'm afraid such niceties don't always apply to us. Freedom of information, the right to strike, health and safety, restriction on working hours – these are not things that are vouchsafed to us. If they were, we'd never get a damn thing done now, would we? So, the report, if you don't mind.'

Anna sighed and fished in her briefcase, pulling out a file the size of a fashion magazine that she passed across the desk to the serious-faced Addis.

'It's all in there,' she said. 'Everything I could discover, anyway.'

'Good,' Addis replied, finding the temptation to run his fingers over the file too much to resist. 'And he suspects nothing?'

'I don't think so, but I can't be sure. He's clearly of a high intellect. I tried to interview him a couple of times, but he saw me coming and clammed up. Most of my findings were through straight observation and speaking to his colleagues.'

'And what did that tell you?'

'It's all in the report.'

'I'm sure it is, but perhaps you could give me a verbal summary to be going on with?'

'Very well. As I've said, he's intelligent, highly observant and determined. I wouldn't call him a natural leader, but his subordinates seem to follow him willingly. They clearly believe in him. He's anchored by his wife and children. He may not spend much time with them, but they're enormously important to him and his ability to deal with what he has to deal with. Just knowing they're there is crucial to him – even if he doesn't always know it himself. He possesses an extraordinary ability to combine his imagination and experience, and this enables him to visualize past events.'

'What does that mean, exactly?'

'It means he can recreate events that have occurred at the crime scenes he attends. In his mind he can see what happened there.'

'Is he psychic?'

'No – and personally I don't believe anyone is. He simply has a highly developed sense of projected imagination. It's probably not as uncommon as you may think in police officers – especially detectives. If you see something enough times and then later solve the riddle of how it came to be, then eventually you'll start to see crime scenes differently. You'll start to see what happened there even before the evidence or witness testimony explains it.'

'And that's all he's doing?' Addis asked. 'Combining experience with imagination?'

'Largely.'

'But not entirely?'

'No. Not entirely.'

'So there's something else? Something that enables him to have these . . . insights?'

'I believe so. Is there anything in his past, some event in his service history that may have caused him psychiatric problems? Something that may have left him suffering from post-traumatic stress?'

Addis shook his head. 'No. A few minor injuries and some close scrapes, but nothing particularly unusual.'

'His service history shows he infiltrated a paedophile ring while working undercover. Things appear to have got a little out of hand during the operation. Could that have affected him?'

'I'm familiar with that operation,' Addis assured her. 'Corrigan was returned to normal duties without the need for any special . . . arrangements.'

'Really?' Anna quizzed. 'Only, I noticed the report said the officer in charge of the undercover side of the operation, DS Chopra, had sufficiently serious doubts about DI Corrigan's psychological welfare during the operation that he considered terminating it?'

'An overreaction,' Addis answered. 'The operation was successfully concluded and Corrigan did his job. So, something else then? In his past perhaps? Before he joined the service?'

'It's possible,' she admitted. 'But if there is anything of that nature he's buried it so deeply I couldn't find what it is. I can only guess.'

'And what's your guess?'

'It's in the report – better to read it in full.'

'Very well,' Addis agreed. 'I shall look forward to it.'

Since she'd watched Louise Russell being dragged from the cellar hours ago Deborah Thomson had been unable to do anything other than stare through the thin grey light at the cage he used to keep her in, its door hanging open as if to torment her. She'd prayed to hear the cellar door wrenched open, to hear their voices descending towards her and watch as he imprisoned Louise in her wire crate once more – anything rather than being all alone in the bleakest of dungeons. But in her gut she could feel the truth – that Louise was never coming back, never coming back to anyone.

She'd cried for so long, abandoned in the virtual darkness, that she couldn't cry any more. Dehydration had dried her tear ducts and made her skin thin and vulnerable. She couldn't remember the last drink she'd had and her mouth and throat burned with thirst as her gums began to shrink back over her teeth. Another day or two without water and they'd start to split and bleed while her non-essential organs would begin to slow down and eventually cease functioning as her body sent what little moisture there would be to the most vital organs – the brain, heart, lungs and liver. She chastised herself for having wasted so much valuable water on self-indulgent tears – water that had long since fallen on the stony ground and dried away. What would her brothers have thought if they'd seen her feeling sorry for herself, huddled in a corner crying like a baby when she should have been planning her escape – the next attack on the bastard who'd brought her here? They would have been ashamed of her – their tough little sister, scared of some loser-freak. Next time she had a chance she'd make it count, even with her broken kneecap. She'd almost got the better of him the first time. If it hadn't been for an unlucky slip on the stairs, she'd have been off.

Deborah vowed not to make the same mistakes again. Next time, instead of being in a rush to get away she'd stand her ground and beat the living shit out of him – make sure he was totally incapacitated before getting out of the cellar and finding help. Or maybe she'd just call her brothers and tell them what the bastard had done to her. They'd see to it that he paid. No need for police to be involved – no interviews and court appearances. Her brothers would make him suffer – suffer like he'd made her suffer. And once she decided he'd had enough, they'd take him somewhere he'd never be found and bury him alive in a six-foot hole and that would be the end of the bastard.

Her fantasy of revenge and punishment made her feel temporarily brave, but the clang of the padlock on the cellar door being tampered with brought the terror flooding back, vanquishing all thoughts of her brothers and escape. For a brief moment she imagined it could be someone other than him fumbling at the lock, the excitement of the possibility rushing through her, almost making her cry out for help, but the lack of voices warned her to stay silent. A few seconds later she heard the dreaded sound of the metal door being dragged open, followed by the slow, steady tread of his feet on the stairs. She continued to stare at the empty cage opposite her own. She was alone now. He couldn't be coming to see anyone else. Louise was gone. He was coming for her.

Sally pulled the car to the side of the quiet, tidy street in Catford. The small, newly built houses were arranged at strange angles to each other in an effort to give the occupiers some feeling of privacy. Sean climbed out of the car without speaking, moving as if he was somehow hypnotized by 16 Sangley Road – its new brown bricks and white PVC windows with a small garage to match – the front door hidden from passers-by. Sally appeared at his shoulder.

'Looks familiar,' she said, but he didn't answer as he drifted towards the front door, his head thumping with possibilities. He was about to meet for the first time the woman who was a goddess to the man he hunted, but couldn't help but feel he'd already met her twice – yet never while she was still alive. As he walked along the short driveway he experienced the same disorientating sense of déjà-vu – the same sense of the killer's presence he'd had at the other scenes, and knew he'd been here and why.

He rang the doorbell, stepped back and waited, sensing movement inside – hearing muffled voices. After a couple of minutes a face warped by the thick glass of the door approached, moving quickly and confidently, not like someone who was living in fear of being stalked. The door was pulled open without caution and a young woman with short brown hair smiled at them, her green eyes shining with life.

'Hi,' she greeted them without a care in the world – it was Sunday and the sun was beginning to poke through the low cloud. Her hair was still wet from the shower and strands were sticking to her temples and brow. Sean remembered gently brushing the hair away from Karen Green's face when he'd been alone with her in the woods. He hadn't expected to be so vividly reminded of the women, now dead, that the killer had taken to replace the one standing in front of him.

'Is there something I can help you with?' Sam prompted him, her smile fading a little.

He suddenly remembered why he was there and pulled his warrant card free, flipping it open for her to see. 'Samantha Shaw?' he asked.

'Yes. That's me. Is something wrong?' The smile disappeared from her face.

Sean ignored her concern, her obvious fear they were there to deliver bad news about someone she loved. 'I'm DI Corrigan and this is DS Jones. It's about Thomas Keller,' he told her. 'I need to find him. Do you know where he lives?'

She looked over her shoulder before answering. 'Tommy? This is about Tommy?'

'Yes,' he answered. 'Do you know where he lives?'

'Why would you ask me that? I haven't seen Tommy since we were kids. Not since . . .'

'We know about what happened back then,' he assured her. 'And we know he was harassing you—'

She cut across him. 'No – watching me, but not harassing me. My parents reported it, not me.'

'You sound as though you still have a lot of affection for him,' Sean almost accused her.

'Tommy's childhood was hell. I felt sorry for him – thought I could help him, that's all. I didn't want to make things worse for him, even after . . .'

'Can we come in and talk about it?' Sally asked.

'No, I don't think so,' she said. 'Ian doesn't know anything about it and I'd like to keep it that way.'

'Have you seen Thomas Keller since?' Sean persisted. 'Since the assault and the harassment?'

'No,' she replied, and he believed her. 'They took him out of my school and last I heard he was still in the children's home. But I never saw him again and quite frankly, until now, I'd pretty much forgotten about him – which is exactly how I want it to be. Tommy's not my problem any more.'

'After what happened to you, when you were still a child – you're telling me you forgot all about it, about him?'

'Yes.' She was a bad liar, but Sean decided to let it go. 'The only thing I heard was from an old school friend I bumped into a few years ago. They said they'd seen Tommy and that he was a postman now. I was happy for him, you know. I thought maybe things had turned out all right for him, despite everything. I'm sorry, but there's nothing else I can tell you.'

'I understand,' Sean said, eager to move the questioning on. 'Just one more thing. Have you had any break-ins in the last few months or maybe even longer ago? Anything unusual gone missing?'

She looked truly concerned for the first time since she'd opened the door. 'Is Tommy in trouble? Did he do something? Is that why you're here?'

'My question,' he reminded her.

'No,' she snapped. 'I haven't had any break-ins and nothing's gone missing.'

'I need you to think really hard,' he insisted. 'Not necessarily an obvious burglary – maybe just small items that have gone missing?' He saw a flicker of something in her eyes. 'You can't go on protecting him, Samantha. You're not twelve any more, and neither is he. He's dangerous now – more dangerous than you can imagine. I need you to answer my questions.'

She sighed and shook her head. 'OK. A few months ago I'd just had a bath and was in my bedroom. I went to use my body cream, but it wasn't where I always left it, on my dressing table. I looked everywhere, but couldn't find it. I asked Ian if he'd moved it and he said no. We'd just taken on a cleaner, because we both work, and I guess I thought she might have taken it.'

'Did anything else go missing?'

'A few silly things – a bottle of perfume.'

'Black Orchid. And the body cream was from Elemis, wasn't it?'

She gawped at him, mouth hanging open, eyes clouding with suspicion. 'How did you know? How could you possibly know that?'

'Lucky guess,' said Sean. 'You said other things went missing too. What things?'

'Some of my clothes: a skirt, blouse and a sweater, I think. But you know how it is, things go missing all the time, lost at the dry cleaner's, left at work. It happens to us all.'

Clothes. Of course, he thought, berating himself for having not seen it earlier. He dressed them in her clothes – that's why the bodies had been naked or nearly so, because he was recycling her clothes, using them on victim after victim, taking them from one to give to the next as his belief that they were the real Samantha Shaw faded and died.

'Did you report it to the police?'

'Are you kidding? They would have thought I was mental.'

'But did you think it could be Tommy? In your heart, did you think it could be him? Did you see him in your mind coming into your house, your bedroom, and taking the perfume – the cream?'

'I . . . I don't know what you're talking about,' she faltered.

'Yes you do,' he said. 'But burying the past mattered more to you than telling anyone the thing you feared – feared more than anything else.'

'And what would that be?' she asked calmly.

'That he was back,' said Sean. 'That after all these years, Thomas Keller was back.'

'You don't know anything about my fears,' she warned him, still icy calm.

'I know more than you think.'

Sally had seen Sean in many guises, but this was a new one, even for her. 'This isn't getting us any closer to Keller,' she said. 'If you have no idea where he is, then you can't help us any further. Thanks for your time. We'll be in touch.'

She turned to look at Sean, as if willing him to walk away,

but he stood rooted, eyes locked with Samantha Shaw's, convinced there was more information she could give, even if she didn't know it herself. He let his eyes alone ask all the questions, until eventually she answered.

'Listen, the only other thing I can think of is that Tommy always talked about getting himself a farm when he grew up. That's all I can tell you.'

Sean suddenly looked at the ground, his hand rising towards her face, fingers spread wide like a net, as if he was trying to catch her words before they escaped and were lost for ever. 'What did you just say?' he demanded.

'I said Tommy wanted to live on a farm. I suppose he wanted to be away from people . . .' She was still talking when he turned from her, not listening any more, walking away tugging his phone from his pocket and searching for Donnelly's number. It was answered within a few ring tones.

'Guv'nor.'

'Are you still in the office?'

'Aye.'

'Thomas Keller. I remember where I've seen his name,' Sean told him. 'It was on an information report. A uniform patrol checked out a farm – the man living there gave his name as Thomas Keller.'

'You sure?' Donnelly asked. 'We must have checked out more than a hundred smallholdings, not to mention the hundreds of other information reports with name after name on them.'

'Samantha Shaw just told me that Keller always wanted to live on a farm. As soon as she said it, I remembered – remembered seeing it. But I can't remember the address. The report should still be in my office. I need you to search for it – go through every last scrap of paper till you find it.'

'Fuck me, guv'nor – have you seen your office? That could take days.'

'No,' Sean insisted. 'The information reports from property searches are in a separate pile, as are the ones from door-to-door, as are the ones from roadblocks, as are they all. The pile you're looking for will be smaller than the others. I'll stay on the line while you check.'

Donnelly eased himself out of his chair and headed to Sean's office. 'On my way – hold on.' He scanned the stacks of reports until he found the pile he was looking for. 'Here we go,' he said, sitting at the desk in front of the reports. He puffed out his cheeks and began to scan through them, checking the names while Sean waited silently, his hands shaking with anticipation, listening to Donnelly discounting each useless report. 'No.' A few seconds later. 'No.' More seconds later. 'No,' until finally Donnelly's tone changed completely. 'Fuck me,' he declared. 'How the hell did you remember seeing that?'

Sean didn't have to ask if Donnelly had found it. 'What's the address?'

'It's in Keston, Kent, off Shire Lane in what appears to be a disused poultry farm. He showed the uniform patrol his driving licence as ID, which by all accounts checked out. Do you want me to scramble TSG, or maybe a surveillance team – make sure he's holding Deborah Thomson at the same place?'

'No,' Sean insisted. 'For all we know it could be another part-time address. I'll check it out first quietly. Once I know he's there, I'll call you – then we'll think about the TSG.'

Donnelly didn't believe a word of it. 'OK, guv'nor. If that's how you want to play it.'

'It is,' said Sean, and hung up. He sensed Sally by his side. 'We've got his address.'

'How?'

'I'll explain on the way,' he promised and strode towards their car.

'On the way to where?'

'Where d'you think?' he asked, oblivious to her fears. 'To Keller's home address, of course.'

'Just the two of us? Shouldn't we wait for the TSG or at

least have some of the team meet us there? We know he has access to electrical weapons and he lives on a farm – God knows what else he's got down there.'

'Don't worry,' he assured her, 'we're not going to arrest him. We're checking out the address, that's all.'

She watched him duck inside the car, leaving her with a sickness deep in the pit of her stomach – a feeling of dread that he was leading her towards places in her own soul and consciousness she wasn't ready to go to yet. But she could see he had the taste for the hunt and his quarry was close. Like an out-of-control freight train, nothing could stop him now.

The pain had been almost as unbearable as the humiliation – his stinking, sweet breath panting in her ear, her body too racked with exhaustion and pain to resist after he'd stabbed her with the cattle prod again and again until she'd finally succumbed. At last her torture was over and he crawled from the cage, dragging her filthy mattress with him and all of her clothes except her underwear. She reached down and pulled her knickers up as best she could with one hand, sobbing a tearless cry – his voice behind her, out of breath and merciless.

'That's what you wanted, wasn't it, you little whore? Feel better now, don't you? You fucking whore – you disgust me.' He slammed the cage door shut and locked it with the padlock, gathering up the mattress and clothes. 'I need to have a shower,' he told her. 'I need to wash your filth off my body. The smell of your cunt makes me feel sick.' He headed for the stairs, stopping and looking back at her lying on the cold stone floor. 'I thought you were different to the others,' he said through gritted teeth. 'I thought you were her, but you're not. You lied to me – you tricked me. You'll fucking pay for trying to make me look like a fool. You'll all pay.'

With that he tugged the cord, turning off the electric bulb, and slowly climbed the stairs walking through the streams of sunlight that flooded into the cellar, his body cutting a silhouette into the light.

'Don't get too close,' Sean warned Sally as they drove along Shire Lane towards the outcrop of buildings they could see one hundred metres ahead. 'I don't want to spook him. Pull over here.' Sally let the car roll silently to a standstill at the side of the dirt road, the surrounding trees and hedges camouflaging them well enough. 'We'll walk from this point,' he said, 'follow the treeline and double back around on ourselves. That'll bring us right on top of the place – we'll be able to see anything moving.'

'I don't think this is a good idea,' Sally argued. 'We should wait for assistance, or better still let someone else take him out. Once we know he's secured we can search the place safely.'

'No,' he insisted. 'I want some time alone with him first.'

'You'll have time with him when you interview him. You can ask him anything you want.'

'What, when he's surrounded by solicitors, appropriate adults and the Mental Health team? I can't talk to him then – not properly. I need to be alone with him.'

'I don't under—'

'I have to know why. Why he did it.'

'You already know,' Sally argued. 'You know more about why he's doing it than he probably knows himself.'

'No, I don't.' Sean was adamant. 'I can get close, but I can't think like him. Not all the way. I need to know how he thinks.'

'But what does it matt—'

'For Christ's sake, Sally, don't you understand? It matters for the next time and the time after that and the time after that. I need to know what makes them feel alive – what they'll do to feel alive – to feel something.'

'What makes *them* feel alive?' she queried. '*Them,* Sean?'

'Come on, let's go,' he snapped, opening his door and

trying to escape. Strong fingers around his forearm stopped him.

'I'm scared, Sean,' she admitted. 'You think I'm ready for this, but I'm not. I'm scared of how I'll react if we find him – if we find Deborah Thomson. I don't know what's going to happen to me. And I'm scared for you, Sean. I'm scared what you might do.'

'What's that supposed to mean?'

'When Donnelly found you with Lawlor, on the railway bank, he told me Lawlor said you were trying to kill him.'

Sean froze, icy fingers stretching into his mind and wrapping themselves around hundreds of dark memories he tried so hard to conceal from himself as much as anyone else. He said nothing, eyes unblinking and staring into Sally's.

'Well, Sean, is it true? Were you?'

He managed to shake his head and even fake a slight smile. 'Someone's talking shit,' he lied. 'Canteen chatter, that's all.'

'Are you sure about that? Because, if there's more to it, then maybe you should think about taking a break from . . . from *this* – the madmen and the carnage, the sadness they leave behind that only we and families of their victims see. If something happened out there, maybe you should step away.'

'Look,' he tried to reassure her, 'Lawlor is scum. He pissed me off and I wanted to scare the shit out of him – that's all, I promise.' She watched him for a while, reading him as she had a thousand suspects before – judging him. 'Come on, Sally,' he said. 'I need you to do this with me. All we're going to do is follow the treeline until we can see the buildings better – then we watch and wait. No more, I promise.'

In the end she agreed, even though she knew he would never be able to just watch and wait, not with his prey so close. She released his forearm and they climbed from the car together, easing the doors shut. Sally followed Sean, occasionally shaking her head in disbelief at what she was doing and where she was. When Sean found a natural break in the trees they headed deeper into the woods that surrounded the ramshackle collection of ugly buildings until they came to a low wooden fence that formed a perimeter. Like the buildings below it had been neglected and was rotting in several places. The panels would be easy to pry away from the holding frames. On the other side there was another line of trees, but smaller and younger than those in the woods behind them. Beyond was a grassy bank leading to the buildings, which were arranged in a circular valley. Sean prised one of the panels away and peered down. He saw nothing moving, but his view was partially restricted. He looked through the gap to his right and saw a better position to spy from.

'We need to keep moving,' he told Sally. 'About fifty metres further round there's a better place. We can watch from there – anything moves, we'll see it.'

'OK,' Sally whispered. 'Lead the way.'

He nodded once and headed off. The sharp fallen branches breaking under his feet and the whip-like limbs of the saplings reaching out for his face made him think of the madman's victims being marched barefoot into the woods in the middle of the night, their feet cut to ribbons, their soft skin scratched and slashed at. And always the faceless, hooded man walking behind them, protected from the elements and the fury of the woods by his shapeless clothing. Soon the madman would have a face and Sean would be staring straight into it. He felt a surge of excitement and adrenalin surge through his body. It was all he could do not to smash through the wooden fence, charge down the grassy hill and flush out Thomas Keller – the hunter becoming the hunted as he finally cornered him and *then* . . .

He reached a place he guessed would be near enough the vantage point and began to ease another panel from the frame, the rusty nails pulling free from the damp wood easily. He propped the panel against the fence and looked through, a satisfied smile spreading across his face as he realized he'd stopped at almost exactly the place he'd intended to, the buildings below being no more than forty metres away and washed in spring sunshine. He could see pretty much everything.

'Take a look,' he whispered, moving aside to let Sally peer through. She took a quick glance then handed the vigil back to him. 'This is our man,' he added, never taking his eyes off his quarry. 'This place is perfect for him – the woods, the isolation. He keeps them here too – close at hand for when he needs . . .' Just in time he remembered Sally was standing next to him . . . 'to go to them. He doesn't want to keep them miles away, having to get into his car and drive to see them – he covets his collection too much. He needs to be able to see them instantly, as soon as he wants to.'

'His collection?' Sally queried.

He was about to answer until a movement caught his eyes, a change in the shadows of an open door leading into a small brick building.

'Someone's moving,' he whispered. As he looked on, the shadow in the doorway stepped into the light and turned into a man. 'He's carrying something . . .'

'What?' Sally managed to ask, her heart pounding, wanting to be anywhere but there.

'. . . a mattress and . . . and clothes – some sort of clothing. Here,' he said, his excitement matching her anxiety.

Sally took a peep. 'Looks like an outside toilet to me.'

Sean peered back through the gap in time to see the man place the items on the ground and lock the door with a padlock before recovering the clothing and mattress and heading off across the forecourt towards a dilapidated bungalow he guessed was his living quarters. 'That's no outside toilet,' he said. 'You don't padlock an outside toilet. And the mattress and the clothes – it must be the entrance to an old bomb shelter or cellar.' He filled his lungs and pushed himself away from the fence. 'He keeps them in there,' he told himself as much as Sally. 'Deborah Thomson's down there.'

'Are you sure it's him?' Sally asked. 'Thomas Keller?'

Sean pulled up the image in his mind: the employee photograph of Thomas Keller that Leonard Trewsbury had shown him little more than an hour ago. 'Hard to tell – he's older now and we're too far away. But yes, I think it's him.'

'Fine,' said Sally. 'Let's call in back-up and take him down.' Her head was beginning to pound as the sickness in her stomach started to spread to the rest of her body. She wanted to run – run back to the car and drive away, keep driving and leave the madmen to it.

'OK . . .' Sean appeared to relent, but immediately went on to confirm her worst fears: 'You sort out the back-up and wait here until it arrives. I'm going to fetch the car and drive up to the front of his house. Keep watch and cover my back. If the shit hits the fan, stay put and wait for back-up. Call for urgent assistance if you have to – but only if you have to.'

'This is a really bad idea,' she warned him.

'I'll be fine,' he assured her. 'I've got my ASP and CS spray. If he tries to get the jump on me, I'll give him a full canister in the face.'

'Why are you doing this?'

'You know why,' he answered. 'Because I have to. I have to fill in the blanks.'

Sally nodded. She didn't like it, but she understood. He was the animal that he was and no one could change him.

'Here ' he handed her a standard-issue radio. 'Take this. You'll need it more than I will.'

She slowly took it from him as if it was some precious parting gift, handing him the keys to the car in exchange. He began to walk away.

'Wait,' she stopped him. 'How will I know you're OK?'

'I told you, I'll be fine. I'm going to keep him talking until the troops arrive. As soon as they do, just come charging in.'

'But what if this isn't where he's keeping Deborah Thomson?'

'It is,' he insisted. 'Trust me.'

Determined not to give her another chance to stop him, he strode into the woods, moving quickly and quietly, becoming more accustomed to his rural surroundings, more comfortable amongst the trees – just like the man he hunted. He reached the car and climbed in, fumbling with the keys as his hands shook with anticipation of what was soon to come. Finally he got the car started and headed slowly towards the farm and Thomas Keller, swallowing drily, his mouth parched and sticky. He pulled the CS spray from its leather holster on his belt and slid it into his right-hand coat pocket where it would be easier to reach in a desperate moment. The car passed through the tumble-down gates and rolled to a gentle halt in front of the breezeblock bungalow.

Sean took a moment to compose himself before getting out of the car. The realization that he'd reached the end of the deadly game brought a sudden peace and calmness to him. It was over – almost. Gently closing the car door behind him, he spent a few seconds looking around, vivid images of Karen Green and Louise Russell being marched from the cellar before being driven away to their deaths played in his mind, but nevertheless he remained icy calm. Images of Thomas Keller heading towards the cellar armed with his cattle prod and alfentanil, intent on the rape and murder of innocent women, followed, but still Sean remained calm. When he was ready, he walked purposefully to what appeared to be the front door, his warrant card already in the palm of his left hand while his right rested on the CS canister in his coat pocket. There was no doorbell, just a thin door with a plain sheet of glass covering the top quarter. He tapped gently on the window and called into the house. 'Hello. Is anyone home? It's the police.' He stood back from the door and watched through the glass, listening for sounds of life, imagining the jolt of panic his voice must have delivered to the man he knew was lurking somewhere inside. Imagining Keller breaking out in a cold sweat of terror, he savoured his own moment of cruelty before stepping forward and tapping on the glass again. 'Hello. Police.' This time he stayed close to the door, pretending to be looking away, in case he was being watched, using his peripheral vision to look through the window. He saw a shape dart across a doorway inside, on the other side of what looked to be the kitchen. 'Come on, you son-of-a-bitch,' he whispered to himself. 'Open the fucking door and let me see your face.'

It was unfortunate the front door appeared to lead directly into the kitchen, where knives and heavy metal objects would be easily to hand. He covertly checked his ASP was still attached to his belt. If it came to a close-quarter battle, the CS spray would be no good – it would blind them both. Better to go with the ASP. Again the shape inside darted across the doorway opposite. 'Fuck this,' he said, almost too loudly, and reached out for the door handle. He rested his hand on the faded chrome and slowly pressed down on it, wary of a possible booby trap. As the handle depressed further he heard the click of the door opening. Clearly Keller hadn't been expecting company and had left the door unlocked.

Sean remembered the clothes he'd been carrying and imagined what Keller had been doing when he'd first heard the knock at his door – holding the clothes against his naked skin, rubbing their scent all over himself, especially his private parts, lying on the soiled mattress and drinking in the smell of his victims, relishing their fear and his power over them. Sean wondered whether Keller had pissed himself when he heard the knock at his door.

He pushed the door and let it swing open, intently surveying the room for anything that could be used as a weapon or a hiding place, listening for the sound of a pit-bull that had been trained to lie silently in wait for an unsuspecting trespasser to enter its domain. As satisfied as he could be that there were no immediate hidden dangers, he stepped inside.

He felt powerful and dangerous intruding into Keller's sanctuary – doing to Keller what he had done to women he'd taken – invading his home, his most sacred place, and shattering all his faint illusions.

'Thomas Keller,' he called out. 'My name is DI Sean Corrigan. I need to speak to you, Thomas. You're not in any trouble – I just want a word with you. I'm doing a follow-up visit – two of my uniformed colleagues came to see you a couple of days ago. They thought you might be able to help me with a certain matter I'm looking into.'

Suddenly he was there – the madman, Thomas Keller – standing in the doorway he'd been ghosting past seconds earlier, those same burning brown eyes Sean had seen in the Post Office ID photograph, their intensity not even slightly diminished by the passing of the years since the picture was taken. Sean could see Keller's chest rising and falling with the exertion of whatever he'd been doing before his arrival. The effort of trying to appear unconcerned that a policeman was standing in his kitchen was only adding to his strain. He watched Keller's tongue curl from his mouth like a cat's and lick the beads of sweat from his upper lip.

Sean faked a smile. 'Hi. The door was unlocked so I let myself in,' he told the madman. 'I was worried something might have happened to you. You don't mind, do you?'

'No,' Keller stabbed his answer, using the back of his sleeve to wipe the sweat from his brow.

'Are you OK?' he asked, enjoying the torture, knowing Keller was anything but OK, knowing that he would be dying inside. He saw Keller's legs momentarily twitch, as if he was about to sprint away, and realized he was moving too fast. He wanted to speak to Keller, not end up chasing him across ground the madman would know better than him – into the woods where he felt so comfortable and empowered. No, he needed to keep him here, in the confined space he himself was already growing accustomed to.

He pulled an old wooden chair from under the littered kitchen table and slowly sat down, his eyes never leaving Keller, the false smile still keeping the madman disorientated. 'You don't mind if I sit down, do you?' Sean asked. 'It's been a long week.' Keller said nothing. 'Hell of a place you've got here,' Sean continued, 'lots of space. Not easy to find in this neck of the woods. Must have cost plenty?'

Sean held his silence and his nerve, knowing Keller had to be the next to speak or the game would be over before it started. While he waited, he studied the thin, unimpressive man standing on the other side of the foul-smelling kitchen – a man who would be feared by no one who saw him in the street, a man who looked like one of life's victims, yet a man who the media and public would soon be branding a monster. What name would they create for him, Sean wondered: *The South London Strangler? The Keston Rapist? The Keeper?*

'I got it cheap,' Keller's weak voice brought Sean back from his musing. 'It used to be a poultry farm, and they slaughtered calves here, for veal. It put people off wanting to buy it.'

'But not you?' Sean asked, trying to keep him talking.

'No. Not me, but I don't suppose you came here to talk about how much my land cost,' said Keller, stepping into the kitchen, his eyes wandering around the room, avoiding contact with Sean's.

'No,' he agreed. 'It's like I said, I'm doing a follow-up to the visit by my uniformed colleagues. Do you remember them?'

'Of course,' Keller answered, still standing, his back to a tall, narrow, built-in cupboard he clearly didn't want to be too far away from.

Sean sensed that the cupboard spelled danger. Was it where he kept his cattle prod and the stun-gun? Years of experience searching suspects' houses had given him a sixth sense of where the threat would come from. If Keller went for the cupboard, he would have to move fast, unthinkingly, hit him hard and stop him before he got the door open. If he hesitated he could be dead. He needed to get Keller away from there.

'Why don't you take a seat?'

'No,' Keller replied, 'I'm fine. Thank you.'

'Suit yourself,' he said calmly, despite his soaring heart rate, his eyes flicking between Keller and the cupboard. 'Did the other officers tell you why they were here?'

'They said it was about some prowler?'

'That's right,' he said, managing to sound flippant and friendly. 'But we're also looking for some women who've gone missing,' Sean told him matter-of-factly, hoping he could panic him into running and confirming his guilt there and then. 'We're up to three women – so far.' He let the smile slip from his face, but only for a few seconds while he listed their names. 'Karen Green, Louise Russell and Deborah Thomson. Those names mean anything to you?' Again he saw the twitch in Keller's legs.

'No,' he replied. 'Why should they?'

'No reason, other than they've been on the news a lot and in the papers – local and national.'

'I don't watch television,' Keller answered truthfully.

'Ever read the papers?'

'Not really.' Another truthful answer.

'Then you probably don't know that we've already found two of the women, both dead. Both slaughtered, just like the animals on this farm used to be.' He waited for a reaction, but Keller was blank.

'That's very sad. I'm sorry for their families.'

'Sorry for their families?' Sean probed. 'It's the women I'm sorry for. I'm sorry for Karen Green and I'm sorry for Louise Russell. And unless I find her soon I'm going to be sorry for Deborah Thomson – it's strange you're not.'

'That's not what I meant,' Keller stammered. 'Listen, I'm very sorry, but I can't help you and I'm really busy, so if you don't mind . . .'

Sean ignored him. 'What happened to your face?' he asked. Keller's hand involuntarily reached for the deep gouges Deborah Thomson's nails had made. 'Cut yourself walking in the woods round here?' Sean knew the marks had not been left by a tree, but he didn't want to panic his prey – not yet. 'Me too,' he continued, pointing to the cut on his own cheek, left by the branch of a tree at the scene of Louise Russell's body drop.

'Something like that,' Keller answered.

'Who would have thought walking in the woods could be so dangerous?' Sean asked. Keller said nothing. 'I think my uniform colleagues were a little worried they hadn't searched your land properly – checked inside the other buildings and maybe the woods that seem to surround you here.'

'Why would they want to do that?' said Keller, his eyes blinking fast.

'I don't know. I suppose they thought you've got a decent amount of land and plenty of outbuildings. Lots of places to hide things.'

'Like what?'

'You tell me,' Sean inched closer. Keller said nothing. 'Maybe we could take a look around now, together – see what we can find.'

'I . . .'

'Check the outbuildings together. Check the cellar or bomb shelter or whatever it is.'

'No. I . . .'

'What did you do with the clothes and the mattress?' he suddenly asked. 'The clothes and the mattress I saw you with?'

'I don't know what you're talking about,' Keller lied, every muscle in his body tensing, the shotgun in the cupboard behind him so close, already loaded and primed to fire.

'You know who I spoke to, just before I came here?'

'No.'

'Samantha Shaw, Thomas. I spoke to Samantha Shaw.'

Keller nodded slowly and silently. He understood now.

'You do remember Samantha, don't you, Thomas? We don't forget our gods, do we? I just wanted to talk to you, you know – alone, before the world falls on you, Thomas.'

'Why? Why do you want to talk to me? We have nothing to say to each other.'

Sean remembered his interview with Jason Lawlor, the gaps in his own imagination that Lawlor had been able to fill – the things he'd felt, the things he'd desired that Sean never could or would. 'After you've raped them, could you go on smelling them, smelling their sex? Did you avoid washing your private parts for days after so you could still smell them on you?' He watched the madman's eyes narrow and then grow wide and round, his nostrils flare as his breathing intensified. 'God, they smelled so good, didn't they? Tell me, what was it like, being in their houses, their homes – taking them from the place where they felt safest of all? My God, that must have made you feel so . . . so powerful – so *alive*. And keeping them close, so you could go to them whenever you wanted to – whenever you needed to . . . Was it everything you dreamed it would be? Did you feel accepted by them, when you forced yourself inside them? Did you feel loved?'

'No!' Keller shouted, taking a step towards him and then stopping, almost making Sean leap from his chair and spray blinding CS gas into his eyes. 'No. They disgust me. I can't stand the smell of them on me.'

'Then why?' Sean pushed, knowing he must be running out of time, knowing Sally would have called for assistance almost as soon as he left her and that any moment half the Metropolitan Police would be crashing through the thin door behind him.

'They made me do it,' Keller answered. 'They're whores – all of them. They tricked me. They made me . . . be with them, but they disgusted me. I scrubbed myself in the shower, but still I could smell their stench. They're whores. They're nothing and I treated them like nothing.'

'But what about Samantha? She wasn't a whore. She wasn't nothing.'

'Don't you talk about her,' Keller warned him, tears welling in his eyes, spit spraying from his thin, white lips. 'She's not like them. They tried to make me believe they were her . . . the . . . the way they cut their hair – the clothes they wore, everything, but they were just whores. Meaningless whores.'

'So you killed them. You drugged them and you took them into the woods and you killed them.'

'No,' Keller screamed, taking another step forward, but Sean held his ground, acting as the bait to draw him further away from the tall cupboard.

'And how did that feel, Thomas? Killing them? When you slipped your hands around their beautiful, delicate necks and sank your thumbs deep into their throats – how did that feel?'

'You don't know anything,' Keller screamed.

'When the life ebbed from them, when you held them even after they were dead, when you stared into their lifeless eyes – how did that feel, Thomas?'

'No. No. No!'

Sean's fist hit the table hard, making the myriad items littering its surface jump and scatter. 'Damn you – tell me how it felt.'

Hatred poured from Keller's eyes, his face twisted and deformed, his stained teeth bared and threatening, primeval weapons readied for use, his entire body a coiled spring about to explode all over Sean. 'Fuck you!' he screamed so loudly he shattered the very air in the dingy room, spinning quickly and smoothly, reaching the tall cupboard in micro-seconds and throwing the door open.

Sean was already on his feet, his right hand pulling the CS

spray from his coat, his left planted on the underside of the table, lifting it upwards and hurtling it out of his way, providing him with the shortest route to the madman, cups and plates, half-full glasses flying through the air. It seemed to happen in slow motion, but it was the shotgun Keller was reaching for that Sean saw above all else – its wooden stock and shortened black double barrels. He moved as fast as he'd ever moved in his life, but as he watched Keller's right hand wrap around the pistol grip of the stock he knew he hadn't moved fast enough. Keller spun back towards him, the black holes of the gun barrels bearing down on him. The two men were only three feet from each other, simultaneously firing their weapons. The CS canister soaked Keller's face in burning liquid, instantly blinding him and arresting his respiratory system, while the outside arc of the shotgun blast pounded into Sean's left shoulder, knocking him backwards through the air and throwing him to the ground, dozens of red-hot lead pellets feeling first like a punch, then like the feet of a hundred crawling insects before turning to the searing pain of a thousand wasp stings.

He looked up at the madman, thrashing and wailing, clawing at his own eyes with one hand, unwittingly pushing the caustic liquid deeper into them, salivating uncontrollably, sweeping the shotgun back and forth across the room, trying to see Sean through blinded eyes, listening for him, finger wrapped around the trigger. It wouldn't be long before Keller's eyes began to clear, leaving him a sitting duck, lying on the floor with only one good arm, the CS he'd been holding long since dropped and lost amongst the wreckage from the table he'd upturned. He grabbed the first thing of size he could reach, a small saucepan, and threw it across the room, sending it crashing into the cupboard next to the sink. Keller spun towards the noise, pointing the shotgun at the place he thought Sean had to be, his finger squeezing the trigger, but then easing off, some animal instinct to survive telling him to save his last shot until he was sure.

Sean groaned inside as he realized his plan had failed and now he was on the floor and at least eight feet from Keller. He swallowed the searing pain in his shoulder and managed to hold his useless arm across his chest while crouching into the starting position of a sprinter, bursting into a full charge, keeping low as he saw the shotgun sweeping in his direction, Keller's watering eyes growing wide as they tried to focus on the dark shape covering the short distance between them. Sean powered his right shoulder hard into Keller's midriff, carrying him backwards with him until they smashed into the tall cupboard. The shotgun blast exploded above Sean's head as they fell to the floor, the cupboard falling on top of them and catching Sean a glancing blow on his temple, knocking him temporarily senseless. It was all he could do to hold on to Keller as they wrestled on the filthy floor, but the blow to the head, the blood loss and the shock of being shot were beginning to tell, beginning to overwhelm his instinct to survive.

Suddenly Keller was on top of him, overpowering him, his face fading away to be replaced by the face of his father, sneering and lascivious, before it faded back to Keller's. A hand grabbed him around the throat and began to squeeze, the thumb pressing hard on his trachea and making him cough and gag for air, the fingers of his good arm desperately trying to pull the hand away from his neck, loosening it just enough so he could breathe as the madman stared down at him, eyes wild with hatred, his teeth stained with blood from a cut somewhere inside his mouth, making him appear demonic. Sean was powerless to act as he watched Keller pull his right fist back and then ram it into his injured, bleeding shoulder.

Sean screamed out in pain and anger. Keller drew back for a moment then once more smashed his fist into Sean's wounded shoulder, then repeated the action again and again. As the blows raining down on him added to his blood loss and accelerated the effects of shock, Sean's vision began to fail, the man above him little more than a silhouette. Finally the blows stopped and Keller leaned close and whispered in his ear.

'Time to die.'

He felt the same long, bony, strong fingers that had strangled Karen Green and Louise Russell closing around his throat – two hands now, squeezing the life from him. But just as he felt he was on the verge of blacking out, the hands released him and the silhouette seemed to rear backwards, a pathetic scream of pain leaking from his mouth, closely followed by a whimper as the madman toppled off him and lay next to him on the floor, clutching at the back of his head.

Sean coughed and gulped for air, the oxygen partially restoring his vision as he blinked his eyes clear enough to see Sally pulling her handcuffs out and bending over the stricken Keller. She set her ASP baton on the floor next to Sean while she rolled Keller on to his front and pulled his hands behind his back, inflicting as much pain as she could in the process. She clicked one of the cuffs around his wrist then dragged him a few feet to a thick metal radiator pipe running along the length of the wall just above floor height. She fed the cuffs around the back of the pipe and secured his other wrist, then recovered her ASP from the floor and knelt beside Sean.

Through his shock and confusion Sean was able to piece together what had happened, the dark hairs, sticky with fresh blood stuck to Sally's ASP told their own story. He felt his head being lifted as Sally placed her rolled-up coat under it.

'Don't try and talk,' she told him. 'You've been shot.'

'You don't say,' he answered, laughing in spite of the pain at the absurdity of her observation. Sally smiled and shook her head. 'Get me up,' he ordered.

'You shouldn't try to move,' she argued.

'I'm fine,' he lied. 'Prop me up against the wall – where I can watch him from.'

'You don't have to worry about him,' she said. 'I'll watch him till back-up arrives. I'll call you an ambulance.'

'No,' Sean insisted. 'You're going to get Deborah Thomson out of that fucking dungeon.' He fumbled for his jacket pocket with his one good hand and retrieved his phone. 'I'll call my own ambulance. You get her.'

'Christ,' she complained as she helped him crawl to the wall, propping him up limply where he could see the sobbing Keller slumped against the adjacent wall.

'The door to the cellar's locked,' he reminded her. 'You need to search him for the key. I think he still has it on him.'

'OK,' she nodded, cautiously approaching Keller, her ASP in hand. 'Try anything and I'll cave your fucking head in,' she warned him – and meant it. She patted the outsides of his trouser pockets until she felt what she was searching for, carefully slipping her hand inside his tracksuit and recovering two keys. She turned and showed them to Sean. 'I've got them,' she announced gleefully.

'Good,' he answered. 'You know what to do.'

She recovered her coat from the floor and placed it over his wounded shoulder. 'Try and keep this pressed against the wound. It'll help stem the bleeding. The coat's ruined anyway,' she added, making him smile through the increasing nausea and drowsiness.

'Don't worry about me, I'll be fine. Take the keys and go.'

'OK,' she said and was halfway out the door when Sean stopped her.

'Hey,' he called as loudly as he could. 'I thought I told you to wait outside until back-up arrived.'

'You did,' she agreed, 'but I got bored.'

He managed one last faint smile and waved her away. As soon as she left the building his eyes flickered and his head fell forward. A few seconds later – the darkness came.

Sally picked her way across the forecourt of Keller's dilapidated collection of old brick buildings with their rusty corrugated-iron roofs, the smell of CS gas from the kitchen still clinging to her clothes and making her eyes sting and water. She held them as wide open as she could to let the mixture of sunlight and spring breeze clear the gas in the safest and quickest way. Several times she almost tripped on the debris that littered her route towards the small building Sean was convinced was the entrance to Keller's private dungeon and torture house. Coughing CS gas from her lungs, its taste acrid and caustic on her tongue, she paused to peer into an old oil drum with burn marks around its rim. The smell of lighter fuel and petrol rose from inside the drum, causing her to examine it closer. She could make out the remnants of burnt clothes at the bottom, the occasional fragment of colour. 'This is not good,' she muttered.

Reminding herself that Keller was cuffed and secured under Sean's watchful gaze, she forced herself to approach the door of the brick outbuilding. Taking a deep breath, she studied the keys in the palm of her hand and then the padlock. The first key she tried didn't fit. A strange sense of relief washed over her, brought on by the possibility that she wouldn't have to descend into the monster's subterranean labyrinth – into the darkness that held nothing but fear for her. She sighed as she tucked the failed key into her jacket pocket, looking at the next one, willing it not to fit. But it slid into the slot smoothly, turning easily and popping the padlock open.

Sally's throat suddenly constricted. She tried to swallow but couldn't. The time had arrived when she would have to either walk through that wall of paralysing fear or risk never again being the person she once was. She wriggled the lock free and placed it carefully on the ground, aware that it would eventually play its part in forming the chain of evidence that would convict Keller of the murders and abductions.

The metal door felt as heavy as it looked once she started to pull it open, the terrible metallic scraping noise catching her by surprise and making her release the door and jump back, clutching her chest. 'Fuck,' she cursed loudly, feeling better for it. 'This is not good,' she said again and took hold of the door, vowing not to let go, no matter what happened. She pulled hard and kept pulling until the door was fully open, revealing the darkness inside and the stone steps that led down deeper into the well of her fears and nightmares. Her immediate reaction was to recoil from the darkness, retreating a few steps, but she managed to stop herself. 'Shit,' she cursed again. 'This is fucking great.'

She paused, listening for the sound of approaching sirens, but there were none. 'Bloody sticks,' she complained. 'I hate it out in the sticks.' Most cops did. The inner cities might be dangerous, but assistance was never more than a couple of minutes away. Out here, you could be on your own fighting for your life for ten to fifteen minutes before anyone got to you. 'Come on, girl, get a grip,' she told herself, drawing her ASP – more for comfort than in the belief she would need to use it. It was stained with Keller's blood – a fact that somehow made her feel better, bolder.

After several deep breaths to control her breathing and heart rate, she moved into the doorway and began her descent, squinting in the gloom, moving as silently as she could, cursing every scratch and scrape her shoes made on the hard stairs, her hand stretched out in front of her, feeling her way, ready to push aside any dangers, until at last her eyes adjusted to the gloom. Only another dozen or so steps and she would be at the end of her descent. But the further she went, the more she left the fresh air behind her. Now she was breathing in the sickening stench of unwashed humanity – urine, sweat, excrement and semen mixed into a foul, ungodly brew. She covered her mouth to stop herself gagging, desperately fighting the urge to flee back to the clean air above and abandon whatever creatures lay below to their fate. Halfway down she had to stop and lean against the wall to chase away the rising panic in her chest, her head turning towards the light. But it was in the darkness below her that salvation lay, and she knew it.

'Come on. Come on,' she urged, cursing herself for not having thought to bring a torch, afraid she would never be able to force herself down these stairs again if she returned to the house to find one. 'Steady as she goes,' she muttered, relieved to feel the panic fading somewhat, seizing the moment to push away from the wall and continue her descent, keeping the wall at her back. There was always the possibility that Keller had an accomplice or accomplices, or that he kept vicious, half-starved animals in the cellar.

It seemed to take a lifetime, but eventually she reached the bottom stair and stepped on to the floor of the underground prison. Inching her way around the room, back pressed to the wall, she moved away from the stairs. The sound of trickling water disorientated her; it felt as if she was in a natural cavern rather than a man-made shelter. As her eyes continued to adjust she made out a hazy, square object, maybe ten feet in front of her, but she needed to get closer to see it properly. Counting down from ten, she pushed herself off the wall and into the free space of the cellar, feeling instantly giddy, as if she was standing on the edge of a cliff. After a few seconds the dizziness wore off and she was able to shuffle onward, her feet not trusting the ground underneath them, convinced she would at any second feel her stomach leap into her mouth as she fell into some unseen bottomless pit, but the feeling of falling never came.

As she drew closer and closer to the square object she began to realize what it was – a cage, maybe four foot wide and high, six feet long. Worse, the door to the cage was open. Her breathing became instantly short and laboured like a panting dog, as she convinced herself she was trapped in the cellar with some escaped wild beast that was now circling her in the gloom, clinging to the edges of the room where it couldn't be seen, preparing to pounce as soon as she ran for the stairs.

Then she heard it, a noise away to her right, something moving, the animal positioning itself to attack, the terror of her situation freezing her rigid. But eventually she forced her head to twist towards the sound, at least enough so she could see out of the corner of her right eye, another large box silhouetted in the gloom, a shape huddled in one corner – an unthreatening shape – something that feared her more than she feared it. She turned fully and headed towards the box until she could see it was an identical cage to the first one, only this one's door was shut and there was something inside – something alive, cowering.

Sally shuffled slowly forward, her ASP gripped tightly at her side, moving endlessly towards the cage before suddenly freezing again and looking from the empty cage to the cage with the thing inside. The image of Keller coming from the door above carrying a mattress and clothes flashed in her memory, the fear lifting and allowing her to think, the realization of where she was and what she was seeing flooding over her. The true awfulness of what must have happened down here suddenly dawned on her as she covered her mouth with her free hand to try and disguise her words. 'Oh my dear God,' she said, louder than a whisper. 'Oh my dear God.'

She almost ran the last few feet to the cage and kneeled by its side, peering through the wire at the wild-eyed creature trapped within as she simultaneously fumbled for the key she knew would fit the lock. 'I'm a police officer,' she told the filthy, terrified woman trying to hide in the corner of the cage. She fished her warrant card from her pocket and pressed it against the wire mesh. 'You're Deborah Thomson, yes? I've come to get you out of here.'

The woman didn't reply, her eyes full of mistrust and fear. Sally moved quickly around to the cage door and wrestled to free the lock, struggling to find the slot for the key in the dim light. Finally it popped open and she was able to pull the door free and swing it ajar.

'I think it's time to get out of here. Don't you?' she said.

The woman remained where she was, cowering virtually naked in a corner of the cage.

'It's over,' Sally reassured her. 'He can't hurt you any more. It's over.'

The woman's bloodied lips finally cracked open. 'Who are you?' she asked, her voice hoarse and barely audible.

'My name's Sally.' She stretched out her arm, offering Deborah Thomson her hand. 'Detective Sergeant Sally Jones.'

Kate sat tiredly in the staffroom hidden in the corner of Guy's Hospital Emergency Department, watching some hideous Sunday afternoon cooking programme and drinking instant coffee – her sixth of the day. She'd had to dump the kids on her mum again, thanks to Sean's unscripted absence. No doubt he wouldn't be home until well after she'd picked the kids up, taken them home, fed them and put them to bed. She was beginning to feel like she was doing two full-time jobs without a whole lot of support and she was having to try harder and harder not to resent it. It wasn't as if Sean was being paid a fortune as a detective inspector. Worst thing he ever did was take promotion – at least as a sergeant he got paid overtime, some compensation for never being around. Now he seemed to work more hours for less money.

Hearing the staffroom door open, she looked up and saw Mary Greer, the A and E manager, enter. Ignoring the other people slumped around the room, she made a beeline in Kate's direction. Kate smiled, but Mary didn't smile back. Her own smile faded as she recognized the expression on the other woman's face. It was an expression that said she was the bearer of bad news – personal bad news.

Kate's first thought was that it was one of the girls, the fear almost stopping her heart. But if it was the children, surely Sean would have come? No matter what was going on at work, he would have dropped everything to be here . . .

In that second she realized she'd solved the puzzle. Her hand covered her mouth as tears pooled in her eyes and her throat swelled almost shut. Mary crossed the room quickly and held her gently by the shoulders. 'I'm sorry,' she told her. 'It's Sean. He's on his way in. He's been shot.'

Mostly it was darkness – silent darkness, but the nightmares found their way through – the orange blast of a gun pointing towards him, faces too close to his own – his father's, sneering and leering – Thomas Keller's, his red teeth gritted in hatred, eyes blazing with evil intention – Sebastian Gibran, mocking him with laughter – Sally lying in the hospital with tubes snaking down her throat – Kate crying and pleading with him not to leave her – the faces of Louise Russell and Karen Green, their dead eyes staring at him, their lifeless blue lips parting to whisper to him: *Why didn't you save us? Why didn't you save us? Why didn't you save us?* – their faces slowly changing, growing younger and younger until they became the faces of his own daughters, their eyes also the eyes of the lifeless, their lips as pale blue as the lips of the dead women who'd spoken to him from beyond the grave as they lay broken in the woods – *Why didn't you save us? Why didn't you save us? Why didn't you save us?* Then the darkness came and brought him peace – peace like he'd never known before – peace like he'd never had since being forced from his mother's womb.

Three Days Later

He heard sounds though he couldn't see anything other than light. Sounds in the distance, surreal and difficult to make out. A few seconds later his eyes flickered and opened and he remembered where he was. Kate was sitting by his bedside, dressed in her hospital uniform, loose blue cotton trousers and shapeless blue top, her name tag clipped to her breast pocket. 'You fell asleep again,' she told him. The sun shone brightly through the window of his private room. He'd only escaped intensive care the night before.

'Sorry,' he murmured, his mouth painfully dry.

'Don't be,' she assured him. 'It's the painkillers. You'll be dopey for a few days yet.' She lifted his covered water beaker and eased the straw between his lips. 'You're still pretty dehydrated. You need to try and drink.'

He nodded he understood, sipped the water and looked around the room, even in his present state able to process the information his eyes were passing to his brain. Since he'd recovered from his initial surgery he'd been waking for brief periods and nearly every time she'd been there, waiting for him, snatched conversations before he drifted away, emotional and tearful at first, but increasingly calm as the gut-wrenching fear faded somewhat.

'A private room?' he asked, the straw still in his mouth.

'Press got wind of your *heroics,*' she said. 'They were sniffing around all over the place dressed as everything from surgeons to porters. We thought we'd better ferret you away somewhere out of sight.'

'Thanks,' he said, pushing the straw from his mouth with his tongue and relaxing back into his pillow, the movement making him wince with pain and turn to look at his shoulder wrapped in heavily layered white bandages with a thin tube disappearing under them.

'It's a self-administering morphine feed. If you're feeling any pain, just press this switch.' She pointed at a grey box close to his right hand. 'It's regulated,' she added, 'so you can't overdose.'

He nodded he understood. He'd only been awake a couple of minutes, but already felt exhausted. His eyes were beginning to roll back into their sockets when Kate's voice cut through the morphine and other opioids, the fear in her voice acting like smelling salts. 'Sean . . .' He forced his eyes to open and focus, like a drunk trying to stay awake on a train. He could see the tears she wouldn't allow to escape in her eyes.

'That was too close, Sean, way too close. When they told me you'd been shot and you were being brought in – my heart, Sean – the pain in my . . .' She couldn't finish. He gave her a few seconds to compose herself. 'I've been checking out the New Zealand Immigration website. I'd have no problem getting a job there, and neither would you. You could even transfer over as a DI. Listen, Sean – London, this job you're doing – it's too much. We have to think of the girls. A new life. A better life – for us all.'

'Maybe . . .'

A knock at the open door saved him. Sally appeared,

smiling in the doorway. Kate took it as her cue to leave and stood, bending over him and kissing him on the forehead.

'Promise me you'll think about it,' she pleaded and headed for the door, brushing past Sally on the way out.

'How you doing?' Sally asked.

'I'm fine, thank you,' Kate replied with a forced smile before hurrying away along the sterile corridor. Sally shrugged her shoulders and crossed the room to Sean, slumping into the chair Kate had just vacated.

'You look well,' she told him with a wry smile. He shook his head and grinned as much as he could. 'She's hardly left your side, you know. When they first brought you in, they tried to keep her away, but she wouldn't have it.'

'Did you tell her what happened?'

'I told her you're a bloody idiot.'

'And what about everybody else?'

'I told them you went to the front of the house while I covered the back – that we didn't think he was at home, which is how he managed to get the drop on you. There were a few awkward questions about why we didn't wait for back-up, etc.'

'And . . .?'

'I said that we believed Deborah Thomson was in clear and imminent danger, so we had no choice but to go straight in and get her out.'

'Anyone buy your story?'

Sally gave a shrug. 'Keller didn't contradict my account of events.'

'You interviewed him?'

'Yeah.'

'With Dave?'

'No. With Anna.'

'Anna? Jesus.'

'She asked some good questions. She was useful.'

'And Keller – what did he say?'

'I'm guessing you already know.'

He nodded. 'He said nothing.'

'He said less than nothing. He's gone catatonic on us – won't even say his name. Another future guest for Broadmoor, courtesy of our good selves.'

'Best place for him,' Sean pointed out, his voice beginning to fade. 'Maybe Anna can interview him again as a patient.'

Sensing his distrust, Sally said, 'She's OK. Anna and I are becoming something like friends.' Sean raised his eyebrows. 'She's been helping me, you know, with things.'

'You fixed yourself,' he told her. 'It's what we do, remember?'

'I'm seeing her privately. No one at work knows about it. I'd like to keep it that way.'

'Fair enough,' he agreed, wilting under the influence of the medication that kept the pain at bay. Sally saw him drifting and stood to leave, her last words sounding warped and dreamlike in his head.

'You and I both sailed too close to the wind these past nine months,' she whispered. 'The physical stuff heals, Sean, but we're not the same after. We'll never be the same people we were. But then again, maybe that's not such a bad thing.'

He blinked slowly twice – then the darkness came.

Epilogue

Detective Superintendent Featherstone sat in his office at Shooters' Hill police station poring over the reports generated by the investigation and arrest of Thomas Keller. With Corrigan still cooped up in hospital, he'd inherited a lot more paperwork than he cared for. Waste of time, he told himself – the shrinks would say Keller was barking mad and the courts would agree. There'd be no trial, just a plea of not guilty on the grounds of diminished responsibility that the CPS would accept. Then Keller would be marched off to Broadmoor for the rest of his natural. Waste of everybody's time and money.

The phone ringing on his desk made him look up from Sally's written account of Keller's arrest and Deborah Thomson's rescue, an account that had caused him to raise his eyebrows on more than one occasion. He snatched at the phone. 'Detective Superintendent Featherstone speaking.' He never tired of using his full rank on the phone – or anywhere else, for that matter.

'Alan, it's Assistant Commissioner Addis here.' Featherstone rolled his eyes and sank deep into his chair. 'You need to know, a lot of people are asking a lot of questions.'

'About what, exactly?'

'DI Corrigan,' Addis answered.

'Such as?'

'Such as will he ever be fit to return to duty?'

'He'll need another operation to repair his shoulder, but I'm led to believe he'll make a full recovery.'

'Good. How soon?'

'I don't know – a few months, maybe less.'

'Let's make it less, shall we.'

'I don't understand,' said Featherstone. 'What's the rush?'

'Maximizing the use of assets, Alan,' Addis explained. 'I want him in place and ready for the next time. Special Cases only – understood?'

'Yes, sir.' Featherstone listened to the line go dead, Addis's words playing in his mind.

The next time. The next time.

Acknowledgements

Firstly I would like to acknowledge and say a huge thank you to my agent – Simon Trewin, now at William Morris Endeavour, for the incredible belief he showed in this untried, untested and untrained author. The work he put in to make my first book – *Cold Killing* – a viable piece of literature was miraculous, as were his efforts to secure fantastic publishing deals in Britain, the Commonwealth, America and beyond. Without Simon there would have been no first book, let alone a second. I'd also like to mention his assistant at the time and now agent in her own right – Ariella Feiner at United Agents, for all her work thus far.

Secondly I'd like to say a massive thank you to all the staff at HarperCollins Publishers for everything they've done for me, especially Kate Elton for having the courage to take such a big chance on an unknown quantity like myself and to Sarah Hodgson who's not only been my fantastic editor, but also my chief liaison officer and guide in what to me is still the weird and wonderful world of publishing. A hearty thanks also to the rest of the team – Adam, Oli, Louise, Tanya, Kiwi Kate, Hannah and everyone else. Many, many thanks.

LD